Agnes Short was
parents and stud
University. She has worked as a teacher, a secretary, a research assistant and in the editorial offices of a Sunday newspaper, and has lived in London, Oxford, Wiltshire and Malaya before settling in Old Aberdeen.

Also by Agnes Short

The First Fair Wind
The Flowing Tide

The Dragon Seas

Agnes Short

HEADLINE

For Philip and Katharine

First published in Great Britain in 1988
by Constable and Company Limited

First published in paperback in 1989
by HEADLINE BOOK PUBLISHING PLC

ISBN 0 7472 3181 8

Printed and bound in Great Britain by
Collins, Glasgow

HEADLINE BOOK PUBLISHING PLC
Headline House
79 Great Titchfield Street
London W1P 7FN

The Dragon Seas

Part I

Aberdeen
June 1834

i

Pearl Duthie looked up in surprise from the close-written ledger to see a man's shape blocking the doorway. 'Can I help you, sir?' The quill pen in her hand was well-worn, its feathers chewed.

'I'm seeking a ship,' he said, without ceremony.

'Oh?' Pearl raised an eyebrow, quelled the urge to point out he might have better luck finding one in the sea, and said, politely enough, 'Which ship? The *Steadfast* is in London meantime and the *Rachel Christie* . . .'

'Nay, lass, 'tis not a particular ship I'm seeking, so much as any ship.' The stranger stooped under the lintel and stepped inside. His boots were new leather, Pearl noted, his jacket best nankeen cloth, and the pin in his white cravat had the look of a pearl about it, a large pearl, set in gold. As an afterthought, he removed his tall hat, revealing thick, dark hair flecked with grey, and held it at an angle, left elbow crooked. He bowed briefly with a mixture of impatience and self-parody. Manners, he implied, were for the leisured or idle, not men of action like himself. Though it was the restlessness of inaction which coloured his speech as he continued.

'I've had my master's ticket these twelve years now and most of those spent running between India and the China seas. I'm here to look after my employers' interests in the matter of a ship on order, but I'm finding I don't take kindly to shore leave. Three months' idleness is enough, so, as I said, I'm needing a ship.'

'Then I am sorry, Captain, but you have come to the wrong place,' said Pearl, a gleam in her warm brown eyes. She did not like his manner of speaking, nor his manner of looking at her, as if she were an erring midshipman or a bungling cabin boy. 'Unless your name happens to be Christie?'

'Duncan Greig,' he said curtly. 'And proud of it. And you'll oblige me by telling me where I can find Mister er . . .' He tipped his head round the door, studied the brass nameplate outside, and bobbed in again. 'Christie.' He stopped as her words sank home. 'Ah, I see. Then you know fine I'm no Christie. Or do you not know your own master?'

'Oh yes,' said Pearl sweetly, dipping her pen into the inkwell, examining its point, then resuming her careful calligraphy. 'I know my uncles well enough. I was merely warning you that you'll find no ship to captain here.'

Greig flushed with anger, any pretence at courtesy forgotten.

'Hear this, woman.' He reached forward and seized her wrist in a strong, firm grip. 'I'm the best captain in the China seas – ask any man in Macau and he'll tell ye the same. There's no Englishman nor American nor Chinese neither as can get the better of me and I'll not be turned away before I've stated my case to the man himself. So ye'll kindly leave your scribbling and fetch him – now.'

'And you will kindly release my arm,' said Pearl, looking up at him with an unwavering gaze in which there was surprise, but no fear. He was younger than she had at first thought – no more than thirty-five – but drawn about the mouth and eyes and with a greyish tinge under the tan. But of course, he's been ill, she thought with compassion. Ill and lonely and lost. She waited, silent, until slowly he removed his hand, then she said cheerfully, 'This scribbling, as you call it, is the bill of lading for the *Anya*, master, William Christie. This ledger also contains details of the *Steadfast*, master, George Christie, the *Rachel Christie*, master, Alex Christie, and the *Bonnie Annie*, master, James Christie. So you see, Captain Greig, why I said you are wasting your time. It is company policy only to employ Christie men to captain Christie ships and we have men enough. I am sorry,' she added, her voice friendly. 'But that's how it is. You could try the Farquharson company, or the Aberdeen and Leith . . .'

But the newcomer showed no sign of leaving. Instead he began to range the room, looking at the half models of ships' hulls on the wall, the charts, ship's compasses and sextants in the corner cupboard, the whalebone scrimshaws. Pearl's eyes followed him, taking in the lean shoulders, the weather-tanned skin and the fan of fine lines around the eyes. A man acquired such lines by looking into the horizon, or squinting at the stars – all her uncles had them – but those other lines, she knew instinctively, were caused not by seafaring but by suffering, or grief. She studied the stranger more closely. Pearl Duthie knew most of the shipmasters of Aberdeen harbour, of Leith and Dundee too, for that matter, as well as most of the foreign captains who sailed regularly from the Low Countries, but this man was a complete stranger. Duncan Greig had a Scottish enough name, though she could not place his accent. He had stopped, now, at the globe by the window, and was apparently studying it, turning it idly between his hands. Then he looked up and caught her watching him.

'Why are you staring?' he demanded.

'I'm committing your features to memory,' she said coolly, 'so I'll know you again. We Christies have rivals, who are not above using agents to spy on us, with or without their knowledge.' She put up a hand to smooth back a strand of straying hair.

The movement tightened the cloth of her bodice and stopped his angry retort. She was a well-set girl, trim but rounded, with a clear complexion and lively eyes. Intelligent, he thought, assessing her now with closer interest, confident, level-headed and reliable. But with a touch of spirit and a cheerfulness which would go far to balance the boredom, irritations and plain discomfort of living. Most of all, she looked strong.

'I'm no spy, lass,' he said. 'Merely a sailor restless for the sea. So you must forgive my manners. I'm not used to company and have been too long away from civilisation. I don't know the proper ways o' conducting things. But I'm thinking,' he went on with deliberation, 'that I've sailed half the world for half my life and I havena seen a better favoured lass for many a year.'

'Then your travels have been unlucky,' said Pearl with composure, 'or you have not looked about you. And there is no need to pay me compliments. That's not the Christie way of conducting things, so you can forget your fancy talk and relax. You said you are on shore leave, Captain Greig. From which ship?'

'From none you've heard of.' But he mastered his temper and went on, after a moment, 'I work for a commercial firm out east. I sail the coastal route and have done for years, but there was sickness – and death – and they sent me home by the mail boat to recuperate.' He paused and Pearl felt unspoken grief wash over her like an unexpected, icy wave. 'I've a ship order to supervise,' he went on. 'Alexander Hall's are building the vessel and I am to sail her out east when she's ready. But I am restless and the ship's no more than half built. It'll be months yet and I need a deck under my feet again.'

'Alexander Hall?' said Pearl indignantly. 'Then you

have only yourself to blame if you're restless. You should have brought your order to Christie's. We'd have built you a ship twice as good in half the time and for less, too, I'll warrant. What are they charging you?'

'And what would you have charged, for a steam yacht o' 58 tons, 82 by 17, a hold of 9 foot 5 deep and with paddle wheels?'

'A steam yacht?' Pearl was suddenly deflated. 'We don't deal with steam. But it's a real pity. We'd have built you a beauty of a yacht, a swift, graceful bird of a yacht to sing over the surface of the water and gladden the heart. But if it's steam, ye'd best go to Hall's after all. Unless you can wait a year or two till we've our own Christie engineer?'

'Whether I could wait or not is immaterial,' said Greig. 'Jardine's can't. They're needing the yacht for the coastal trade, to beat the competition. To carry company messages and intercept the mail boat before she touches land!'

'Jardine's, did you say? But they are . . .'

'Aye, that Jardine's. And they didna make their millions by waiting a year or two. For myself,' he went on deliberately, 'I reckon I could cruise in these waters happily for a year or so – Aberdeen, London, Leith – for, compliments apart, I like the cut o' your jib. Tell me, are you a Christie too?'

Working as she did in her uncle's shipping office, Pearl was used to seamen's banter and undisturbed by even the coarsest remark – though such were rare in the Christie office and never made if a Christie man were present. But there was something almost sad about Captain Greig's compliments. She was tempted to show him the door – cut of her jib indeed! – but instead she said, with unconscious pride, 'Of course. My Da, God rest his soul, was Uncle James's brother and though my name's Pearl

Duthie Noble I'm as true-blooded a Christie as any o' them.'

'I thought so, from the proud set to your head and the loyalty in your voice. I value loyalty.'

'So do most people.' She busied herself with her papers, trying to ignore the way he was looking at her, but he did not take the hint and go.

Instead, after a moment, he said thoughtfully, 'Pearl. There's a river named for you at the other side o' the world. Did ye know that? The Pearl river at Canton.'

'Do you know Canton?' She pushed back her chair in excitement, hostility forgotten. 'How? Why? have you sailed there? Do you know the Factories? That is the name they give to the tea-traders' offices, isn't it? And Lintin Island and the Bogue?' Abandoning the ledger, she hurried to join him at the globe. She was smaller than he had expected, her head barely reaching his shoulder, but she more than made up in animation for any deficiency in size.

'Here is Canton, is it not?' she said, pointing with an inkstained finger. 'And here is Macau. Is it true what they say, that traders may only live in Canton half the year and must spend the rest of the year at Macau? Is it true that the tea trade is only in the winter months and that if a ship misses the market, for whatever reason, that is a year lost? Is it true that . . .'

'Steady, lass! How can I begin to answer when you give me no pause to speak? Besides,' he said, the first hint of a smile in his eyes, 'I did not come here to be quizzed. I came in search of a job which, it's plain to see, I'll not find here. So I'd best up anchor and leave.'

'No, please, Captain Greig, don't go!' cried Pearl. 'Not yet. Perhaps Jardine's would like another yacht, or a brig for the tea trade? Maitland's working on an idea at the moment. See, here is the sheer.' She reached for a rolled chart from the pile in a wooden rack beside the desk.

'I have no power to order ships, lass, much as I would like to.'

'Then at least,' finished Pearl, with pleading now in her eyes, 'at least tell me about the tea trade, Captain Greig? We are hoping to send a ship to Canton ourselves one day and must find out the best way to go about it for we hear there are such things as squeeze money and quotas and all sorts of smuggling and a group of Chinese merchants called the Cohong without whose permission it is impossible to do anything. And you never know, Captain, we might have a spare ship. We are always repairing or refitting or buying vessels for resale and sometimes they need to be delivered. I could speak to my Uncle James about you and he might . . .'

'Your Uncle James might what, Pearl?' said a quiet voice from the doorway and they turned to see a tall, serene-faced woman in her mid-thirties, a baby on one hip and another as yet unborn swelling the crisp linen of her apron. Her calm eyes were untroubled, but at the same time there was a strength about her which marked her as no ordinary housewife.

'This is Captain Greig, Aunt Rachel. He is from the China seas and needing a job, but I told him we only employ Christies. He's here to oversee an order for a steam yacht at Alexander Hall's.'

'And you, if I know my Pearl, were trying to persuade him to switch to the Christie yard? To jettison the engine? Or to order Maitland's latest? I thought so. You must forgive my niece, Captain Greig. She always has the Christie interests at heart, but in this case you are right to go to Hall's. We are a family firm, as no doubt Pearl has told you, and must wait for a family engineer before we can undertake a steam vessel.'

'Captain Greig sails for Jardine's,' put in Pearl eagerly. 'You know how prominent they are in the tea trade. Even when the East India Company still had the monopoly they managed to make a fortune, and now that the trade is open to all comers, Jardine's must be in the best position to make another.'

'And no doubt will keep their information to themselves,' said Rachel, with a smile. 'I am sorry we cannot help you, Captain Greig.' She stood aside, waiting for the captain to leave.

'And so am I, ma'am. That's a fine wee boy you have there.'

'Davy?' Rachel looked down at the child who had been named for Pearl's father, dead long ago, and her face irradiated love and pride. 'Yes, praise God. We have been blessed.'

Abruptly, Captain Greig left.

'Without so much as a goodbye! What a strange man,' said Pearl, looking after him with open mouth. 'One minute bragging, one minute hectoring, one minute attempting awkward compliments, and the next – gone! Oh well.'

'He will be back,' said Rachel Christie. 'A man with time on his hands won't turn his back on a sympathetic audience, especially if that audience is young and pretty.'

'Nonsense,' said Pearl briskly, though her cheeks were pinker than usual. 'If he comes back, it will be because he wants a job. I think he is unhappy, though,' she added thoughtfully, 'and not just because he is a seaman ashore.'

'And if he has any troubles, you will find them out, like the sympathetic listener you are,' teased Rachel. 'But that is no excuse for bullying the man.'

'Why not? It was all in the way of business.'

'The business being a steam yacht at Alexander Hall's?' Rachel Christie looked steadily at her niece, who looked steadily back at her until they both spontaneously laughed. Pearl plucked young Davy from his mother's hip and swung him in the air before cuddling him close. 'Besides,' she confessed, 'he was so serious, poor man. It is a pity, though, that we could not have built his ship,' she went on, subsiding into a chair so she could dandle the child on her knee. 'Steam is growing daily in popularity and I know we have not the knowledge nor the equipment but I wonder whether it is not time for us to acquire them, now, before we are left behind?'

Rachel Christie busied herself with the open ledger on the desk and said nothing, but her niece knew she was rehearsing the old arguments over and over inside her head, arguments that inevitably led to the same conclusion. 'Either we take in strangers, or we wait for Tom.' The Christies had met with too much treachery in the past to trust to strangers and though their worst enemy, Atholl Farquharson, was dead now, his son still lived and traded in the same harbour.

'Tom may be only fourteen, but he's learnt a great deal already,' said Pearl, reading her thoughts. 'After two years on the *Jessica* he knows the workings of an engine inside out. All right, the *Jessica*'s not as good a ship as the Christie yard would build, and no wonder when they sent to Glasgow for her, but she's a bonny enough steamboat and Tom says he reckons he could fit an engine "nae bother" into one o' Maitland's designs.'

'Maitland's dream lies with sail, Pearl. You know that.'

Something in her voice made Pearl look up in surprise, but Rachel had turned away and was apparently studying the nearest half-hull on the office wall – the model of the *Bonnie Annie II*, built thirteen years ago to commemorate the first *Bonnie Annie*, sunk in the Baltic on her maiden voyage.

But it was not the model which had touched her voice

with sadness. It was the reminder of Jessica Abercrombie, for whom the *Jessica* steamship had been named, by old George Abercrombie himself, in gratitude for the birth of his first – and only – grandson. In their childhood, in the fishing community of the North Square in Footdee, Jessica and Rachel had been friends, but since Jessica's marriage into a prosperous city family and Rachel's own marriage to James Christie, enmity had grown between them, though that had been none of Rachel's doing. As the Abercrombie interests had grown and flourished, George Abercrombie had put money into the Christie shipbuilding enterprise, and had championed Christie's against their rival Farquharson for years. But the coming of steam had introduced a disruptive element and when George Abercrombie needed a steamship to mark wee Finlay Abercrombie's birth, the Christies could not supply one and Abercrombie had turned to Farquharson instead. But he had not withdrawn his patronage. On the contrary, and it was entirely due to George Abercrombie that young Tom had been apprenticed on the *Jessica*.

Rachel had not been happy about that, fearing some sort of devious dealing or secret persecution which would harm her Tom. But so far Jessica had lain low. If she felt any antagonism for the Christie lad, she had not shown it. In fact, Jessica had been surprisingly sober and dutiful in her behaviour – in public anyway. But Rachel remembered too vividly the days when Jessica Abercrombie had flaunted her new status as wife of a prosperous city trader and daughter-in-law of the Christie patron. She had been in the habit of visiting the Christie yard, uninvited, in her most flamboyant clothes, behaving in a high-handed and flirtatious manner, unsettling the menfolk, disrupting the work in hand, and leaving jealousy and suspicion behind her. It was James she had been after then, in spite of her husband, Fenton Abercrombie, and Jessica was used to getting what she wanted.

During all those barren years Rachel had felt the threat of Jessica's restlessness, though now, with her dear son Davy a healthy 18-month-old, and another child kicking in her womb, she should have felt secure. Those days were *over*. Jessica was changed, matured, a respectable matron and pillar of Aberdeen society. There was no harm she could do the Christies now.

'All right, Aunt Rachel,' persisted Pearl, breaking in upon her thoughts. 'Maybe Uncle Maitland dreams of sail, but what of Uncle James's dream?'

'You know that. A ship for every Christie man and a Christie master for every ship – though ye'll have to wait yet a while for your wee boatie, Davy lad,' she said, shaking off apprehension and retrieving her son with a laugh. 'For they'll not take an infant apprentice in steam or sail.'

'The next had better be a quine,' said Pearl, reaching for her bonnet. 'I'll not be here for ever and you'll be needing a daughter to help you out.'

No, thought Rachel with a stab of sadness. Pearl would not be with her for ever. She was a girl ripe for marriage and with lads enough knocking already at her door. Alfie Baxter, ship's carpenter on the *Bonnie Annie*, was particularly persistent. But Dr Andrew made them mind their manners and Pearl herself had been sensible enough – so far.

'Besides,' went on Pearl, tying the ribbons firmly under her chin, 'Aunt Louise needs me in the dispensary. Amelia is no help at all and as for Booky, all he can think of is the Bursary competition.'

'Aye,' sighed Rachel. 'Andrew must be glad of your help right enough.' Dr Andrew Noble had married Pearl's mother Isla years ago, and when Isla died, had married

Rachel's dear friend Louise Forbes – a forthright, sensible girl almost as conversant with medical matters as Dr Andrew himself. In childhood Pearl had spent as much time in the Christie home as in her own and had been as a daughter to Rachel, helping her with her firstborn son, Jamie, now fourteen, and her adopted son Tom. More than that, she had been a loyal and cheerful companion during James Christie's long absences at sea, and an invaluable help in the shipping office. Marriage, of course, was inevitable and after all Pearl was seventeen. Many girls were mothers by that age. At least, thought Rachel with optimism, she will marry a local boy and live close by.

'To tell you the truth, Aunt Rachel,' said Pearl cheerfully, 'as long as the medicines are prepared when he needs them, his notes in order and his reference books to hand, I don't think Dr Andrew notices me. But Aunt Louise is good for him. They talk together for hours.'

Not like poor Isla, thought Rachel, remembering. But there was nothing of Isla's pitiful dependence in her daughter Pearl – only her affectionate nature and her loyalty.

'I'm sorry I have not quite finished,' said Pearl, indicating the ledger, 'but you know how Amelia is and there is no one else to meet her today.' Ever since the night of the burning of the Anatomy Theatre when the streets of Aberdeen had been thronged with rioters and Isla Duthie had died, Amelia had been frightened to walk in the town alone, even the short distance from her school to the Nobles' house in the West End. 'I will come back and finish it for you as soon as I've seen Amelia safely home.'

'Don't trouble, dear.' Rachel kissed her on the cheek. 'You have enough to do and I can easily finish the work myself. Young Davy here will help me, won't you, my pet?'

'You'd best give him to Kirsty to look after,' said Pearl

as the child lunged for the inkwell and almost upended it. 'Ye'll find the work goes twice as fast with two hands instead of four.' Then she was gone, hurrying along Trinity Quay towards the town and Mrs Ellison's school.

Left alone, Rachel felt a sudden draught of loneliness. Whatever would she do without Pearl?

'I wish I was at school,' said India Abercrombie, drumming slippered feet against the sofa leg and picking aimlessly at the threads of the upholstery. She, her two sisters and her mother, were in the drawing room awaiting the arrival of various ladies and their offspring to take tea.

'Well you're nae, and stop fidgeting,' snapped her mother. Jessica, at thirty-seven, was a buxom woman, as well upholstered as her own sofa and covered in a similar finery of red brocade. Her dark hair was still satisfyingly thick and unspecked by any hint of grey, her skin as clear as when she was India's age and hawking fish through the streets of Aberdeen. But that was a part of her life she had pushed firmly behind her since her most satisfactory marriage into the Abercrombie 'empire'. At least, she amended, remembering certain private aspects of connubial habitation, it had been satisfactory till young Finlay's birth and that stupid Mairi's blabbing. Since then, Jess had concentrated on consolidating her suddenly precarious position by a display of domestic vigour and social good works. She joined all her mother-in-law's committees as well as working all hours in her father-in-law's emporium. She supervised her daughters' music with a mercifully toneless and indiscriminate ear, oversaw their inept attempts at watercolours with similar lack of expertise, and decked them, like herself, in the brightest and most flamboyant materials her husband's money could buy.

Her husband remained unmoved, but by now Jess had given up expecting him to change. She lavished all the affection her husband spurned upon their son, Finlay, and unloosed all her frustration on her daughters – usually on India.

'You drive a body wild with your shifting and picking,' she said now. 'Why ye canna do a wee bit sewing like your sisters and try to look ladylike, I dinna ken. I've Mrs Henderson and Mrs Cruickshank coming, and they'll likely bring their girls, dolled up to the eyeballs and simpering fit to crack their jawbones, so ye'll not disgrace me by behaving like a . . . like a fisher lass.'

'But weren't you a fisher quine yourself, Ma?' said India innocently.

'*Mamma*,' corrected Victoria quickly before her mother could draw breath. 'And sit up straight. You've a back like a dromedary.'

'Dromedary yourself,' retorted India, and put out her tongue. 'And it's *true*,' she added defiantly. 'Nana Brand . . .'

'I've warned you . . .' began her mother, but Augusta said quickly, 'It's all right, Mamma, take no heed of her. She's only trying to torment you and you don't want to make your complexion all red, do you? Not with Mrs Henderson always looking so pale and elegant.' Augusta, at sixteen, was a placid replica of her mother, but much shrewder than she looked. Besides, Augusta had her eye on the eldest Henderson boy, and whereas she found her youngest sister as infuriating as her mother did, recognised that it was in everyone's interest to present a calm and united family front.

'Why don't you let Victoria play to us, Mamma?' she went on before her mother could speak. 'It will sound lovely when the door opens.' Victoria had had piano lessons for three years.

'It is a pity you don't learn from your sisters,' muttered Jessica, glaring at India with something close to venom, as Victoria, a slender, pale-haired and vaguely discontented-looking fifteen-year-old in fuchsia pink, scrabbled in the piano stool for her music.

'I don't want to play the piano – not like Victoria, anyway,' India added *sotto voce*. Victoria, as she had been meant to, heard and slammed her fingers down viciously on the keys. Jessica winced.

'Play that nice wee tune, Victoria. You know the one. With the twiddly bits and the pedalling. It's real elegant, that one. And you, India my lass, can shut your mou' and listen.'

Victoria, after an uncertain note or two and a glare in India's direction, embarked on a painstakingly careful and pedestrian rendering of a Bach exercise. India put her hands over her ears and shuddered. This was too much for Jessica, complexion or no.

'*India*! You'll do as I say in this house or I'll put you over my knee and personally tan you black and blue. Do you hear me?'

'Yes, Ma.'

'*Mamma*,' corrected Augusta and Victoria in virtuous unison. India ignored them, her eyes on her mother in the usual battle. She knew Jessica meant what she said, and also, to her cost, that she wielded a devastating switch. Nevertheless, she dared to add, humbly enough, 'But I don't want to have painting lessons, or music lessons, nor dancing lessons neither. I would rather . . .'

'*You'd* rather? Listen to me, my lass, and listen well,' said Jessica, rising to the challenge. 'You'll have lessons like your sisters and like it. How else are ye ever to be a lady and marry a real gent?'

'But I don't want to be a lady – not if it means boring things like painting bad pictures and murdering music.

Besides, all ladies don't have to do that. There's Dr Andrew's wife Louise. She's a lady and she *works*.'

'Aye, and look at her. Plain as a pig's arse and she had to wait till his first wife died afore she finally caught a husband.' Poor sod, she added under her breath, though you had to hand it to the woman for persistence. But then, anyone with a face like hers would need to be persistent. At least India was not plain.

'All right,' said India defiantly, 'then what about Mrs Christie? She is not plain. She has been married years and years, too, and she doesn't paint or play the . . .'

'Shut yer mou' or I'll skelp your backside,' cried Jessica in fury, aiming a smack at India, who ducked. 'You know fine your father's forbidden you to speak that name i' this house.'

'Yes, Ma. *Mamma.*' India realised she had gone too far. She picked up the stretched hoop of embroidery at which she had been working with little achievement for months and stabbed at it in silence while Victoria laboured to the end of her piece and, at a nod from her mother, embarked on a second and Augusta, at the window, kept a watchful eye on Union Terrace below.

A fly droned against the window pane and it was oppressively warm. Old Mrs Abercrombie never lit a fire from April till October, replacing coals with folded paper fans and expecting her guests to shiver and survive, but Jessica refused to do likewise. It was a needless economy, in her opinion, and town in summer could be dreary enough, without adding to the gloom by an empty grate. 'I like a good fire,' she would explain and add complacently, 'After all, Fenton can afford it.'

One day, she vowed, he would 'afford' them a house in the country like county folk, so they too could flit to Culter or Skene for the summer months and leave the town to those who knew no better. Meantime, she'd keep a good fire and a good table, if only to prove they could afford any style of life they chose, when they chose. But today it was certainly hot.

'Are they coming yet, Augusta?'

'No, Mamma. At least, I can't see them.'

'Then ye can stop yer playing for a while, Victoria. Give yer hands a rest.'

'Thank goodness for that,' muttered India. Jessica chose to ignore her.

'Do you think Iain Henderson is back from Edinburgh yet?' asked Victoria, joining her sister at the window. 'Well move over, can't you, and let me see too.'

'There's no need to shove,' retorted Augusta, but amiably enough. She rarely found it worth the effort to squabble. Besides, the mention of Iain Henderson had set her curiosity galloping, and a moment later the two sisters were whispering and snorting with suppressed glee. Boys and their activities formed the bulk of their conversation, day in, day out, to their younger sister's profound disgust.

But India's turn would come, thought Jessica, glowering at her youngest daughter. She'd grow out of her tempers one day and marry like the others, or else . . . But the child looked docile enough at the moment, red head bent over grubby embroidery, and Jessica allowed herself to relax. She began to rearrange her hair at the gilt-framed mirror above the mantel-shelf, a task in which she was happily absorbed until India announced loudly, 'I've finished my pansy. Please can I go?'

'Go?' Jessica rounded on her in astonishment. 'Of course ye canna go. Ye'll stay and behave like I telt ye to behave. Ye can help hand round the ratafia biscuits and the wee scones.'

'But Ma, I hate ratafias, and anyway, I'll spill them.'

'She will, too,' put in Victoria maliciously. 'Out of spite.'

'I'll only be in the way, Ma, and you won't be able to talk about the same things if I'm there,' she added, child's eyes innocent, small freckled nose appealing. 'Grown-up things, I mean.'

'Well . . .' Jessica hesitated and India continued quickly, snatching her advantage, 'I could help Nana Abercrombie in the shop.'

'She's nae at the shop.' Jessica herself still helped in 'Abercrombie's' but on an elevated basis. She advised on 'fancy' foods, and recommended as the latest thing all the extravagances she persuaded old Abercrombie to order. But her department made a profit, 'new-fangled rubbish' or not, and she was an official partner now, on a level with Fenton, with her own share of the profits. When she saw the way her husband's mind was working, she'd made sure of that. By the time Fenton heard about it his father had already drawn up the agreement and it was too late for him to prevent it. If he'd wanted to. For Jessica had no means of telling what went on in her husband's head. Any contact between them was on a purely practical, day-to-day basis: domestic arrangements, the children's schooling, tradesmen's bills. There was little exchange of opinion, let alone thought, and she had no idea any more what he felt – for her or for their children. It made her uneasy.

'Then can I visit Nana at home?' persisted India, breaking in on her thoughts.

'No ye canna. She and yer Grandpa have gone to visit Clementina.' Clementina, Abercrombie's daughter, was married to the Farquharson boy and, since old Atholl Farquharson's death, had moved into enviable prominence in city society – at least, it would have been enviable were it not for the perpetual interference of the dowager

Mrs Euphemia Farquarson, an old and infuriating friend of Mrs Abercrombie senior.

'Then can I visit Nana Brand?' dared India recklessly. 'I haven't seen her for . . .'

But at that moment Augusta squealed, 'They're coming! I can see them turning the corner into Union Terrace. Mrs Henderson's wearing yellow . . .'

'What a colour for a woman her age!' put in Victoria.

'. . . with some sort of pink sash, and Anne's carrying a parasol . . .'

Jessica turned on India and said, with concentrated fury, 'You can visit your bedroom and stay there, if ye canna hold yer peace, ye infuriating wee tyke.' Then she flew into action. 'Quick, Victoria. Play that wee tune again, but quiet-like when you hear them on the stairs, and you, Augusta, sit i' the window with yer sewing, sideways to show yer profile. Aye, that's it. I'll sit here. Or maybe here . . .'

In the scramble to take up suitably impressive positions, India was forgotten and, seizing her opportunity – for hadn't her mother mentioned the bedroom? – she slid quickly out of the room and round a corner of the landing to hide until the guests were safely inside and the maid returned to the kitchen quarters. Then she shot downstairs and out into the street.

After all, her mother had not said she could not go. Not in as many words. And Nana Brand would be delighted to see her. She would call at the Christie house first, ostensibly to see if Kirsty's Annie was in – Kirsty's Annie's Nana lived in Footdee too – then they could go to the Square together. She knew she was not supposed to speak to the Christies, let alone visit them, because of some stupid family feud from way back, but no one would know and Jamie Christie was her friend. Singing happily to herself, India set off jauntily along Union Terrace towards the Castlegate and the Quay.

Number 3, Trinity Quay was a tall, narrow house, rubbing shoulders with a similar house on either side, and all of them standing watchful guard over the new stretch of quayside and the multiplicity of ships in the inner basin. Harbour development had extended and deepened the channel so that large ships could berth practically in the city centre instead of mooring in deep water and unloading into lighters as had previously happened.

In the days when the Christies had lived in the North Square at Footdee, on the edge of the grey North Sea, they had been away from the centre of shipping commerce, though near to their own shipyard and slipway, and to the fishing which had once been their livelihood. But with the consolidation of the shipyard and the slow build-up of the Christies' own fleet – four ships now – a shipping office nearer the town had seemed essential if they were to keep abreast of commercial and shipping developments, and keep a good eye on their competition.

The move from the one-roomed cottage in North Square had been an ambition James Christie had inherited, with the responsibility for the Christie clan, from his father, and an ambition he had for years set aside as he sought to establish shipyard, repair yard and trade links on an unshakeable foundation. But Christie's now employed some thirty men, produced a steady run of sailing ships for the local market – brigs of 80 tons or so for the most part, for the coastal trade – and, at regular intervals, a larger, carefully designed and beautifully executed addition to the Christies' own small but growing fleet.

But when harbour development extended the water inwards, and at the same time extended the quay, from the Fittiegait and the Shiprow, the new houses had seemed to James ideal, providing as they did extensive accommodation for his growing family, an office on the Quayside, and a perfect view from the upper windows of every shipyard in the basin, from Pocra to the Inches, and of every ship in harbour, from the smallest fishing smack to the largest emigrant ship for the Americas, from the most elaborately fitted whaler with her row of whaleboats slung on davits on the deck and her protective cannon, to the latest steam packet of the Aberdeen and Leith line, with her gaily decorated cabins for the ladies, her neatly dressed attendants and her smoke-belching funnels which so offended Maitland.

From the Christie window one could also see the constant activity of the quay – the loading and unloading, the shore porters threading the crowds with hand-barrows, the trundling of barrels, bales, portmanteaux, cabin trunks, the herding of cattle or horses, the arrivals and departures. The departures were the saddest – whole shiploads of emigrants, driven by eviction or economic necessity to seek a better life in Canada or America, their families weeping or stoically white-faced, as they watched their menfolk out of sight. Sometimes there was money enough for the whole family to go – often at the cost of selling everything they and their relatives possessed and leaving them with nothing except the clothes on their backs – though often, as Alex Christie soberly reported, it was not the whole family that arrived at the other side. With malnourishment, overcrowding, the incipient fevers or dysentery which cramped, insanitary conditions too soon exacerbated, death at sea was all too common. Though not, Rachel Christie was proud to remember, on the Christie ship which had been named for her and which regularly in the the spring and summer months took emigrants out to Canada and brought timber and other commodities back. They did not make the profits the Farquharson ships did, but at least, as James Christie said, they could hold up their heads in St Clement's Church of a Sunday without shame. But then it would take more than a few dozen dead emigrants to cause some folk shame . . .

Robert Farquharson had none of his father's shrewd business sense or ruthless drive, yet the Farquharson Shipping Co. still flourished, and still presented formidable competition, particularly on the London route where they had introduced another steam packet.

Steam . . . it was a subject that recurred with increasing urgency.

After Pearl had left to meet her half-sister Amelia from school, Rachel Christie finished entering the men's wages into the cash book, checked the total, and finally locked the office door. Then, Davy on her hip, she mounted the stair to their apartment on the first floor.

The ground floor of the building was reserved for James's twin brothers, William and George, when they were ashore, for the Office, and for general storage purposes – useful when they needed space to assemble ship's provisions, or to keep passengers' baggage safe. Rachel had also fitted up a small waiting room for the use of ladies meeting, or waiting to embark on, the *Anya* or the *Steadfast*, the two Christie ships which regularly plied the London run, taking goods of all kinds from live cattle to the most delicate of fancy stockings, as well as any passengers who wanted a reliable, courteous and comfortable passage without the dirt and danger of steam.

Steam again. There seemed to be no way of escaping it, thought Rachel as she opened the door on the first landing and stepped into her home. From the floor above came the usual bickering and squealing of Alex's children

– six of them now – and the sound of Kirsty's voice raised in sudden exasperation. Poor Kirsty, thought Rachel as she closed the door behind her and stepped into the sunlit peace of her own front room. Those kids of hers were quite a handful. Alex Christie had married Kirsty Guyan twelve years ago, with James and the Minister practically frog-marching him to the altar the moment he came back from the Greenland whaling. Kirsty's Annie had been born a mere three weeks later. Alex Christie, the youngest of the Christie brothers, had given up whaling two years ago in gratitude for Riga Tom's recovery from the fever and had rejoined the family fleet. He had successfully captained the *Rachel Christie* ever since.

Rachel put Davy down on the floor and moved to the hearth, to see to the fire and the kettle before setting about preparations for the family tea. The *Bonnie Annie* was due any moment – she had been spotted in the roads off Greyhope Bay in the late forenoon – and that meant young Jamie and his father would be home.

Jamie Christie was approaching fifteen, a tall, cheerful-faced boy who delighted his mother's heart – and set half the young female hearts in the harbour sighing for him whenever he stepped ashore. So far, however, to his mother's relief, he remained impervious, preferring the company of his brother Tom and his cousins, or, thought Rachel with a stir of unease, of India Abercrombie, Jessica's third daughter and, though a trifle tomboyish, the best of the three.

They had met in childhood in the days when Abercrombies and Christies freely mixed and, in spite of parental interdicts, still managed to meet somehow or other, as friends. But after all, Rachel told herself briskly, where was the harm in that? India was only a child – a normal, lively twelve-year-old – and in spite of his height and his broadening shoulders, her Jamie was still a child too in many ways. She moved to the window to check the seas eastward, towards Pocra, for the outline of the *Bonnie Annie*. Her husband, she knew, would have work to do before he came ashore, but he invariably sent Jamie home the moment the hawsers were secured. But before her eyes had moved over the tangle of masts in the inner basin to the clearer waters beyond, a movement in the foreground of her vision caught her attention.

As if the thought of Jamie had created him, there was the familiar figure striding jauntily along the quayside from beyond the Weigh-house. Rachel snatched up wee Davy and held him up at the window.

'See, Davy. There is your big brother Jamie. Wave to him like your Ma.' She knocked happily on the glass, but Jamie did not hear. His attention was on something further along the quayside, in the direction of Trinity Hall. Rachel turned her head to follow the line of Jamie's smiling gaze and saw a slight, red-headed lass in a yellow dress who, even as Rachel watched, broke into a laughing run and a moment later flung her arms round Jamie's waist.

Abruptly, Rachel turned away from the window, the light unaccountably gone from her afternoon.

India was turning the corner at the foot of the Shiprow when she saw him – a tall, shock-haired lad with the loose gait of someone whose limbs have grown faster than he can quite cope with, especially when he has spent three weeks on board ship and only just stepped ashore. She would have known him anywhere, in spite of the new jersey he was wearing and the new 'moustache' which shadowed his upper lip. She saw him stop as he drew level with the Weigh-house, saw him speak to someone and laugh before moving on again, whistling now, a bundle slung over one shoulder. Suddenly she could contain her impatience no longer.

'Jamie!' She forgot all female decorum and broke into a happy run, skirts and hair flying anyhow, eyes laughing and arms outstretched to hug him with exuberant affection.

Blushing, Jamie loosed her arms and drew away, glancing in quick embarrassment to either side to see who might have witnessed their meeting, but it was only momentary embarrassment, born of his burgeoning manhood and the awareness of what was expected of a midshipman who would one day be a ship's master in the Christie fleet. James was an uncomplicated boy, happy-natured and affectionate, and as fond of the girl he had known all her life as he was of his own brothers and cousins.

'Hello, Indy. Have ye come to the Quay especially to meet me? Or are ye here on an errand for yer Da?'

'Neither,' said India happily, falling into step beside him and slipping her hand into his free one. This time he did not pull away, but held hers tight and even swung it a little as they walked. 'Ma has visitors today and I was bored so I slipped out when she wasn't looking. Oh, I know I shouldn't have, but she won't notice. Not when she's busy telling Ma Henderson or Ma Cruickshank what new clothes she's bought and boasting about her new china tea set, "a' the way from Delft. That's in *Holland* ye ken,"' and India give a wicked imitation of her mother's native speech overlaid with what India scathingly called 'West End Social'. 'And the others won't notice either. All Augusta and Victoria think about these days is boys. I wouldn't mind that if they were interesting boys, like you and Tom, but they are all spots and starched collars and they stammer and go red if you so much as look at them. I hope our Finlay doesn't grow up to be like that . . .'

Jamie hardly listened. He was absorbed, as usual, by the shipping life of the Quay and anxious to catch up on any harbour gossip he might have missed in his four-week trip to the Baltic – longer than usual this time as they had spent some time with Tom's old grandparents outside Riga. Now, he made no comment, but slowed his steps the better to study a newly berthed three-master through whose open hatch could be seen a stack of tea-chests stamped 'Congou' and 'Best Bohea'.

'We'll have a ship of our own on the China run one day,' he said conversationally. By common consent they stopped to watch as the derrick swung out across the deck, the chains were lowered and hooks attached to the roped chests. 'Yon tea's come via London and a London broker. But now the monopoly's over, my Da says, in no time at all there'll be ports licensed all round Britain to take direct imports.'

'Grandpa gets his tea from London,' put in India knowledgeably.

'Aye, on our ships. But some of they London dealers are real rogues. There was a laddie caught gambling of a Sunday wi' money he'd earned picking "tea-leaves" in the hedgerow! Only they were nae tea, but all kinds of weeds to add to the real tea and make it go further. Your Grandda couldn't be doing with yon kind of carry-on, could he? But when we've a ship on the China run, he'll be able to get his tea direct from Canton, nae bother. So my Da says. I reckon I'll have served my apprenticeship by then and I mean to captain her myself.'

'Oh Jamie, will you really?' India looked at him with worshipping eyes. 'Will you really sail all the way to *China*?'

'Reckon so.' Jamie tried to look offhand about the

matter, but for all his efforts, could not keep the excitement from his voice.

India had a sobering thought. 'How long will it take to sail to China and back?'

'Eight months? Ten? A year maybe if we have to hang around for the tea auctions.' Jamie had heard his da and his Uncle Maitland discussing the matter. 'Of course there's other trade to be done out east to pass the time, if you arrive too soon. For instance I might take a look at Singapore,' he said nonchalantly, 'or Bombay.' He readjusted the bundle on his shoulder and added, 'But I'd best be getting on. Ma's sure to have seen the *Bonnie Annie* dock and she'll be expecting me.'

Dawdling along at his side, past all sorts and sizes of ships in all stages of preparation for sea-faring, India was silent, awed by the way Jamie referred to places she had barely heard of and then only as names on the schoolroom globe. Then she had a happy inspiration.

'I will come with you,' she announced. 'By the time you've served your apprenticeship I will be grown up anyway. I will tell Grandpa to appoint me his agent and I will buy his tea for him in Canton and ship it home on your vessel.' When Jamie made no reply, his attention apparently on the ship they were passing – a 90-ton brig loading salt-herring – she went on, 'You are lucky, Jamie. You can sail to the Baltic or to London or even Nova Scotia whenever you want to, and when you are at home you can look out of your window and see all these ships.' She sighed with envy. 'All we see is that old bleaching green and trees and things. "Such a peaceful outlook," Ma says, boasting. She says she wouldna live on the Quay if you paid her – though nobody ever would! – "not wi' the stink o' yon boilyard and the fish," but I think it's lovely and I hate a peaceful outlook! The only time I like it is when the fair is in town and sometimes we see jugglers or quack doctors and once there was a wee bear that danced.'

'That reminds me, Indy.' Jamie stopped, swung the bundle from his shoulder on to the nearest bollard and began to rummage in the contents. 'I have a wee gift for you somewhere in here. I have something for Davy, too, and for Tom of course, but . . . ah! Here it is. Close your eyes and hold out your hand.'

Obediently India squeezed her eyes as tight closed as they would go and, face radiant with excitement, held out her small, grubby hand, palm upwards.

'There. You can open them now.'

For a moment, India was silent with wonder as she gazed at the tiny, perfect wooden bear in the palm of her hand.

'Vanya Priit carved it,' said Jamie awkwardly. Vanya Priit was Tom's grandfather. 'I hope you like it.'

'Oh Jamie, he's lovely! Thank you, thank you!' and she reached up, pulled his face within reach, and kissed him on the cheek.

Fenton Abercrombie, emerging from the forward companionway of the Leith steam packet as the vessel breasted the swell of the harbour bar and slipped safely into calm water, saw the exchange and caught his breath on a mixture of anger and heart-stopping fear. But he was still a fair distance from shore. Perhaps he had been mistaken? After all, Aberdeen was full of young men in fishermen's jerseys and seaboots, with bundles over one shoulder, and the dockland was notorious for brazen womenfolk of all ages.

But in spite of the expanse of choppy water, the tangle of masts and resting ships, the clamour of gulls over garbage and the usual wharfside bustle, in spite of all reasoned argument, Fenton knew he was not mistaken

. . . He would know his youngest daughter anywhere, even were she disguised as a blackamoor in a fair-day side-show. No one else had her particular quicksilver vitality, her bright red hair and gangling limbs, and as for the lad . . . Fenton quivered with ancient humiliation and anger. He could smell a Christie in a multitude, in the dark and blindfold. He forgot Edinburgh, forgot the new shop in the Canongate that was doing so well, forgot the samples of best pipe tobacco he had brought back for his father to approve, and saw only his daughter, with a Christie.

Yet it was not entirely true to say that he had forgotten everything relating to his Edinburgh trip, for the sight of India, young and undeveloped though she was, had reminded him in an oblique way of Mrs Ballantyne – Mary Ballantyne whom he had just appointed over the heads of several older and more experienced male applicants, to a position of responsibility and trust.

Fenton could not have said where the comparison lay, except perhaps in their youth, but Mrs Ballantyne was twenty-five, not really young at all, and her hair was pale and drawn into some sort of neat coil whereas India's was unruly and red. Mrs Ballantyne was trim and demure, India invariably dishevelled. Perhaps the resemblance lay in their eyes? Clear, candid grey eyes, though India's held a hint of green. Or in their air of honesty? Or perhaps it was the figure? Mrs Ballantyne was slender, almost boyish in build, yet with a hint of delicious roundness at the bosom, as of a younger girl's budding breasts . . .

But the thought of breasts brought the blood rushing to his cheeks with mingled shame and anger. India was only twelve and a child, but in too few years she would be a woman – and she had kissed a Christie in the public street. In his haste he almost fell down the gangplank at the steamboat quay and, forgetting both bag and cartons of precious samples, pushed his way violently through the crowds on the wharf in pursuit of that strolling, brazen pair who, to his horror, he now saw were holding hands.

He caught up with them just as they reached the Christie office, seized India from behind, and tugged her viciously away so that she stumbled and almost fell.

'You bastard! I'll . . .' Jamie moved instinctively to defend her, but stopped, confused, as he saw the face of her supposed attacker. 'Sir . . . I thought . . .'

'Come home,' breathed Fenton in a voice of such quivering fury that India for a moment was speechless. Then, as he jerked her roughly forward, his fingers digging painfully into the flesh of her arm, she found her tongue and cried, 'Why, Papa? Jamie was only . . .'

'I said, come home! How dare you disobey me? How dare you speak to that . . . that . . .'

'But it was *Jamie*, Papa!' cried India, her eyes blurred with tears, as much of confusion as anything else. She did not understand what she had done wrong. 'Jamie Christie.'

'Never speak that name again, do you hear me?' Heedless alike of the startled passers-by and his own reputation as a mild, compassionate man, he almost threw her up the first stretch of the Shiprow, her feet slipping and stumbling on the cobbles as she struggled to twist free. Not until the Quay was obscured by the first bend of the street and they had passed the Farquharson office did he slacken speed. 'Were you walking with him?'

'Yes, but . . .'

'Were you holding hands?'

'Yes, but . . .'

'Did you kiss him?'

'Yes, but only to say thank you, Papa. For this.' Rashly she opened her hand and showed the little carved bear. Fenton snatched it from her and almost in the same movement ground it to splinters on the cobbles, under his heel.

'No!' shrieked India. 'It was mine. You had no right!' She struggled and struck out, but the normally quiet-tempered Fenton was inexorable.

'Never again, do you hear me? Never see him, speak to him, walk with him, *touch* him again. *Do you hear?*'

'Yes, Papa,' cried India, terrified by her father's rage, then she looked back at the pitiful remains of Jamie's gift and screamed in answering fury, 'Why? Why? *Why?*'

Fenton made no answer, but continued to propel her ahead of him up the slope towards the Castlegate, then into Union Street and on towards Union Terrace, while the blinding mist of scarlet fury gradually faded and cleared and the pounding blood quietened at last in his ears. Only then did the sense of India's words sink in, India who would have been his favourite daughter had he allowed his heart to open to any of his children, and who, he realised, was crying. India, who rarely cried and never for her own pain, was sobbing uncontrollably, tears blotching her face, eyes swollen and nose red, lips muttering in pitiful anguish, 'You insulted him in the public street. You shamed me and yourself. You had no right. I hate you. You stole my bear. He'd brought it all the way from Riga for me and Tom's grandfather made it himself. For *me*. You stole it. You destroyed it. You are a wicked, cruel *vandal* and I hate you. I hate you for ever and ever and I will never forgive you. You had no right. It was mine and you stamped on it. You are wicked. Wicked. I'll never forgive you. Never. Never . . .'

Listening to the stream of pain and humiliation, Fenton felt his own shame engulf him. India was right. He had been unforgivably cruel. He might at least have left her her little carved bear. Why he had ground it underfoot he did not know. He had never in his life done anything so senselessly destructive. He had thought himself a gentle, considerate man, a man who would never willingly inflict pain, especially on a child, and now he had damned himself in his daughter's eyes for ever and was ashamed. Irrelevantly, he wondered what Mrs Ballantyne would have said, had she seen him in the Shiprow, and knew she too would have looked away in shame.

But I had no choice, he thought bleakly, when his brain was clear and cold again, all grief, all anger spent. Poor child. One day, perhaps, she will understand.

'What was that disturbance, Jamie?' asked Rachel when her son had embraced her, swung young Davy in the air, tickled him and put him down again, spooned a ladleful from the hot-pot on the hearth, blown away the steam, tasted with eye-rolling appreciation and swallowed before Rachel could rescue it, and finally helped himself to a hunk of newly baked bread which he was now happily munching in the intervals of feeding pieces of it to his small brother.

'What disturbance, Ma?' countered Jamie, deliberately obtuse. 'Do you mean yon fishwifies mis-calling each other? Or Piddly Willy at the Weigh-house, wi' a skinful and singing?'

'You know fine what I mean, Jamie,' said Rachel in the quiet voice she always used when something serious was under discussion. 'Wasn't India Abercrombie with you? And before you deny it, remember I have a pair of eyes and can use them and a window with a fine view of the Quay.'

'What if she was?' said Jamie after a moment's pause. 'There's nae harm in that, surely? She was on her way to visit her Nana Brand, she said, i' Footdee.'

'And changed her mind?' prompted his mother.

'Aye, I reckon so.'

'Just as well,' said Rachel, 'considering I know for a fact her Ma has forbidden her to go to the Square unless she goes with her parents, in the family carriage. Kirsty told me.'

Kirsty Guyan, Alex's wife, was a fisherman's lass and in the Square one man's news was public knowledge within the hour.

'Eattle ottle, black bottle,' chanted Jamie, tickling Davy's tummy to the infant's intense delight.

'And?' said Rachel. 'You can stop pretending you don't know what I'm on about, Jamie. I saw Mr Abercrombie as well as you did. And leave Davy alone. You'll make him sick. You might as well tell me, lad, for you will get no peace till you do.'

Jamie sighed. It was not that he wanted secrets from his Ma – he told her everything and always had – but there were some things he thought it better she should not know. Things that, in his short experience, brought a frown to her face, or spread what he called her 'sad' look. It was a look she had worn for years until wee Davy's arrival and one which had always distressed him. Now he said evasively, 'Indy's Ma had invited a few wifies in for a "fly" cup and seemingly Indy should have been there. Her Da told her to get along home, sharp like.'

'I see.' Rachel spoke quietly enough, but Jamie sensed the unspoken question as clearly as if she had uttered it aloud.

'No, he didn't say it was my fault, Ma. He said nothing to me. Only to Indy.'

'I see,' said Rachel again, in the same abstracted voice, but this time Jamie knew he was not required to comment. Nevertheless her silence left him with a question of his own. Why had Indy's Da been so angry? When he told his Ma Mr Abercrombie had said nothing to him, it was the truth, but what he had not said was that Mr Abercrombie's face had expressed clearer than any words could what he thought of Jamie, or that he had heard Mr Abercrombie order Indy never to 'speak that name again'. Why? puzzled Jamie. The Christies are honest enough and well-liked, in Square or Town. So *why*? But five minutes later the arrival of his father from the *Bonnie Annie* and of his Uncle Maitland from the Christie shipyard put all other thoughts from his mind. Gifts were bestowed, news exchanged, and a multitude of questions answered before the family settled into any sort of calm. Then, as always, the talk reverted to the one question uppermost in every Christie man's mind: the China trade.

'But will Aberdeen be licensed for direct tea trading?' Maitland demanded, as he had done repeatedly over the last weeks.

'Bannerman got us the Lord Commissioner's despatch, remember, approving Aberdeen as a Warehousing Port for the East India trade.' Bannerman was their MP. 'China will be next, you'll see.'

'But when, James? And even if we are approved, if the Government doesn't revise the tonnage duty, will trade be worth anyone's while? A shilling a ton on every British ship entering Canton is crippling, especially with the extra seven shillings per cent on all exports and imports.'

'It certainly gives foreign competition a free rein,' said James, 'and the Americans in particular will gobble up the market, given the chance.' James Christie, at forty-one, was a sober, sensible family man, reliable and honest, yet still with a spark of the old adventurous spirit left in him, in spite of past injury and suffering. His strange, mis-matched eyes, one brown, one crystal-blue, had always held a hint of mystery and teasing and sometimes, as now, a disconcerting sparkle. 'But they won't have that chance. Did you know the *City of Aberdeen* reached the gulf of Guinea, all well, by mid-March? If she keeps as good time she'll reach Canton well ahead of the tea auctions, and with plenty of time to find her bearings.'

The *City of Aberdeen*, sent by a group of city merchants to try the market now the East India Company's monopoly had ceased, was to be a kind of test.

'But she's a small ship,' said Maitland. '260 tons at the most. She'll not make the profit a larger vessel could.'

'Maybe not, but she'll have the speed and a lower tonnage duty.'

'I meant to tell you,' put in Rachel, removing the empty stewpot and replacing it with fresh bread and a slab of cheese from the morning market, 'Pearl had a visitor this afternoon. A sea captain in search of work. A Captain Greig.'

'I hope she sent him packing,' said James, with a smile. He knew his niece's competence and her ability to take care of both herself and the Christie interests.

'Not exactly . . .' Rachel waited till she had both men's full attention before adding, 'He's here to see to yon wee steamship Alexander Hall's are building and to sail her out east when she's ready. The vessel's for the China trade, seemingly. For Jardine's, in Canton.'

She watched their expressions change from wary interest to open curiosity.

'Why didn't ye say so, woman!' cried James and Maitland in unison. Then, with one accord, both men emptied their ale mugs, pushed back their chairs and rose from the table.

'We'll away to the shipyard. Someone's sure to have heard where the fellow's berthed. Captain Greig, did you say?'

'Duncan Greig,' supplied Rachel, handing James his seaman's jacket and woollen hat. 'Mind and dinna catch a chill now. It may be June, but there'll likely be a nip in the air by the time you come home.'

'Dinna fuss, woman.' But James was grinning as he kissed her.

'Can I come too, Da?' Jamie was already on his feet and reaching for his jersey.

'No. Your uncle and I will likely call in at the tavern when we've taken a turn round the quay. Time enough for that when you're sixteen. You stay here with your Ma.'

'But Da . . .' wailed Jamie. 'I want to . . .'

'You'll do as you're told,' said his father sternly. 'Dinna forget you've signed papers. You are apprenticed to me, lad, and like any other apprentice you'll obey the rules. No taverns. You can think yourself lucky you're not confined to below decks, wi' ship's biscuit and water. So ye'll stay at home, lad, and see to yer Ma. Understand?'

'Yes, Da.' Jamie subsided, crestfallen, into his chair. He knew his father was right, but it made no difference. He would have given anything to have gone with them to the tavern, to look for Captain Greig of the China seas, and to talk men's talk till the moon set and the first light paled the morning sky. At the door, James Christie relented.

'Dinna look so glum, laddie. When we track down the China captain, we'll hook him fair and square and bring him home for a meal, maybe, or a dram. Ye'll get to talk to him one day.' Then he was gone, Maitland at his side and both of them whistling.

'I am sorry, Jamie,' said Rachel, seeing his disappointment. 'But your Da's right, you know. Here, hold wee Davy for me while I see to the dishes, then you can tell me all about Riga so I can tell Tom if you're away to sea again before he's back.' The *Jessica* steamship plied regularly between London and Aberdeen and often the boys' paths did not cross for weeks. 'Did you see Vanya Priit and Friida? How are they? And did they like the cheeses I sent them and the knitted stockings?'

While he told his mother all he could remember of the Riga trip – and she needed to know every detail – he wondered with a secret part of his mind whether Indy's father was still angry with her. Poor Indy. But at least she had liked the little wooden bear.

'Why was your daughter walking the streets with that Christie boy?' Fenton's voice was quiet, but cold as Greenland ice, and Jessica looked at him warily from under lowered lids before attempting a reply.

Her guests had stayed gratifyingly late, one way and another, what with all there was to talk about – 'Toria and Gussy needing to know about Edinburgh fashions and then who was going to wear what when the new season started in the autumn, and Mrs Henderson's cousin's sister-in-law's daughter having ridden in a steam omnibus on the Paddington road at ten miles per hour and been terrified quite out of her mind. Then Mrs Cruickshank's eldest daughter's husband was thinking of standing for the Town Council what with all the changes and no one having any say and Mrs Henderson had said if he did, he should see the streets were kept cleaner. It was a disgrace the way some folk tipped garbage into the street at any hour when anybody knew the scavvies were finished by ten in the morning. Altogether it had been a happy afternoon – until Fenton arrived home with India, blotched and dishevelled, shouting some rubbish about bears and insulting her father, there on the steps, for all the street to hear, let alone Jessica's guests who were just leaving – and Mrs Henderson looking so smart, too. Jessica could cheerfully have strangled India on the spot

– and Fenton too when he pushed past her without a word of common courtesy to herself or to her guests.

Jessica had seen the looks exchanged between Mrs Cruickshank and Mrs Henderson and knew exactly the course their conversation would take the moment they were out of earshot. It would be a combination of condescension and pity, and a huge self-satisfaction that their own husbands and daughters at least knew how to behave.

But Jessica had smoothed over the incident as best she could. 'Poor Fenton is so busy these days,' she had confided, 'with the new Edinburgh branch taking up so much time and then he is such a *family* man. It is not easy, you know, to find time for both. But with "Abercrombie's" so flourishing, we really musn't complain.'

Even as she uttered the words, Jessica knew that were the profits of the Abercrombie shop ten times what they were, it would not compensate for her guests' affronted feelings, nor obliterate the picture of the angry-faced father and the rebellious daughter. Speculation on that score would continue well into next week, by which time, no doubt, India would have been credited with the blackest of imaginable sins.

'Well?' said Fenton ominously. 'I am waiting for an answer.'

'Yes dear.' Jessica gathered strength and managed to look her husband calmly in the face. After all, it was not her fault. 'You obviously know more than I do,' she said daringly. 'I thought India was upstairs in her room.'

'You *thought*! You will do more than "think" in the future. You will *ensure*. Do you understand? You will ensure that India behaves in a decorous and ladylike fashion at all times. And that she has nothing to do with that family.'

Patience was never Jessica's strong point and what little

she had was exhausted. 'It's no good going on at me, Fenton, it's her you should go on at. You try telling Indy what to do if she doesn't want to do it and see how you get on. She's a disobedient wee bitch. I've telt her a thousand times and she pays not the slightest . . .'

'Surely you can control your own daughters?' interrupted Fenton. 'You are a grown woman!' He strode to the sideboard and poured himself a large brandy before continuing. 'I would remind you, Jessica, of certain obligations on your part, namely to care for *our* children as I direct you.' The irony of the 'our' was plain. 'I ask a simple thing of you and it seems you cannot even oblige me in that. Must I take this to mean you are no longer prepared to co-operate?'

'No, Fenton,' said Jessica as humbly as she could manage.

'Then I will tell you again, as you seem not to have understood me clearly. The children are not to consort with that family. I forbid it. Kindly tell India so.'

'Tell her yourself,' snapped Jessica, needled beyond endurance. But the moment the words were out, she regretted them. Gone were the days when she could wheedle and twist Fenton at will. Ever since the day of wee Finlay's birth when he had found out a thing or two about her past, or thought he had, she had been treading uncertain ground. Fenton had moved a bed into his dressing room and the door between his room and hers had remained locked ever since – on his side of the door. She had tried cajoling, tried humility, tried solicitude and long-suffering amiability. She had tried self-abasement and defiance, coaxing and neglect. Even, when he was well-wined and, she had hoped, susceptible, open seduction. Nothing worked, till in the end she had settled into a sort of sporadic sniping, but always from a safe distance.

With the family firm flourishing and her life as comfortable as money could make it, she was not going to risk being put into the street, and Fenton's moods were unpredictable.

Now, as she waited, with held breath, for an outburst he merely frowned in private silence till his brandy glass was empty then, holding its bowl in his two hands, he tipped it slowly this way and that, staring into the glinting well before saying at last, 'How old is Augusta?'

'Sixteen, of course.'

'And Victoria?'

'Fifteen next month. Surely you . . .' but Fenton interrupted.

'What have you done about finding husbands for them?'

'Nothing,' said Jessica, astonished. 'They're hardly out of school and . . .'

'Then start. Augusta is old enough. Arrange it. Speak to my mother and see to it between you. Someone *suitable*. You understand me?'

'Yes, *dear*,' said Jessica with heavy irony. 'And in return perhaps you would kindly tell me why you have suddenly decided to sell off your daughters as child brides?'

'Hardly that. Where you come from, I understand a girl is practically "on the shelf" if she is unmarried at seventeen.'

'Well this is not Footdee and your daughters are not fisher quinies, so I see no reason to . . .'

'I do. And why, I hear you ask. Because I'll not risk having them walking the streets, that's why! Do you realise she actually *kissed* the boy? On Trinity Quay, for all the world to see?'

'The wicked wee tyke,' exploded Jessica. 'Wait till I lay my hands on her. I'll tan her disobedient backside so hard she'll not sit down for a week. See if I don't. I am sorry,

Fenton,' she said, switching from anger to wifely sympathy in the drawing of a breath. 'No wonder ye're so put out. I don't know what's got into the lass these days, she's that feckless and wild. I canna think who she takes after . . .' She stopped, too late, and continued hastily, 'And you are quite right about Augusta. Of course she'd best start choosing a husband and then next year when 'Toria's sixteen, she can follow.'

Fenton was not deceived. He could read every devious twist and turn of his wife's mind and only marvelled that he had been duped for so long. But on that fatal day of his son's birth, his eyes had been opened and his love destroyed. He could not even love his children any more, though it would have been more true to say that he forbade himself to love them and certainly refused to show affection lest that small concession loose the flood gates of his love. And he had loved, once. He had loved his wife and then his children, one by one, with an all-consuming tenderness and adoration which still troubled him, on bad days, with persistent memory.

Augusta had been adorable, so sweet-natured, so affectionate, with her mother's black-haired, rosy beauty. But with adolescence Augusta had grown as silly as the next girl. Victoria was as bad. They said her fair looks were the image of his sister Clementina, though 'Toria had more spirit and could have been clever had she applied herself – or, prompted the voice of conscience, been given more encouragement. He thought fleetingly of Mrs Ballantyne, fair and slender like Victoria, but calm and self-contained, with intelligence in her eyes. Of course, there might still be time to steer Victoria's interests, and Augusta's, into more rewarding channels than Jessica's fashion plates and gossip. They were not unintelligent and he would have enjoyed exploring the classics with them, even discussing serious topics like the new factory laws or the plight of the dispossessed crofters, watching their young faces brighten with lively interest. Abruptly he slammed the door on that dangerous avenue of thought and closed his heart. Marriage was the answer.

'You should have no trouble arranging it,' he told Jessica now. 'It is public knowledge that the Abercrombies are making a tidy profit and they are neither of them actually plain. If they giggle and simper and doll themselves up half as ridiculously as they usually do, you will marry them off in a week.'

Married they would be safe. First Augusta, then Victoria. And eventually little red-headed India. Remembering her tears and her passionate imprecations, Fenton's heart twisted with aching compassion – then into his mind came a picture of his daughter and the Christie boy, hand in hand and laughing together in some private world, and the hair rose on the nape of his neck.

'See to it, woman,' he finished, and strode out of the room.

Captain Greig was nowhere to be found in the harbour that night, though the Christies scoured every tavern. 'He's likely found accommodation,' they agreed, with a knowing wink, 'and gone early to bed.' But wherever he had spent the night and with whom, he was at the Christie office the next morning, looking, he told Rachel, for James Christie.

'I heard as how he's ashore,' Greig explained.

If Rachel was surprised to see him back so soon after his abrupt departure of the previous day, she did not show it. Instead she noted the way his eyes ranged over the office, taking in panelled walls, map stand, leather-topped desk, then the globe of the world on a stand near the window, the corner shelves of nautical instruments and the half-models of ships' sheers on the walls. Whatever he had been seeking, apparently he did not find it, for he finished, restlessly, 'After what Miss Noble said, I thought I'd call in by and ask if he is maybe needing an extra hand?'

Ah, thought Rachel, with an inner smile. It's that way the wind lies, is it? But she said, courteously enough, 'Of course, Captain Greig. I know my husband would be delighted to meet you, though I cannot promise anything in the way of work. Unfortunately he has already left for the shipyard, with his brother Maitland, and as I am alone in the office today, I cannot take you myself, but if you will just wait a moment I am sure my son would be happy to accompany you there.'

She stepped past him into the stairwell just as the door on the landing opened and Jamie Christie ambled out, a slab of bread in one hand, an earthenware jug in the other. 'Kirsty's minding Davy, Ma,' he began, then saw the captain and stopped, mouth open in mid-chew.

'Don't speak with your mouth full, Jamie, and remember the ale is for your father, not you. Take it straight to the yard and hurry. You're late.' She spoke with apparent severity and it was not until she spoke again that Jamie realised he was not in trouble, but the opposite. 'And if you will take Captain Greig with you, I'm sure he will be happy to tell a young midshipman all about his adventures in the China seas on the way.'

'Yes, Ma!' He leapt down the stairs and slithered to attention as best he could with the heavy ale jar in one hand.

'Captain Greig, sir?' He looked from the waiting Greig to his mother and raised questioning eyebrows. 'Pearl's Captain Greig?'

His mother gave a quick nod before saying courteously, 'Captain Greig is from Jardine's, in Canton,' then to the captain, 'My eldest son, Jamie. Take the captain to the shipyard. He'd like a word with your father. And when you find my husband,' she went on, smiling, 'please tell him I would be happy if he would bring you back to eat with us when your business is settled.'

'Thank you, ma'am.' Again Captain Greig looked round the office as if expecting to find something he had lost, then reluctantly turned for the door.

'Where is the young lady today?' he asked Jamie when they were outside on the Quay and moving eastward towards Pocra.

'Young lady? Oh, you mean Pearl. At home, I expect. Captain Greig, sir. Is it true what Pearl told Ma, that you know all about the China trade?'

'Maybe.' Greig sounded preoccupied and when Jamie stole a sideways look at him to gauge his temper – maybe Jamie had spoken in too familiar a fashion? He wasn't sure how a mere apprentice was supposed to speak to a China captain – he saw that Greig's brows were drawn together, apparently in thought. He looked both authoritative and forbidding. Jamie noted the weather-tanned features, the grey hairs in his black side-whiskers, the slightly hooked nose and the long scar above one eye. He wished he dare ask how the man got that scar. Pirates perhaps? Chinese opium smugglers? He felt awe and humility and a desperate desire to ask questions, coupled with a crippling shyness. He hoped he had not offended the captain already by asking about China. They strode on in silence for some dozen steps, Greig still lost in thought, Jamie increasingly anxious, while the ale slap-slapped in the jar and he felt his face growing red with embarrassment. Then Greig spoke.

'Does Pearl, Miss Noble, work regularly in the office?'

'Yes,' said Jamie, surprised. 'At least, I suppose you'd call it regularly. She comes when she can, you see – when Dr Andrew doesn't need her, or Aunt Louise.' When the captain made no comment, Jamie went on, as much from nervousness as from the wish to impart information, 'Pearl likes babies, you see. She comes to help Ma and play with wee Davy and she's very good at accounts, too. Ma says she's better than any bank clerk. But sometimes she has to meet Amelia from school and help with her lessons and sometimes she has to work in the dispensary, mixing tonics and things. Or help with a wash week. Or make jam. But mostly,' he finished desperately, praying Captain Greig would say something before it was too late and they reached the shipyard, 'mostly she comes to us.'

'Good,' said Greig, and smiled to himself. 'Tell me, lad, what exactly is it you want to know about Canton?'

'Everything,' said Jamie happily, and prepared to listen, for weeks and months if necessary, till he had soaked up every scrap of information the captain had to offer.

ii

The schooner *Jardine* progressed steadily from wooden skeleton to sleek-curved hull, a sailing vessel, as Maitland pointed out, with paddle wheels. In fact, the two steam engines were not to be used at all on the passage out, apparently, and the paddles and paddle boxes were to be stowed below.

'We could have built her for you, easy,' boasted Jamie to Captain Greig on a day in late October, 'and twice as fast. Yon engines are only extras anyway.'

'And more trouble than they're worth, seemingly,' put in Pearl, ladling broth from the family pot and putting a brimming dish in front of the guest. 'Take some bread, Captain Greig. It's fresh baked today. All yon engines do is take up good cargo space.'

'Maybe,' said Greig. 'But they'll earn their keep in the Pearl river. This broth is splendid, by the by.' He nodded his apprcciation to Rachel, then to Pearl as both women busied themselves with filling the menfolk's bowls, replenishing the ale jar, and slicing bread. 'They reckon yon wee engines will give a speed of seven knots, wind or no wind. She'll be the first steamship in the delta – and what "face" that will give to Jardine's. It'll be the Hoppo's turn to kowtow then.'

'If they don't turn their guns on her as spawn of the foreign devils,' said James Christie with a grin.

'Surely they would not do that?' Pearl had set Davy on

her knee and was feeding the child with broth from his own wee bowl, but now she looked at Greig in alarm, the spoon suspended halfway to Davy's mouth.

'Why not?' said Greig. 'But there's no need to look so worried, lass. If they do, they'll miss, like as not. They may have invented gunpowder while we folk were still killing each other with sticks and stones, but their guns are no match for ours, nor their fighting skill neither. I remember a fellow telling me about an incident off the coast of Lintin Island . . .' and he launched into a tale which held the company spellbound till well after the meal was over.

Since that first encounter with Pearl when he had demanded work, Duncan Greig had become a familiar face at the family table and though he had been given no Christie ship, he seemed content. He found occasional work in the harbour – piloting or a coastal run – and, on one occasion, shipped passage to London on unspecified business. But always he would reappear, put his head round the door of the Christie office and, if Pearl was there, come in and, as he put it, 'renew acquaintance'. If she was not, he would nod to Rachel, ask after the Christie menfolk, then stroll eastwards towards the shipyards, first to inspect the *Jardine*, then to find Maitland or Christie himself, in the Christie yard.

For though still wary of strangers, both brothers welcomed his experience of the China seas and his advice on rigging and freight-space suitable for the typhoon-lashed oceans of the East and the delicate cargo they planned to carry. Maitland's next ship for the Christie fleet was destined for the China run and the plans must be perfect. Meanwhile, Greig's own ship took shape until he confidently predicted a launch in April of the coming year, or early May.

By then, the Christies agreed in private – for friend

though Greig had become, he was still an outsider and not to be entirely trusted – the *City of Aberdeen* should have returned from Canton, with her precious cargo and a wealth of first-hand experience for them to draw upon to corroborate or contradict Greig's tales. Then, they agreed, they would be able to settle the final details of their own tea-ship – and lay down the keel.

Meanwhile, the days shortened, the seas roughened and the coasts were raked with the usual winter storms. The *Bonnie Annie* took upwards of five weeks from Riga when boisterous weather obliged them to seek shelter in a Norwegian port, east of the Naze, and kept them there a fortnight or more, with some fifty other vessels. Young Jamie revelled in the excitement, in the strangeness of the Norwegian sailors, and in the company of the other ships, but James Christie was less happy. He worried for Rachel, who he knew would be anxious and who was near her time.

In late November, Rachel's child was born – another healthy son, whom they named Maitland after his uncle, but who was instantly dubbed 'Matt'.

Tom, on the *Jessica*, fared better than Jamie, for with the onset of the first bad storms, the Farquharson management decided to beach her, for alterations. The Aberdeen and Leith company had recently refurbished their *Duke of Wellington* with a sumptuous new 'Ladies' Cabin' and numerous other comforts and Euphemia Farquharson would not rest content until the *Jessica* had not only the same, but better.

So it was that on a day in late January Tom called at the Nobles' house to see Amelia and found her, with Booky and Pearl, bundled up in plaid, muff and leather boots and obviously dressed to go out.

Tom, at fifteen, was smaller than his adoptive brother Jamie and slighter in build, but with a strength about him that was hard to define. Born in Latvia and orphaned a year later, Toomas, as was his original name, had been given by his grandparents to James Christie, the sailor they had found shipwrecked and unconscious in Riga bay, and nursed back to life. They hoped that with him, across the seas, the child might have a better life than they could hope to give him. He had repaid the Christies' generosity with unswerving loyalty and love. Quick-witted, intelligent, with a lively, inquiring mind, when his father had signed him to the steamship *Jessica*, he had quickly earned the respect of the rest of the crew and though only an apprentice, like Jamie, had early established a niche for himself in the boiler room, when ship's duties did not require him elsewhere. After two years at sea, he could have stripped and reassembled the *Jessica*'s engine blindfold and knew exactly the changes in engine noise which heralded trouble. His only regret was that the *Jessica* was not a Christie ship, but one day, he was sure, there would be a Christie steamship for him to sail. Until that day, he would be loyal to the *Jessica* and to George Abercrombie who had arranged his apprenticeship – but his chief loyalty remained, as it would always do, to the Christies whom he loved.

But Tom had another, private love, which he mentioned to no one, not even Jamie from whom he had few secrets. Ever since childhood he had loved Amelia Noble, Dr Andrew's daughter and Pearl's half-sister.

Amelia was four years his junior. Always a timid child and more so since her mother's death, her fair hair, blue eyes and pink-and-white complexion merely increased her air of fragility, though in reality she had a stubborn streak as strong as steel. 'If that quinie wants a thing, she'll get it,' the long-suffering Pearl had commented years ago, 'by wile or guile or just plain dogged obstinacy.' But Amelia tearful or Amelia smiling were equally irresistible to Tom and brought out all the protective chivalry in his young heart. So, when he found himself ashore with time to spare, he often walked to the Nobles' new house in the West End to offer his services as escort – Amelia did not like to walk to or from school alone – or merely to exchange news of what had happened since his last sea trip.

'We were just leaving for the Exhibition,' Pearl told him when he arrived that January afternoon. 'It's the last week and Booky wants to see it again.'

'It's the Oxy-hydrogen Microscopic Exhibition,' said Amelia carefully. 'Little living creatures in a drop of water made to look enormous, so Booky says.'

Happily Tom fell into step beside her as the group turned eastward towards the wide stretch of Union Street. There was a powdering of new snow on the ground under a pale, frost-clear sky. Sunlight sparkled from the granite of the house fronts and again from the snow underfoot. Amelia took Tom's hand, in case she slipped, and Pearl linked arms with young Andrew 'Booky' Noble, a year younger than Tom and to sit the Bursary Competition for Marischal College in September. He would probably win, too, thought Tom without envy. Booky was clever. Usually he preferred his books to other company, but today the Exhibition was of sufficient interest to lure him away and he was earnestly explaining to Pearl what they were about to see.

'. . . a screen of 300 square feet on which is thrown a picture, magnified . . .'

Tom hardly listened. He was absorbed by the picture of Amelia in her outdoor plaid, her cheeks bright with cold and exercise, her breath visible in small white clouds before her face as she spoke. Her little feet, in their thick, hand-knitted stockings and sensible boots, scurried to keep up with Pearl's brisk pace. They had passed Union

Terrace and the bridge, its parapet still capped with snow, passed Belmont Street and the Aberdeen Hotel, and were almost at the door of the Exhibition when a voice called from across the wide expanse of street.

'Miss Noble! Tom!'

They stopped, looked about them, and saw on the far side of the street the tall, spare figure of Duncan Greig, waving. He threaded his way through the carriages, water-carts, errand boys and muffled pedestrians to join them, stamping his feet on the rutted mud and snow and clapping his arms briskly across his chest.

'A bit colder than Macau,' he said cheerfully, looking round the small group with a nod of greeting. 'Are you walking far? Going to the Quay perhaps?'

'We are going to the Oxy-hydrogen Microscopic Exhibition,' said Amelia politely. 'It is one shilling, but only sixpence for children and Papa said we might go.'

'Then I would be happy to join you. I havena seen an exhibition like that for many a year, if ever, and at least it should be warmer than the street. That is,' he said, suddenly awkward, 'if it would not be an intrusion, Miss Noble?'

'The Exhibition is open to everyone,' she said coolly. 'I could hardly stop you going in if I wanted to. But I don't mind,' she added hastily, seeing his expression. 'Join us, by all means. You can tell Booky about sea creatures. I gather the projections resemble serpents and crocodiles and all kinds of monsters, but are really only tiny wee beasties, normally too small for us to see.'

Captain Greig felt in the pocket of his thick serge jacket and pulled out a handful of coins. 'Allow me,' he said and, stepping in front of her to the ticket-window, paid for them all. Pearl tried to protest, but he brushed away her arguments with 'Save your money to buy sweetmeats for the wee ones,' then they were inside, in a new, strange world.

'I don't want to go to a mouldy old Exhibition,' said India rebelliously.

'What you want or don't want is nobody's business, my lass,' said Jessica, wrenching at India's bonnet ribbons as if she meant to strangle the child. 'You are going and that's that.' She inspected India through narrowed eyes, gave her a shove between the shoulder blades and said, 'You'll do. Augusta. Victoria. Get moving, the pair of you. The carriage is waiting.'

'Why do we need a carriage when it's only five minutes' walk away? It's silly,' grumbled India.

'Why? Because we're nae getting our clothes wet in the snow, you stupid quine, nor our feet soggy and our faces froze when we can ride in comfort, that's why! Mrs Henderson will come in her carriage, see if she doesn't, and she's as close as we are. Closer, in Belmont Street. Well, go on with you,' she snapped as India deliberately hung back at the step. 'We dinna want to keep folk waiting.' India quickly scrambled up beside the driver, knowing she was not allowed, but gambling that once her mother and her two sisters were inside, they would not want to squeeze their skirts up to make room for her. She was right, and when the coachman touched his whip to the horse's flanks and the animal moved obediently forward, the carriage creaking and swaying more than usual and the wooden wheels trundling in a spray of slush, India felt her spirits rise in spite of her resolve not to enjoy herself. She had been dragged around with her sisters all winter, to theatres and lectures and exhibitions and teas, all of them boring though mainly, she admitted, because of the company. Anything would be boring if the Hendersons and the Piries were there. But they always were – and if not them, the Cruickshanks.

Now she sat high on the seat above the horse's swaying rump, the crisp air clean and fresh in her face, the wide swath of Union Street snow-bright and cheerful under the winter sun. There were other carriages abroad, and horsemen, gentlemen in from the country on business, or city lawyers perhaps. And the usual crowd of people on foot – servants with covered baskets, busy about their employers' business, errand boys, pedlars, townsfolk taking the air. Perhaps she would see Jamie? Or Tom? It was weeks since she had been allowed near the Quay, and the last time Ma had visited Nana Brand in North Square, India had been left behind with Mairi, and dire threats of what would befall her if she disobeyed her Ma and set so much as one toe over the threshold. She was beginning to feel like a prisoner.

They passed the splendid new frontage of her grandfather's shop, with 'Abercrombie and Son' in red and gold letters a foot high above the door, with brown spirals and green leaves and a space carefully left for the crest they meant one day to win – a Royal 'By Appointment' crest on which Nana Abercrombie had set her heart. There were jars and bottles in the windows, and a huge, red-lacquered tea caddy with a black pagoda and little bridge. Then the carriage drew up at the doorway of the Exhibition, and Jessica made her regal descent, her daughters behind her, just as the Henderson carriage arrived. India groaned. It was going to be every bit as boring as all the other outings had been. But as Jessica, in full finery, stepped into the shadowed doorway, she found her passage blocked by another party coming out.

'Excuse *me*,' she said loudly, then stopped, momentarily taken aback as her eyes adjusted to the half-light inside and she saw who blocked her way.

'Hello, Mrs Abercrombie,' said Pearl politely. 'I hope you enjoy the Exhibition.'

'It is really most interesting,' said Booky earnestly. 'Did you not think so, Captain Greig?'

'You don't know the Cap . . .' began Pearl politely, but Jessica had recovered her dignity and rudely interrupted.

'Allow me to pass, if you please.' She pushed Pearl aside and swept through into the dimly lit exhibition room where, on the wall beyond, worm-like creatures gyrated and interwove, saying over her shoulder to Mrs Henderson, 'Some folk have no manners, speaking to their betters without so much as a by-your-leave and blocking folk's paths.' She took a peacock-feather fan from her muff and fanned herself ostentatiously, saying loudly, 'What a stench! It's always the same i' thesc places where they let *anybody* in.'

'I say,' said the Henderson boy, looking back over his shoulder, 'who's the girl with the blonde hair? She's uncommon pretty.'

'Yon pale wee thing wi' the rabbit-fur muff?' said Victoria scornfully. 'I suppose if you like whey-faced looks and girls with nothing to say for themselves, she'd pass.'

'Don't be unkind, 'Toria,' said Augusta, taking Iain Henderson's arm and smiling up at him. 'Cradle-snatcher!' she teased. 'But you're quite right. She is pretty, and if she's quiet it's because she's only a child and her Ma died. She's Dr Noble's daughter.'

'Oh, I *see*.' Everyone knew Dr Noble's first wife had died on the night the Anatomy Theatre burned down and the doctor himself had been lucky to escape with his life. 'Poor wee lassie.' He turned to look over his shoulder again at Amelia and instead of her sweet face, encountered the stony-faced glare of a boy in a fisherman's jersey and heavy serge trousers, with the look of the sea about him. The boy had one arm protectively round the blonde girl's waist and the look in his tawny eyes made Henderson flush and turn away.

'Go *on*,' said Victoria and pushed him, none too gently, in the back. 'I want to see and there's such a crush in here, wi' all these folk.'

Tom, checking to make sure the objectionable youth was not still staring at Amelia, saw only the back of his head as the crowd closed behind the group. Tom was inwardly trembling with shame and rage and love – how dare those people treat Pearl and Amelia like dirt? How dare they stare and make patronising remarks? If that boy had looked at Amelia once more, Tom would have . . . would have . . . But he found no words to fit the turmoil in his heart.

'Come along, Amelia,' he said, trying to shield her from the pressing crowd. 'The others are outside already. They'll be wondering where we are.'

'Wait!' A hand clutched his arm and he turned to see India Abercrombie, dishevelled from elbowing her way through the crowds, her bonnet awry, but such a look of appeal in her eyes that he resisted his first impulse to shake off her hand. It was not India's fault, after all, that her mother and sisters were so offensive.

'What is it, Indy?' he asked, civilly enough. 'We can't stop, though. Pearl's waiting.'

'How is Jamie? He's not with you, is he? No, I know he's not. He's at sea still, isn't he, and I'll never see him. Never. Ma won't let me out and I . . . Oh Tom, what am I going to do?'

Tom looked at her in astonishment, but she did not wait for an answer.

'Quick,' she said, looking swiftly from side to side. 'She'll miss me any minute now. Tell Jamie I'm not allowed. Tell him I wanted to visit him but I couldn't. *She* won't let me. Tell Jamie . . .' She stopped and for a horrified moment Tom thought she was going to cry.

'Tell him what, Indy?'

'Tell him . . .'

'*India*! Come away this instant!' India was suddenly seized from behind and yanked almost off her feet by the irate Jessica. 'If I've telt ye once I've telt ye a thousand times, ye're nae to speak to the likes o' *them*.' Her hand slapped once, hard, against India's ear, then she propelled the girl in front of her towards the inner room. 'They are not our class o' person,' she went on, in a different voice as she remembered her audience. 'But then, what can you do when folk accost you in public? Some people just don't know their place . . .' Her voice receded, unctuously grumbling, to be lost in the general chatter occasioned by the magnified wonders they had all paid their shilling to see.

Outside in the chill gloom, for the sun set early on a winter's afternoon, Captain Greig waited with Pearl while she assembled her small party.

'Who's the Spanish galleon wi' the temper?' he asked, one eyebrow raised. He had seen women like that all over the world, but usually in circumstances he could not mention in the company of ladies.

'That was Jessica Abercrombie,' said Pearl, her eyes angry and her checks red with mortification. 'Born Jessie Brand, a fisherman's daughter in the North Square, but since she married money she thinks herself too grand to speak to the likes of us. I am sorry she was so rude,' she finished unhappily.

'Dinna worry yourself, lass,' said Greig. 'I've met folk like her before. They're not worth troubling about. But where's that brother o' yours got to? Come here, Booky,' he called, spotting the lad in a nearby doorway, reading a handbill which had been pasted to the adjacent wall. 'I want you to tell me exactly how yon magnification works. He's a bright lad, your brother,' he added kindly. It had troubled him to see a hardened bitch like the Abercrombie woman trample young Pearl underfoot like that. And Pearl had minded, for all she pretended it didn't matter.

'Yes,' she said, brightening. 'We hope he will win a bursary to the College one day.'

'It is done by the projection of light through a magnifying glass, Captain Greig,' explained Booky earnestly. 'But of course you know how a telescope makes distant things seem close.'

'Light through glass can do rare things,' agreed the Captain. 'I've seen a man strike a light with only a scrap of glass and a heap of dead leaves and sawdust – and the sun, of course. Useful if you've no tinder box, but dangerous too, especially in a drought.'

'Well, there's no chance of a drought today,' said Pearl. 'It's offering to snow again any minute. Ah, here come Tom and Amelia at last. We'd best go straight home, before we get caught, and it's growing darker by the minute. Would you like to come too, Tom? If your Ma can spare you?'

'Yes please, Pearl. And ye needn't worry about Ma. She'll know where I am.'

'What about you, Captain Greig?' said Pearl, with some idea of making restitution for Jessica's rudeness. 'Would you care to come home with us and share a bite to eat? I know Dr Andrew would be glad to meet you. He has made a study of tropical fevers and will have a hundred questions to ask you.'

'That's very kind, Miss Noble. I would be honoured to accept your invitation.' Greig offered her his arm and though he spoke to Booky, on his other side, most of the way home, Pearl was content. With Captain Greig's arm to lean on and the comforting sight of Amelia and Tom in front of them, walking hand in hand, she felt her spirits rise so that by the time they saw the lamp-lit entrance of the Nobles' house, with snow glinting golden on the path, and more light from the uncurtained windows on either side, she was her old, cheerful self again.

'So, Captain Greig,' said Andrew Noble, leaning back in his chair and pushing his empty plate aside. 'I understand you have spent some years in the East?'

'Aye, and most o' them at sea, avoiding the pirates. Or beating up the Pearl river to Canton, avoiding the typhoons and the Hoppo.'

'And when you are not at sea, Captain Greig, what do you do then?' asked Louise, Dr Andrew's wife. She was a plain, spare woman of forty or so, but with a lively, intelligent face and a disarming warmth which made her question seem not impertinence, but genuine interest. For a moment, however, she thought Captain Greig had not heard, or did not wish to answer.

Then he said curtly, 'Live ashore and wait to put to sea again.' As if realising his rudeness, he went on, with obvious effort, 'You see, Mrs Noble, the all-powerful Cohong require foreigners to live in Macau from April till October and only allow them in Canton during the winter months, for the tea trading. Of course, for a firm like Jardine's, there is always other trading when Canton is "closed", but there is, of necessity, quite a settled community in Macau.'

'And does this settled community include a doctor?' asked Dr Andrew, scenting interest.

'If we are lucky. We have missionaries in plenty and occasionally one of these has other qualifications and can be of some real use. As interpreter or medical aid.'

'You are sour, Captain Greig,' said Louise. 'And cynical.'

'You should see the Protestant graveyard,' he said, with sudden savagery. 'There is a whole wall set aside for child graves. And wives,' he added, as if to himself.

The long pause was broken suddenly by a cannonade of questions, and the awkward moment passed, but not before Pearl had noted the private pain in Captain Greig's expression. He told them about the missionaries, about the school for blind orphan girls, run by one of the wives.

'I will go to China one day,' said soft-hearted Amelia, 'to work with the little orphans.'

'Then you will need to grow first, lass, and learn the pidgin.'

Pidgin, he explained, was the lingua franca though Mandarin was the official language of the rulers and the law. There was a shortage of interpreters who could speak and, more important, write Mandarin, though the common pidgin was easy enough to pick up, and if a missionary arrived who was conversant with Mandarin, he was much prized by the trading community and guaranteed a job. But the Chinese were forbidden to teach foreigners their language so translators were few.

'I shall learn pidgin *and* Mandarin,' announced Amelia, but Greig was telling them about the Chinese attitude to foreigners.

'They think us scum for the most part, but then if you believe, as they do, that you are born into the Middle Kingdom, on your way to Heaven, you are bound to be arrogant.' He told them about tea-money and 'squeeze' and the strict rules of protocol; about the races in Macau, and the summer season, and whenever he flagged, Louise or Pearl would refill his glass and Booky would ask about dialects or Dr Andrew about malaria. Then, in a small pause of contentment, with the glow from the fire touching the half-panelling with velvet and casting gentle shadows over bookcases and gilt-framed oils, to mingle with the warm glow of the lamps and the brighter glow of the heaped oranges which were all that remained, with the decanter and glasses, on the polished table, Amelia dared a question of her own, about schooling for girls.

'Think yourself lucky you were born in Scotland, lass,' said Greig, smiling with port-fed indulgence on the earnest-faced child. 'Had you been Chinese, you might not have survived, let alone gone to school.'

'Whyever not, Captain Greig? Do girl babies get ill?'

'Nay, lass, not ill. Leastways no more ill than the boy babies.' He looked round the table at the doctor and his wife, not rich perhaps, but certainly comfortable compared to many, at their son Booky's absorbed, intelligent face, at Pearl, all homely warmth and good sense with the bloom of health about her, and at Amelia, gazing trustingly at him from clear blue eyes, her blonde hair and flawless complexion almost ethereal in the lamplight, and, no doubt, her heart as idealistic and unreal as her beauty, and his brief mood of well-being vanished, swallowed into the old pain. What could these people know of that other life?

'Not ill,' he repeated, his face hard as his voice and addressing all of them now. 'But you must understand the Chinese value women differently. Sons are always needed, daughters not, when the requirements of domestic help are fulfilled. Female infanticide is still common, I am told, in many regions, in spite of the missionaries' zeal. In Peking, for instance, one missionary reported, and I see no reason to disbelieve the story, that there is a special cart collection in the early morning for unwanted female infants. They are dumped in a pit outside the city walls where the missionaries search out and rescue any still alive – but after a night in the common street, where dogs and swine are loosed before the cart, you can imagine . . .' He stopped as Amelia clapped a hand to her mouth to stifle a scream, scrambled up from the table and ran out of the room. Tom started to his feet, but Dr Andrew stopped him with a hand on his arm and a shake of the head.

'I am sorry . . .' began the captain, but Pearl did not stay to hear. She hurried after Amelia, to hug her and comfort her till at last the child shivered into silence and Pearl was able to settle her into the bed they shared, tuck the heavy quilt around her and finally promise to come straight back, 'the moment I have said goodbye.'

But when she rejoined them downstairs, she found both Tom and the captain gone.

Pearl was at work in the Christie office some days later when she looked up to see Greig in the doorway, studying her.

'I didn't hear you come in,' she said. 'You should knock.' She lifted a hand to pin back a strand of hair with the familiar gesture and added, 'Have you been standing there long?'

'Long enough to see what a neat hand you write and that you bite your pen when puzzled.'

'That's not fair!' Pearl felt her privacy had been invaded and could not help blushing, in spite of her anger. 'You should not spy on people. It's impertinent.'

'Then I am sorry. I did not wish to disturb you when you were obviously engrossed. But nor did I want to upset you, lass, which I have obviously done. Please forgive me.'

Pearl did not answer, but busied herself with her papers, moving them without apparent purpose from one pile to another.

'I did not realise you were spring cleaning,' he said after the silence had stretched too far. 'Would you like me to leave?'

'You had best tell me why you came in the first place,' she retorted. 'Or was it merely to stare at other folks working when you are not?'

'I came,' he said slowly, 'to apologise for my insensitivity the other night. I am sorry if I upset your sister.'

'If? You *know* you upset her. She is young and soft-hearted. It was thoughtless of you to . . .'

'I know it was, damn it!' He crashed a hand down hard on the desk top. 'That is what I am saying, isn't it? That is why I came . . .' He paused, took a long breath, and continued, more quietly, 'But those things happen. Those conditions exist. Not to speak of them does not make them go away. I have seen such horrors, such humiliations and pain – but should not have spoken as I did before a child. Please forgive me.'

Pearl was unaccountably touched. She had been angry with him for hurting Amelia. Had thought him crass, insensitive, cruel. But Greig was a proud man, she knew, and quick-tempered. It must have cost him great effort to humble himself as he was doing. 'Thank you,' she said, with a sudden smile. 'And in spite of Amelia's distress, I am glad you spoke of such things. I had no idea female infanticide existed and if I had known, would not have understood. I am grateful to you for opening my eyes. I would like to hear more about Macau, too, and the missionaries. There must be so much work for them to do.'

'Work?' said a voice from the doorway. 'There's plenty work to do in the Yard today and that's a fact.' Maitland Christie leant against the door jamb and ran a hand through his hair, making it more dishevelled than before. He looked tired, his face pale with lack of sleep. 'I've more orders than I can cope with and two of the men off sick and now there's a new order come in for a repair job on a fishing smack and they want it by dawn tomorrow so as not to miss a day's fishing. By dawn! The men will have to work all night, I reckon. Have you seen Tom?'

'Not since yesterday,' said Pearl. 'But I was late this morning. Is he not on the *Jessica*?'

'Likely,' said Maitland, with a sigh. He straightened, collecting what strength remained, and said, 'No matter. I thought he might lend a hand, but we'll have to manage. I was forgetting the lad's signed papers.' He turned to go, but Greig stopped him.

'I'd be glad to give a hand, Christie. I've nought else to do today and I'd welcome the occupation. I've been a ship's carpenter in my time,' he added, 'so you needn't look so chary.'

'Shouldn't you be at Hall's, on Jardine business?'

'Aye, but inspecting yon wee ship will not take long.'

'Tell you what,' said Maitland. 'I'll come with you to Hall's and run a professional eye over yon ship they're building for you. Maybe even hurry them up a bit. Then we can go on to the Yard. I'm working on a design for a new bow whenever I get the chance and I'd welcome your experience of the China seas to guide me. And your strength wi' the fishing smack repair.'

'And what about Miss Noble?' asked Greig. 'Would you like to come too?'

'And me with this pile to get through?' Pearl indicated a heap of papers. 'Tomorrow maybe. Or next week. But today I'm helping Rachel out, first with these, then I've promised to take the wee ones off her hands for a while, to give her peace.' She turned back to her work and, after a moment's hesitation, Greig shrugged and followed Maitland out on to the Quay.

'A good man, that,' said Maitland to James Christie late that evening, when Greig had been and gone again, after inspecting Maitland's half-models and the rough drafts he was making for what they all called his China ship, as well as lending a skilled hand in the repair shop till the breached fishing boat was patched, well caulked and returned, once more watertight, to its owners. If the Christies had had doubts about Greig's competence, that day's work dispelled them – and if Greig had had doubts about the competence of the Christie shipyard, that visit opened his eyes. For not only was the repair work skilfully done, but the office was adorned with elegant half-hulls of all the Christie ships, as well as with beautifully drawn sheers of all kinds of vessels, from a 50-foot smack to a 500-ton whaler conversion. The desk and over-mantel gleamed with snuff-boxes and silver tankards engraved with the thanks of grateful clients and an air of confidence and efficiency overlaid the jumble of plans which littered every available space. In the yard itself, two half-built and beautifully fashioned hulls reared up against the winter sky to the tune of cheerful whistling and a steady cacophony of purposeful noise.

'I hope you didn't tell him everything.' James Christie glanced quickly at the office door – closed – then at the window – blank – before saying, with the habitual wariness, 'We don't want our private business discussed all round the harbour. Not with trade what it is and the competition for tea getting tighter.'

'But it's tea he can help us with,' insisted Maitland, leaning back in his chair and tucking thumbs into waistcoat pockets. 'Greig says there are huge profits to be made if you know your way around, in spite of the Government taxes. The main thing is to get the tea home, fast, before the competition. But wi' this new model I'm working on and your skill . . .' Maitland launched into a complicated explanation of water resistance, hydraulics, the relationship of mast height to deck length, and the square yardage of canvas.

James Christie listened, but he had heard most of it

before and if he hadn't, would still have had absolute faith in Maitland's judgement. Maitland was the designer of the family and as long as his brothers reported to him every detail of how their ships handled, he could convert such information into models on a page. As long as Rachel and Pearl told him what cargo space they needed for what kind of freight, he could design the hull accordingly. The result was invariably a ship better than the last – and the tea-ship he was designing now would, James knew, be the best of all.

But was it *right*? Ought they to be thinking of importing tea when they were doing well enough on the routes they already covered? Was it right to hazard ship and crew on a journey half-way across the world to a market set about with strange customs and protocol of which they knew nothing?

'There's no more news of the *City of Aberdeen*,' he said, when Maitland paused for comment. There was no need to explain the connection. Both men knew that the first ship from Aberdeen to Canton would hold the answer to a hundred questions on its return.

'No, but news takes months to travel from the East.'

'A piece of news that has come through is disturbing, though,' continued James. It was something that had been troubling him ever since he heard it that morning. 'There was some mix-up of protocol when Lord Napier arrived there in the summer and all British trade was suspended.'

'Does that mean the *City*'s gone all that way for nothing?' Maitland was appalled.

'I hope not. News is old and stale by the time we get it. I reckon they'll have sorted things out before any ship of ours ventures that far. And if they haven't,' he finished, coming to a decision, 'then we stick to routes we know and your fine new ship will have to content herself wi' Riga or St John's.'

iii

Both routes, though familiar, could be dangerous. On the last run from Riga, James had encountered weather so boisterous that he had been obliged to seek shelter off the Norwegian coast, and Alex, bringing the *Rachel Christie* homewards from St John's after safely delivering some ninety emigrants, had encountered heavy gales 100 miles eastwards of Newfoundland and, while battling for his own survival, had come across a vessel in distress. The *Earl*, from Quebec for London, had capsized in a heavy gale. Her crew had managed to right her again by cutting free the masts and the deck loads, but she had been drifting helpless ever since.

'The captain was killed, poor devil,' said Alex, regaling the company with the tale. 'Fell from the masthead to the deck.'

The Christies' living room was packed. For once, all the Christie men were ashore together, and the family gathering was augmented by friends from harbour and Square, including Duncan Greig. Firelight glanced over familiar faces, ale and whisky flowed, with bread, oatcakes and cheese. Alex's family had joined them from upstairs and while Kirsty moved among the menfolk, helping Rachel and Pearl to replenish mug or plate, the children played, or slept, or leant against indulgent adult knees, listening, thumb in mouth. Tobacco smoke wreathed in comforting spirals over the company to add to the general atmosphere of security and well-being in which Alex's tale of death and shipwreck in icy winter seas seemed to relate to a different world.

'The second mate was killed with him,' he went on, 'and seven of the crew drowned. The rest had been tossed and battered, helpless, at the mercy of the seas for nigh on a week till we came upon them. Took off seventeen crew though it was a tricky operation, wi' their ship out o' control and threatening to take us wi' them to the bottom o' the sea. But were they glad to see us! I've had three letters o' thanks from grateful families already, and I reckon there'll be a dozen more afore I put to sea again.'

Rachel, listening in the background, shuddered. She knew as well as any of them that the *Earl* could have been the *Rachel Christie*, that the dead captain could have been Alex – or James. Any one of her menfolk could meet the same fate, on any voyage, be it to Leith or to St Petersburg – or merely going out for the day, as they still occasionally did, with the fishing fleet from Footdee. But tonight they were all here, safe – James with wee Davy curled on his lap, Tom and Jamie, Maitland, the twins, and Alex. A rare meeting. How long would it be before all of them met together again? A draught came from nowhere to send a shiver across her back and she held baby Matt closer to her breast for comfort. But Alex, apparently, felt only exhilaration.

'I reckon the *Earl* would have broken up in another night of gales,' he was saying cheerfully. 'There was waves rearing up, high as a steeple, and troughs like nought you've ever seen.'

'Nor will neither,' muttered some disbeliever, but he was quickly squashed. There was nothing folks liked better than a yarn of an evening, with a pint of ale and a good fire, and sailors, like all tale-tellers, were expected to embellish for their audience's benefit.

The talk moved from Alex's storm to other boisterous weather and, by natural progression, to typhoons in the China seas. Captain Greig was called on to give his experiences, which inevitably led to other tales, of piracy and double-dealing and strange Chinese customs. He told them of ancestor worship and the dragon dances, of Tin Hua, goddess of the fishermen, of good 'joss' and bad 'joss' and the paper money cast on the sea to bring good luck. As Alex listened, his own vainglory fizzled into envy. Alex was always restless during the winter weeks when the *Rachel Christie* was laid up for careening and necessary repairs before, with the first sailing of the season in March, the regular run was resumed. Now, hearing Duncan Greig's tales of the China seas and the devious intricacies of eastern trading, his restlessness took a new channel.

'I'd like fine to try the China run, James,' he interrupted suddenly, when Greig paused to let Pearl refill his mug. She had stayed on after her office work was done to help Rachel, as she often did, with the cooking and the children. 'Will ye give me the command when we send our first ship east?'

'No.' The unqualified refusal washed the confidence from Alex's face.

'Why not?'

'Because I reckon I'd best do that myself. Besides, you know the Canada run better than any of us now, lad. You're doing a fine job there.'

'But I want a change. I can handle wicked seas, winds, tides, rocks – even icebergs, if I have to.'

'Ye'll nae find many o' them in the China seas, laddie,' said someone and the company laughed. Alex, red-faced, said, 'I can handle anything you can, James. You know no more of China than I do and I can learn, as well as you. Let me go. We could both go, together?'

'One day maybe,' soothed James, 'but Kirsty wouldna want her man at the far side of the earth for ten months out of twelve, would she?'

'Nor would Rachel,' countered Alex, 'or any wife, come to that. 'Tis the same for all of them.'

But James was not prepared to discuss such matters with others present. 'The ship isna built yet, Alex,' he said lightly. 'We'd best not tempt fate by manning her before she's masted. There'll be time enough for such things when she's in the slipway.'

'And when will that be?' challenged Alex. 'This year? Next year? Never?'

'Come away, Alex,' called George, the broken-nosed twin. 'A penny to a pound o' tea her keel'll be laid afore the year's out.'

'Or Maitland will be selling puddings for a living,' added William, the gap-toothed twin. When Alex opened his mouth to argue afresh, they stood up with one accord, took an arm each and steered him for the door.

'I reckon we'll tak' our wee brother to cool his temper in a pint o' Ma Hogg's best,' said George.

'Failing that, a quick drink o' the sea might not come amiss,' added William cheerfully.

'Take care,' called Rachel, reminded suddenly of an incident long ago when the twins had 'dunked' someone else, but it had been a Christie enemy that time, and Alex had been there to help.

'Dinna worry, Rachy, we'll care for him like a baby.' Then they were gone, Alex still protesting, half laughing, between them.

Pearl reached for her plaid. 'I must go home, Aunt Rachel. I had no idea it was so late and Dr Andrew will be waiting to lock up. Besides, I promised Louise I'd help in the dispensary tomorrow so I'll need to be up early.

Goodbye, and thank you.' She bent to kiss wee Matt, then Rachel.

'Goodbye, my dear. Jamie and Tom will see you home, won't you, boys?'

'I reckon I'd best be going too,' said Greig, pushing back his chair. 'I've taken your hospitality too long already and ye'll be wanting to get to your beds. And to save any more o' ye turning out this late at night, I'll be happy to see Miss Noble home myself. That is, if you would allow me?'

'Thank you,' said Pearl, surprised. 'But there is really no need. Jamie and Tom can . . .'

'No, no. Let the lads save their feet and enjoy their own fireside while they can. She will be safe enough with me, Mrs Christie,' he assured Rachel, 'and I'm thinking you don't often have all your family at home together.'

'No,' agreed Rachel, smiling. 'But if you are sure it's no trouble . . .'

'None at all.' The Captain made his brief farewells and ushered Pearl out into the dank darkness of the February street.

Haar hung low over the water, blurring the outline of mast and prow, and from beyond Girdleness came the muffled boom of the fog horn, regular and forlorn. There was light on the Quay and more on the ships in the inner basin, though even here the mist blurred everything into shapeless gloom. Pearl shivered as the damp air crept round the back of her neck and she drew her plaid tighter about her shoulders. Moisture glistened from the cassies underfoot and as they turned into the upward slope of the Shiprow, she stumbled.

'You'd best take my arm,' Greig said, 'unless you'd prefer to fall?'

'Thank you, Captain Greig,' said Pearl. 'It is a mite slippy.'

'Could you not call me Duncan? It's a fair time since we met and I hope we are at least friends.'

'All right. Duncan it is,' said Pearl, testing the name. 'But if we are friends, as you say, I know precious little about you in spite of all the weeks and months you've been in and out of the Christie house.'

When Greig did not answer, she went on daringly, 'For instance, do you have any family?'

'None.'

After another silence, she ventured, 'Why did you never marry?'

At first she thought he was not going to answer, then he said, with difficulty, 'I did. My wife died.'

'Oh Duncan, I am sorry! I would not have spoken if I'd known.' Her heart filled with tenderness. 'I have been crass and cruel. Please forgive me. You must have known such grief and I open all the old wounds with my thoughtless questions.'

'It is no matter. I should have told you. You were not to know.' But her spontaneous compassion swept aside his reserve and when she asked him gently, 'Were you married long?' he told her.

'Four years. Elspeth was a sea captain's daughter, from Dundee. She should have been strong. She was young, healthy, wi' fair hair and a complexion like yours. She had a fine figure, too . . .' He paused and Pearl waited patiently as they walked on in silence. When he spoke again it was with an edge of anger to his voice, as if he had said the words over and over to himself countless times. 'I thought she was strong. She looked strong. But somehow in Macau the heat and the airlessness wore her down. I couldna be there all the time, could I? Not wi' company work to do. I *had* to leave her. And there were others there. She was not alone. How could I know she would catch the fever? It is humid, you see, out there, as well as hot and unless the sea breezes freshen the air, it can be oppressive. There are bad fevers. Not only typhoid and the fevers we know here, but other, tropical fevers for which only the Chinese know any cure and often even they can do nothing. Then there is dysentery and the flux. Children die . . .'

Again he paused and they walked on in renewed silence, Pearl's boots sounding unnaturally loud on the deserted cobbles. It was the first time Greig had spoken of his private life and his voice held such bitterness and pain that she dare not ask further questions in case she touched on deeper wounds, but her young heart swelled with compassion. The lamp was still lit over the Athenaeum doorway when they reached the Castlegate, and they stood a moment looking about them at the shadowed Plainstanes and the market cross. A carriage loomed out of the mist to the east, a lantern swinging from the coachman's box, in a rumble of wooden wheels.

'Shall I try to find us a carriage?' offered Duncan, with something of his old authority.

'No. I would rather walk. That is, if you do not mind?' she added, remembering the distance they had to go. But Greig had already swung westwards into Union Street and was lengthening his stride so that Pearl had to cling tighter to his arm and scramble to keep up. When he spoke again, it was on an apparently different tack.

'The Christie family seem very close.'

'Oh yes. We are a tight clan,' said Pearl with pride.

'You do a lot for them.'

'For us,' she corrected. 'My Da was a Christie, remember.'

'But you said he died before you were born.'

'Aye, poor man. I'd have liked fine to know him. He was always happy, folks say, and cheerful.'

'And you? Did you mind being an orphan and then your ma marrying again?'

'Mind? What's the use of minding something you can't correct? I've the rest of the family still. Aunt Rachel has always been good to me. Besides, Ma needed me even when she married Dr Andrew. She wasn't strong, you see. Oh I don't mean in her body,' she explained hastily. 'She was healthy enough. It was just that she had no strength for setbacks. The sort of difficulties other folks shrug off used to oppress her and weigh her down. She needed me to cheer her and reassure her. She had too much fear in her heart, poor Ma.'

'Elspeth was something like that,' said Greig, musing. 'I hadn't thought of it in as many words before, but I reckon fear was her trouble, too. Anxiety and worry so she couldn't rest, and then the illness.'

'The poor thing.' Pearl's eyes were moist with sympathy. 'She must have been so lonely, too, all that way from home.'

'Aye.' Duncan strode on in silence for some five minutes before saying, offhand, 'And you. Would you be lonely and afraid?'

'Me?' Pearl laughed. 'Maybe. But if I was, I'd not show it. Besides, I'd be far too busy. For it seems to me that if even half your stories are true there is plenty of folk out there needs looking after and especially the wee orphan lassies. Then surely you don't think I could be in Macau and not lend a hand with the Christie business? No, no. The more I think of it the more I reckon I'd best stay where I am, for I'd be run off my feet in yon Macau – and it's not the place for running, I'm thinking, not with it being so hot.'

Greig laughed, in spite of himself. There was something irresistible about Pearl's wholesome cheerfulness, her matter-of-fact capability, and her loyal heart. When they reached the Union bridge, they stopped to lean on the parapet and peer into the darkness below.

'That's the Dark Briggie,' said Pearl, 'and the road to the Green. We used to go that way to the Square when we lived near the hospital.'

'Really?' said Greig. He slipped his arm round her waist and when she turned her head in surprise, he kissed her.

iv

Pearl sang as she wrote out the usual announcement for the *Aberdeen Journal*. 'The *Rachel Christie* now loading for New Brunswick . . . elegant cabin accommodation for passengers . . . commodious and comfortable steerage. For terms apply to the Christie Office, Trinity Quay. She will sail the end of March . . .'

'Why not sooner?' demanded Alex impatiently. 'The weather's not too bad and I can handle heavy seas no bother.'

'But what about the poor passengers?' said Pearl. 'They would not only be frightened out of their minds, but also very sick.'

'But that's what they expect, isn't it? They canna find a new life in a new world without going through a bit o' hardship to get there and there'll be a preacher among them. There always is.'

'Alex Christie, you are a hard-hearted bully and I'm ashamed of you,' said Pearl cheerfully. 'I expect my uncles to be more kindly and considerate.'

'Bah!' said Alex and kicked the desk leg. 'How can I be "kindly" when I'm driven near mad with boredom? James'll not let me sail, but expects me to work alongside Maitland all day, sawing and hammering, when all I want is the open sea.'

'You used to enjoy carpentry, and ship's design, too, once upon a time. I remember you . . .'

'Years ago,' interrupted Alex. 'Before I was . . .' He stopped and went on carefully, 'Before I had a ship of my own.'

'You were going to say before you were married, weren't you, Uncle?' Pearl rarely called Alex that, as he was a mere thirteen years older then she, and usually only when she wanted him to be serious.

'Aye, well, it's the same thing really,' he blustered.

'No it's not. You went to the whale fishing for years before James gave you a ship.'

Alex was silent. He moved restlessly around the small office before bursting out at last, 'I can't abide waiting around. I need to be sailing. I told James I'd take the *Bonnie Annie* to St Petersburg for him but no, he must do it himself because "he knows the traders". He just doesn't trust me, Pearl. After all these years you'd think he would forget and give me a chance.'

'That is not fair, Alex.' Years ago, when Rachel and James were newly married, Alex had sailed to Riga with James on the first *Bonnie Annie* and had disgraced himself by misbehaving ashore when James needed him aboard. The *Bonnie Annie* had been scuppered and James nearly drowned, but it was years now since the incident had been mentioned. 'James has given you a position of trust. The *Rachel Christie* is a valuable ship with a valuable cargo. You are responsible for a hundred souls on every voyage, Alex. How can you say he does not trust you!'

'Then why won't he let me go to China?'

'Because,' said Pearl patiently, 'we have no ship.'

'But when we have, he'll still not let me.'

'How do you know?' she challenged, and before he could answer, said, 'But I would not blame him if he didn't let you the way you're behaving now. Just like a spoilt child who can't get his own way. You'd best watch

James doesn't take the *Rachel* away from you, you great baby!'

Alex looked at her for a startled moment, open-mouthed, then laughed, and aimed a playful smack at her head. She ducked and grinned back at him.

'Away with you to the Yard and let me get on with my work. I've promised to be home in good time today.'

'Oh?' Alex looked at her speculatively, one eyebrow raised. 'It wouldna be anything to do wi' the fact that Captain Greig's expected to dine wi' Dr Andrew, would it?'

Surprisingly, Pearl blushed. 'It's really a secret, Alex – but Duncan's going to speak to Dr Andrew tonight – about me, I mean.'

'Is he, by God? Well, at least his intentions are honourable.'

'Of course they are! He is a fine man, brave and honest, and you know yourself what splendid tales he has to tell.' Her face was flushed with pride and excitement now, her eyes bright. 'And he knows all there is to know about the China seas. He may be a little brusque sometimes, but that is only his manner. You see, Duncan has known much sorrow. But I mean to cheer him and care for him. We have discussed everything and . . .' She stopped, her face suddenly anxious. 'You won't tell Aunt Rachel, will you? Not yet?'

'No.' He winked and grinned. 'Time enough for that when you've actually landed him!' Then, whistling nonchalantly, Alex thrust hands into pockets and strolled out on to the Quay to find company and entertainment in one or other of the Quayside bars.

The study in the Nobles' West End home was a comfortable, book-lined room with a coal fire, leather armchairs and a big, leather-topped desk covered with papers. On one wall was a life-size drawing of a human skeleton, on another the blood circulation and muscle systems. A microscope stood on a side table and beside it various coloured bottles of liquids and a heap of glass plates. A similar plate was positioned under the microscope, and Dr Andrew was adjusting the light and the focus when Captain Greig arrived. He straightened, studied his visitor briefly over half-moon glasses, and waved him to one of the chairs by the fire.

'Please excuse me for one moment, Captain. I am just examining this blood sample from a young patient.'

'Dr Noble. I wish to speak to you.'

'Yes, yes, in a moment. Please sit down.'

Andrew Noble at forty looked little different from Andrew Noble ten years earlier, still lean, spare, ascetic, with pale hair and an air of gentle abstraction. Even the months spent as ship's doctor on the *Rachel Christie* after his first wife died had not altered his air of other-worldly scholarship or hardened the kindly compassion in his eyes. A scar over one eye from the fracas on the night the Anatomy Hall burned down, and a few sorrow-lines around the eyes and mouth were the only indications of age. Now he waved a hand vaguely in the direction of a chair and turned back to his microscope.

'Dr Noble.' Andrew looked up in surprise as Greig cleared his throat, before continuing with his carefully thought-out speech. 'I am thirty-five years old. I have a good job as captain in the Jardine Matheson fleet, with a half-share in one of their ships and permission to trade on my own account as well as theirs. I'm a free man – though I was married once, and widowed – with good lodgings above the Praia Grande and sufficient income to support a wife. I am asking you now if you will give your permission for Pearl to be that wife. I have spoken to her and she is willing.'

Andrew Noble stared at Greig in astonishment, microscope slide forgotten. When the man had arrived early for dinner and asked for a word in private Andrew had assumed it would be about some personal ailment, possibly something disreputable, picked up in the tropics and too embarrassing to mention except in strictest privacy. But marriage had never entered his head. And to Pearl!

'Well, I . . .' he began, completely taken aback.

'She is of age, I think,' said Greig. 'At least, of an age to marry.'

'I really don't know,' said the doctor helplessly. 'How old is she? I think perhaps I had better . . . Yes.' He crossed the room, opened the door and called, 'Louise! Could you come in a moment, my dear? Louise will be able to help you,' he said, with relief, turning back to his visitor. 'But let me pour you something. A whisky perhaps? Or brandy?'

'Nothing, thank you.' Greig still stood stiffly to attention, his hat held tight across his chest, his black side-whiskers newly trimmed and his hair still damp from the washing he had given it before setting out. 'I would prefer to wait until I have your answer.'

'Yes, I suppose . . . ah, come in, Louise, and shut the door. Captain Greig has just asked me if he may marry Pearl.'

'Really?' Louise looked hard at Greig, her plain face carefully expressionless. 'Then tell me, Captain Greig, have you also asked Pearl?'

'Of course.' Greig's manner grew more brusque the longer he was kept waiting for an answer.

'And what was her reply?'

'She accepted me – provided Dr Noble gave his permission.'

'Then that is splendid news!' cried Louise, her face breaking into the smile which transformed her. 'I did wonder for a moment if you were planning the dear girl's future behind her back. That, of course, would not do, but now that I hear she is party to the arrangement we give you both our heartiest congratulations, don't we, Andrew? She is a dear, warm-hearted, loyal girl. I hope you value her.'

'Then you give your permission, Dr Noble?'

'Apparently I do,' said Andrew, smiling at Louise and slipping an arm around her waist. 'I rely on my wife's judgement entirely where the children are concerned. But . . .' A thought struck him. 'I am only Pearl's step-father and her mother is dead. Her own father, as you know, was a Christie. Perhaps you should also ask Rachel and James? In many ways, Pearl has been as much a daughter to them as to us.'

'Rachel will miss her,' said Louise, 'as we all will. But I am a believer, Captain Greig, in women taking charge of their own fates, and if Pearl has accepted you, then we support her decision – and wish you well. Come along, Andrew, what are you thinking of? This calls for a special celebration. I will call the others while you fetch the wine.'

'It will be lovely to have a wedding,' said Amelia, looking particularly appealing in pale blue cotton with daisy sprigs. 'When will it be?'

'The *Jardine* is promised for the end of May at the latest,' said Greig. 'So we thought a wedding in April.'

'Or early May,' said Pearl. 'It will depend what there is to be done first.'

'April or May, we sail the moment she's launched,' said Greig.

'*Sail?*' Louise was taken aback. 'But I had thought . . . Surely Pearl will live *here*, while you are at sea?'

'Oh no, Aunt Louise. You see Duncan does not often sail home. He is usually employed in the China seas, working the China coast and the Pearl river delta, for Jardine's. If I stayed here, I would never see him.'

'And what use is an absent wife, Mrs Noble?' said Greig with a smile at Pearl. 'No, we will live in Macau.'

'*Macau!*' Louise was horrified. 'But you can't, Pearl. How would you survive? You will be homesick and lonely and . . . besides, what will the Christies do without you?'

'They'll not be without me.' Pearl sounded determinedly cheerful. 'When the tea-ship is built and trading, I will be their China agent. Maitland's plans are almost finished, he says. He hopes to lay the keel before the year is out. So you see, Aunt Louise, I will see Uncle James every year and maybe more of the family, too.'

'I will visit you,' announced Amelia, her face lit with secret excitement. 'As soon as I am old enough for Papa to let me come. I may visit you, mayn't I, Pearl?'

'Of course, my love. You may all visit us, whenever you choose. And I am going to be so busy out there, one way or another, that there will be no time for regrets, isn't that right, Duncan?'

Greig drained his glass before saying lightly, 'It has not been the custom for foreign women to work.'

'Well it will be when I arrive,' announced Pearl. 'I mean to find out all Uncle James needs to know and more, so that when the Christie ship sails into Macau roads, she will find a right royal welcome. With Duncan to help me, it will be easy. So you see, Aunt Louise, there is really no need to worry about me.'

'I know I said women must be responsible for their own decisions, Andrew, but I hope she is doing the right thing,' said Louise later, in the privacy of their bedroom. 'There is something cold about that man.'

'Which is why he has chosen Pearl, my dear. Pearl is a warm-hearted, capable girl who will brighten his hearth and his heart. He has known loneliness and pain.'

'Which, I suppose, is why Pearl has chosen him,' sighed Louise. 'And I had hoped that nice Baxter boy would speak for her – the red-headed one, Alfie I think. But trust Pearl to find out a lame dog and coddle him. I only hope he appreciates her.'

'I thought you approved,' said Andrew. 'You agreed outright, with no demur. But if you have serious doubts, perhaps you would like me to speak to Captain Greig? To withdraw my permission?'

'No, no. You cannot do that. It is Pearl's choice and I meant it when I said she should be allowed to follow her own chosen path even though it leads so far away. But I shall be interested to hear what Rachel has to say about it.'

'Are you sure, Pearl dear?'said Rachel, blinking back unexpected tears. 'It is a huge step to take.' When Pearl had announced her news, Rachel had to bite hard on her lower lip to quell the trembling.

'I am sure, Aunt Rachel. Oh, I know you think I should have taken one of the lads from the Square, someone nearer my own age instead of a widower almost old enough to be my father – but you see, Duncan needs me. He isn't really as crusty or as brusque as he seems. It is just that he has been hurt and ill. He needs a wife to comfort him. I think I can do that, Aunt Rachel.'

'I know you can.' Rachel put her arms round Pearl and hugged her. 'But you have been like a daughter to me and I shall miss you, dreadfully. So please ask yourself, very carefully, if you are absolutely sure? China is a long way away.'

'I am sure, Aunt Rachel,' said Pearl quietly. 'Besides, there is work for me to do there,' she went on, brushing away a tear, 'Christie work for when Maitland's ship is launched. Then I will see one or other of you every year, even young Davy one day, and baby Matt. Perhaps you will even come yourself, with James, for a visit?'

'Perhaps.' But Rachel felt as if Pearl was already lost to her and the ache in her heart was a physical pain. 'You will write to me often?'

'I will write by every mail boat,' Pearl promised. 'And you must write to me, too, or I shall be homesick.'

'I will send word every month, my dear, and think of you every day. But this won't do,' said Rachel, brushing her eyes with the back of her hand. 'We should be thinking of practical things like bedlinen and light cotton petticoats. You will need to take suitable clothing with it being so hot out there. It is no good asking men about such things. We will need to put our heads together and do as best we can ourselves. There's a new batch of spotted muslin arrived at Mackie's only last week and you'll need at least one good dress. Then cotton's always cool in the heat and smart enough for everyday. You will need pillow cases and table linen, too, and at least three pairs of good sheets. I'll ask Kirsty to help me and maybe her Annie and your Amelia can help by stitching a plain seam or two? It is March already, so we have not much time. I expect you'll find a woman handy with a needle when you get there, but it's best to go provided if you can. Besides, you will need clothes for the voyage and James says you cannot hope to reach China in less than four months.'

'Then I'd best take plenty o' sewing with me,' said Pearl cheerfully, 'to pass the time.'

After the initial sadness, for she was a popular girl, the Christie family took Pearl's news with equanimity and even a touch of envy. Alex in particular was openly jealous.

'I wish I was coming with you, Pearl,' he said, coming into the office on an afternoon a few days later. 'There's

Jamie away to St Petersburg and Tom in London and the twins aye flitting about the ocean like a pair of herring gulls and me – where am I? Stuck here in Aberdeen with the blessed *Rachel Christie* not loaded yet. We should have sailed last week. I swear I canna wait another day.'

'You'd have to wait two more months if you came with me,' said Pearl evenly, 'and think what your temper would be like by then. Poor Kirsty would likely throw a pot at you.'

'She's done that already,' said Alex, grinning. 'But seriously, Pearl, I'd give anything to be in your shoes.'

'What? Married to Duncan?'

'No, ye daft quine! On the China run. With the flying fish and the dolphins and the green seas of the equator. I'm fed up with ice and snow.'

'I thought you were a Greenland man at heart,' she said, straightfaced. 'You were telling everybody so last night.'

'That's different. There's excitement in whaling. It's the emigrant run that's depressing. People, all moaning and groaning and complaining. When they're not weeping and wailing, they're being sick over the side, or praying fit to give a man the creeps.'

'Alex! Don't be so unfeeling!'

'I'm not. Merely accurate. Then it's wood, wood, wood all the way home. And the same seas and the same stars and the same boards under one's feet. I feel restless, Pearl, and that's a fact. I reckon it's the call of the East.'

'Jealousy, more like,' she said with equanimity. 'If you want a change, why not persuade James to let you take a ship to Jamaica, for the sugar?'

'I've tried. He says he's not having Christie resources diverted when we need all we have for Maitland's blessed tea-ship.'

'Then suggest he buy up an old brig and adapt her, for

the tropics. I reckon she'd more than pay for herself on the first trip, especially if you brought back cocoa and tobacco.'

Alex grinned. 'Pearl, you're a grand lass! I can always count on you for ideas. I'll away to the yard now, to see what Maitland says, then I'll tackle James. Bless you for an angel – and tell Greig he's a lucky man!' He kissed Pearl exuberantly before striding jauntily out on to the Quay and eastwards towards Pocra.

Sighing, Pearl packed up her things, locked the office, called up the stair to Rachel, and left. Amelia would be waiting for her at the school. I wonder how they will manage without me? she thought, then pushed the idea aside. Of course they would manage. She was not indispensable. More important was how she would manage to get everything ready before the wedding.

'I hear that Christie girl is to be married,' said Mairi, thumping the soup tureen down on the table and spattering the polished wood. She smeared the blots with a corner of her apron and went on, 'to a sea captain twice her age, wi' a black brow and a blacker temper, so folks say.'

'Mairi, how many times must I tell you not to gossip,' said Jessica in her best lady-of-the-house voice. 'And you can leave me to serve the soup. You've spilt enough already wi'out sloshing more.'

'Please yoursel'. I just thought you'd be interested, that's all. Wi' you and the Christies being acquainted.' She flounced out of the room, slamming the door unnecessarily hard behind her. Victoria and Augusta giggled, but hastily composed themselves at a glare from their mother.

'That woman will really have to go,' said Jessica, ladling broth. 'There you are, Finlay, love. You shall have yours first so it can cool. Mind and blow, so ye dinna burn yourself, though. She cracked one o' my best cups yesterday, that Mairi did, though she swore it wasna her, *and* there's a teaspoon missing.'

'Slipped down the drain,' contributed Finlay, slurping his soup unnecessarily loudly. 'Saw it.'

'Yes love,' soothed his mother, with a look of open devotion. 'Maybe ye did, but it's her should have stopped it. She'll go at Michaelmas.'

The door opened without ceremony and Mairi entered with a gigot of lamb on an ashet, swimming with grease. 'I heard that,' she said, glaring. 'No gratitude some folks. Nigh on twenty years wi' the family and "she'll go at Michaelmas". Why wait? I'll pack my bags now. Or do you want me to carve this beast afore I go?'

'The mistress did not mean it,' said Fenton wearily. Jessica was right. Mairi was far from satisfactory. But she had been with them since the day they were married and knew too many family secrets to be turned loose into someone else's kitchen where she would, no doubt, spread the lot, suitably embellished. She had done mischief enough as it was, though Fenton had to admit, through stupidity rather than malice. But she was loyal in her fashion and she adored young Finlay. She would stay. 'Just do what you have to do and go back to the kitchen as usual.' He laid aside his soup spoon, took up the book from beside his place and opened it.

Fenton Abercrombie invariably read at table, though his family were forbidden to do the same. Not that Jessica would be able to, being practically illiterate. But Fenton had found the printed page the best refuge from the obligations of social discourse. The alternative, silence, had long ago proved too uncomfortable to sustain for long, and, with relief, he turned the pages of *Rob Roy* till he found the place and began to read. The womenfolk exchanged glances, then imperceptibly relaxed.

'Thank you, Mr Fenton sir,' said Mairi with an aggrieved glare at Jessica, but her news was too juicy not to share and after only a token moment's huff, she continued conversationally, as she sawed away at the joint, 'Aye, Greig's his name and there was half the Square thinking as how Alfie Baxter would get her, what wi' him doing so well on yon *Bonnie Annie* and they having been friends like since childhood, but no. It's a stranger she wants, and from China, too. There you are, Finlay love. I've given you the wee marrow bone so ye can chew it and suck out the best bits. They reckon yon Greig's a good captain,' she went on, passing a loaded plate to Jessica. 'But ye never can tell wi' they foreigners. He's been to London twice, seemingly, "on business". But we know what *that* means.' She sawed away at the joint before adding, with relish, 'A mistress, like as not.'

'Mairi!' Jessica managed to sound convincingly shocked, though her eyes were alive with curiosity. No one noticed the slow flush which had spread over Fenton's cheeks and up to the roots of his hair.

'Well it's true,' said Mairi defiantly, making for the door before she could be told to go. 'I had it from Ma Hogg's maid. Her at the tavern. All married men are the same, she said, and widowers worse. I reckon yon Pearl Duthie Noble or whatever she calls herself had best watch out.' The door slammed behind her, only to open again for Mairi's parting shot.

'He's likely got a string o' women, one in every port.'

There was a moment's silence before Augusta said, with interest, 'Then why does he want to marry a plain, dull body like Pearl?'

'She's not dull,' cried India. 'And she's not plain

neither. *And* she's a deal more intelligent than the two of you put together!' she added, with a glare at her sisters.

'And what do you know about it, lass?' snapped Jessica, looking quickly at her husband, fearing his intervention, but though rather more flushed than usual, he was still apparently absorbed in his reading. 'I thought you were forbidden to have any truck wi' yon family.'

'I am,' said India, 'but Pearl is a Noble not a Christie, and she's nice. Besides, I can't help knowing what half the town knows anyway.'

'Well, the other half, the *best* half, knows otherwise,' sneered Victoria. 'She's taking him because she's nae chance of a better, but I wouldn't marry her China captain if he was the last man on earth.'

'No, cos he wouldn't ask you!' retorted India. 'He'd rather die celibate!'

'What's a selly butt?' asked Finlay, looking up from the solemn business of polishing the last drop of grease from his plate with a hunk of bread. But his father had recovered control.

'Unmarried,' he snapped. 'And your daughters,' he went on, addressing Jessica, 'look as if they will all remain celibate unless you stir yourself more. Pearl Duthie is no older than Augusta, and less well provided for.'

'Actually,' said Jessica haughtily, 'Augusta is a year younger. And for your information she's invited to the Assembly on Thursday next, wi' the Hendersons. I reckon if she plays it right,' and she winked at her daughter, 'she can get the boy to speak. I've ordered her a new ball dress,' she went on, pressing her advantage. 'I knew you'd want her to look her best. Pink figured muslin, wi' bows of gauze ribbon and gigot sleeves – real pretty. And then wi' Victoria and me as chaperons, like, we couldna let her down, so I'm having a new . . .'

'Spare me the details,' interrupted Fenton, with an

impatient gesture. 'Just so long as you do not bankrupt me before they are off my hands. No doubt the Henderson boy – he is the one with the stammer and the expensive taste in gloves, is he not? – will expect a large settlement if he's to relieve me of Augusta? Not every man is gullible enough to take a wife for nothing.'

'What a charming way of putting it!' Jessica coloured with annoyance, knowing he referred to their own courtship. 'Augusta's a good enough match for anyone, with or without a dowry.'

'Do you suppose Pearl Duthie has a dowry?' speculated Victoria idly. Since her father's veto on all mention of the Christies, the family had acquired an illicit fascination which they had never had before, and the fact that Pearl's name, at least, was not Christie allowed her to mention what she otherwise would not have dared.

'She has some lovely clothes,' sighed Augusta. 'The assistant in Mackie's was telling me all the materials she's bought and the styles they're to be made up in and they sound real smart. There was a lovely flowered foulard and a length of jaconet muslin in pale blue, with spots, and a plaid cashmere, she said, for travelling.'

'You will have twice as much, and better,' promised Jessica, 'when you're wed. And you won't have to go traipsing off to China, neither. The Hendersons have a house in Monymusk,' she told Fenton who was no longer listening, 'as well as a house in town.'

'I'd like to go to China,' said India, remembering Jamie's promises. 'I'd like to see new places and strange sights. There's snakes in China and dragons and temples and men called Mandarins with their hands in their sleeves and pigtails. You have to bow to them.'

'Well I'm not bowing to anyone,' declared Victoria, 'and you can go to China for all I care,' she added as India put out her tongue. 'And good riddance.'

Fenton slammed his book closed and pushed back his chair.

'Are you not waiting for dessert, dear?' asked Jessica.

'No. I have had enough.'

In more senses than one, he thought, when he had closed the study door behind him. But his book-lined haven with its coal fire, leather armchair and comfortable, cluttered desk, its red-patterned Turkey carpet and polished wooden shutters, closed now against the cold March night, failed to calm his spirits. He felt restless and guilty, lonely and at the same time warm with a private memory he wanted to shout to the whole world and yet knew he dare not share. When Mairi came in some time later to make up the fire with fresh coals, he said, 'Pack a bag for me, Mairi. The small portmanteau will be sufficient. I find I need to go to Edinburgh tomorrow. I will take the early morning packet.'

'You was in Edinburgh last week,' she said, clattering the fire irons with no attempt at quiet. 'But please yoursel'.'

'Thank you, Mairi,' he said with weary sarcasm. 'I will. I will also,' he added for the benefit of the neighbouring servants' kitchens which Mairi regularly regaled with family gossip, 'buy in new tea from the Melrose warehouse at the special discount they are currently offering.' He tapped the open newspaper with a pointing pen. 'And check the week's takings at the new branch. It's best to keep a sharp eye on things, right from the start, don't you agree? I will be back again on Thursday.'

'Then ye'll nae need a clean shirt. Your linen'll do fine for two – three days.'

'It will not. Those steam packets are uncommon dirty at times. You will pack me a change of linen and my good cravat.'

'Dinna mind me,' she remarked, giving the fire a final

kick with her foot. 'I've nought else to do but scrub at shirts folk change before they've worn them.' She flounced out of the room, slamming the door behind her – only to open it a moment later to add, 'Anyone'd think you was going courtin'!'

'*Goodnight*!' thundered Fenton. Mairi fled.

'I am sorry I cannot give you more, Mrs Ballantyne, but I hope you find the rooms comfortable.'

'Oh yes, Mr Abercrombie. More than comfortable.' In fact, she thought, as she looked round the sunlit, high-ceilinged room and remembered the other, smaller but just as bright, which led off the entrance hall, it was the most elegant accommodation she had ever enjoyed. 'I know I shall be very happy here.' Mary Ballantyne smiled at him with the grey-eyed, dimpled smile that had first made his heart lurch with excitement and hope.

She is lovely, he thought for the hundredth time. Sweet, intelligent, ladylike, demure, and with an air of sadness that went straight to his heart. It was that, more than anything, which had first attracted him. That, and her courage. A widow, she had told him, after barely a year of marriage and left, on her husband's sudden death, with neither relatives nor means. Her small salary from Abercrombie's was all she had in the world. The thought made Fenton's heart ache with protectiveness. She was such a slight, helpless figure and so vulnerable. But as she stood in the centre of the small sitting room he had found for her, a shaft of evening sunlight touching her hair with gold, she looked as happy as a child and he was reluctant to interrupt her mood by speech. Instead, he studied her with the yearning pleasure which had grown familiar during the weeks she had been working for him, in Abercrombie's Edinburgh branch.

She wore the tight-waisted, dove-grey skirt and jacket

she had worn to work, with a high-necked silk blouse and soft lace cravat and her hair was pinned up in a sort of chignon, low on the nape of her slender neck. Tendrils of hair, curling like a baby's, framed her forehead and temples and her ears, small and delicate as sea shells, were adorned with the discreetest of pearl drops. How different from Jessica's flamboyant taste.

Her face, when she turned to him, was radiant. 'I am so very grateful to you, Mr Abercrombie. You cannot know what it means to me. I felt I could not endure that dreadful room in the Cowgate a moment longer, though I know it was cheap and convenient for work. But the filth and the overcrowding and the noise at night, with the tavern so unpleasantly close, made it quite intolerable to me. Perhaps I should not have spoken to you about it, Mr Abercrombie, but I am glad I did. I cannot thank you enough for finding this little haven . . . so clean and new.'

'This part of Edinburgh is indeed "new", Mrs Ballantyne, with so many newly laid out streets spreading northwards and westwards, in space and air.' He stood at the window, looking out over green fields and gardens to the sparkling strip of the Forth estuary and the misted hills beyond. His back to her, he added quietly, 'I hope you will allow me to visit you here. Often.'

'Of course, Mr Abercrombie. You will be always welcome. That is . . .' she looked down at her hands, neatly gloved in grey kid, before continuing, 'You have not told me the rent. It may be more than I can afford.'

'The rent is taken care of. You did not think,' he continued hastily, before she could protest, 'that Abercrombie's would allow a member of their staff to suffer merely because she had no home of her own? And to put your mind at rest, I may as well tell you that the rooms belong to me. I bought them for family use, in the future. I have no need of them at present and you would be doing me a favour by airing them and keeping them fresh and clean. You may regard the accommodation as part of your salary, if you wish, and the care of them as part of your duties. Though of course the rooms are yours to do with as you please.'

'You are very kind.' At the softness of her voice he turned and saw her looking at him with an expression which lifted his spirits to jubilation.

'It is no more than you deserve, Mrs Ballantyne. And now, if you will allow me, I will send to a place I know for dinner to be brought round, for two? And a bottle of champagne, perhaps, to celebrate?'

V

Pearl Duthie was to be married in May. The week before her wedding, news came from Leith that the *Isabella* had arrived safely after a passage of a mere 130 days, having left Canton on December 17th with a cargo of the new season's best teas. She brought upwards of 8,000 packages, the first direct import of the new crop into Scotland, and the news of her safe arrival was greeted with relief and renewed hope in the Christie yard. One ship on the stocks was almost finished. Soon they would have a free slipway and plans for Maitland's ship were practically complete. He talked of a launch, if not in time for this year's crop, then certainly for next.

The first tea leaves were picked in early April, with a second picking in mid-May, a third in late June and even, if the season was a good one, a fourth picking in August. Some growers even squeezed in a fifth, but that picking would be poor stuff compared to the rest. The tea had to travel cross-country from the inlands of China so that it was October before the first spring teas arrived in Canton, with the bulk of the crop arriving in November, December and January. These were the main trading months, when the big tea auctions were held and the principal trading companies did business. It was imperative, therefore, that ships hoping to trade arrive in Canton in good time, for if they missed the opening auctions, they might as well go home again – or be content with others' rejects and the tail-end of the market.

Maitland's aim, as was most enthusiasts', was to send his ship to catch the first tea crop and race home again ahead of the rest, not just to make a better profit by getting into the home market first – that was James's and Rachel's side of things – but to test his skill in ship's design against the best.

There were, however, voices of dissent: not everyone was as enthusiastic as Maitland about the benefits of free trade. But then, he approached the idea solely as a shipbuilder. Free trade gave him both the challenge and the opportunity he had long been waiting for. It was left to merchants such as Abercrombie to argue the commercial merits and demerits of such an enterprise. For more than fifty years the East India Company had monopolised the tea imports of Britain and provided the dealers with a steady market, a more or less steady price, and teas of variety, quality and, most important of all, the kind the customers wanted to buy.

Now, however, all that was changed. London was no longer the only favoured port for tea imports. Bristol, Liverpool, Hull, Glasgow and Leith were also to be allowed to import direct from China. Traders were scrambling to charter ships, others to order their own. But few of the newcomers had the experience and expertise of the London brokers who could not only judge all varieties of teas to a nicety, but could also gauge the tastes of different markets round the country. For instance, a Hyson, much valued in London, would hardly sell at all in Glasgow where black tea was favoured over green. Here the brokers' experience was invaluable. But tea-tasting was a skilled profession, requiring years of practice in which the apprentice learnt to taste and distinguish all the infinite varieties and qualities of teas until he could set his 'chop' unerringly on any parcel of tea to certify its uniform quality. 'Charactering the tea' was as skilled as wine-tasting and not to be acquired by the stamp of an official seal on a document authorising free trade.

The Christies could handle the shipping side easily – Maitland's skill was incomparable – but they knew they would need the advice and help of experts if they were to make any kind of profit. But Abercrombie already had connections with the tea-brokers of London – he had bought from them for long enough – and undertook to find them a reliable tea-taster to act for them in Canton, when the time came. Rachel was not entirely happy, being wary of any undertaking not initiated by themselves, but Pearl reassured her.

'I will be there myself, very soon, Aunt Rachel, and I will keep my eyes and ears open. I will soon find out who is trustworthy and who is not. Duncan says the womenfolk are not allowed to live in Canton and must stay in Macau, down river. But in the summer, when trading stops, everyone must move to Macau anyway, and I will find out what you want to know, don't you worry.'

'It will be as good as having our own agent,' said Rachel, fighting back the desolation which welled up whenever she let herself think of Pearl's departure. 'Our own Christie office, in Macau.'

'Hardly that, Mrs Christie,' said Greig, politely enough. 'It is not like it is here. There is a certain protocol to be observed. Different customs. Women have not the same freedoms and must tread warily.'

'Of course,' said Rachel quickly. 'A foreign country must necessarily be different. But Pearl will quickly adapt. She is very sensible, aren't you, dear?'

'You don't need to worry, Duncan,' said Pearl, smiling up at him. 'I will be discreet. But surely you cannot expect me to forget the Christie business? Not when I have worked in the office for so long. And when Maitland's ship is ready, I hope to do the same work for them in Macau as I do here. So there is no need to frown in that disapproving fashion. Besides, there are other British people there and you cannot tell me all the womenfolk do nothing but sit at home and wait for their husbands?'

When Greig made no comment, Rachel quickly turned the conversation to the *Bonnie Annie*'s latest trip to Riga which had been achieved in excellent time and the news of Vanya Priit and Friida. Seeing Greig's silence, a small stir of unease had moved at the back of her mind, but was lost in a different anxiety as James spoke.

'They were both very pleased to see us, but they are very old,' he finished, with a frown. 'I think Tom should go and see them, soon. I will speak to George Abercrombie to ask leave for him to go with us on our next trip. But not until Pearl's wedding is over and her ship sailed.' The whole family must be there, on the Quay, to wave her on her way.

Pearl was married in mid-May, at a gathering of Christies, Nobles and mutual friends. Afterwards, Duncan went home with Pearl to the house in the West End and took her straight to bed. If she was taken aback by the wordless hunger of his lovemaking, or the rough and ready speed, she did not show it. If she yearned for words of tenderness, she pushed disappointment aside and told herself cheerfully, he is a sailor after all, not a poet. Besides, she had tenderness enough for both of them. A week later, on May 19th, the *Jardine* sailed for China.

Half the town, it seemed, was assembled on the Quay to see the wee ship on her way, including India Abercrombie.

India had not seen Jamie Christie, except once in the distance across the Castlegate, since he had given her the little wooden bear which her father had destroyed. Not even Tom had crossed her path since she had been so ignominiously hauled away by her mother at the Oxy-hydrogen Microscopic exhibition in January, before she could even give Tom her message. She had half-thought of going to Pearl's wedding. There would so many people coming and going, laughing, drinking, and later, dancing, that no one would know who had been invited and who not. India would dress in her Sunday best, she decided, and join Kirsty's Annie, or Kirsty's Annie's cousins from the Square. They would all be there, surely, and with so many children no one, she reasoned, would notice one more. Except her grandfather, of course, but she would keep well out of his way, and her father, by some blessed chance, was away in Edinburgh again, 'on business'. That left her ma and sisters to deal with. Her brother Finlay didn't count. She could make him do anything she wanted.

But in the event she had lost her nerve. Besides, by then her grandfather Abercrombie had promised to take her and Finlay to the launch, 'So ye can see how a China ship sets out for the Far East, though she's nae a Christie ship, more's the pity, and wilna be using her engines. But Pearl's a grand lass. I'd like her to have a fine send-off, for Lord knows what she'll find at the other end of her voyage.'

Abercrombie had taken a dislike to Duncan Greig, for no reason except that, in Abercrombie's opinion, he was 'a mite too full o' his blessed China seas and his own seamanship'. This was untrue, for Greig on the whole was a reticent man, but something in his manner when he did speak had antagonised Abercrombie from the outset and the fact that he was removing Pearl Duthie to the other side of the world was an added injury. George Abercrombie was fond of Pearl and knew the wrench it must be to

Rachel to part with her. But if he could not dissuade the lass – and he had tried on more than one occasion without success – he could at least see she had a good send-off.

'So ye'll all come, Jessie lass,' he announced, arriving unexpectedly on the Union Terrace doorstep just as Jessica and her two eldest daughters were setting out for the town.

'Well . . .' began Jessica, swiftly weighing up the pros and cons of annoying her father-in-law by refusing, and antagonising her husband by accepting. 'If it's the nineteenth, then the girls and I are spoken for already, at the Cruickshanks. I suppose we *could* cry off, but . . .' She paused fractionally before saying, 'There's India and wee Finlay. It'd be a rare treat for them to see a launching and wi' the crowds and all, Gussie and 'Toria wouldna really enjoy it. They canna be doing wi' crowds, can ye?'

'No, Mamma,' chorused the two obediently. Victoria, for one, had no objection at all, particularly if the crowd included young men, but she stood too much in awe of her ma's right arm to contradict.

'Humph!' growled Abercrombie, momentarily put out. 'There's nae *crowds*, I take it, at yon Assemblies you're aye attending, nor at the theatre, wi' standing room only?'

'Finlay's never seen a launching,' said Victoria quickly. 'He was saying only yesterday how he'd love to go.' Seeing her grandfather's face, she added, 'We'd love to come too, if we could, Grandpa, but as Mamma says, we've already accepted and it'd be rude to cry off.'

'Aye, and it would keep India out of mischief,' said Augusta piously. 'Being with you, I mean, Grandpa.'

'Aye, well, if that's how you feel.' Abercrombie glowered at the trio of beribboned and bonneted females with their silken skirts and flounces and yon silly mantle-things. There was nought wrong wi' good woollen cloth and a sensible plaid, in his opinion. Then, from behind them on the stair, came a cry of 'Grandpa!' and India came bounding down the steps two at a time to hurl herself at him with a joyful hug. Her hair was unpinned, her apron awry and one stocking hung in grubby folds around her ankle, but she irradiated such welcome and love that all impatience left him. 'Aye, well,' he repeated in quite a different voice. 'In that case, I'll gladly take Finlay and young Indy here. That is if ye'll come, lassie?'

'To what, Grandpa?' It was only a token question, born of bubbling excitement, for whatever it was, she would go. But when Abercrombie said, 'To the launching o' the *Jardine*, to wave Pearl Duthie on her way,' she hugged him again with a delighted 'Yes!'

Jessica felt a disagreeable stir of unease. Fenton had forbidden all contact with the Christies. Then she pushed the thought aside. It was Fenton's fault for spending so much time in Edinburgh. He could not expect her to watch the child twenty-four hours a day. Besides, if he did say anything, she could always claim she had no choice. His father had insisted. Having shifted the blame quite satisfactorily on to other shoulders, she smiled graciously, took her leave of her father-in-law and swept into the Terrace, a daughter on each arm.

'Go in wi' Indy, if you like,' she said over her shoulder. 'Tell that Mairi to get ye a drink o' something and a wee bite to eat.'

'Thank you,' said Abercrombie solemnly, with a large wink at India, 'I think I will.'

So it was that India found herself in the Christie party, side by side with Jamie, with Tom, Amelia, Booky, Kirsty's Annie and all the others crowding round them as the *Jardine* made the last preparations to sail. There was much sniffing and gulping in the company and many tearful faces. Even Jamie looked suspiciously red-eyed.

But then he had known Pearl all his life. Even at four, she had been a motherly, protective child and had taken charge of her wee cousin to help Rachel out. Pearl had been a loving elder sister to Jamie ever since and, grown lad that he was, the idea of such a parting brought the tears to his eyes.

'I'll miss her, and that's a fact,' he confessed to India, blinking hard and squeezing her hand. 'Pearl's aye been good to me. But I'll see her again soon enough.' He brushed an arm across his eyes. 'When Uncle Maitland's built his fine ship I'll be out there, visiting her, in the snap of a sail. Da says he'll take me with him,' he finished, pride almost defeating that threatening lump in his throat. But when Pearl hugged him in farewell, the tears welled up unchecked.

George and William, the Christie twins, were weeping too, quite openly and unashamed. 'Mind when we tickled wee Pearl as a baby?' one said. 'Aye, and played "Eattle ottle" wi' her?'

'I'm a grown woman, now,' said Pearl gently. 'I must go with my husband. But I'll not forget you, dear Uncle George and dear Uncle Willy. Nor you, Tom,' she said, turning to Jamie's adopted brother who stood white-faced and silent, concealing his deepest feelings as he always did. But when she put her arms around him, he clung to her for a brief, intense moment, before saying, 'Nor I you.'

Rachel Christie watched the leave-takings with a mixture of pride and grief. She was glad the family was united, glad they were bound by strong mutual affection. Pearl might be a thousand miles away, but at least she would know she had a loving family, wherever she might be. Rachel would miss her. She could feel the heavy ache already.

'Don't be sad, Rachel,' said James at her side. 'You must try to look cheerful, for Pearl's sake.'

'Cheerful? When the poor girl is leaving us for the other side of the world?'

'He's maybe glad to see the back of her?' managed Alex, attempting levity. He, too, was fond of Pearl.

'Well, she does have a very attractive little back, I grant you.'

In spite of her grief, Rachel smiled, as James had meant her to do. Together they lifted up Davy and wee Matt to watch the sailors carrying last-minute bundles on board.

'Well, lass,' said George Abercrombie when Pearl came to take her leave of him. 'I'll miss you and that's a fact. The Christie office'll not be the same without your bonny face to cheer it. Here, lass,' and he thrust something into her hand with a wink. 'That's for you and the bairn, when it comes. Not for that husband of yours, mind, so keep it safe and secret.'

Pearl felt the soft leather bag of coins and knew they were sovereigns. 'Thank you, Mr Abercrombie, but really you shouldn't . . .'

'And why not?' he demanded. 'Cannot an old man please himself what he does with his money? You're a good lass, so take it and dinna argue. I wouldna want to think of you stranded, on the other side o' the world, wi'out the means to come home. So buy yourself a dress or bonnet or whatever you lassies like and put the rest by, in a safe place, for emergencies.'

'But Mr Abercrombie, there's really no need to . . .'

'Nonsense. Do as you're told, lass. And give an old man a kiss afore ye go.'

'I wish I was going too,' sighed Amelia unexpectedly. The quayside was packed with people – spectators, sailors, shore porters – for, while crowds collected at the point where, on board the little *Jardine*, Captain Greig was making final preparations to sail, the rest of the harbour continued with the day's normal business. Seagulls wheeled and screeched, somewhere a tug boat chugged and smoked into the clear May air and from the shipyards on the Inches came the steady hammering and sawing of men at work. Nobles, Abercrombies, Christies, Baxters all jostled and chattered together as Pearl moved among them, making her last farewells. She was a popular girl and no one wanted to be left out of her leave-takings.

'I'd love to go to China,' said Amelia.

'Maybe you will one day, if you marry a China captain,' said India helpfully. She liked Amelia, in spite of her soppy yellow ringlets and her easy tears.

'I'm not going to marry anyone,' said Amelia. 'I have a different plan.'

'What plan?'asked Tom, in a strange voice. He looked pale and almost ill.

'I can't say,' said Amelia. 'It's a secret. But I might tell you one day,' she added, relenting. 'When everything is ready.'

Tom did not answer. He hardly spoke again until it was time to say the final goodbye. The hatches were battened down, Pearl's trunk and portmanteau aboard, the last-minute stores safely packed away in the tiny galley. The cumbersome engine and paddle wheels were out of sight below decks, the new sails crisp and clean, only waiting to fill with a good wind to carry Pearl and Duncan Greig to the other side of the world. The ship gleamed with varnish and new paint, the freshening wind whipped the surface of the harbour water into a thousand cat's-paws and set it slapping busily against the prow.

'She looks so small,' said Rachel, trying to keep the tears from her voice.

'Pearl? Or the ship?' said Maitland, deliberately cheerful. But Maitland, of all the family, felt Pearl's departure the least. For him she was an envoy, going ahead to test the waters where his ship, when she was finally built, would follow. Sorrow at parting was mingled with excitement and hope. But it was harder for Rachel.

'Both, I suppose,' she said now, attempting a smile. 'The *Jardine* is only fifty-eight tons. The *City of Aberdeen* is five times the size. Do you really think she's safe to sail all that way?'

'Why not? Mind you,' said Maitland, teasing, 'I'd have been a lot happier had she been one of the Christie ships. But I reckon Hall's have made a good enough job, considering. They had to, wi' us Christies keeping an eye on them. Come on, Rachel,' he added, in a different voice. 'It is hard enough for Pearl as it is, without you breaking down.'

Rachel did not break down. Maitland was right. It was harder for Pearl, leaving her home, her family, and all she had ever known behind her to sail into the unknown with a stranger. She watched the girl bravely making her farewells of Dr Andrew and Louise, of Booky and Amelia, then finally it was Rachel's turn.

'Goodbye, Pearl,' she managed, clasping the girl tight against her breast. 'You've been better than any daughter to me. I'll never forget your loving cheerfulness, your . . . oh Pearl, I'll miss you.' For a shuddering moment they clung to each other, speechless, then Rachel said, 'Write to me often.'

'I will, Aunt Rachel.' She turned to James. 'Goodbye, Uncle James. Thank you for all you have given me. I'll not forget.'

He hugged her close, then said gently, 'And we'll not forget you, Pearl. Come, lass, we canna have tears. We'll see you soon enough. Remember Maitland's building a ship so we can visit you.'

'I'll be waiting for you, Uncle. For all of you.' Then Duncan Greig took her arm and led her aboard.

They watched in silence as the hawsers were loosed, the sails set and the little ship slipped into the channel, gathered speed, and headed for the open sea. They watched until the small figure waving from the stern dwindled to a pinpoint and vanished.

'Pray God he's good to her,' murmured Rachel. James added, 'God keep her safe.'

The *Jardine* had not sailed twenty-four hours when news came of the approach of the *City of Aberdeen*. But the long-awaited tea-ship from Canton found less than a welcome from her home port: as the privilege of direct trade from China had not yet been extended to Aberdeen, she was refused permission to discharge her precious cargo and instead had to up anchor and proceed, wearily, for London. But not before news of her sufferings had reached the harbour.

'Ten of the crew dead,' reported James, his face sombre. 'Some in China, some on the passage home. From sickness, fever, ague, the flux. They reckon it added six weeks at least to the passage time.' He sounded worried, and no wonder. When the Christie ship sailed east, she would be manned by Christie men and crewed by friends.

'The sea hazards are bad enough without that,' said Rachel, her face pale. No one answered. Fresh in everyone's mind was the picture of a tiny, 58-ton sailing ship on her way to Canton. But even if she got there safely, what would she find?

Part II

Macau
September 1835

i

The *Jardine* arrived at Macau on an early morning in mid-September. In sight, scent, sound and flavour it was like nothing Pearl had known, not even in Bombay where they had anchored briefly, nor in Singapore, though the people there had been as strange and the seas as silkily green.

They came upon the place almost unawares, after a calm passage through a chain of green-hilled islands, with a backdrop to the north and east of higher hills, already shimmering pale against a strengthening sky. Heat quivered from the white wood of the deck, from the turquoise water all around them, and from the rocky outcrops of the wooded islands strung like blobs of green froth over the bluer sea.

The *Jardine* kept her distance from the coast, in the safety of deep water, but closer to shore Pearl saw a score of native boats of all sizes, from the bobbing saucer of a fishing coracle to heavy wooden junks with their ridged sails, like slatted banners, or dragon's wings. Off the island of Coloane one such junk sailed close across their path so that Pearl saw every detail of the red and gold paintwork, the dragon swirls and the all-seeing eye. The junk had a square stern, high out of the water, and a long, pointed prow. Like a medieval lady's slipper, thought Pearl, noting details to write in her letter home. Maitland, she knew, would be interested. As the junk passed, slipping smoothly in a curl of parting water, she saw a man naked to the waist, in a wide straw hat, squatting on deck, paring some sort of fruit with a villainous-looking knife. The blade flashed bright as wildfire when it caught the sun.

'Pirates,' said Duncan. 'Off duty.'

He shouted an order, the boom swung, the sails quivered and filled again as they altered course, then they rounded the last headland and Pearl saw Macau. On the shore, a fringe of sand-coloured buildings, two or three storeys high, with here and there a larger, porticoed mansion. A fort on a small hill, a church tower and gardens, and behind them, hill after misted hill, quivering colourless in the summer heat, and reaching ever northwards, on and on, into the infinity of China. Pearl caught her breath with awe and the first small prickle of fear.

The *Jardine* dropped anchor in deep water, in Macau roads. Pearl heard the rattle of the anchor chain, the swish of folding sails, the usual shouts of the crew, though with the prospect of dry land again, after four months at sea, there was a new cheerfulness in their voices as they furled sails, coiled ropes and made everything shipshape. Duncan Greig was a stern taskmaster; in spite of the long and often taxing voyage, the *Jardine* would be delivered to her new owners in mint condition. As Pearl stood at the rail of the little ship which had grown so familiar to her and surveyed that tiny foreign town, all her resilience and optimism drained away. The *Jardine* was her last link with home and all she loved.

'I'll leave Masterson in charge,' said Greig at her side. Masterson was the mate. 'And take you ashore at once. You will want to see your new house, and settle in. There's no need to look so apprehensive,' he added, noting her expression. 'You will soon pick up the way of things.'

Then he was gone again and Pearl stood alone, with only the *Jardine* and that busy ant-heap of Macau between herself and the vast and alien country which was China. She had not known it would be so large. At the thought, a new and unexpected sickness touched her vitals – not the head-swimming, gut-rising nausea of seasickness which had racked her for the first weeks of her journey, till she had wanted only to die, but a different, more piercing malaise of the heart. For a moment she knew panic. Then she set her chin and deliberately studied the town which from henceforth was to be home.

Ashore, the Praia Grande swarmed with people – little, yellow people, with strange, loose garments and wide, pointed hats. Hunched peasants in black shuffled, bent double under swaying bamboo poles supporting ornamented sedan chairs; others trotted under bamboo yokes, bearing less human burdens. Their dusty yellow feet were fleshless as a hen's claws, their faces leather-yellow and inscrutable. At her anchorage, sampans slid like lurking crocodiles around the *Jardine*, weaving in and out, jostling for position. A cacophony of unintelligible chatter rose on all sides. Pearl could not have said what it was about the place which sent a shiver of apprehension up her spine, or which made her glad she had Duncan at her side.

But he was calling her. It was time to leave the safety of thc *Jardine* and go ashore. A rattan-roofed sampan, like a long, old-fashioned cradle, had drawn alongside. Men were swarming on board, jabbering; someone snatched the portmanteau from her hand, two more took her cabin trunk and swung it somchow over the side into the waiting boat.

'Don't worry,' said Duncan at her shoulder. 'They are Company men.' He shouted orders of which Pearl could make out nothing but 'quick-quick'. Then it was time to follow her luggage over the side and into the waiting sampan, Duncan close behind her. Too soon they were crossing the sand-coloured strip of water towards the shore.

'It's not far,' said Duncan, when they stood on the Praia Grande some ten minutes later, their trunks and portmanteaux beside them. 'We'll walk.' He looked to either side of him with a wary alertness which, rather than reassuring Pearl, filled her with unease. 'Put up your parasol. The sun is hot. Watch the baggage. And keep a tight hold of your purse.'

The strange procession set off, Pearl and Duncan at its head, a string of laden coolies following. First along the Praia Grande, then away from the seafront and up, through narrow, cobbled streets raucous with traders. Pearl saw wooden stalls heaped high with noodles, like tangled knitting wool, sardine stalls, dried fish, fried fish, innards, snakes, more noodles, bones, biscuits, herbs, strange vegetables and tropical fruits. On either side were red-roofed houses, heaped haphazard, like the card houses her uncles George and Willy had made for her when she was a child, and teetering towards each other as if to gossip across the street, as the cobbled path grew narrower and steeper.

'Most of the cobbles came from Portugal,' Duncan told her. 'As ballast.'

Birds sang from cages on rickety balconies, brilliant with flower pots and poles of washing. On one such balcony, on a level with Pearl's parasol, an old, old man in black pyjamas squatted, knees behind ears, apparently asleep. His wispy white beard was so sparse she could have counted the hairs.

Then they reached a junction with a wider street and turned right into a sort of square, with air and light and gardens and, above them on the crest of the hill, a fortress.

'That's the Monte Fort,' said Duncan. 'You can see the whole of Macau from there, and a large chunk of China, too. And this is home.'

He indicated the peeling arched facade of a building across a courtyard, shaded by lush green branches and the thin spikes of a palm. An ageless Chinese woman in black trousers and a white tunic top, a tight black pigtail swinging well below her waist, materialised silently out of the shadows and shuffled on wooden shoes to meet them.

'Ah May,' said Duncan. 'She speaks no English, but understands enough. This Missee Greig,' he said slowly, indicating Pearl. 'New Missee belong Taipan Greig. Ah May fetch tea, chopchop.' He clapped his hands and the woman dipped in obedience, before shuffling off into the shadows of the house.

'She will soon learn to obey you too,' he said, offhand, to Pearl. 'Stand no nonsense from her. Be firm.' Taking her arm, he led Pearl inside. 'The house belongs to a Portuguese,' he explained. 'But I rent it on a permanent basis.'

The arched entrance led into a cool and tranquil hall, high-ceilinged and tiled to shoulder height with beautiful blue and white tiles.

'Portuguese,' said Duncan. 'You'll see them everywhere. Remember Macau is a Portuguese colony.'

Pearl had forgotten, if she had ever known, but the tiles were lovely. On the far side of the entrance hall, shallow stone steps led to a little inner garden with a well in one corner and a statue of Our Lady. More steps led upwards, in a sweeping double curve, to a large, bare room with more blue and white tiles, a gleaming tiled floor, and two arched windows which overlooked the courtyard. The green slatted shutters were propped open on bamboo poles, like the skylight windows of an attic, at home. Only these shutters were large – more like the sails of that pirate junk they had seen, off Coloane. It was a disturbing comparison.

'The servant quarters are across the garden,' Duncan was explaining. 'You will have little need to go there. Our rooms are in this part of the house. This room, the bedroom next door, and a couple more. You'll soon find your bearings.'

Under the high ceiling, the room was mercifully cool after the sweat-drenching heat of the streets. There was a heavy wooden table, one or two solid chairs in the same dark wood, a cane chair or two, and little else. A spartan room, thought Pearl in surprise. She had expected some signs of domesticity, bequeathed by the first Mrs Greig, but there was nothing. Not even a sampler or a stitched linen cloth. As if nobody lived here. Empty. And peaceful, with the tranquillity of death . . . Unexpectedly, Pearl shivered.

Ah May arrived with tea, in tiny shallow bowls. It was surprisingly refreshing. While Pearl sipped at the pale amber liquid, Greig went below to direct the coolies in the disposal of luggage. He returned after barely five minutes, Ah May a shadow at his back.

'They have put the things in the bedroom and gone. All undamaged and correct as far as I can tell. But if you find aught broken, shout at Ah May. She'll understand.'

With that enigmatic instruction, he turned for the door.

'Duncan! You are not leaving me?' Panic gripped her as she met Ah May's inscrutable eyes. Duncan was the one familiar point in an alien world.

'Of course.' He looked at her in surprise. 'What would I be doing here? Unpacking is women's work. Besides, I have business to attend to if the *Jardine* is to be ready to sail tomorrow.'

'Sail? *Tomorrow*?' Pearl felt her mouth go dry with

fear. 'But I thought . . .' She stopped, appalled, as realisation rose like bile in her throat.

'Thought what, wife? That the *Jardine* would deliver herself to Lintin?' He was blustering, half-teasing, but there was an edge of irritation to his voice which warned Pearl that she must not protest. 'I've been absent long enough as it is. The Company's waiting for my services as well as the *Jardine*'s and we've had no chance to test those engines yet. If they perform half as well as promised, we should be able to cut the time between Canton and here by half. It'll be an eye-opener for the Hoppo.' He sounded almost gleeful at the thought. 'So, now you're settled, I'll go to Lintin and conduct steam trials at once.'

'But . . .' Pearl fought against hysteria. She wanted to scream, to beg, to implore him to take her with him. Anything, so that she need not stay alone, in that alien house, with that alien servant in that dreadful, stifling, alien town. But of course she must not. That hint of anger would have warned her, had she not already known it.

'I'll be back this evening,' Duncan was saying. 'Tell Ah May to have a meal ready. I could tell her myself, but you had best show her from the start that you are Mistress here.' Then, without another word, he was gone.

She stood at the open window, ready to wave to him, but he strode across the small courtyard and out into the sunlit street without a backward glance. Behind her, she heard the soft shuffle of Ah May's feet receding into the vaulted silence of the empty house and for a moment courage left her. Into her mind came a picture more vivid than any Macanese street, a picture of Trinity Quay, with Rachel and the children at the fireside, Uncle James and Uncle Maitland and the dear, daft twins, George and Willy. There would be firelight and laughter and the comfortable companionship of people who had known each other most of their lives. It would be autumn at home. The leaves would be turning and there would be a touch of frost in the air. Soon, Dr Andrew would wear his greatcoat when he went visiting and Amelia would need her fur muff for school. Someone else would have to remind her now. Booky would be studying, by candle-light, late into the night, working for the Bursary competition, and Aunt Louise would not mind. She never grudged candles for book learning. Would he win a bursary? Pearl would not know until months had passed and the news was old and stale. She missed them all – their familiar faces, their company, their cheerful busy lives. Most of all, she missed their warmth. Here, there was nothing. Homesickness engulfed her with unbearable pain.

Oh God, what have I done?

But after that moment's bleak despair, she squared her small shoulders and set her chin higher. Was she not a Christie? A Christie never gave in.

She swallowed, moistened dry lips and called, in a voice that wavered only slightly, 'Ah May!'

No sound. Only a distant twittering of voices from a far street and, close at hand, a canary singing valiantly into the stifling air. To reinforce her courage as much as her order, she clapped her hands loudly, twice, and called again. '*Ah May!*'

It was late when Greig returned. The sun had long set and a welcome coolness crept across the courtyard, with the evening shadows. Lights sprang up in the town as lamps were lit. The smell of charcoal fires wreathed the air, with frying garlic and incense from the bunched joss-sticks and candles at hundreds of tiny shrines, Catholic and Buddhist, side by side. The Portuguese were Catholic, though Duncan had assured her there was also a Protestant church, 'So you need not think you have come entirely among heathens.' Somewhere in the town a church bell rang.

Bats wove silent, swooping patterns over the courtyard and somewhere a toad boomed its melancholy call. Other, invisible creatures moved busily about their business, rustling undergrowth, creaking branches, tap-tapping lightly on wall or window glass and when Pearl lit the lamp so she might occupy herself with sewing till her husband's return, a thousand flying ants beat themselves against the lamp glass and fell squirming in death-agony on to the tiles. Pearl felt sick and had to look away.

But the emptiness and the silence, made louder by the busy activity of the night town, filled her with a nervousness she had never felt at home. She remembered the pirate ship, the strange carved idols, the joss-sticks and the snakes, until every shadow became menacing, every sound a threat.

Once, she ventured downstairs, with some idea of crossing the courtyard to the outer door to watch for Duncan, but when she turned the stair at the half landing which led from hall to inner garden, she stopped, heart thumping loud against her ribs. The entrance hall was eerie with moonlight, the tiles black-patterned now instead of blue, and in the doorway between the hall and outer courtyard a black shape stirred.

'What are you doing, Ah May?' called Pearl, her voice sharp with fear and relief.

The woman muttered in Chinese, then added, reluctantly, what sounded like 'Ah May wait Taipan Greig.'

Pearl returned to her loneliness. She would have liked to wait with Ah May. To talk, gently, of family matters and of home. But how could she begin to talk to anyone, when she knew no other language but her own? I will learn, she vowed. Tomorrow I will go to the servant quarters and ask Ah May to tell me the names of things.

It will not be difficult. But she knew in her heart that it would.

That night she clung to Duncan with new need. Always till now she had been the comforter, the giver, but this time it was Pearl who needed his reassurance and his strength.

'What is it, Little One?' he said, with rare endearment, when she held him close long after they had loved, and would not let him go. 'I have to sail early, remember. And I will be back.'

'Soon?'

'Of course, woman! I'm only going to Lintin.'

Still she clung to him, in silent need, until roughly his body answered hers. But afterwards, as she lay wide-eyed in the darkness, her loneliness and fear were unassuaged.

He would not let her go to the Quay to see him off. 'It is not necessary,' he said. 'Besides, you would have to walk home alone and that would not do.'

'But I have not said goodbye to Mr Masterson and the others. I want to thank them, and to wish them well.'

'I will do it for you.'

Meekly, Pearl acquiesced, but only because she had come to a private decision of her own.

When Duncan had left, in the cool silence before sunrise, Pearl waited till the sky had paled from a dark bronze against which trees and buildings were no more than black silhouettes, to a paler splendour of misted gold. Then she took her parasol, for the sun would soon be baking hot, and left the house. Taking careful note of every twist and turn, she followed the path upward towards the Monte Fort which Duncan had pointed out to her and from which, he said, one could see all Macau. She would wave goodbye to the *Jardine* from there.

* * *

The path was steep and narrow, twisting round and up, sometimes with steps, sometimes not, till the jumble of red-roofed houses, some no bigger than hen-coops, lay below her and she could see across their crowded rooftops to the sea. But she wanted to see further. Doggedly, she climbed on.

When Pearl finally reached the Fortress she was flushed and out of breath. A slow rivulet of sweat ran down between her breasts and the hair on her brow was wet with perspiration. She took off her straw hat and fanned herself vigorously while she looked around her.

A cannon guarded the entrance to the Fortress and more were positioned at the corner of the battlements, their barrels pointing out to sea.

Pearl followed the direction of those iron barrels and caught her breath in awe. Below her lay Macau, still in morning shadow, but with here and there a wisp of woodsmoke rising straight into the motionless air. The sky was gold and green now, streaked with red, and the sea a vast burnished plate with here and there the darker blemish of an island. She could see the ships in the harbour and more already at sea. Tiny fishing boats, some with their stake-nets already set, a larger sampan making for the sea. But no *Jardine*. Then the sight of the hills caught the breath in her throat. To the north and west, as far as the eye could see, were layer after layer of regal hills, gold-washed, ethereal – no wonder China thought of itself as the Middle Kingdom. It would be easy enough to see heaven as a mere step over that highest mountain. And Canton was somewhere beyond those near hills, in the valley of the Pearl river, some eighty miles to the north. She followed the coastline east from Macau till it vanished behind the headland. The mist had lifted, the dawn gold paled to turquoise and the sea was no longer bronzed but turning as she watched to a deep, unearthly blue.

'You are admiring our view, I see,' said a soft voice at her back. Pearl spun round in alarm to see a mild-faced man of perhaps forty dressed severely in black.

'I am sorry if I startled you, Mrs Greig. It is Mrs Greig, is it not?'

'How did you know?' Hastily Pearl replaced her bonnet and smoothed her dress. She was both flattered and a little alarmed that he should know her name.

'We are a small community in Macau. English, American, Dutch, and, of course, Portuguese. We know each other. The *Jardine* arrived yesterday, with Captain Greig's new wife aboard. So you see, it is really not so miraculous after all.'

'No.' Pearl smiled with relief. There was something comforting about the phrase, 'a small community'.

'But if I may give you a little friendly advice, Mrs Greig?' He looked at her seriously, his brown eyes troubled. 'Do not walk out alone. This is not Scotland, where you are among your own people, and it is not wise. Your husband would not like it.'

'I wanted to see the view – and to see him sail,' explained Pearl. She had no need to justify her actions to a stranger, but he spoke with courtesy and kindness and she would have been grateful merely to hear an English voice. 'My husband leaves for Lintin this morning.'

'So soon after your arrival? No wonder you wish to see him sail. But I fear you may be too late. No matter. I will point out our more notable landmarks, if you will allow me, so your outing may not be entirely fruitless. Robert Morton, by the way.' He held out his hand. 'I am considered something of an expert on the colony's history. The Monte Fortress, behind us, is more correctly the Citadel of Sao Paulo do Monte, built by the Jesuits in the early sixteenth century. Legend says they did not keep it long. The Governor invited himself to dinner one night – and refused to go home. Instead, the Jesuits were invited to leave and as the Governor owned the cannon, what else could they do? That cannon was very useful, however, when the Dutch tried to capture Macau. A cannon ball landed in the Dutch magazine and made them change their minds. See, my dear. There is the plaque put up in 1622 lest anyone forget. I will translate for you. "Stop. Take heed. Consider for a moment the beautiful history of our country. Enter proudly and hold your head up high." The colony had much to be proud of then.'

'And now?'

'We are a tiny outpost in a vast and heathen wilderness and there are many evils.' His face was momentarily troubled, then he smiled. 'See, Mrs Greig. You can follow the line of the ancient city walls from the Fortress as far as Sao Francisco fort, there, on the northernmost headland of the bay of Praia Grande.'

'And where is Lintin?' she asked, searching the sea for a familiar sail.

'Lintin, my dear, is in the Pearl river estuary, some forty miles away. One can sometimes see it from here, but I think . . . yes. The clouds are gathering. We would be well advised to seek shelter.'

Pearl noticed, with surprise, that the sky had unaccountably lost its light, the sea the same, and a turbulence of treacherous cloud was racing rapidly across the sky from its concealment in the hills. She felt the first drops of rain on her face and heard a low growl of menace. Mr Morton took her arm and steered her under a nearby archway.

'We had best wait here till the storm has passed. These tropical storms come quickly at this time of year – and are quickly over, but one can be throughly soaked if caught unawares.'

The air grew heavier, the drops larger, the thunder more ominous, until lightning slashed the sky with blinding fire. There was a thunderous explosion almost overhead, and the air became solid water. Clouds crashed and split in titanic combat, while the hills reverberated with roll after roll of thunder and Pearl's eyes hurt with the brilliance of that stabbing fire. No Dutch siege could have been more violent. The path was a bubbling sheet of water, splashing a hundred tiny fountains as the rain streamed down and the entire seaview was a sand-coloured haze. Then, as suddenly as it had come, the cloud lifted, moved on and diminished into the distance as the storm passed out to sea beyond Coloane and there was a new freshness in the cool, clean air.

'Tin Hua is angry,' said Robert Morton lightly. 'I should not have spoken disparagingly of her kingdom.'

'Tin Hua. Who is that?'

'Goddess of seafarers and fishermen. You will see elaborate ceremonies in her honour in the springtime, Mrs Greig, and small shrines all over Macau. But her finest temples are at Barra Point, at Lin Fong Min. There you will find mazes, corridors, moon-gates and tiny gardens. Tin Hua sits between her Generals, Thousand-Li Eye and Favourable-Wind Ear, and her gates are guarded by dragons.'

Pearl looked at him with wary eyes. Was he spinning a tale? As Uncle Alex would elaborate from the depths of his boasting imagination? But Robert Morton's face was grave.

'You may well look disbelieving, Mrs Greig, but the Chinese have gods for all occasions and all possible needs. Idolatry is colourful and imaginative among the heathen and many of the artifacts have great beauty. The lion-dog, for instance, and the less obese of the jade Buddhas! But what am I thinking of? You must be chilled and thirsty. Now that the storm has passed, let me escort you home. But not before I have shown you our Christian monument, though of course it is of a different persuasion.'

He took her arm and led her out of the protection of the Fortress arch on to the path where the ground was already steaming under the sun's renewed heat and everywhere sparkled with a fresh-washed intensity of green. Below her, over the battlements, the balconies of the nearest houses were whiter, the flowers more vibrant, the roof-tops more red. In the distance towards Barra Point the pink and white facade of some dignitary's residence sparkled like sugar icing. But it was a different facade that brought her up short as they rounded the corner of the Fortress wall and looked down on an open space, a huge flight of steps, and the burnt-out shell of a cathedral of which only the great, carved front still stood intact.

'St Paul's,' said Morton quietly. 'Once the most beautiful church in Asia and now only a singed facade crowned with the Dove of Peace. Closed when the Jesuits were suppressed, and used as a barracks till it burnt to the ground in a typhoon a year ago.'

Pearl shuddered, remembering the fury of the morning storm – Tin Hua's storm, Mr Morton had said, and the Christian cathedral had been destroyed . . . 'I am sorry.' It was an inadequate response at best, but what else could she say?

'Perhaps our God was angry? Like Tin Hua? Perhaps we have not fought strongly enough against the heathen? But it is a sadness and it does our cause no good.'

'Your cause?' Pearl was baffled.

'Christianity, Mrs Greig. Did I not tell you? I am a

missionary, unofficially of course. Officially I am a clerk with a trading company. I have some fluency in the Chinese language and my services are useful as interpreter. But my real work is God's. But it is not only Tin Hua who will be angry if we stand about in damp clothes,' he said, suddenly brisk. 'Take my arm, Mrs Greig, and I will see you home. Then I advise a change of clothing, an invigorating rub down – even a bath if your household can produce one at short notice – and a cup of China tea. Your maid will know what is best.' As he left her at her own door, he said, 'My wife will call on you, my dear. Very soon.'

It was almost noon before Mrs Morton arrived, but when she did, she brought an air of wholesome cheerfulness which did much to restore Pearl's spirits. She was a tall, thin woman whom the climate had made angular. Her dark grey alpaca dress hung loosely over her bones, her bony feet were long and looked more so in the black pointed boots she wore, and the paisley shawl about her shoulders had a fringe which matched the straggling side-wisps of her hair exactly, being a mixture of grey and black and white. But the face under the plain straw bonnet was fresh-washed and cheerful, her brown eyes lively and her cheeks surprisingly pink and youthful for a woman who had spent ten years in Macau and, as she readily admitted, would not see forty again.

'No wonder you look so pale,' she said, when she had introduced herself and settled comfortably into the chair opposite Pearl's, in the room Pearl had already learnt to call not the drawing, but the tea-room. Now Elizabeth Morton studied Pearl critically, head on one side. 'It does not do to go gallivanting about the town alone at the best of times and certainly not with a storm threatening. Robert told me all about it. You will catch all sorts of fevers, you know, without proper care. And what is this about your husband leaving you? You are too young to be alone.'

'I will be all right,' said Pearl quickly, sensing a criticism of her husband. 'Duncan will be home very soon, and I will have plenty to occupy me. You see, I am not here merely as Duncan's wife,' and she told Mrs Morton about the Christies, about Rachel and James and their plans for the future, about the ship Maitland was building for the tea trade.

'When the ship is finished, Uncle James will sail her here himself,' she finished, her eyes shining. 'He might bring Jamie with him, even perhaps Aunt Rachel, so you see I will see them again very soon.'

'Yes, dear,' said Mrs Morton, but her voice was troubled.

'Meanwhile,' continued Pearl happily, 'I shall do what I can so that everything is ready for them here. Perhaps I could even set up an office here? There is room enough.'

'I see you will be a credit to us, my dear,' said Mrs Morton, smiling. 'And I am glad you have come. We are a small enough community and in need of new young blood. You will find the time passes well enough. The Portuguese are very sociable, and then there are the British traders and the Navy. You will be surprised how many dinners there are, and concerts, dances and such like, especially in the summer months. I do not go to many myself, but a young girl like you . . .'

'I do not expect I shall go to many either,' said Pearl quickly. She could count the dances she had been to so far in her life on the fingers of one hand – and those had been weddings. 'I am not used to such things. I prefer to be working.'

'My dear, perhaps I had better warn you, as I am sure your husband must have done already, that things are not quite the same here as at home. Wives are not expected to interfere in business matters.'

'But I don't interfere! I do the books for Aunt Rachel. I draft the advertisements. I order the . . .'

'Yes, dear. But here there are men to do all that. After all, when the tea-trading season opens the ships will all be at Canton, where the factories are, and everyone knows no women are allowed there. Not even wives.'

Pearl was too polite to contradict her guest. But she knew Mrs Morton was wrong. Pearl had come half-way across the world to pave the way for her uncle's enterprise and had it been an impossible hope, then surely Duncan would have told her so?

But when Mrs Morton had gone, promising to call again tomorrow and to send her friends, Pearl's optimism faltered. The house was large and lonely, the air humid, the heat oppressive. From the window of the tea-room she could see across the courtyard and over the roof-tops of the town to the sea. It was the same sea, she told herself over and over, that flowed to Scotland, the same water that lapped the quay at Pocra and filled the inner basin under Trinity Quay. But the thought brought no comfort and when she saw a returning boat, serene against the evening sky, it was the unfamiliar tall sail, the high square stern and pointed prow of a Chinese junk, not the outline of the little *Jardine* or the more graceful lines of a Christie ship. And when at last she went to bed, it was not the bed she had shared with Amelia for as long as she could remember, nor the pallet bed at Aunt Rachel's, nor the narrow wooden bunk of the *Jardine* with Duncan folded round her and the crew divided only by a few wooden boards, nor even the love-bed of her first night ashore, but a wide, hard bed with a carved wooden tester and with netting draped all round it, to keep out the mosquitoes. Like a nun's veil, she thought, and shivered in spite of the lingering heat which hung, airless, over the white sheet, the eerie white netting and the moonlit room beyond.

She lay a long time listening to the night sounds – the mewing of bats above the courtyard, the distant bark of a dog, and closer, inside the room, a dozen different scufflings and scrabblings and once, the tap tap of an insect's back against the ceiling. There were strange scents in the air – the cloying perfume of frangipani, the tang of joss-sticks and incense, the faint odour of decaying undergrowth, and, underlying everything else, the stench of nightsoil from the seething, overcrowded town. Somewhere in the distance a church bell rang, to be answered by the jangle of temple bells and a slow and sombre drum.

Pearl shuddered and cringed deeper under the sheet. It was the first time in her life that she had slept alone.

ii

The winter of 1835 was a bleak one for the Christies. They missed Pearl more than they had expected, and had so far heard no word. The usual winter gales and lashing storms added to the anxiety, with one or other of the menfolk always at sea. But at least they were not on whalers – the *Middleton*, with several others, had been trapped in the Arctic ice and had no hope of escape till spring. There were shipwrecks off the east coast from Buckie to Dundee and beyond as far as Lowestoft, Yarmouth, Hull. The Canada route was as dangerous and the Baltic, with a hurricane blowing off Amsterdam and many ports blocked by ice. As if that was not worry enough, news came of a ship attacked by pirates off Singapore, on her way to Canton, her captain and crew manhandled, her cargo stolen. And still no word reached them of the *Jardine*.

'Such things take time,' James assured her. 'Be patient and have faith. It is a long passage, after all.' But it was almost eight months since Pearl had sailed and Rachel could not help being anxious.

Maitland, too, was restless. He was not satisfied with the progress of his tea-ship. The wood was badly seasoned, the men slow and too often required in the repair shop, or to work on the other slipway – a ship for a client willing to pay over the odds for a quick delivery. Privately, James thought it no bad thing. There was, after all, no hurry. The setback with the *City of Aberdeen* had been a warning, and they said there was trouble brewing in Canton between the British Superintendent and the Chinese Viceroy. Something to do with opium, but it was bound to affect all trade, one way or another. The Glasgow merchants had already petitioned those in Aberdeen to help them bring about changes in trading conditions in Canton. It could do no harm to wait.

'I'm feeling old, Rachel,' he confessed. 'And a little tired.'

'It's the winter, that is all, dear,' she said, reassuring. 'Things will look better when the days lengthen.'

'Aye. Maybe.' And by the spring, thought Rachel, we might have news of Pearl.

Mairi hummed tunelessly as she thumped the flat iron over the petticoat she was pressing on a trestle table set up for the purpose in the girls' bedroom. A dour fire struggled in the smoking grate – the wind was in the wrong direction – and the sky beyond the unshuttered window was grey with threatening snow. But the room was bright enough. Heaps of silk and taffeta garments in blues and pinks and yellows littered chairs and window seat. There were more in the open wardrobe and a smell of lavender and rose-water permeated the chill air. Although it was not even mid-day, an oil lamp burned on the mantelshelf, to aid Mairi's efforts, and its light was reflected in the polished sides of the oak chest and the brass handles of the tallboy.

'They say the whaler men are so thin you can count their ribs through their clothes,' said Victoria with lazy relish. The first of the *Middleton*'s survivors had just arrived home. She reached for another sugared plum from the plate on the bedside table and put it whole into her mouth. They had been sent to their bedroom to check over their various outfits while their mother dealt with an unexpected caller, but in Jessica's absence were not getting very far. Mairi had been pressing the same petticoat for the last ten minutes, Victoria sprawled idle on the bed, while India perched on the window seat, knees drawn up under her chin, and more than half her attention on the street below. Augusta was trying on various garments from her trousseau, one by one, in front of the mirror.

'Some of the men,' went on Victoria, lying back on the coverlet, hands folded behind her head, 'have no toes or fingers left. Eaten off in the frost.' She raised one foot high in the air, so that her skirts fell back to show her stockings, and studied her ankle with obvious approval.

'Poor things,' said Augusta complacently. She looked at herself sideways in the mirror, hands on hips. 'Do you think this new corset pushes me out too far at the front?'

'Like a pair of cheeses,' said India in disgust. 'Watch you don't go near the Green or someone will offer to buy them, two shillings the pound.'

'She's just jealous,' said Victoria, 'because she's only a pair of pimples herself.'

Mairi sniggered.

'Well I'd rather have pimples than *udders*,' retorted India. 'I've seen better udders on a cow!'

Augusta hurled a slipper at India, who ducked, and it struck the window-glass dangerously hard, just as her mother entered the room.

'India! I've telt ye a hundred times to stop capering! Break a window, lass, and you'll soon know it!'

'But it was Augusta, Ma! She . . .'

'Don't tell me what's what! I've eyes in my head and I can see. As I telt yon butcher's lad. I wasna paying for best sirloin when any fool could see it was skink. As for you, Indy, you've done nought but get under our feet all week. I'd have thought you'd take more interest in looking nice for your sister's wedding and you nigh on fourteen. It'll be your own turn afore you know it.'

'Who would marry her?' jeered Victoria from the safe distance of the bed. Jessica had turned her attention to Mairi's ironing, so she went on, apparently to the ceiling, 'She's a temper like an alley cat and the looks to go with it. No decent man would look at her.'

India flushed in spite of her resolve to ignore Victoria's taunts. Ever since Augusta's engagement, Victoria and she had been inseparable, whispering, giggling, talking clothes and jewellery, and when the Henderson family came calling they were even worse. India could not bear to watch their simpering and silliness and her mother was as bad. Boasting about Augusta's non-existent talents, or openly pushing Victoria at the Pirie boy or the Cruickshank boy or any other she decided was 'suitable'. Victoria would soon be seventeen and from the way her mother went on about it, you'd think she was on the shelf already. What surprised India was that her father did not stop them. She had thought he had better sense. But her father was always in Edinburgh these days and when he did come home, he spent most of his time at the Union Street premises or the office. Business, apparently, was going well. As Jessica was quick to remind them.

'Of course they'll look at her,' she snapped, overhearing. 'And get a move on wi' that petticoat, Mairi. Anyone'd think you were at a wake. No, Victoria,' she went on sententiously, returning to her theme. 'Any man would be glad to marry one of you girls, even Indy, with your father's standing in the town and the Abercrombie money. Even county folk could do worse.'

'Do you really think so, Mamma?' said Victoria, with new interest. She sat up, consciously posing, one foot tucked under her, one ankle exposed. Like a Quayside whore, thought India with disgust and then glanced uneasily at her mother. She was not supposed to know about such things. But her mother was launched on her favourite subject, the eligibility of her daughters as matches for 'county folk'.

'Any one of you,' she finished triumphantly, 'could be wife to a county gent, easy as winking.'

'It's too late for Augusta of course,' said Victoria innocently, 'but I'm willing. I've a fancy for a country house, with a lodge and a paddock maybe, and a drive the length of Union Street.'

'I haven't,' said India. 'I shall marry a sea captain, like Pearl Duthie did.' Only my sea captain will be Jamie Christie, not a stranger. Jamie will get his master's ticket and marry me and we'll sail to the ends of the earth. But she knew better than to speak Jamie's name in her mother's presence. 'You two can marry who you like, but I shall sail to China and have adventures, like Pearl.'

'How do you know she's had any adventures?' said Augusta. 'They've had no letter yet. Come over here, Indy, and pull this corset a bit tighter for me. I can't manage.'

'That's right,' put in Mairi helpfully as, with a resigned sigh, India uncurled from the window seat and went to help her sister at the mirror. 'News came that the ship had arrived safe, but no letters. They reckon the mail boat's becalmed or maybe pirates have attacked it.'

'Who would want to steal letters?' said Augusta, in astonishment. 'Anyway, India, you'd be seasick. Look at that time you were sick all over Mairi in the carriage just because it was swaying about.'

'That was the lobster – even Ma said so – and anyway I was only young then. And if I was seasick, I'd not be for long.'

'Maybe not,' said Victoria innocently, 'you'd get scurvy instead. Or yellow fever.'

'Or diarrhoea,' contributed Mairi with relish. 'Some o' they whaling laddies back from Greenland died of diarrhoea. On the ship, afore they reached Shetland.'

'Well there's no call to talk about it here,' said Jessica sharply. 'We've better things to do than discuss common folk's insides. There's Augusta's wedding clothes to be sorted. If you've done that petticoat at long last you'd best press the bodice o' this pink foulard and dinna take till next week to do it.'

'Yes, *ma'am*.' Mairi was always sarcastically formal when reproved. 'But it's nae easy wi' yon fire. The iron heats up a deal faster on the kitchen range.'

'You will not press Augusta's best clothes in the kitchen. They'd stink o' fish or onion in no time and you wouldna want that, would you, Augusta?'

But Augusta and Victoria were still teasing their sister. 'Weevils,' 'Scorpions,' 'Cockroaches in your shoes,' 'And a husband like a salt herring, pickled with the sea air and stinking.'

'Anything would be better than marrying some long-nosed, spotty-faced nobody,' cried India, needled beyond caution, 'just 'cos his father sells spanners to the gentry. Half a dozen nails and a chamber pot, if you please, my good fellow,' she mimicked and tugged, too hard, at a corset string. It snapped. Augusta whirled round and smacked her, hard, on the ear. With a squeal of pain, India retaliated, while Victoria fell back on the bed, laughing.

'That's right, Indy. Kick and scratch. You'll make a fine fishwife one day.'

'Stop it!' roared Jessica, clouting Augusta, as the nearest, then India who was not quite quick enough to escape. 'I'll nae have you fighting like a pair of Billingsgate wifies, and look at Augusta's corset! Burst all up the seam and newly bought only last week!' She turned on India as the cause. 'Get out from under my feet, ye pesky wee bitch. I can see we'll get nowhere wi' you in the room and now we'll have to buy new laces for Gussie's stays. As if we hadna enough to do.'

'Yes, Ma.' India retreated hastily to the door. 'I'll fetch them for you if you like. I'd be glad to.' She had been waiting for an excuse to get out of the house for days. The incessant teas and social calls, the dressmaking visits, the fittings, were unendurable, and the constant talk of weddings even more so. Her brother Finlay didn't seem to mind. He hung about the women, waiting to be patted on the head and given sweetmeats or sugar biscuits and when they stopped cooing and drooling over him, he settled quietly into a corner with his spoils and they didn't notice he was there. It was different for her. Whatever she did was wrong. She had only to open her mouth to be shouted at, only to appear in the doorway and some silly woman would say, 'When will it be her turn?' or 'She doesn't look like Augusta at all.' Then her mother would push her out again with a hissed command to 'Make yourself decent before you come in here!'

And if she stayed in her room and avoided them, it was worse. 'Our company not good enough for you?' her mother would say, with that exasperated look India knew too well. 'Well listen to me, lass, and listen well. When my visitors come a-calling, I want my daughters around me. We're a family, remember. I'll not have you behaving like your father, sneaking off to your own amusements whenever there's entertaining to be done. You'll sit with me, and like it.' But today, there was just a chance.

'And I could buy that ribbon you wanted, Mamma,' she added. 'For Gussie's bonnet.'

Normally her Ma would not let her out of the house

alone, but now with so much to do before Augusta's silly wedding and with her father away, she might relent. India had noticed that her Ma was not always as strict with her when Papa was in Edinburgh, as he often was these days. At least, not until it was time for him to come back. Though as often as not when he did come home, Papa went straight into his study and closed the door. India did not mind. In fact, she was glad. Ever since he had crushed her little wooden bear she had hated him. It would serve her father right if she did marry Jamie – and she would, one day, whatever he said.

'Can I, Mamma? I'll come straight back.'

'Why not? We've an account at Hay's so you'll not need money and at least you'll be doing something useful for once. Where's that sample, Mairi? You'd best give it to the lass or she'll likely come back wi' purple instead of sky blue.'

'Are you sure it's safe to send her, Mamma?' said Augusta, with an infuriatingly superior air, as of one matron to another. 'You know what she's like. She's sure to find mischief of one kind or another the moment she's out of the house and I'd be so ashamed, what with my wedding and all.'

'Even I can hardly get into mischief buying ribbon,' said India, with heavy sarcasm. 'But if you'd rather buy it yourself, I'll not bother.'

'Get on with you, Indy, and stop irritating folk,' said her mother. 'You are to buy a yard and a quarter, exact, mind, and put it on the slate. Then come straight back. And behave yourself!' she called after the girl as India scurried downstairs and out of the house before Jessica could change her mind. Her mother was particularly irritable today, thought Indy, idly wondering why. But at least she had let India go out.

James Hay's was near the Castlegate and India made

the journey last as long as she could, dawdling along Union Street, looking in shop windows, scanning every face she passed in case it might be Jamie or Tom. Even Amelia Noble would do. But she saw no one remotely connected with the Christies until the ribbon had been chosen, measured, and tied up in a neat packet. Then, as the assistant entered the transaction into his book, a huge, cheerful-faced old woman in purple and black waddled into the shop, trailing children of various sizes behind her.

'Why if it isn't our Jessie's Indy,' she cried, oblivious of the other customers' turning heads. 'Large as life and twice as pretty! Give us a hug, lass.'

'Nana!' shouted India delightedly and ran to her grandmother who hugged the girl in an exuberant embrace, redolent of whisky and perspiration, before holding her at arm's length and studying her, head on one side. The old woman's eyes were bright as little jet buttons in the mottled folds of flesh which squeezed her eyelids to slits and hung in great rolls under her chin, and shrewd as any bird's.

'Where've you been all these months, lass? I havena seen your Ma since I don't know when. I reckon she forgot Auld Yell this year, or maybe she's too busy with her county folk and her fancy teas to remember her own Ma and Pa. Mind you, lass, we had rare fun wi'out her, but I'd have liked fine to see you, Indy, and wee Finlay. You should have come.'

'I wanted to,' said India, truthfully enough. 'But I was not allowed. Ma's very busy,' she added hastily, not wishing to give offence, 'what with Augusta's wedding and all the things to be done.'

'Reckon she'll not be asking me,' said Mrs Brand with a sigh of brief regret, 'but no loss. I like a good wedding wi' whisky and dancing where ye can kick your heels a bit. Not yon po-faced affairs wi' tiny morsels o' this and that on plates that crack if ye look at them, and sips o' wine like gnat's pee.'

India giggled. She liked her Nana Brand and the brood of children and grandchildren which always seemed to follow her about, like chickens with an elderly hen. There were three or four with Mrs Brand now, though India was not sure what relations they were of her own. Cousins of some kind, probably.

'We're away to the Panorama when we've done my wee bit messages,' went on Mrs Brand. 'Why not come too? I'd be glad o' your company, lass, and ye can help keep an eye on this lot. Wee Eppie's a mischievous devil. Yon's Eppie wi' the black hair and the sugar-plum.' She indicated a skinny child with an assortment of ill-fitting clothes, obviously hand-me-downs, and an air of wiry insolence. Hearing her grandmother's introduction, she removed the sugar-plum long enough to put out her tongue at India, then resumed sucking.

'I can't, Nana,' said India with genuine regret. 'Ma's expecting me back, quick, with this parcel. And if I went home and asked her first, she'd be sure to say "no".'

'Would she now?' A gleam of mischief brightened the old woman's eyes. 'Well then, I'm thinking I've a right to take my grand-daughter out if I've a mind to, so this is what we'll do.'

'A lad from the shop brought this, ma'am,' announced Mairi some half an hour later, throwing open the drawing room door without ceremony. 'It's they ribbons you was wantin'.'

'A lad from the shop? Where's Indy? I'm nae paying a lad to bring what that wee pest was sent to get. Fetch her this minute and I'll . . .'

'There's a note,' interrupted Mairi. 'Here.'

'A note?' Jessica waved it away. 'I canna be doin' wi'

notes. Give it to Victoria. Read it aloud to me, 'Toria, there's a pet. I'm that tired with all this fuss, I canna see straight.'

'It says India's gone to the Panorama, with Nana!' "Do not trouble yourself about her," it says, "I know you will be glad to have her out from under your feet with all the preparations you have to make. Her grandfather will return her safe to you tomorrow."'

'*Tomorrow*?' Jessica felt first relief, then wariness, as she remembered Fenton's instructions. But Fenton was away, as usual, in Edinburgh. She was beginning to suspect he had a private reason for visiting so often – Mairi said he was most particular about having clean shirts and all, and he had been, well, different lately. As if he had a secret world of his own where he enjoyed himself a deal more than he did with her, at home. Fear and frustration mingled to produce a sort of virtuous annoyance. It was his fault for being so obstinate in the first place. After all, she'd been prepared to forgive and forget years ago, and to start afresh, but no, he would have none of it. He insisted on harbouring his grievance till it infected everything. As for this business with India and the Christie boy, Jessica couldn't say she wanted the pair to meet, not with the Christies being unfriendly like, and the lad only a seaman's apprentice, but there was no harm. To hear Fenton, anyone'd think the Christies had the plague, or worse! As to watching India every minute of the day, Fenton should try it himself and see how he got on. No, Jessica would be glad of a bit of peace for once with the child out of the house and Fenton could hardly object to her staying with his own father.

'There now,' said Nana Brand gleefully when the note had been composed, by her and India together, and written in carefully standard copperplate, by India, with pen and ink supplied by the shop. 'That'll keep us right. It'll be her fault if she reckons it's from the Abercrombies, nae ours. Now, which o' you wee tykes would like another sugar-plum, or maybe a piece o' mutton pie afore we see yon Panorama?'

'I would, please,' said India, in no way ashamed to be lumped together with a rabble of noisy, grubby-faced infants, and when, toffee in mouth and hand-in-hand with a cousin on either side, she set off towards Crown Street and the Panorama, she was happier than she had been for days. For the next twenty-four hours she would be free to go where she liked and do what she liked. Nana Brand wouldn't mind – and her mother would not even know.

'Are ye coming for the mussels wi' us?' asked Eppie as they settled down for the night in crowded but cheerful squalor. 'We'll need to be up early, mind.'

They had spent a happy couple of hours in the room in Crown Street where the Panorama was on show before making their noisy way home to North Square and the one-roomed cottage which was the Brands' home. Fishing nets, coiled lines, and assorted baskets were stacked in the rafters, amid a faint odour of fish and old seaweed. A grubby sailcloth partition supposedly separated the room into two, with various beds in one half and in the other, a table and benches, all the paraphernalia of cooking and feeding, and a wooden rocking chair, Nana Brand's pride, beside the fire. Once she had squeezed her vast bulk into this chair, she sat rocking to and fro, beer tankard in hand, while her family milled noisily around her, occasionally receiving a well-aimed clout on ear or backside if they came too boisterously close.

India was fascinated by Nana Brand and even more so when the old woman lit up a clay pipe and puffed at it with cheek-sucking concentration. Grandpa Brand was, as usual, out.

'At Ma Hogg's tavern,' Eppie told India. 'He spends all day there, seemingly, when he's not out in the boat.'

But Grandpa Brand, or Bosun as he was known in the Square, was over sixty, with enough sons and grandsons to take the boat out without him – a course they often preferred, especially if old Bosun had been too long at Ma Hogg's. Unfortunately, that was when he was most likely to become maudlin about the old days and insist on recreating them by taking the family boat to sea himself. Then, only Nana Brand could stop him – or plain physical force. India was a little afraid of Bosun. But he had been out when they arrived at the Square and by the time he appeared, India had merged into the background and was helping Eppie and two other girls to bait the men's lines for the next day's fishing.

At first Eppie had sneered at India, mocking her accent, her clothes, her ignorance of what seemed to Eppie to be the simplest things such as how to spear the mussel flesh on to the hooks, and how best to coil the line so the hooks did not snarl in the skull. But India was quick to learn and did not give herself airs. By sundown Eppie had accepted her as a friend.

Then there had been supper and singing, neighbours drifting in and out, children squalling. India had heard gossip of half the Square and the Quay, too, for good measure, including the disappointing information that Jamie Christie was at sea. But it did not matter. For once she was enjoying herself too much to mind. The Square was so different from home, so much more lively and interesting, and tomorrow Eppie had actually asked her to go collecting mussels. That meant she was accepted into the clan.

'Yes, I'll come, Eppie,' she said eagerly.

'She canna,' jeered a sibling. 'Nae wi' her posh clothes.'

'I can so! I can tuck my skirts up,' retorted India, 'and I'll leave my legs bare, like you. I'll manage fine.'

'She will that,' called Nana Brand from her seat by the fire, and choked on her own pipe smoke. When she could draw wheezing breath again, she added, chuckling, 'My Jessie was a rare one for the mussels and isn't she my own Jessie's wee lass?'

Dawn broke late in February, at least compared with the summer months. But the Brand household rose early whatever the season. The men were gone before first light, to the fishing, leaving the womenfolk to the usual round of preparation for when they returned, with, if they had been lucky, fish to sell in the city markets, and lines to be cleaned and baited for the next day's fishing. But first, the bait had to be collected.

'Mind and take care, now,' warned Nana Brand, as India, Eppie and a handful of others wrapped plaids round small shoulders, took pails in hands and prepared to leave. 'Keep a sharp eye open for yon Harbour mannie.'

'Who is that?' asked India when they were outside in the half-light of the Square. The sky was still dark, but to the east, beyond the sea-line, a golden glow spread slowly upward, staining sky and sea with turquoise and trails of morning pink. The thatched roofs of the cottages were dense black silhouettes, tinged here and there with light. There was an edge of frost in the air and when they rounded the corner of the Square on to Pocra Quay a seabreeze which set India's cheeks tingling. Other figures, muffled as they were and also carrying pails, were gathering now from all round the Square, moving silently and most of them barefooted, towards the quay. It was a weird and eerie sight.

'Who?' she repeated, tugging at Eppie's arm. 'What "mannie"?'

'I telt ye, the Harbour mannie,' whispered Eppie crossly. 'Who else? Ye dinna want to get caught, do ye?'

India felt a shiver of mingled excitement and fear. She had expected it to be wet and cold, expected to have to rake about the slippery rocks for mussels, and to endure Eppie's jeers if she found none, even anticipated cuts and bruises from the rocks themselves. But not actual danger.

'Why should we get caught?' she faltered. 'I thought mussels were free?'

'Aye, sea-mussels are free enough, but they're nae so easy to find. Ye'd be raking around till all hours to fill yon pail. But the town's got a mussel bed in the Spillwater over there, where we can fill our pails nae bother. Only thing is, the town'd rather we paid for them! So keep your eyes open for the Harbour mannie, like I said, and if ye see him, run!'

India nodded, looked nervously over her shoulder once or twice, then decided she could safely leave survival to those more skilled than she in the business of evasion. For the group had swelled to a couple of dozen, obviously well practised at traversing the harbour basin. The tide was out, the mud-flats gleaming, the Spillwater channel south of Pocra pink now and shimmering as the sun rose higher. India could see dark shapes on the rocks beyond that thread of water and more, splashing through the shallows ahead of them.

'Hurry,' urged Eppie, skipping nimbly from one sand hump to the next, 'or yon Torry quines will have taken the lot afore we get there.'

To the east, the dark mass of the lighthouse marked the entrance to the harbour with, across the narrow harbour mouth, the green hump of the headland above Torry. Inside, within the harbour, the deep water by Trinity Quay stood dark and quiet, its ships still sleeping at their moorings, with, at their backs, the shipyards on the Inches stirring into life. But Trinity Quay was waking, too, and the town beyond. India could see lights in the Shiprow. On the south side of the inner basin, beyond the Inches, the river meandered in a scatter of untidy sandbanks towards the harbour mouth and the sea and it was here, along the banks of the Spillwater, near Point Law, that the Harbour trustees had lain down mussel beds, at considerable expense, in order to supply bait to the fishermen at a cheap rate.

'Why should folk pay for something that's always been free afore?' finished Eppie, with incontrovertible logic.

Why indeed? India splashed happily behind Eppie, oblivious of the icy water on her bare legs, till they reached the mussel scarp and joined the rest of the scavengers – a silent, urgent group, with none of the cheerful banter usual in such a gathering. Sounds carry over water. India straightened momentarily to ease her back, noted that there were about fifty of them now, strung out along the banks, women of all ages from five- or six-year-olds to grannies, and even a few men, too old for the fishing or, in some cases, too simple. But all were concentrating in silent haste on filling their pails. India looked at her own almost empty bucket and marvelled at their speed and skill. Eppie had shown her how to run her fingers along the rock's surface, find the exact spot on the mussel's shell to give the best purchase, then twist and tug. India's fingers were crisscrossed with cuts, but so numb with the cold seawater that she felt nothing and her feet and ankles were dead. But there were some mussels in her pail. She looked at them proudly, admiring the blue-green sheen, the plump curve of the shell. Eppie's bucket was almost full, she noticed, and bent over her own rock with renewed concentration.

She did not see the warning signal from a fishing boat in the channel, did not hear the warning hiss. Then someone pushed her roughly in the back. 'Town Sergeants! Run!' Eppie snatched up her bucket and was gone, up the bank, over the grass, racing like a hare for the open shore at Torry. For a shocked moment India stood, ankle deep in the shallows, while all around her the dark shapes scattered, draining away into the sea or shore or sand dunes till only a handful remained. Then she seized her precious pail and ran – along the Spillwater, up the bank, over the scrubland, dipping, twisting, dodging, hair streaming, bare feet flying. She felt the ground thud behind her, heard a man's voice shouting, then another. She rounded a scarp of rocks – and ran straight into the Town Sergeant's outspread arms.

'They caught only three of them,' chuckled old Abercrombie. 'Fifty or more on the mussel scarp and they couldna catch but three! And they wouldn't have caught Indy, if she'd had more practice. But rocks are treacherous to those who don't know their way around them. Next time she'll get away, no bother.'

He had claimed her from the town jail, for that Fenton was grateful, had taken her back to his own house in the Guestrow and actually fed her porridge and hot toddy, 'to get her circulation going again, she was that cold, the poor wee lass', while Mrs Abercrombie's maid heated water for a bath. Now, warmed, dried, freshly clad, apparently unrepentant, India sat at her grandfather's fireside, for all the world like a favoured child, instead of a disobedient jailbird. What the town would say when the news got about, Fenton dreaded to think. It would be all over Aberdeen by sundown, and Augusta's wedding imminent. What it would do to Victoria's chances, let alone the child's own, was too awful to contemplate. But what distressed Fenton as much as anything else was that the old man seemed to regard the whole incident as highly entertaining. In fact, if you listened to him you would think the child's sole sin had been to get caught.

'Dinna look so glum,' his father was saying now. 'It's time yon lass had a taste o' real life instead of spending her time doing daft things like stitching samplers nobody wants and sitting on her behind all day. There's plenty fishergirls her age running a household and earning their keep.'

'But she is not a fishergirl, Father.' Fenton had heard the arguments before, about each of his daughters in turn.

'More's the pity! I'm right disappointed in you, Fenton lad. When you chose a fisher lass for a wife I thought you'd done the first sensible thing of your life. Then she goes soft on you and brings her daughters up soft. It's nae right, Fenton. But then your own Ma was a fisher lass and look what happened to her.' He sighed briefly, before saying, 'It's no wonder the lass wants a taste of the life her ma and her grandma knew.'

'Maybe, Father. But it is not right that she should disobey her parents to do so!' Fenton was appalled by the incident, appalled that India should want to stay in the Square in the first place, appalled by the deceptions, and most of all appalled by Jessica's ineptitude and gullibility. Anyone of any intelligence would have recognised that the note was written by India herself. But then Jessica was barely literate. Not like Mary Ballantyne. He allowed himself one brief memory of Mary, in dove-grey silk, reading in the window seat of the elegant little apartment he had bought her. She had looked up as he opened the door, the soft-leather-bound book open in her lap, and he had watched her face change in an instant from rapt absorption to joy.

'Well, what do you say, Fenton?' demanded his father, breaking in on his thoughts.

'About what?'

'About Indy, of course. What else, ye daft loon? You're aye away wi' the fairies these days.'

Hastily Fenton banished Mary Ballantyne to the deeper recesses of his mind. It would not do for his father to suspect anything. As for India . . . He looked up to see her watching him with that closed, accusing look that had become familiar ever since that shameful incident when he had lost his temper in the public street and crushed her wooden bear. He had been in the wrong and they both knew it, but it was too late to go back.

'Didn't ye hear me?' said Abercrombie. 'I'll have her wi' me in the Union Street shop. She can learn the trade from the bottom, no soft treatment, no difference between her and the others, no favours, but if she learns well and earns it, she'll get all the promotion she wants . . . What do you say, lass?'

'Oh yes, Grandpa! I'd like that and I'd work really hard, honest I would.'

'I know you would, Indy love. So ye can start straight in tomorrow. I'll put you in the groceries first. Ye'll be a rare hand at weighing out sugar and flour.'

'No, Father.' Fenton put both hands on the chair arms and stood up. 'No,' he repeated, looking down at his father with unwavering eyes. 'India will go away, to school.'

The moment the words were out, he knew it was the right choice. At boarding school she would be safe from the Square, safe from the Christies, and safe from her mother's ignorance. At boarding school she might even learn to be a lady.

But Abercrombie was on his feet too, now, and glaring. 'I've not heard such a daft idea since I don't know when. Indy will work in the family business, for me.'

'I shall call on the Bonningtons at once,' said Fenton, impervious. 'Their girls were at boarding school. With their recommendation, India should be able to travel south almost immediately.'

'Aye, that's an idea,' said Abercrombie with a sly look in his eye. 'She could travel south with you and maybe learn the business in the Edinburgh branch. I hear folks like lady assistants in Edinburgh, pretty young assistants, with apartments of their own.'

'I'd rather stay here, Grandpa, with you,' said India, slipping her hand into his. Neither man heard her. They were glaring at each other in silent combat. Grandfather and grand-daughter stood hand in hand on the turkey hearth rug, the firelight bright behind them and Mrs Abercrombie's crystal candelabra gleaming on either end of the mantelshelf while Fenton felt the slow flush of guilt spread upwards to engulf him.

His father knew. Oh God! If the old man were to tell anyone . . . Then Fenton squared his shoulders. His life was his own, to live as he chose. It was no business of his father's, or anyone else's. As for his daughter, she was his business too, to deal with as he chose. But letters south would take time. There would be the question of guardians, so far from home, and other matters to settle. It was not a good time to travel, with the weather still unpredictable. Spring would be better. Or summer. Meanwhile, if India were kept occupied . . .

'Well?' his father was saying, with that challenging look in his eye.

'India may start work in the shop tomorrow,' said Fenton coldly. 'Until I make other arrangements.'

But the other arrangements were frustratingly slow to materialise. Fenton inquired of the Bonningtons, wrote off an exploratory letter, and eventually, when he had almost given up hope, received a letter in return apologising for the delay which was due to sickness in the school. An outbreak of measles meant they were virtually in

iii

In May, letters arrived from Pearl – a bundle of them, collected somewhere *en route* and obviously delayed. The Nobles gathered at the Christies' house to share the news. Since Louise Forbes's marriage to Dr Andrew and her involvement in his work, Rachel had not seen so much of her friend, so it was an added pleasure to spend an evening in her company, though obviously the news from Pearl was in the forefront of everyone's mind. Even Booky's. He was a student now, at Marischal College, having won a bursary in the October competition. As Rachel looked round the crowded room, she felt something of the old happiness, before Pearl's marriage. In fact, she realised with private alarm, before Duncan Greig. But she could not and must not lay all the family's troubles at his door just because he was a stranger come among them, even though aspects of Pearl's letters troubled her with doubt. For instance, it sounded as if she was too much alone: and Pearl was a gregarious girl who needed company. But it is not my business, she told herself firmly. He is Pearl's chosen husband and Pearl is happy. Certainly her letters were full of fascinating information.

'She says the Chinese called the *Jardine* a smoke-ship,' said Jamie, slurping at the broth his mother had put before him. 'They fired on it and banned it from Chinese waters, Pearl says. So much for your precious steam,

Tom. It's no good having engines if you're not allowed to use them, is it?'

'What did Pearl say about the trials in your letter, Aunt Louise?' asked Tom, ignoring him. Tom was used to Jamie's teasing and knew as well as any of them that it was only a preliminary to brotherly banter and horseplay, but today he obviously had thoughts only for the steam engines – and, thought Rachel, noting the way the boy's eyes strayed over and over again to her absorbed face, for Amelia Noble.

'Here, Tom. Read it for yourself,' said Louise, handing over the letter, already much read and pored over since its arrival the day before, by the London packet.

'Loud! Loud!' chanted Davy, who, at four years old, considered himself every bit the sailor his brothers were.

'Please, Tom,' added Amelia, fixing him with limpid eyes. 'Read it aloud.'

Tom blushed, fumbled with the letter, scanned its closely written pages briefly, then said, 'Pearl writes that when the Chinese banned the ship from Chinese waters, the *Jardine* was sent to Singapore to be sold, then "a steam picnic was arranged so that prospective buyers could see the vessel's prowess. Unfortunately, the expedition was arranged for Friday, an unlucky day as you know, and this Friday was no exception. The *Jardine* set off under only half steam and lopsided, so that Duncan was obliged to throw overboard a great deal of the heavy wood fuel which had been supplied. Then, under full steam at last, the kettle boiled . . ." That is the engine's kettle, Davy, not like Ma's – " and the *Jardine* stuck on the mud. As you may imagine, Duncan was not pleased . . ."'

'I'll bet he wasn't!' put in Jamie, grinning.

'". . . but after heaving off with a kedge anchor the party proceeded, though at a very disappointing speed.

An engine lever fractured, one of the iron davits gave way and eventually Duncan had no alternative but to set the sails. Even then there was trouble as various ropes and things were apparently missing, but fortunately there was no deficiency of beer, champagne or claret and also a very good larder. The picnic party returned home in two yachts which came to the rescue and Duncan has been obliged to order a thorough overhaul of the engines and to fix new trials. He tells me he must stay in Singapore till these are over and the *Jardine* sold. I cannot help but think that had the ship been ordered from the Christie yard, none of these troubles would have happened, though I may not say so."'

'Dear Pearl, she was always so loyal,' murmured Rachel and busied herself at the fire so that no one should see her emotion.

'She is right, too,' said Jamie. 'Yon steamboats are all very well, on canals and so on, but for real sea-sailing, give me canvas every time. And Christie canvas at that.'

'No one's offering to give you anything,' said Tom, 'nor me neither, yet a while. But I am interested in these trials Pearl talks of. I wonder why that engine lever fractured? Perhaps if the bolts were screwed too tight and the machinery not sufficiently oiled . . .'

'What does Pearl say next?' interrupted Jamie. 'She'll maybe tell us.'

'Let's see . . . "I cannot help thinking," she says, "that there will be more troubles before the ship is disposed of. It is an annoyance to Duncan who would prefer to be in Chinese waters and as for me, I would prefer to have him here. Macau is still strange and alien to me. But when my child is born I will have more to occupy me and less time to think of home. Which I do every day, with loving affection, and always will."'

'She's expecting a child!' cried Jamie. 'Why didn't you

say so, Ma? Do you think he will have slit eyes and yellow skin along of being born in China?'

'Daft!' Rachel slapped him playfully on the head. 'Of course he won't.' But even if he did, we would not know, she thought with a wave of fresh sadness. Who will care for Pearl when her time comes? The thought of Pearl alone, among strangers, when her labour pains struck was a sobering one. Rachel had heard Greig's tales, had heard him and Dr Andrew talking of tropical diseases and primitive nursing care and hadn't Greig mentioned a graveyard once, with a row specially set aside for the children? Tom had been particularly upset, she remembered, to hear that. Rachel felt a nameless chill at her back and could not prevent a shiver. When she looked up she saw Tom watching her and when he said, 'Suppose it's a girl?' something in his voice told her he shared her fear.

But a moment later he was talking of engines and horsepower and when Jamie challenged him, the two launched into the usual amiable argument of steam versus sail and Rachel decided she had been mistaken. Tom was too young to be apprehensive about such things. She had merely been projecting her own anxiety on to him, and groundless anxiety at that. Pearl would have friends to help her – other captains' wives or that Mrs Morton she mentioned, and one of the missionaries was a qualified doctor. There was no more need to worry than if Pearl had been giving birth here, at home.

But Rachel had been right in one respect. When Tom called at the Nobles' house some days later, as he often did when he had free time ashore, he found Amelia alone in the drawing room, poring over some papers at the writing desk. She covered them with her hand when he opened the door, but when she saw who it was, she relaxed, smiling.

'Oh, it's you, Tom. Come in. I'm just finishing off some work I had to do. I won't be a minute.'

'That's all right, Amelia. I didn't mean to interrupt you. You finish what you are doing and I'll easy wait. That is, if you don't mind?'

'No, no.' She bent over the desk and resumed writing while Tom watched her, admiring the sunlight on her golden hair, the narrow curve of her shoulders in the plain blue calico dress. It was a large, high-ceilinged room, with white walls on which hung several oil paintings in gilt frames. The tall windows overlooked a short drive, with flowering trees and a neat stretch of lawn and somewhere a blackbird was singing. It was quiet in the room, except for the soft scratch of Amelia's pen, the slow tick of the grandfather clock and the occasional stirring of coals in the grate, but it was a restful quiet in which Tom felt no impatience. He sat down on one of the mahogany chairs and waited, content to be in Amelia's company and confidence.

After five minutes or so she shut her books, tucked her papers into a neat bundle and closed the desk. 'There,' she said with satisfaction. 'Booky will be proud of me. I promised him I would study for two hours every day and I have. He says it is the only way I shall ever learn anything, and he is right.'

'What is it you are studying?' asked Tom, interested in anything concerning Amelia.

'Oh, just lessons Booky set for me,' she said evasively. 'Shall we go in the garden? I want to show you my little rosemary bush. Pearl gave me the cutting which she begged from a lady in Ferryhill and it is growing beautifully.'

Behind the house, and sloping gently southwards, was a kitchen garden with neat rows of vegetables and, in one corner, a patch of herbs with mint, thyme, sage and the bright blue flowers of borage. Amelia's rosemary bush was no more than six inches high, but healthy enough and already sprouting tiny lavender-coloured flowers.

'Rosemary is for remembrance,' said Amelia seriously. 'I look at my little bush every day and think of Pearl.'

Tom took a deep breath and voiced the fear which had been with him ever since he had read Pearl's letter. 'If her baby is a girl, will she be properly treated, Amelia? I don't mean by Pearl and Captain Greig, though whether he approves of daughters or not I don't know. But Pearl says she has a Chinese servant and you remember those dreadful tales Captain Greig told us about female infanticide.' Tom and Amelia had discussed the question often since that appalled evening when Amelia had rushed, gagging, from the dining room of the Nobles' house. Tom had walked home with Captain Greig and had asked further questions. When next he saw Amelia he had deliberately brought up the subject so that she could discuss her fears with him and together they had explored the terrible insensitivities of a culture so alien to their own.

'And yet,' Tom had said, 'at its simplest it is practical. If there is not enough food, and too many children – '

'People should not have children if they cannot feed them,' Amelia had declared. 'Louise says there is no need. There are ways of not having children, though she will not tell me what she means until I am older.'

Tom had blushed and talked quickly of other things, but the image of those little dead girl babies had stayed with him and, he knew, with Amelia too.

'I shall go to Macau,' said Amelia now. 'Not yet, because I am only twelve and Papa will not let me. But as soon as I am old enough, I shall go. I shall live with Pearl and work among the orphan girls.'

Tom listened indulgently, as he had listened to all her

childhood dreams for as long as he could remember. She had always spun dreams of one kind or another, and he humoured her, knowing each dream would merge into the next until, with age, reality would creep in. This dream was like the others, spun from Pearl's departure and her letters. Soon a different one would take its place. But Amelia was looking at him with a strange expression, almost of excitement.

'Shall I tell you a secret, Tom?'

Tom looked at her eager face, her golden hair and blue-eyed innocence, and wondered whatever it could be. Another private daydream? 'Yes, please,' he said, smiling.

'Promise on the Holy Bible, cross your heart and hope to die, that you will never tell? Not *anyone*?'

'I promise.'

She looked back at the house, as if its blank windows might harbour eavesdroppers, then at the vegetable patch and the apple tree beyond. The tree was in blossom, the air scented with the pink and white clusters which hung, bee-laden, from the green-leafed branches. One or two petals had already fallen, like pink snowflakes, on to the grass or on to the freshly turned earth of the vegetable garden where a thrush rooted busily between the rows of sprouting kale. A butterfly hovered over the tiny rosemary bush, then lifted and moved on to the richer nectar of the borage flowers. There was no one in sight. Satisfied, Amelia reached up, put her arms round his neck and pulled him close. Then she whispered her secret into his ear. Tom bit his lip with shock.

'Promise you won't tell?' Dumbly he shook his head. She would change her mind, like she always did. She must . . . When she was older, he would show her how much she meant to him. Then her secret would not matter any more. Then, surely, she would forget her childhood plans and . . . and . . . But Tom dared not tempt fate by putting words to what he hoped, even in the privacy of his own thoughts.

Vanya Priit died that summer. A mere three weeks later, Friida followed him. Jamie and Tom went to the funeral with their father. When the *Bonnie Annie* returned to Aberdeen, both boys looked older. Tom, in particular, had a new air of maturity about him.

'They left us everything, Ma,' he said, indicating a cloth bundle. 'But they had so little. Priit was carving a wee dancing bear for Matt, see.' He took out a piece of half-carved wood and set it on the table. 'You can see the head and the shape of the legs. Then he died.'

'He was very old,' said Rachel, in what comfort she could, and held Tom close. Rachel had never met Tom's grandparents in their simple wooden hut in Riga bay, but they had been part of her family for too many years for her not to feel their loss. 'They both were. And you gave them great joy.'

But afterwards, when the boys had gone to bed, James held her close. They both knew that the old pair's death had altered things.

'We need not limit ourselves to Riga now,' said James the next day, putting Rachel's thoughts into words. 'As long as the old ones were alive, it was only right for us to visit them. Now perhaps it is time to reassess the routes of all our ships. Move them where they will find best profits. Even go further afield. With a growing family, we need to expand.'

Rachel was expecting again, but there was not only their own young family to consider. Christie's was a family firm and Alex's six children must be taken into account, too. Alex's twin sons were growing fast. If they were to be seamen, they would have to be apprenticed and a premium paid.

'With the Yard in full production and the repair shop with more business than we can handle,' said James thoughtfully, 'we'd best look to the trade side of the business for expansion.'

'China,' said Maitland absentmindedly. 'Then possibly Australia. Or across the Pacific to the west coast of South America, then round the Horn and home. My *White Bird* will circle the earth one day.'

'Aye, one day. But we've missed this year's season and who's to say we'll catch the next? If we could find a suitable ship to buy in, I'm thinking we might shelve work on your tea-ship for a month or so and copper bottom a brig for Jamaica or Brazil.'

'Oh please, James,' cried Rachel. 'Don't stop work on Maitland's ship. Not now, when she's almost completed. Pearl's child will be born by now and I know she is longing to see a Christie ship sail into Macau harbour. Maitland says he can finish the ship by December if he has the men. Allowing for trials and delays, she could sail by May. Please, James? I suspect Pearl is homesick, though being Pearl, she does not say. If I could tell her Maitland's ship was on her way . . .?'

'Very well.' James smiled indulgently at his wife and put a protective arm around her shoulders. 'Another month and we'll see.'

But before the month was out, disaster struck.

The summer of '36 was uncommonly hot. The bathing huts on the beach were in constant use, the shallows loud with splashing children and girlish squeals. Sand pies and more ambitious edifices dotted the shore where normally only seagulls roamed, or Eppie and her friends from the Square in search of mussels or mischief.

India often thought of that early morning February raid on the town mussel beds, of the icy water on her hands and feet, of the slippery grey heap in the bottom of her pail, a heap which grew respectably larger in memory as the months passed.

'I'd well nigh filled my bucket,' she told Jamie proudly, 'when the Sergeant nabbed me. If it hadn't been that the rocks were so slippery, I'd have got away, too.' Fortunately Eppie was not around to dispute her story. India had seen neither Eppie nor Nana Brand since February, though once she thought she recognised one of the Brand tribe, buying flour. But Jamie she saw often, if not in the shop where he came regularly on some message or other for Mrs Christie, then on the Quay.

For India had persuaded her Grandpa Abercrombie to show her the business in all its stages right down to the warehouse which housed his stores on the Quay, the Weigh-house and Customs house and the ships which brought his orders to Aberdeen. Christie ships as a rule, though since the Farquharson steamship *Jessica* had been in operation he had transported certain things via her, 'in the interests of family harmony,' his daughter Clementina being married to the Farquharson boy. Besides, he told India, that way he could keep an eye on young Tom Christie and 'see he's treated right'.

India liked Tom and on the days when she accompanied old George Abercrombie to the Quay and Jamie was away at sea, she would talk to Tom instead. Tom was interesting. He knew about steamships and London and he had seen the East India docks. He had even seen a steam omnibus on the Paddington road. He told her about the freight they carried on the *Jessica*, too, so that she could discuss it intelligently with her grandpa. Once they transported the very animal that won the prize for the best beef in Smithfield. But best of all was when her grandpa called in at the Christie office and she went with him. Sometimes she felt a twinge of guilt about that, for hadn't her father forbidden her all contact with the Christies? But her grandfather seemed to think it all right for her to accompany him, and as her father was in Edinburgh as often as not and believed India spent her days in the Union Street shop, he did not object. He would have objected had he known, of course, but India firmly pushed aside that guilty thought and rejoiced in the opportunity those visits gave her to share, if only on the edges, in Jamie's life.

But life was altogether more interesting now that India was not cooped up in the house all day, with her mother and sisters, and when the summer days grew oppressively hot and her mother announced that she was going to spend a few weeks with Augusta and her new husband, in the Henderson house at Monymusk, and take Victoria and young Finlay with her, India was delighted. India, of course, was supposed to go too, but when she refused her mother made no objection. The invitation, as they both knew, had been merely a token gesture. So India moved in with Nana Abercrombie and went to work each day with her grandpa, hand in hand. Even then her father said nothing except 'Remember what I told you, India, and behave.' Then he told Mairi to pack his usual portmanteau, for Edinburgh.

India reckoned he spent more time in Edinburgh these days than he did at home. But then with the Aberdeen house empty except for Mairi, why not? India herself would have been happy to stay on indefinitely with her grandparents, but she knew the end of summer would put an end to that.

At the moment, however, the cloudless skies and shimmering warmth seemed set to last for ever. Sales of lemonade and cinnamon water were gratifyingly high and there was a correspondingly brisk trade in ginger ale and other cooling drinks. India helped her grandpa fill the stone bottles from the barrels in the back shop and soon became expert at not spilling a drop.

She liked working in the shop, liked the sacks of flour and sugar and rice with their little metal scoops with which to weigh out the customer's requirements. She liked the rows of glass jars containing spices and pickles. Liked the heaps of raisins and almonds, the boxes of oranges and the stone jars of pineapples or stem ginger in thick sugar syrup. She soon grew adept at twisting the squares of paper into neat cones into which to spoon the demerara sugar or the raisins. Then she would fold the top down and tie the packet with string as swiftly and as neatly as any of the other assistants. She even liked slipping her hand into the cool slime of the egg barrel if the supply of fresh eggs ran out and someone wanted a pickled egg or two to tide them over. Grandfather Abercrombie was pleased with her and said so.

'As long as you remember always to be polite to the customers, however annoying, you'll do, lass,' he said and India glowed with pride. But there was one customer she was in no danger of offending.

'Hello, Indy.' India looked up from the sugar she was carefully weighing out for an order, brass scoop poised over brass balance, then her face lit up with welcome.

'Jamie! You're back. You must have had a swift passage this time. I thought with the calm weather and no wind it might have taken you longer, but I'm right glad to see you. Have you come to buy something, or just to chat?'

'Both,' he grinned, and wiped his forehead on the back of his hand. 'My, but it's sweltering outside and nae much better in.' The shop was almost as crowded with customers as it was with produce in spite of the baking summer heat, for Abercrombie's was a well-known rendezvous for half the town. You could get practically anything in Abercrombie's. Though it might not be quite as cheap as elsewhere, at least you were sure of a friendly welcome and a bit of a chat, for as like as not you would meet an acquaintance and, failing that, the staff were always ready for a wee 'news'. And now, since the heatwave, you could even get a cool drink if you felt the need.

'Would you like a glass of water?' offered India. 'I could put a dash of whisky in it, if you like, Grandpa wouldn't mind.'

'Thanks, Indy, but I'd best not. I'm to fetch whisky for the Yard and I dinna want Uncle Maitland thinking I've been sampling it on the way. The men are working extra hours on our tea-ship and Uncle Maitland's giving them all whisky and water, for the heat. He's a barrel o' fresh water in the Yard, from the water-cart, and he ladles it out himself wi' a tot o' whisky in each mug, but the whisky's done and he's sent me for more.'

'Is the tea-ship nearly finished then?' India had been following the progress of the Christies' latest ship with close interest, especially as her grandfather talked of putting money into the venture. Lately, though, there had been disquieting news from Canton – something about the new British Superintendent and relations with the Chinese authorities. Trade, apparently, was not running smoothly. In fact, some reports said it was positively bad. There was talk of a clampdown on opium trafficking. India was not quite sure how that affected the tea trade, but apparently it did, and there was even talk of urging the Government to send gunboats to protect British ships and property. But such rumours only added to the excitement, as far as India was concerned, and gave an extra glamour to the Christies' tea-ship.

'Aye, she's coming on fine,' said Jamie proudly. 'Uncle Maitland says it's only a matter of weeks now before she's finished. Would you like to see over her?'

'Oh Jamie, I'd love to!' India's face lit up with excitement and joy.

'Well, why don't you come to the Yard with me now? I'll ask Mr Abercrombie if you like, when I get the whisky jar.'

'No, you'd best not.' Into India's mind had come the memory of her father's fury on that other occasion when she had walked with Jamie on the Quay. Suppose he were to see them again? To be sure she did not know if her father was in Edinburgh or Aberdeen at the moment, but it was not worth the risk. 'I am working, you see,' she said hastily as he turned away. 'But I could come as soon as I'm finished.'

'As you like.' Jamie shrugged good-humouredly. 'It's all the same to me. I just thought you might like to see over her, seeing as how you're always so interested.'

'But I *am*, Jamie. I'd like to see her more than anything. So as soon as I've finished here, I'll come to the Yard and you can show me. That is, if you'll still be there?' she finished, uncertain whether she had offended him or not.

'Aye, I'll be there. We'll all be there, like as not, if the good weather holds. But I'd best be off or Uncle Maitland'll be sending out a search party!'

India watched him stroll across the crowded shop towards the wines and spirits, nodding a cheerful greeting here, exchanging a word there, till his tall, young figure disappeared through the arched doorway into her grandfather's domain.

With new enthusiasm and a mounting excitement, she resumed her sugar weighing and, when old Mrs Farquharson insisted on having her order weighed twice over *'for discrepancies*', India smiled cheerfully and said only, 'Of course.'

'What was the old bag complaining about this time, Indy?' said a pert voice, a little too loud, as Eppie from Footdee, with a gaggle of friends, erupted into the shop.

'Mind your manners, lass!' called a warning voice from the inner regions, 'and see ye keep your hands to yourself and nae in my toffee jar!'

Eppie Brand pulled a face behind Mr Abercrombie's back, then winked at India. 'Me and my friends are off to the beach, Indy, for a picnic. Want to come?'

'I'd love to, Eppie, but . . .'

'But you're not allowed? No, well, ye wouldna be, would you? Ye'd likely get caught by the Town Sergeant, stealing the sand!' Eppie and her friends squealed with delighted laughter at Eppie's wit. 'Ye'd best leave picnics and suchlike to respectable folk like us. I'll take a quarter o' treacle toffee, and no short measure.'

India glared. It still rankled with her that Eppie and her friends had escaped capture on the mussel beds while India, who had thought herself as nimble-footed as any of them, had not. 'With nuts, or without?'

'Oh I reckon we can afford nuts the day,' said Eppie grandly. 'And a pint o' best ale. We've our own bottle, see. Nae your stone jar, but real glass. So kindly fill it, my good woman.'

Eppie was enjoying herself. When India returned a few moments later and handed over the bottle, with a look of lofty scorn, Eppie said graciously, 'Thank you.' Then added, teasing, 'Don't you wish you was coming too? Nana Brand's given us two whole shillings to spend. We're going to buy buns at the baker's and maybe some strawberries, and sit on the sand like holiday folk.'

'Well mind you don't drown while you're at it!' snapped India and turned her back. She would have liked to go with them, liked to paddle and splash and forget everything except the pleasure of bare feet on warm sand. Then she remembered Jamie and her ill-humour vanished. When the shop closed, she was going to meet him in the Christie yard to see Maitland Christie's China ship. That was worth any picnic, any day.

Maitland Christie was pleased. In spite of the heat, work was going well. The repair shop was temporarily empty and he had been able to move extra men on to the building of his tea-ship. The hull was complete, the decks in place, and the hold which would carry the precious tea chests fitted his measurements exactly. Now, carpenters were at work inside the hull, fashioning the cabin fitments, while others planed the deck planks smooth or fitted the cleats which would hold the yards. The masts had been ordered, the sails spoken for at the sailyard, the rope-works knew what was required of them and the anchor was already cast and awaiting only its chain. Everything was moving smoothly into place. There would be the tests, of course, once she was launched, and the provisioning, then the hiring of a suitable crew, but even with all that to take care of, his tea-ship should be more than ready to sail for the East in the spring. This time next year, his ship would be on the high seas, in the Indian Ocean perhaps, or the Malacca Straits, speeding towards Macau and well in time for the next season at the end of the year. If he were not such a bad sailor, he would have insisted on going himself. As it was, the moment this tea-ship was on her way, he would start on another – and another after that. Tom and the Farquharsons could keep their steam. It was sail every time for him.

But the work force must be cosseted at all costs. He could not afford illness or defection at this stage. So Maitland saw to the men's extra refreshment himself, ladling out fresh water laced with whisky – the best drink for hot weather – three times day. Some men brought their own bottles, of course – shipbuilding was thirsty work – and at mid-day the gates opened to admit a flood of wives and daughters with their menfolk's dinners, and closed after them half an hour later when they left again, taking empty basins and bottles with them – Maitland was a stickler for tidiness and with the current drought you couldn't be too careful. But the women did not complain, for as well as the debris of the dinner, they each took a bundle of wooden offcuts and shavings for kindling, with the compliments of the management.

From the direction of the shore came the squeals and laughter of children playing and the different cries of the gulls, circling hopefully for scraps. To the east, beyond the boundary fence, he could see bright patches of colour on the marram grass where the fishwives had spread blankets and bedlinen to dry and from the harbour rose the smell of new varnish and paint where one of the Aberdeen and Leith Company ships was being refurbished. Maitland whistled happily to himself as he checked the specifications for the master cabin and waited for Jamie to reappear with the men's afternoon whisky. Pearl would have teased him for wasting good money, but it was money well spent if it kept the men happy, especially as he wanted them to work till sundown today. And sundown was late in high summer.

Her grandfather kept India working later than usual in the shop.One of the assistants found a hole in a flour sack and the entire contents had to be sifted. 'It wouldna do for the likes o' Mrs Farquharson to find mouse droppings in her flour, would it?' he told India and added, with a wink, 'Mind you, she's blind as a bat these days and if we told her it was currants, she'd likely believe us. But best not risk it.' So India sifted scoop after scoop of the flour till she had transferred the lot into a fresh sack – and a good job, too, as there *were* mouse droppings, half a cupful of them.

It was late when she finally dusted off her hands, removed apron and cap, and asked her grandfather if she could see him later at the house instead of walking home with him as she usually did.

'I'll not be long, Grandpa. But Jamie said he'd show me the new tea-ship if I went to the Yard. It's nearly ready for launching.'

'I'd come wi' you myself, lass, if it wasn't for the shop. But I've the cellars to check yet. So you run along. Dinna be long, mind, or I'll have your Nana Abercrombie after me for losing you!'

'Thank you, Grandpa,' and India stepped happily out into the street. But as soon as she was outside, all decorum forgotten, she looped up her skirts and ran. The sun was still above the horizon, but the sky to the west, at the top of Union Street, was already streaked a dying green and crimson and gold and the shadows of the tenements in the Shiprow were long and cold. She hoped Jamie wouldn't have gone home.

She was out of breath when she reached the Quay and had to slow to a walk before breaking into a run again when she saw the arched entrance of the Christie Yard. She was almost there when a crowd of children swirled round the corner of Christie's Wynd and all but sent her flying.

'Little tykes!' called someone furiously and Maitland Christie appeared, red-faced and breathless in the entrance.

'Whatever is it, Mr Christie?' asked India, nervously. She was almost sure Nana Brand's Eppie had been in the group.

'Vandals!' he spluttered. 'Hooligans! Found them dodging about in the wood store, stealing like as not. Said they were making sawdust castles because the tide had come in and spoilt the sand. Liars! It's mischief they were after if you ask me.' Then he stopped, noting who she was. 'I'm sorry, India. It's not your fault. Have you come to see Jamie?'

'Yes, please.' India was a little in awe of Maitland Christie. Everyone knew he was very clever, designing ships right out of his own head. He had a room full of snuff boxes and silver dishes and things, too, from the people who had bought his ships, so they must be as good as everyone said. And now he was building a tea-ship that would be the best of all. So Jamie said, anyway. 'Jamie said I could come,' she added, in case he thought she was after 'mischief' like Eppie. 'To look at the tea-ship.'

'Did he?' Mr Christie was still glaring after those running children who, as he watched, disappeared round the corner into Pilot Square. 'Horrors,' he said, with feeling. 'I'll tan their backsides if I catch them here again. Clambering over my best timber . . .'

'Has Jamie gone?' asked India politely. 'I know I am a little late.'

'No, he's not gone, though most of the men have. If you promise to behave, young lady, you can go in and find him. But I'll lock the gate behind you, if you don't mind. I don't want that lot back again. Not that gates will keep them out if they're set on mischief. I reckon they came over the fence anyway.' Still grumbling, he disappeared across the yard and into the office building leaving India standing alone.

She had not been in the Christie yard before. It was still warm with the day's sun and larger than she had imagined, with sawdust everywhere and a huge pile of timber the length of one side, though it seemed to be stacked in special piles, with numbers and different thicknesses and colours. She could smell pine resin and pitch. On her left was the office building, with what she supposed was the planning loft and, opposite it, on her right as she stood at the gate, between her and the harbour waters, the slipways for two ships. They were supported on wooden brackets, the nearest no more than a keel and a few curved planks, the other a huge, gleaming hull, apparently complete. There was even a figurehead of some sort, though India could not quite see what it was. There was no one in sight, but somewhere someone was whistling.

Happily, India set off across the yard towards the tea-ship, the scent of sawdust rising warm to her nostrils and, from the direction of the sea, the first hint of an evening breeze.

'Jamie?' She rounded the stern of the ship and saw a ladder, its feet in the foothills of the timber mountain, its head resting against the gunwales of the tea-ship. 'Jamie?' The whistling stopped and a moment later his cheerful face appeared above the deck.

'Oh, it's you, Indy. Sorry I wasn't at the gate, but the watchman's gone home for a bite to eat and I said I'd hang on till he gets back. He'll not be long. But come on up and I'll show you round. Can you manage the ladder?'

'Of course I can!' A moment later, India was on the deck beside him and Jamie began his proud tour of inspection.

'She'll be about 300 tons register, Uncle Maitland thinks,' he said, standing where the helm would be, and for all the world as if he were already ship's master. 'A bit bigger than the *City of Aberdeen*. 101 feet by 26 by 18 or thereabouts. But come below and I'll show you the cabins. They're not finished, of course, but you'll be able to get an idea.'

The next half hour passed in blissful exploration. India could find no fault and Jamie could not have asked for a more attentive audience as he propounded his pet theories of navigation, the routes he would follow to China, and how he would deal with the inevitable hazards of the voyage.

'We will carry firearms, of course,' he said nonchalantly as they regained the deck. 'For pirates. I suppose we should really think of cannon, too, but then we need all the space we have for the cargo. Just think, Indy,' he went on, his eyes shining. 'In three more years I'll be finished my apprenticeship. I reckon my Da will give me a ship of my own, too. Then I'll really see the world.'

'I will come with you,' said India.'I'd love to see far places and I can help you with the sailing.'

'Maybe,' said Jamie, hardly listening. 'In the China seas there's flying fish, Pearl says, and the pirate junks have sails like dragon's wings, all ridged and creaking.'

'I'll plot those courses you were telling me about,' persisted India. 'I'll cook and keep lookout.' She moved to the side of the ship, where the ladder rested, and turned her face to the breeze as if already on the high seas. The breeze was strengthening as the sun set, sending cat's paws across the harbour water and stirring the bent grass on the headland. The sky to the west had darkened to a copper and turquoise glow against which the roofs of the town were etched black as jet. She caught the familiar scent of seaweed on the wind and of drying fish, and something else, vaguely familiar.

'Jamie, what's that smell?'

'What smell?' But even as he spoke, she realised why it was familiar – Mairi, in the bedroom, pressing linen with an iron that was too hot – or the smell of singed paper, just before the fire took hold. At the same moment she saw the pale plume of smoke from the timber stack and heard the ominous crackling as the wind fanned the smouldering spark into sudden flame. They looked at each other in dawning horror. Then Jamie cupped his hands to his mouth and bellowed '*Fire!*'

He leapt down the ladder and raced for the planning loft, shouting as he ran, with India flying close at his heels. Men emerged from nowhere – Maitland, the watchman, then more men came running from the open street, rattling at the locked gates to get inside and help. Valuable time was lost as the key was fetched from the office, the lock turned with fingers clumsy with haste, to let the men stream in. Workmen, neighbours, strangers. No one wanted the fire to spread. Too many warehouses, dwelling houses, shipyards stood too close and after the dry season everything would flare up at the smallest spark. A water chain was formed from the drinking-water barrel while someone ran to fetch a water cart, someone else to call the fire engine, though by the time it had trundled its cumbersome weight from Union Street the fire would be out – or out of control. India found a pail and helped as best she could. No one stopped her. There were other women helping and men of all ages, some with brooms, beating at the flames which had roared now into jubilant splendour as they found sun-parched wood and a kindly wind.

Then the wind changed direction, veering ever so slightly south, a pyramid of blazing wood capsized in a shower of scarlet sparks which arched like a firework display high above their heads – and fell on the deck of Maitland's helpless tea-ship.

Jamie saw it first and leapt for the ladder, India close behind him. Together they stamped and beat at the sparks, extinguishing what they could. Then another spar of timber fell across the bow of the ship.

'Loose the hawsers!' cried someone. 'Push her into the water!' The next minutes had a nightmarish quality in which colour blazed brighter than life, things happened faster and at the same time in horrifying slow motion so that afterwards, India could, and did, relive every second. She kicked and stamped at the burning timber. Her dress caught. Jamie ripped it away and tossed it over the side, still burning. In only her tattered petticoat and drawers, India snatched up a piece of still-smouldering wood and helped to lever the blazing timber over the side where other fire-fighters extinguished it, while a dozen smaller fires sputtered into life across Maitland's precious deck. A tin of varnish blazed and stank in a black plume of choking smoke, a coiled rope smouldered. Someone tossed up a fire broom, India caught it neatly and laid about her with fanatical, sharp-eyed vigour as sparks caught and blazed in a dozen places at once. 'Close the hatches,' roared Maitland from the Yard where a dozen men were heaving and hauling at the vessel while others strove to remove the restraining wedges from under the keel and all struggled to manhandle her towards the harbour water. James Christie was there now, beside his brother, and Alfie Baxter, with a dozen other familiar faces as word spread up and down the town and friends streamed in from Quay and Square to help. Now one group fought to contain the fire in the timber stack, another to drench and protect the planning shed and a third heaved at the land-locked, smouldering vessel. More raced ahead to clear the way, see the runners were free of obstruction, warn any passing water traffic. All hope of saving the timber store had gone, but the planning loft still stood and must be defended at all costs, and there was still a chance that Maitland's tea-ship might be saved – if she didn't sink!

The ship rocked alarmingly under India's feet, but there was no time for her to scramble overboard, had she wanted to, and the ladder had long gone. Instead, she beat at the sparks with her fire broom, like one demented, laying about her wherever she spotted a flame.

'Over here, Indy!' cried Jamie and she sped to help him attack a particularly venomous outbreak. Then the ship gave a shuddering lurch and hurtled towards the water in a rush of flames and streaming smoke, like a fire-ship, as India reported afterwards, only there was no enemy shipping to set alight. A moment later they felt a hissing, gurgling, stomach-churning violence as the vessel hit the surface before settling, steaming gently, into the safety of the harbour water and subsiding, finally, into silence.

Then other sounds impinged: a steady bubbling from deep inside the ship, the drip, drip of a leak somewhere close at hand. It took half an hour of steady pumping to clear the hold and as long again and more to make it watertight, while every inch of the fabric had to be inspected for lingering sparks. Only then could the first, melancholy assessment begin.

By that time what remained of the Christie's timber store was a heap of half-burnt spars in a sea of ash. But thanks to the eventual arrival of the fire engine, with its water tank and brightly painted fire buckets, the planning loft still stood, singed and blistered on one wall, but apart from that, intact. And the embryo ship in the second slipway, being farthest from the heart of the fire, was untouched.

The destruction of the timber store was nothing, except money lost. The burning of Maitland's beloved tea-ship was something else.

'At least she is watertight,' said Maitland, when he could speak without emotion. 'She'll not sink before morning and that will be time enough to assess the full extent o' the damage.'

'Aye,' agreed James Christie wearily. 'Time enough.

Meantime you'd best all come home. You too, India. Rachel will want to thank you, as we all do, for helping and she can maybe lend you a skirt and help you tidy up a bit. We canna send you home half-clad and streaked like a blackamoor.'

'Oh I don't mind,' said India, glowing under his praise. 'I was only helping.'

'Ay, Da,' said Jamie, 'she did a grand job.' Happily, India slipped a hand into Jamie's and he allowed her to leave it there.

But a familiar figure was pushing his way towards them through the crowd that still lingered on the Quay and India's confidence faltered as she saw her grandfather's angry face. She need not have worried: his anger was directed at quite another target.

'Fools! Mischievous varmints! There's men say a group o' kids was playing in the Yard. One o' them likely had tobacco and a tinder box. Aping grown men, no doubt, wi' out the responsibility.'

'One of the firemen said it could have been the result of sun through glass,' said Maitland, unwilling to damn anyone without trial. 'The heat could concentrate and smoulder in a pile o' dry sawdust and lie low for hours, seemingly.'

With a thud of suspicion, India remembered Eppie's green glass ale bottle. But she did not mention it. Instead, she pushed the hair from her forehead with the back of her hand and said, 'Hello, Grandpa. I'm sorry I'm late but . . .'

Abercrombie stared at her, his mouth open in astonishment, before roaring with laughter. 'If it isn't my wee Indy, black as a New Guinea pigmy and clad in rags. I didna recognise you and that's a fact. But ye'd best not let your Nana see you like that or she'll throw a fit o' the hysterics. What did they do to ye, lass? Throw you on the fire like a Guy Fawkes?'

'We are all very grateful to India,' said James Christie quickly. 'I was just telling her she'd best come home with us so Rachel can clean her up before she goes home. Perhaps you would like to come too? I reckon there's nought else to do now, but drown our sorrows in the whisky jar.'

Rachel had heard the uproar, seen the flames leap above the rooftops of the Quay, and had known, with sickening certainty even before she heard the shouting, that it was the Christie yard. She and Kirsty had herded the children together, left them in Kirsty's Annie's charge, and run, with half the harbour, to see what they could do to help. But the menfolk were doing what they could, and when it was plain that the worst was over, and there was no more anyone could do, Rachel and Kirsty turned back dejectedly to Trinity Quay. The men would be tired when they returned, and dirty. There might be burns to deal with, too, and other injuries. In silence, the women set about boiling kettles for hot water, laying the table for a meal of sorts. Rachel spoke only once.

'Poor Pearl.'

There was no need to elaborate. Kirsty knew as well as anyone that Pearl Duthie Noble was homesick in Macau and lived only in the hope of a Christie ship from home.

It was an equally silent group that arrived back at the house some time later, bedraggled, smoke-streaked and weary, with George Abercrombie in tow and, Rachel was astonished to see, Jessie Abercrombie's daughter India, looking as bedraggled as any of them, with half her skirt torn away, her petticoats dirt-streaked and tattered, and what looked suspiciously like a burn on one hand.

'Whatever have you done to yourself?' she cried, forgetting Jessie's animosity. She had not been close enough to recognise the child in the frantic activity of the fire-fighting, but as she took in the smoke-streaked face, the tatters, the tangled, dirty hair, and the blistering hands, she filled the story in for herself and knew, before Jamie told her, that India had behaved as well as any Christie, in spite of . . . but here Rachel pulled herself up short. The girl was not responsible for her mother's shortcomings.

'Come with me, India,' she said gently. 'I'll see what I can find for those poor hands of yours and make you a little more respectable.'

'Aye, I'd be grateful if you would, Rachel,' said old Abercrombie, a hint of anxiety in his voice. 'She's a grand wee lass. I'd not like her to come to any harm along of tonight's doings. I'm right proud of my wee grand-daughter, but I fear my wife wouldna feel the same if she saw her at this moment – nor her mother, neither!'

'I'll look after her, Mr Abercrombie. You make yourself comfortable by the fire and Jamie will fill your glass. Fetch the best whisky for Mr Abercrombie, Jamie, then you'd best start slicing the ham. You'll all feel the better for nourishment.' But when she returned some fifteen minutes later, with a fresh-washed and cleanly clad India, red hair neatly brushed and red cheeks glowing, the company was sombre enough, in spite of Rachel's ham and pickles and the liberal supply of whisky and ale.

'Is the damage very bad?' she asked, motioning India to a stool by the fire and handing her a steaming bowl of broth.

'Aye,' said her husband. 'Bad enough.'

'The timber yard's destroyed,' said Maitland. 'Any wood that isn't burnt up is fit for nought but kindling.'

'And your tea-ship?' Rachel knew the store that Maitland set upon that ship – so many years of thought had gone into its conception, so many months of plans meticulously drawn, replaced, improved upon, before the work even began; and so many more months of labour – all wasted. James had mapped out his China route to the last degree of longitude and latitude, while Rachel had planned the freight they would carry to the last square inch and Pearl . . . Pearl had waited, hoping, for a ship that never came, and now, perhaps, never would.

Maitland gave a long, quivering sigh, then said, with what spirit he could muster, 'The hull's maybe retrievable. The burnt timbers could be strengthened. The decks replaced. But . . .' He stopped, bit his lip, then crashed his fist on the table. 'Damn it, it's not the *same*!' He held his head in his hands and groaned. No one spoke. After a moment, he straightened, said, 'I'm sorry. It's just that, for me, it's the end of a dream.'

'Not the end, Maitland, surely?' Rachel laid a hand on his shoulder. Maitland, the quiet one, was often withdrawn and silent, but always seemed to emanate an inner excitement which gave him stature and strength. He created beauty out of slabs of timber, gave speed and grace to a heap of planks and was always sustained by the plans taking shape inside his head, plans often two ships ahead of the ones in the slipway. She could not bear to see him bowed. 'You said . . .'

'I expect the vessel could be made seaworthy,' he interrupted. 'I grant you that. But for what? She'll not be fit to carry tea. There'll be the taint of sulphurous ashes always, in my nostrils anyway, and I wanted my tea-ship to be perfect. A pure, white bird of a ship . . .'

'Will there be insurance?' asked Rachel, refilling his mug and moving on to Mr Abercrombie's. The loss of the timber was bad enough, but the loss of two years' work was irreplaceable.

'Some,' said Maitland wearily. 'On the timber anyway. But not enough. And nothing can restore my tea-ship.'

'Maybe it's as well,' said James slowly. He had not spoken for a while, but had sat frowning into his ale mug, apparently deep in private thought. 'Maybe we should stick to what we know and forget China.'

'No, Da!' cried Jamie in horror, amid a stir of protest from the others. 'We've talked of China for years and you practically promised me I could go with you. You can't give up now!'

'Jamie's right,' said Maitland. 'China's not beyond us. And I reckon I could plan the perfect model one day.'

'Aye. One day. But we've spent two years and more on that vessel already and now look at her.'

'That's hardly Maitland's fault, dear,' said Rachel gently.

'I know.' James sighed, drained his mug and set it down with new decision. He looked round the company, collecting their attention, before continuing, 'So I have decided if those years are not to be completely wasted, she had best earn her keep.'

'What had you in mind, lad?' put in Abercrombie. 'I've not said ought yet as it's Christie business and none o' mine, but you know you've my backing whenever you need it. You've only to say the word.'

'Thank you, Mr Abercrombie,' said Rachel, laying a hand briefly on the old man's shoulder. He had been a good friend to them all the years of their marriage, and she knew he would support them in anything James decided. 'What were you thinking of, James?'

'You say you'll never get the smell o' burnt wood and varnish out o' your nostrils, Maitland. I agree that might taint the tea – but there's cargoes no smell could taint. Coal, for instance, or lime. Or even timber. We'll need timber with all our store burnt.'

Maitland looked at his brother for a startled moment, then grinned ironically. 'Aye, you're right. She'd be fine for coal, but I reckon we could make her serve better than that. She'd adapt for timber right enough and the emigrant run is always profitable. She's got the length, and with the hatches repositioned . . . It'd be only fitting, too, and she could fetch yon Canada pine we wanted. Let's see, we'll need to patch her up, refit her, whittle away the spent wood and replace it with new, shore up any weaknesses, though there'll be few of those, I'll warrant you. She's a well-built ship and tough. And there'll be no need for best mahogany for the cabins any more – that'll save on the expense. We'll start work on her tomorrow. She'll not be the elegant vessel originally planned, but she'll not disgrace us neither. A good, solid ship, designed for an honest purpose. And an appropriate one at that. What do we want with tea anyway, when we've a timber yard to restock?'

Rachel was delighted to see Maitland restored almost to his old self again and when he found a scrap of paper and a pencil and began to make notes and tot up figures, she knew one at least of the Christies was on the way to recovery.

'You need timber right enough,' said Abercrombie thoughtfully. 'And if you can fill the ship wi' emigrants on the way over, your pocket'll nae suffer. But it's Pearl I'm thinking of. She'll break her heart wi' waiting if you don't send soon.'

'We'll start on the new tea-ship the moment the slip-way's free,' said Maitland. 'And I think I can promise you she'll be even better than the first, and well worth waiting for. Pearl's a sensible girl. She'll understand.'

But James had more to say. 'We'll need a captain for the timber ship, of course. I'll take her myself, like I always do, on her first voyage, but after that, as we've no

Christie men spare, I reckon young Alfie Baxter is a good lad, loyal and competent. He's done well. It's time he had a ship of his own. And how would you like to go along, Jamie, as first mate?'

'First mate?' Jamie's face was a study of shock, then dawning delight. 'Oh Da, will you really let me?'

'I've taught you all I know long since, Jamie. It's experience you need now, lad, and there's no better way to get it than in a good ship, wi' a good captain, and I reckon we can promise you both. So why not?'

Why not? echoed Rachel bleakly, while the familiar weight settled over her heart. He was a sailor, after all, like his father. It was merely another step along the inevitable road, and if Canada was a longer trip than the Baltic run, at least it was closer than China.

'What'll we call her?' Jamie was saying, his face eager with anticipation. 'She was launched smack into the water, wi' no ceremony and no name, so we'd best give her one, quick.'

Everyone looked at Maitland. 'Anything you like,' he said. 'I had always thought of her as my white bird, but now . . .' he shrugged.

'She's more like a fire-bird,' said India Abercrombie and blushed when Jamie cried, 'That's it! Let's call her *Firebird*, Da? Please?'

'*Firebird*,' repeated his father, savouring the name. 'Aye. It seems appropriate. *Firebird* it is, then. How long do you think it will take, Maitland, to make her seaworthy?'

'Three or four months perhaps. Maybe less. It depends what we find tomorrow when we go over her again.'

'Four months . . . we'll need to check the sea conditions, of course, and the state o' the market, but I reckon that'll do us. And as soon as she's ready, we sail.'

* * *

India was very quiet as she made her way home soon after, to her grandfather's house, his large hand firm in hers. She was proud and sad, elated and at the same time weary with a grief she thought at first was sympathy for the Christies, who had lost so much.

'It's a blow for them, Indy lass, and that's a fact,' said her grandfather, with gruff sympathy. 'They've worked hard and long for yon ship and didna deserve to see all their hopes go up in flames.'

'Not all their hopes, Grandpa, surely?' said India. 'I thought they said . . .'

'Aye, but it's the tea they wanted, lass. Not just another shipload o' timber from St John's.'

At her grandfather's words, she realised what it was that made her feel so weary, and so close to tears. Jamie was to sail the new ship when she was ready.

'How long does it take to sail to Canada, Grandpa?' she asked, in a small voice. He stopped, and looked down at her shrewdly before saying, 'Long enough. But nae as long as to China, I'm thinking, so there's no need to look so glum. You'll see young Jamie again soon enough. Besides, he isna even gone yet. There'll be months o' work to put in on yon *Firebird* o' yours or I'm much mistaken,' and he put an arm round her thin shoulders and drew her close. 'So dinna fret, lass. He'll be in Aberdeen for a while yet and I reckon you and he make a grand pair. I saw the way you fought beside him, brave as any of them. I was proud of you, Indy.'

India glowed with love and snuggled closer into the crook of her grandfather's arm as they crossed the summer darkness of the Castlegate towards the Guestrow. The night sky was faded indigo, so pale you could have read the bill boards outside the Athenaeum without lamplight, though a single lamp still burnt near the Cross, casting patches of pale orange over the cassies. There was another in the Guestrow, though the shadows here were darker, black wedges under area steps, cavernous holes of darkness in archways and wynds. India was glad of her grandfather's reassuring bulk. But even he was powerless to protect her when the servant drew back the bars of the great, studded door and they stepped into the lamplit hall to find Fenton Abercrombie waiting for them.

'*Where have you been?*'

Fenton had spent a blissful summer. The truly halcyon days had been irresponsible, he admitted, but blessed. It was two years since he had first seen Mary Ballantyne, one year and eight months since she had first kissed him. One year and three months since he had installed her in the small apartment in the New Town which she kept so clean, so welcoming and feminine for him. There she had sealed their love by accepting him as her own dear husband, in flesh if not in law. He knew, and remembered, every date to the hour and almost to the minute – and his love for Mary grew till he thought the whole world must see and recognise it, shining from the very pores of his skin. The time he spent in Aberdeen was a tedious impatience – merely empty space in which there was no Mary – and the time he spent in Edinburgh was filled with undiminished glory.

Surprisingly, instead of hampering his work, his new-found love invigorated it. His father, though he might grumble at the time Fenton spent at the Edinburgh branch, could find no fault with Fenton's work – or with the profits which steadily rose – in Edinburgh as much and more than in Aberdeen. Nor could the old man find fault with the books, had he wanted to – and Fenton knew he was neither stupid nor averse to seeking private information should he feel the need – but Mary was as good a book-keeper as any in Scotland, male or female.

And Mary, his Mary was so delightfully, enchantingly female – teasing, demure, intelligent, loving – but never coarse or loud-mouthed, never vulgar. The time when he had actually loved Jessica Brand seemed another life away. She had been his first taste of love and he had known no better. Whereas now, it was as if he walked the paths of a different, enchanted country, with no worries, no responsibilities, only their love to surround them always with sunlight and roses.

It had been a shock when she told him, though he should have known it was inevitable. But after that first shock, it was no more than natural, then even welcome, and now, as he paced the deck of the Aberdeen packet on his way north again, a secret, jubilant excitement pulsed hard within him. Mary was carrying his child. *His*, beyond all doubt. Not like . . . But he thrust all other thoughts aside in the business of planning how to reassure and cosset his precious Mary. She would have to leave the firm, of course, at once. He would put a lump sum into the bank for her, to use as necessary, and more when the child was born. He would look after her better than any husband, and be a better father to her child than . . .

Again he broke off, as that other reality impinged. But Augusta was married, with a generous settlement, and if Jessica was to be believed, Victoria's wedding would follow before another year was out. They didn't need him. As for India, his own father was taking good care of her and whereas the shop was not ideal, it would serve for the moment and the child actually seemed to enjoy it. At least it kept her out of harm's way. She needed him no more than her sisters did and as for his son, Finlay had always been Jessica's child. It had salved his conscience to leave it that way: at least she had Finlay to occupy her.

But the ship's engines were changing tune. He felt the familiar shudder as they rounded Greyhope Bay and saw the twin points of the harbour arms stretched towards them in welcome – and, to the north, at Pocra Quay, a black cloud of smoke above a billowing heart of flame.

'What's on fire?' The question raced through the ship to be answered as quickly by 'Christie's Yard! It must be Christie's!'

The vessel lurched dangerously as everyone rushed to the starboard side to see what they could of the catastrophe, but soon righted again in the scramble for the gangway and the wharf. Fenton wanted nothing to do with the Christies, but some instinct sent him to his father's house before his own – and kept him there till his daughter's return. For there was only one place in Aberdeen that she could be that night and he did not need his mother's words to confirm it. Nevertheless, he gave India the chance to tell him herself.

'*Where have you been?*'

The words dropped like poison into the silence as father and daughter confronted each other and it was as if George Abercrombie was not there. Nevertheless it was the old man who answered.

'We've been at the Christies', ye daft loon, and if ye dinna ken that, you must be the only man in Aberdeen who doesna. And I'll thank you not to block my way into my own house. We've had a long day and we're needing our beds. This lass o' yours has done us all great credit, fire-fighting beside young Christie and as brave as any o' them. You should be proud.'

Fenton ignored him. His father was irrelevant. The contest was between himself and his daughter – this red-haired, white-faced girl whose frightened eyes still defied him and refused to fall before his and whose vulnerability terrified him as nothing else could. He saw the woman she would become – loving, affectionate, true as his Mary was. And, like Mary, she would one day bear a child.

God! The old primeval fear took away his breath. Not young Christie's child! When he spoke again, it was to India and he said only, 'Come home.'

'She's nae going anywhere,' said his father. 'She's going to her bed, here, in my house. When you do me the courtesy of getting out of my way and letting me through!'

'India is coming home, Father, with me.'

'Oh she is, is she? And which home is that? Union Terrace? Or the New Town?'

Fenton met his eyes unwavering. So his father knew. Surprisingly the knowledge only strengthened Fenton's purpose. Let him do his worst. 'Send India's things to the house first thing tomorrow.'

Abercrombie looked at him shrewdly for a long moment, then shrugged. With the child in the room it was maybe best not to argue – but he'd have a thing or two to say to the young stirk in the morning, and not only about his daughter.

'I'll see you tomorrow, Indy love. And dinna hurry. Have a long lie for once. You've earned it and the shop'll manage an hour or two without you, no bother.'

It will manage longer than that, thought Fenton, knowing what he must do.

'Why are you putting the key in the door?' India demanded in alarm, when Mairi came to put out her candle and say goodnight.

Mairi looked nervously over her shoulder and said in a loud whisper, 'Because the master says. He's in a rare queer mood so you'd best not complain. And I'm to bring your breakfast to your room, seemingly. He didna say why – but it's maybe along of you helping put out yon Christie fire. Was it awful, Miss Indy? Were you nae scared?'

Normally India would have relished the retelling of

such a story, but her father's coming had quenched her spirits. She felt nervous, even frightened. 'I'm tired, Mairi,' she said. 'I'll tell you in the morning . . .'

But in the morning it was worse. Apparently she was to be locked in her room till he sent for her.

'Oh miss, he telt me to press all your petticoats and things and to fold your clothes neat and pack them into yon leather trunk,' reported Mairi as she dumped the breakfast tray unceremoniously on the bed and went to open the shutters. 'As if I hadna enough to do wi' him aye wanting clean shirts and taking them off again afore he's had them on. Porridge, the master telt me, and milk. You're to eat it directly and stay here till he sends for ye. He's been up all hours and in a rare black temper. Ordering this and that, writing, sending messages, and me wi' only two hands to my name though you'd think from the way the master's behaving that I'd at least six. He's sent a letter to the mistress at Monymusk, too.'

'Perhaps I'm to go there?' said India nervously, poking at her porridge without appetite. Mairi's porridge always had lumps in it. Besides, she had little stomach for anything after a fitfully sleepless night in which memories of Jamie, of the fire in the Christie yard, and of her father had tossed and turned and mingled till she woke in a sweat of fear, in the airless darkness of her locked room, and lay wishing herself back at her grandfather's, hating her father's presence in the house, fearing what he would do. The Monymusk idea was an unpleasant one, but possible. In those sleepless hours she had remembered her father on that other occasion when he had seen her with Jamie on Trinity Quay. That time he had taken the wooden bear Jamie had given her and ground it underfoot. This time . . . what? She knew he would not overlook it.She remembered his veto on all contact with the Christies. 'Never speak to that boy again.' And she had disobeyed him, openly, for all the town to see. She remembered his face as he had confronted her grandfather and knew he planned some terrible retribution. But Monymusk, with Augusta, newly married, being all important and treating her like a baby, with Victoria teasing her, her mother ordering her about and finding fault, and young Finlay pestering her for attention all the time and nothing at all to do . . . She would far rather work in her grandfather's shop. After all, she had a job there now and her grandfather expected her.

'Did he say what it was about, Mairi?' she asked anxiously. 'Because it's time I was leaving for the shop.'

'He hasna said anything, miss. Yet.' Mairi pursed her lips with ominous relish. 'But you needna worry about the shoppie. Your Da sent word to say you was resting after yesterday's excitement and wouldna be in today. So you'd best eat up and be ready for when he sends for ye. Then ye'll maybe find out. ' With that she was gone, turning the key in the lock behind her.

It was another hour before India was sent for. The moment she entered the study and saw her father's face, she knew she was doomed, but she fought against him just the same.

'I am leaving for the shop now, Papa. I'm late already and Grandpa is expecting me.'

'You do not understand, India. I am sending you to school.'

'School!' India was appalled. 'I don't need any more school, Papa. I've left school.' Her father merely looked at her in silence. All the way from her grandfather's last night he had not spoken. He was often silent at home, but this time there had been a different quality to his silence. He was no longer self-contained, shut away in his private world and impervious to what was going on around him. This time she had known his thoughts concerned her and there had been a threatening quality to the silence which had unnerved her. As it did now. Then he spoke.

'You have left one school, India. Now you will go to another. In Bath.'

'*Bath!*' India cried out in horror. 'I'm not going to Bath. It's in England, hundreds of miles away. The Bonnington girls went to Bath and it was horrible. They told me. They made you wear back boards and sit up straight and dress in flimsy dance dresses even though it's freezing. One of the Bonnington girls was ill all the time and she's *still* ill. Mairi says she'll probably die, Papa, and all because of . . .' But she knew it was no good. He was looking at her steadily, his eyes cold, his face impassive, merely waiting for her to stop.

'You will go to Bath,' he said into the silence. 'I have sent the letter already. And do not think to escape for I intend to take you there myself. We leave by the London steamship. Tonight.'

'Two years,' she told Mairi, through her tears of rage and misery. 'And he will not even let me see anyone to say goodbye.'

'Never mind, miss. Your Ma wouldna want you to miss the steamer. She'll understand.'

But it was not her mother she was thinking of. 'Grandpa wouldn't let him do it if he knew,' she said furiously. 'I know he wouldn't. So you'll tell my grandfather, Mairi, that he is to fetch me back. Promise?'

'I'll tell him,' said Mairi soothingly, though privately she reckoned it would make no difference. Old Abercrombie and the master had had 'words', though what about she didn't know. Them doors were thick and when folks stood by the window on purpose so other folks couldn't hear . . . though she had caught a word here and there – 'Edinburgh' and 'Jessica' and someone called 'Mary' and a whole lot about the Christies that she could make neither head nor tail of, and then she'd heard them moving and had scuttled back to the kitchen, quick, in case one of them came out. One of them did – old Abercrombie – and in a fearful temper for he slammed out o' the house wi'out another word. But a while later a message had come, sly like, to the back door. She felt in her pocket and drew out a packet. 'That reminds me, miss. He sent you this.'

India snatched the packet and tore it open to find a piece of folded paper and a gold sovereign. 'Maybe it's for the best, India love, and the time will soon pass. Write to me often. Your ever-loving Grandpa Abercrombie. P.S. I enclose a gold sovereign for you so if it's not there, tell Mairi I'll skelp her thieving backside.' India might have disbelieved the first half of the note as a forgery of her father's, but the postscript bore the unmistakable stamp of her grandfather. Tears of betrayal welled up in her eyes. Two years. How would she bear it?

'Never mind,' said Mairi soothingly. 'Two years is no time and when ye come back, ye'll be a real young lady. Think o' that. Your Ma will be real proud.'

But India cared nothing for her mother's feelings. She thought only of Jamie Christie and of her grandfather, the two people she loved most and whom she would not see for two long years. And even her grandfather had deserted her. It was not his fault, she told herself. It was her father's: he must have threatened the old man somehow, otherwise he would never have given in. As for Jamie . . . She managed to persuade Mairi to steal paper and ink for her and when she had written her letter, to promise on her honour that she would deliver it as soon as they had gone. And tell no one.

'Cross my heart and hope to die, miss, and I've always wanted that silver chain o' yours. I reckon it looks real nice on me, don't you? But are you sure you should give it me? Wasn't it a present from your Da? Suppose he notices?'

'He'll not notice,' said India with venom. 'And I *want* to give it to you.' I hate it, she added under her breath. I hate everything he ever gave me. I hate *him*. 'Promise you will deliver my letter, Mairi?'

'Aye, miss. I promise.' She hugged the girl to her breast in sudden emotion. 'You're a pesky wee quine sometimes,' she said, swallowing hard, 'but ye're nae a bad lass. I'll miss you.'

'And I'll miss you, Mairi.' And her family and her friends, her grandfather's shop, the Castlegate, everything that she knew. And most of all, the life of the Quay, and Jamie.

'India!' called her father from the hall below. 'The carriage is waiting.'

Dry-eyed, with a calm, closed face and desolation in her heart, India picked up her small portmanteau and followed Mairi out of the room.

Part III

Aberdeen 1837

i

The winter of '36/'37 was worse even than the previous one for the whaling fleet. Six vessels were trapped in the ice, including the *Dee* from Aberdeen, and were not released till way into spring – by which time the toll in lives, and minds, was devastating.

It was the end of April when the survivors reached Stromness, to be put straight into hospital there, and May before a full account was printed in the *Aberdeen Journal*. Again Rachel thanked God that Alex Christie had not returned to the whaling. Though still occasionally discontented with 'that dreary emigrant run' he, like the rest of the Christies, channelled all his hopes into Maitland's China ship and, like them, spent every spare moment ashore in the Christie Yard.

Even the little ones helped, fetching and carrying, running messages. Davy would soon be five and would go to school to learn, as he told anyone who would listen, to be a proper sailor, while Matt, two years younger, echoed everything his brother said and aimed to better it. Both of them, thought Rachel with a mixture of pride and sadness, would follow their father and elder brothers to sea, as soon as they were old enough.

James Christie himself worked to exhaustion point, night after night, on the restoring of *Firebird* till Rachel welcomed the time to set sail. At least at sea James would have some opportunity to rest. His health was not what it had been, though James refused to admit it. His old leg wound often pained him, especially in cold weather, and Rachel feared Canadian waters would only make it worse. But James was adamant. He captained every new Christie ship on her maiden voyage and would continue to do so – till he sailed the tea-ship triumphantly to China.

In mid-June the King died and when the necessary writ eventually arrived from London, preparations were speedily made to proclaim his successor. A platform was knocked up on the Cross, steps constructed around it and the whole edifice decked in scarlet cloth. Barriers were placed across Castle Street to prevent any carriages from tangling up the proceedings and the Plainstanes were surrounded by the scholars of Robert Gordon's Hospital. At noon the grand procession emerged from the Town House and, led by a clutch of trumpeters and the Town Sergeants complete with streamer-decorated halberds, proceeded in dignified splendour to the Cross. The Lord Provost led, followed by Magistrates and Town Officers, Trades Officers, Lords Lieutenant, Principals and Professors of King's and Marischal Colleges complete with gowns and mace bearers, Clergy, Justices of the Peace, Officers of Army and Navy, Esquires, in fact anyone of the slightest claim to status, be it only that of respectable inhabitant!

Trumpeters were ranged behind the Provost on the elevated platform and after the proper flourishes the Proclamation was read, the assembled company cheered and the band struck up the National Anthem. On the Cross and on the barbizon of the steeple the Union flags which had previously drooped at half mast were hoisted aloft to flutter proudly against the clear summer sky while the crowd below waved handkerchiefs and cheered.

The solemn proceedings over, the procession returned to the Town House where the young Queen's health was drunk with three times three, as were the Duchess of Kent her mother's, the Dowager Queen Adelaide's and finally that of the British constitution, all with three times three and hearty cheers.

The reign of Queen Victoria had begun.

The Castlegate was packed with spectators and much of Union Street too as people congregated to celebrate the occasion, not merely out of loyalty to a monarch five hundred miles away whom none of them expected ever to see, but because it was a glorious summer day, most of the shops were closed and a general air of holiday prevailed. After all, it was not every day you could see such a colourful procession or hear so many trumpets blasting away in unison so many times over.

Jessica Abercrombie had debated whether to drive in from the country – where she had once more removed for the summer – and decided against it. There would be more elegant celebrations in Monymusk, she decided, though Victoria and Finlay both wanted to go into Aberdeen and sulked when they were refused. But Victoria knew better than to argue outright – she was enmeshed in a devious intrigue of her mother's to 'catch' the Pirie boy and was required to be obediently demure – and Finlay was soon bribed back to equanimity by the promise of a bonfire party on the village green.

As for Fenton, he preferred to drink his new Queen's health in Edinburgh, in company with Mary Ballantyne and his three-month-old son whom they had named John Fenton.

Fenton adored the child, with a fervour the more intense because it must be secret. But the mere thought of his infant son filled him with an abiding happiness which shone in his eyes in spite of all his efforts and stripped ten years from his middle-aged face.

'You're looking gie pleased wi' yourself,' said Mairi when she opened the door to him some days after the Proclamation. 'Like a cat that's got the cream.'

Fenton ignored her. There were disadvantages to keeping family servants too long. They tended to grow above themselves and Mairi in particular had never been distinguished for tact or discretion. He left his portmanteau in the hall and went into his study. Mairi followed.

'There's letters come while you was away,' she said with an edge of accusation in her voice. 'From poor Miss Indy.'

'I have told you again and again, Mairi, she is *not* "poor",' snapped Fenton, with an irritation which invariably seeped into him whenever he was in the Union Terrace house. 'She is comfortable, well cared for, with plenty to occupy her, in an elegant and cultivated environment.'

'What's the good o' yon culture you're always on about if you're nae happy?' retorted Mairi. 'Poor Miss Indy's homesick.'

'*Not poor!*' Oh what's the use? thought Fenton, taking up the letter from his desk and slitting it open with an ivory paper knife. He unfolded the single sheet and scanned the sparsely covered page. It was, as he had expected, the regular duty letter, supervised and despatched by the school.

'Well?' demanded Mairi, hovering. 'What does poor Miss . . . what does Miss Indy say?'

'She is well,' said Fenton, with exaggerated patience. 'She has been to see the Roman baths. She is reading *Waverley*. She requires new slippers the cost of which will be added to the bill.'

'Is that all?' said Mairi, disappointed.

'That is all.' Fenton laid aside the letter with the familiar feeling of failure and guilt. Mairi was right, of course. India was not happy, but more than that, he knew she blamed him, and rightly, for her misery and harboured an implacable hatred towards him. The reminder doused the joy he had brought back with him from Edinburgh and left the old pain. He did not want India to hate him. He loved her, he realised, as deeply as he loved little John Fenton Ballantyne, perhaps more deeply and with far more pain. More than that, she needed his protection: no one else would guard her from young Christie. And in order to protect her, he must hurt her and incur her hatred. He looked down at the letter for some sign of tenderness. 'Your dutiful, obedient and ever-loving daughter, India Abercrombie.' The correct and accepted phrase held no warmth. He could see, as vividly as if she had been sitting at the desk in his study, the red hair, the clear complexion, the lively, dancing eyes . . . and the clenched teeth and frowning brows of fury as she wrote, to order, those meaningless words. 'Well?' he snapped, seeing Mairi still hovering in the doorway. 'What are you waiting for?'

'I reckon you should let that poor lassie come home and the sooner the better.'

'That is my business, none of yours.'

'Cruelty is any folk's business,' retorted Mairi. 'And I reckon it's cruel to keep Miss Indy in yon place. Mr Abercrombie thinks so too,' she added slyly.

'Cruel or not, she stays and that's the end of it. Now get out and leave me in peace.'

With a glare and a muttered insult, Mairi left, slamming the door behind her so hard the window rattled in its frame. But her words had found their mark. Fenton had had too many uncomfortable brushes with his father on the subject of India and did not want to be reminded.

* * *

The same post brought letters for the Noble household and for the Christies, from Pearl. The two families gathered, at the Christies' this time, to compare notes. Though already the letters had been exchanged, mulled over and re-read till they were known by heart. Now, however, Dr Andrew and Louise, with Amelia and Booky, had joined Rachel and her children for the evening, together with Maitland and the twins, who for once were ashore together, and Alex, newly home from St John's, with his family from upstairs.

The room was packed, though the smaller children had spilled into the adjoining room, with Uncles Willy and George, and were engaged in some riotously disorganised game which involved crawling about on hands and knees and growling. The rest of the adults and the older children lingered round the supper table while the firelight flickered its gentle warmth over the company and through the unshuttered windows the night sky was pale with the half-darkness of midsummer. In the harbour, riding lights prickled in the thicket of gently rocking masts and yards. It was a comfortable scene, warm with the friendliness of people who had known each other a long time and were at ease in each other's company.

It made the bleak sentences of Pearl's letter sound even more forlorn: Duncan was busy, as always, and often away. There was little to do. Business was conducted in Canton where women were not allowed. She worked when she could at an orphanage, but not when Duncan was ashore. He preferred her to be at home. She had lost a baby daughter at birth, but her son Robin thrived. Their servant took good care of him. She was sorry to hear about *Firebird*. She had been so looking forward to seeing them, soon. Now it would be two more years at least. But perhaps by then things would have settled down at Canton. At the moment there was uncertainty. It had been a bad winter's trading. Jardine's had lost money. There were rumblings of discontent. Even talk of gunboats. Duncan told her there was no danger, so they were not to worry, but she hoped *Firebird*'s replacement would be completed *soon*. She did so long to see someone from home.

'Poor Pearl,' said Amelia, when Rachel finished reading her letter aloud. 'She sounds so homesick, and I know she misses us. But those poor little babies! In Papa's letter she says they are thrown away by their parents, like rubbish. Some, she says, are even *sold* to the orphanage. Little blind baby girls. And Pearl says that if they do not agree to buy them they will die. So many of them do, and there is no one to help them but one or two missionaries' wives, and Pearl.'

'Pearl is doing good work,' agreed Louise. 'We are all proud of her.'

'But she needs help,' persisted Amelia. 'If not, think how many more babies may die?' She took a deep breath and said, 'Papa, may I go to Macau to help her?'

Dr Andrew, who had been discussing the new plans for Marischal College with his son Booky and Maitland, looked round in surprise. 'What did you say, dear?'

'Please may I go to Macau, Papa, to help Pearl?' He looked at her vaguely for a moment, then said, 'I expect so, Amelia. One day. When you are older.' He turned back to the diagram Booky had made with knives and spoons on the table, but Amelia persisted.

'I want to go now, Papa. To help.'

'You are too young, Amelia,' said Louise gently. 'You're only thirteen.'

'Besides,' said her father, 'it is so far away, and you cannot even speak the language. In a year or two perhaps. We'll see.'

Amelia caught her brother's eye and he winked. She

smiled to herself before saying, 'Very well. Not now, Papa, but soon. Perhaps I could go on the new Christie ship?'

'Perhaps,' said Louise and Andrew together and Amelia knew it was no more than a soothing formula to keep her quiet until she had forgotten the idea. But I'll not forget, she vowed. And the Christie ship will be ready in another year or so. Two at the most. When she sails to China for the tea, I will go with her. Quietly, she pushed back her chair and went to help Kirsty with the smaller children.

But Rachel had been studying Pearl's letter again. 'I don't like what Pearl says about the tea trade,' she said with a worried glance at Maitland. 'The Chinese sound unreliable and how do we know the new British Superintendent will be able to run things any better than the last? She says the British flag is flying again at the Factories, but for how long? And I don't really understand her references to opium. But one thing is clear – whether the Chinese legalise the trade or forbid it, it is going to have a disturbing effect on the tea market.'

'Aye,' said Maitland thoughtfully. 'Opium buys silver to buy tea. But whether the Union flag flies or not, the trade will continue. British ships will have to buy from American or Dutch again, that's all. There's always a brisk trade in trans-shipping between Canton and Lintin, Pearl says. The profit margin's cut, of course. But if a ship could make up for that by getting the tea home faster . . .'

Maitland's eyes glazed over as he retreated into his private world of ship's plans and rigging. The new ship was developing well, though with the pressure of the shipyard business the keel had only been laid a month.

'I reckon the Navy should send a steamship,' said Tom. 'I've read correspondence in the *Journal* and the Government's being urged to look after our trade interests in the

China seas. Just one steamship would do the trick. Look how nervous they were of the *Jardine* being in Chinese waters. One armed steam frigate in the river delta and they'd draw up proper trading terms soon enough.'

'Tom could sail her,' said Davy, scrambling up on to his knee. 'Tom's clever and he'll be a steam captain *soon*.'

Tom blushed as everyone laughed, but he knew, as they did, that what Davy said was true. Tom had already learnt all there was to know about the *Jessica*'s engines and a whole lot more about steam in general and its application to shipping, in particular. He was a first-class ship's engineer and at seventeen already in a position of trust as junior officer. No one, least of all Tom, had any doubt that he would captain a steam-vessel as soon as his apprenticeship was served.

'Talking of steam,' said Alex. 'What about Maitland's new ship? Maybe we should think of engines for her? I fancy taking a steamship to China, with Tom maybe, and . . .'

'Never!' cried Maitland. 'If you want engines, you'll go elsewhere for them, lad.'

'But look at that new steamer from the Duffus yard. Two hundred and sixty horsepower and plenty of cargo space and she draws very little water for her size. She looks good, too, and I reckon . . .'

'Looks good? Yon lumbering ox of a ship with her insides belching black smoke and her beams creaking and groaning?'

'*And* belting along at a rare speed when other folk are whistling for a wind,' put in Alex, with a wink at Tom.

'Aye – till her coal's eaten up and then what?' It was a familiar argument and one which Tom was normally happy to join in, but today he left it to Alex to uphold the case for steam and looked around for Amelia.

She was sitting in a chair by the fire, baby Martha in

her lap, gently rocking the child to sleep and singing softly, almost under her breath. At thirteen she was already well developed, with neat, round breasts and a trim waist. She would soon be as tall as her step-mother and, suspected Tom, was wishing the process faster with all the will-power she could summon. He remembered that secret whispered to him in the garden of the Nobles' house and knew it was no idle daydream. Amelia meant it.

Now he pushed back his chair and went to join her. 'Did you mean what you said about Macau?' he asked quietly, not looking at her but at the tiny, petal-soft face of the baby.

'Of course.' She looked up at him in mild surprise, her blue eyes unusually mature. 'You know I did, Tom. Or have you forgotten?'

He pulled up a stool and sat beside her, ostensibly to entertain his sister with a cork on a string, but really to try to say what had been choking in his throat all evening, ever since the first mention of Macau.

'I mean to sail to China one day,' he said quietly. 'In a steamship of my own. If you still want to go, then I will take you. If . . .'

'Will you really?' Her face lit up with pleasure and before he realised what was happening she leant towards him and kissed his cheek. 'Dear Tom . . . I'd be so grateful. But you said "if". If what?'

Tom had meant to say, if you will promise to marry me one day. But he knew he would never say it – and if he did, she would laugh at him, with that sweet, tinkling laugh like water in a sunlit fountain, and say 'Dear Tom'. But she would not take him seriously. He knew he could not bear it if she didn't, so he said, 'Nothing.' But he felt the touch of her lips on his cheek for days after.

Rachel saw them from across the room, read the love

in the curve of her son's shoulders and the bend of his head, and felt sadness well up inside her like a physical pain. She knew, instinctively, that Tom was the kind of being who loved only once. He had given his heart to Amelia years ago at an age when other boys thought only of food and mischief. But Tom had always been a quiet child, strangely mature and always intensely loyal. As for Amelia, Rachel could not make her out. She would be delighted if Tom married Amelia – but was that what Amelia wanted? Once, Rachel had thought her a rather silly child, over-protected and spoilt, too timid to walk home from school alone. But lately, since Pearl left – even, thought Rachel, searching for the exact time, since before then, when Duncan Greig arrived on the scene – Amelia had grown more self-possessed, in a quiet, almost secretive way, as if she had a private source of strength and hope.

I wonder what she is up to, thought Rachel, and, more anxiously, I wonder how it will affect Tom? But there was little she could do except hope that time would sort out everything for the best – and pray. As she did night and morning for the safety of her sons and their father, whenever they were at sea.

But the thought of Jamie reminded her of India Abercrombie. She had last seen the two of them as absorbed together as Amelia and Tom were tonight, and now Jamie was on the high seas off Quebec and India miserable, they said, in a boarding school in Bath. Rachel had not at first realised the vehemence of Fenton's antagonism to Jamie, but the girl's banishment to England, with the various reports of what had led up to it as relayed through the kitchens and drying greens of the town, had opened her eyes. With the realisation had come a needling suspicion which, no matter how hard she tried to avoid it, grew stronger. Poor Fenton, she thought with compassion. And poor India. Rachel was fond of India, a bright, lively and affectionate child and certainly the best of the Abercrombie bunch. Rachel suspected that India loved Jamie, but then so does everyone, she reminded herself. Pearl, Amelia, Kirsty's Annie, every girl in the Square. No one could help loving Jamie, one way or another. He was so carefree and affectionate, so cheerfully self-sufficient, so kind. He would survive unscathed, Rachel thought, whatever happened, with or without poor India Abercrombie, but Tom was another matter. Tom, she suspected, would eat his heart out for Amelia whether she deserved it or not. And there was nothing Rachel could do about it. Except wait, as everyone seemed to be waiting in that summer of '37.

Firebird came home sooner than expected. The refitting had taken several months, then bad weather had kept her in home waters, on the coastal routes, but she had finally left Aberdeen in April '37 with the first spring sailing to Canada and a full complement of emigrants in the spacious steerage quarters. She was back by mid-July, with the timber Maitland wanted and a handsome profit on the whole transaction.

'But what a storm we met off Scatterie,' reported Jamie, basking in the pleasure of homecoming. Rachel had laid on a welcome party and everyone was there: family, friends, neighbours, crowding into the Christie rooms which were bright with firelight and friendship. At one end of the table, James was recounting his version of how the new ship handled to Maitland and the Baxter boys, while at the other his son Jamie held the younger ones enthralled. Jamie had changed in the three-month absence from a gangling seventeen-year-old youth to a firm-set, weather-tanned and bearded young man. His voice had deepened too and there was a new maturity about him, but as he told his story of the voyage, he was as cheerfully entertaining as he had always been and, thought Rachel with relief, as natural. Little Davy leant adoringly against his big brother's knee while Tom, beside him at the table and with young Matt on his lap, was as enthralled.

'Forty-eight hours it blew like scissors and thumbscrews,' Jamie was saying. 'Then a snowstorm, thick as feathers from one o' Ma's quilts. We couldn't scarcely keep a scrap o' canvas on her and what there was, was a mass of ice. No sooner was a sail set than it was ripped to ribbons. Stays, shrouds, halyards snapped like cotton, the main foresail in shreds. Even the chicken coop was swept overboard and the sea so solid no one noticed. I tell you we tossed and pitched fit to shake the sticks out of her and it was three days till the wind eased and we got back on course. *Firebird* was splendid, but I reckon the passengers weren't so happy.'

At that moment the door opened to admit Andrew Noble and Louise, with Amelia. She ran to James Christie and kissed him, saying, 'Welcome home, Uncle James.' Then she turned, looked around her, found Jamie and went to kiss him, too. Jamie blushed with pleasure.

'My, what a beautiful lass you've grown to be while my back's turned, Amelia, and you're at least three inches taller.'

'So are you, Jamie. And you've grown a beard.' She studied him, head on one side, before smiling and saying, 'I like it. It suits you.'

But Jamie had been reminded of something. He looked round the company which was shifting and changing all the time as well-wishers arrived and left again, friends moved on, more arrived. Old Abercrombie was deep in conversation with James Christie now and a group of older men. Rachel and Louise were at the centre of a women's group, children drifted hopefully from one tale-teller to another, or played among themselves. But he could not find the face he sought.

'Where's Indy?'

Amelia looked shocked. 'Didn't you know? She's still at school in Bath, learning to be a lady. She hates it and is miserable, but her father will not let her come home again. No one knows why.'

'Poor Indy.' Jamie looked crestfallen and disappointed. He would have liked India to be there, to listen to his tales of danger on the high seas. Then his face brightened. 'I'll maybe visit her, next time we sail south. Bristol's near Bath isn't it?'

'Aye, it is that, but since when have Christie ships sailed to Bristol?' said his father. 'It's a quick turn-around for you, Jamie, then off again and that's the way of it. There'll be no gallivanting off to Bath unless you want to miss your ship.'

Jamie could not risk that, even for Indy. But he hoped next time he was in port, she would be home.

ii

1838

'I'll not stand it a moment longer,' vowed India Abercrombie in the privacy of the empty dormitory where she had been banished yet again, fireless and supperless, for some trivial misdemeanour. What it was she scarcely remembered, there had been so many. Had she tripped in the cotillion? Shown too much ankle or not enough breast? Set to the left instead of to the right? Or vice versa? Had her gloves been too long, too short, too grubby? Her back too arched? Or not enough? Had she spoken too loudly, curtseyed too pertly, even written too quickly? (Suspicious, that.) Probably all of them – or a new, incomprehensible offence of manners or decorum. India knew by now that nothing she did would ever be right.

She did not belong with the vacuous, pale-haired English maidens, nor with the equally vacuous creamy-skinned brunettes, nor even with the sprinkling of foreign girls, many of them titled and all of them rich. Those girls were united by their ambition to marry: apparently whom they married was immaterial as long as they married 'well', and the sole aim of the curriculum was to achieve that end. Each 'good' marriage brought added status to the school – and increased the roll. But the authorities had realised very early in her school career that India Abercrombie, in spite of her father's fortune and her own undoubted good looks, would not be easy to 'place'. Lately they had concluded, regretfully, that she was destined to be one of their rare failures and had it not been that her father seemed willing, in spite of her lack of progress, to continue paying exorbitant fees for India, they would have suggested she go home.

As it was, India stayed and, as naturally she could not be allowed to set a bad example to the other girls, she continued to be punished with increasing exasperation and decreasing patience the longer she remained. The beauties of Bath architecture left her untouched, the finer points of musical appreciation the same. She would not play the piano, could not sing, made deliberate mince-meat of any fine sewing she was given, and showed no enthusiasm for any dances but the Scottish. She did show proficiency in French, her arithmetic could not be faulted, and her reading was as fluent as anyone's in the school, but to these dubious accomplishments she brought a spirit of simmering impatience which turned virtue into vice and she could win no praise.

They don't like me, India realised with cold honesty, and I don't like them. At that moment she decided. She had been one year and ten months in the hated school, with no visit home to succour her and in what holidays there were, only the company of her official guardians, a strict Presbyterian couple from Aberdeenshire, living a life of retirement and repressive rectitude in Clifton. Two years her father had said, but there had been no word of her leaving, though she had asked in every letter to her father for the past four months and today was her sixteenth birthday. Her Grandfather Abercrombie had sent her two guineas and though India knew they would be confiscated into 'safe keeping' as soon as the authorities found out – and one of those prissy-ringleted, simpering sillies would be sure to tell – at the moment they lay safe in her hand, thanks to her only friend in the place, the youngest of the upstairs maids who had met the messenger by chance at the door and had brought India the packet herself.

She looked down at the coins while the decision strengthened to certainty. She was sixteen and her grandfather loved her. He told her so in his letter, said he looked forward to the day she came home, 'very soon'. That settled it. The coins were obviously to be used for that purpose. She would go home to her grandfather and she would go home today.

The rest of the girls, she knew, were in the upstairs drawing room, going through the steps of a new dance with the visiting dancing master. The headmistress would be in her private boudoir, taking tea or, as rumour had it, something stronger, and would not emerge till evening. The household staff would be in the kitchen, gossiping or preparing supper. It was as good a time as any. She could hear a genteel piano-tinkle drifting up the main stair and from the street the distant clip-clop and rattle of a private carriage. Nothing else.

Calmly she packed the barest requirements into the small portmanteau she used for her visits to her guardians. She knotted the sovereigns in a handkerchief and pushed them down the front of her corselet. She selected the plainest of her dresses, a blue sarcenet, the warmest of her pelisses, and the stoutest of her boots. The weather in Bath was mild enough, but by the time she reached home she would need thicker clothing. Then she wound her hair up into the tightest of 'crowns' and topped it with a plain straw bonnet. As an afterthought, she bundled the rest of her clothes with a pillow under the coverlet, in the shape of a sleeping form, and closed the shutters so that the room was in semi-darkness. Then she wrote 'Gone home' on a corner of paper from her grandfather's letter and skewered it to the pillow with a hat pin.

'That'll keep me right,' she said with satisfaction. Then she picked up her portmanteau, walked down the back stairs and out of the house through the tradesmen's entrance.

No one stopped her.

She went up the area steps into the street – a gracious curve of elegant houses of which the school was near one end, and scurried quickly round the nearest corner, out of sight. Then as her lungs filled with the clean air of freedom, she straightened her shoulders and walked jauntily along Gay Street towards the centre of the town. She remembered the coach house from her arrival almost two years ago and it was an easy matter to book herself an outside seat on the London coach which was already standing in the stable yard. She gave the first name that came into her head – Mary Bell – said she was going to London to take up a new position 'in a good family' and settled down happily in a corner of the inn's public parlour to await the coach's departure. Her only anxiety was that it might not leave before her headmistress emerged from genteel torpor and raised the hue and cry.

Once in London she knew exactly what she would do. She would go to the docks where the Aberdeen boats berthed and beg a passage on one of the Christie ships, or on the *Jessica*, with Tom.

Tom spotted her at once. The red hair had worked loose from its moorings and shone bright as any beacon against the blue of her dress. That alone would have caught his attention, but she had beauty as well, and an eagerness which communicated itself across the jumbled and dirty dockside to the deck of the *Jessica* moored at her usual berth in the heart of London's Thames. But it took him a moment to realise that it was India Abercrombie. He had last seen her as a spindly adolescent, grimed and unkempt after the fire in the Christie Yard. Now she was a decidedly beautiful young woman who would have stood out in any crowd.

The city was even busier than usual, alive as it was with preparations for the new Queen's Coronation and as well as the customary clamour of a dockside crowd, there were the hammering of the workmen, assembling wooden platforms to accommodate sightseers along the route of the procession and the clamour of street vendors and charlatans, selling anything from patriotic bunting to sugar biscuits in the shape of a 'V'.

The *Jessica* herself had several bales of bunting in her hold, as well as more combustible merchandise – fireworks for the evening celebrations, and a box of coloured lamps for the new Gas Company's patriotic display. There were extra passengers, too, crowding the decks both fore and aft – Scotsmen going home for the festivities, or enterprising businessmen hoping to make a packet in the crowds.

Tom had seen that everything in the engine room was shipshape and ready for sailing and had come on deck for a last look at London before returning to the sweltering heat of the boilers. But at the sight of India Abercrombie, apparently alone, he shouldered his way quickly through the deck-passengers already settling themselves on bundles and hampers, and made his way ashore.

'India!' he called and had to repeat it several times above the din before she heard him. Then her face lit up with delight and she ran towards him, laughing.

'Oh Tom, I'm so glad to see you,' she cried, hugging him unashamedly. 'I've had such a journey, you would not credit it. I had to pretend I was a servant and that was quite fun at first, but then the inn was horrible and it stank and there were bed bugs, I'm sure of it, and then one of the pot-boys tried to . . . well, I had to hit him!' She giggled delightedly at the memory. 'But after that I dare not go to sleep in case he came after me again and I was afraid all the time that they'd follow me from the school and take me back. Oh Tom, I'm so tired and I have no money left and then I couldn't see a Christie ship anywhere and I dare not go to the Aberdeen and Leith office because of my father. He doesn't know I'm here. So when I saw the *Jessica* I could have cried with relief. Oh Tom,' she finished, pausing for breath. 'I can come aboard, can't I? Grandfather will pay my passage money when I get home and after all, it is half his ship anyway, isn't it?'

'Aye, it is,' said Tom, smiling at her. He had changed, she realised. He had always been quiet and slight in comparison with Jamie. He was still not heavily built, but he had a firmness and strength about him which was strangely reassuring. His tawny eyes were confident and unwavering and the short, fair beard suited him. If he had told her he was already a captain, India would have believed him. As it was, she trusted him instantly, as she would have trusted her grandfather.

'Of course you can come aboard, India,' he was saying. 'I'll see you safe home, don't worry.'

'Thank you, Tom.' She kissed him exuberantly and looked around for her portmanteau. He picked it up in one hand and took her arm with the other.

'We'd best hurry, though, India. We're due to sail any minute.'

'There's something I'd better tell you, Tom,' she said, hurrying towards the gangplank of the *Jessica*.

'What is that?' Already Tom had realised that India ought not to be there, and was preparing himself for some shocking revelation when she said simply, 'I'm *starving*.'

'Is that all!' He grinned with relief, then added, more seriously, 'But you'd best tell me everything, India, before we get to Aberdeen. You may need help and you don't want to risk being sent straight back to Bath, do you?'

That voyage was one of the happiest times of India's life. She stood on the deck with the other passengers and watched the jumble of London slip behind her, Blackwall, Tilbury, the East India docks, and, with it, all the repressive misery of the last two homesick years. Then they were in the open sea, with the bow wave curling, the salt wind sharp in her face, the seabirds wheeling and squealing as they lost heart and fell back astern to mob the next, more hopeful prey – and ahead, the gleaming glory of the open sea.

Tom brought her food when he could, though the engine room required a good deal of his time. But when he was eventually off duty, he brought her rugs and a cushion and found her a sheltered part of the deck, out of the wind.

'I'm sorry the cabins are all full,' he said, 'and I can hardly give you my berth. I share it with the second engineer!'

But he produced a can of broth and a cold chicken and they settled down on a coiled rope to eat while India pumped him for news of home. 'And Jamie?' she finished. 'What is he doing?' It was a secret pain to her that he had never written, but then he was not much of a hand with the pen and, besides, was so often at sea. That reminded her. 'Is the tea-ship finished?'

'Jamie's first mate now, on the *Firebird*, and sails regularly to Quebec or St John's,' said Tom with pride. There was no jealousy between the brothers, at most a friendly rivalry, and Tom himself had risen to first engineer. One day they would both be ship's masters in the Christie fleet. 'As for the tea-ship,' he went on, 'work is going well enough, but she won't be ready for sailing, Maitland says, till at least next year. The Yard has been really busy with orders and after the losses we suffered in yon fire, we've had to take all we can get. We've launched, let's see, it must be three ships since you were home and another almost completed. So Uncle Maitland has to wait – but next year will see the launching, surely.'

'And is Jamie at home now?' India tried to sound unconcerned, but she knew Tom was not deceived.

'He wasn't when I left, but he'll be back for the celebrations. We all will.'

'And now, so will I.' India pulled the rug around her shoulders and settled back happily against the cool wood of the deckhouse.

'India . . .' began Tom hesitantly. 'Are they expecting you at home?'

'Not exactly. But I know my grandfather at least will be glad to see me. It was because of him that I came.' She told him about her letter, the sovereigns, all spent now, and her decision to leave on the spot. 'But Papa always said "two years",' she finished defiantly. 'He just has not had the time to make arrangements, that's all.'

'India,' said Tom quietly, 'that is not all. You know you should not have left without permission, should not have travelled unaccompanied. You know there will be trouble.' He knew, as everyone did, that India Abercrombie had been banished to boarding school for some misdemeanour, though no one quite knew what – some said hoydenish behaviour, others worse. He also knew, because Jamie had told him, that she was forbidden to have anything to do with the Christies and Jamie in particular. This neither Jamie nor Tom could understand, unless it was pure snobbism, and seamen were not considered good enough company for her. But Fenton Abercrombie did not seem a snob and hadn't he married a fishergirl himself? There was something disturbing about the affair and Tom was worried on India's behalf. But there was one person he could trust to handle things.

'I think you had best come home with me when we dock,' he said. 'You cannot just turn up on your own doorstep with no warning. That might cause all sorts of trouble. But my mother will know what to do.'

'Yes,' agreed India happily. 'I knew it would be all right as soon as I saw you, Tom. You are always so . . . reassuring.' With that she closed her eyes and fell instantly asleep.

Tom looked down at her for a baffled, affectionate moment, then tucked the rug closer about her shoulders, gathered up the debris of their meal and left to resume his duties.

They shared all his spare moments after that, exchanging confidences, hopes, ambitions. 'You are so easy to talk to, Tom,' she said with affection.

'And you, Indy.' They settled into an easy companionship in which he almost told her about Amelia, she almost mentioned Jamie, but really there was no need to speak their hopes aloud: they each instinctively understood and were the happier because their dreams were not pinned down by mere words. It was a smooth passage, the May seas kindly, the sun's glare tempered by a cooling breeze, and India was idyllically happy – until they began to approach Aberdeen. Then she grew increasingly nervous and uneasy.

'Don't worry,' Tom told her over and over. 'Ma will see to everything. I know she will.' But India could not be reassured.

'I could not bear it, Tom, if they sent me back. I'd rather *die*!'

'It will be all right, I promise you,' he said, but even so, he felt a touch of her own apprehension as they slipped safely over the harbour bar and into home waters. 'But you'd best keep out of sight till I am free to take you home.'

Rachel, for once, was idle, sitting in her favourite chair at the fireside, gently rocking to and fro and watching the firelight flicker round the edges of the great, cast-iron kettle. From the kettle itself came a gentle purr as the water stirred and simmered, and on a flat girdle at the side of the fire a batch of newly made oatcakes curled crisply brown at the edges.

The window had been opened to let in the fresh summer air and with it came the cheerful sounds of the harbour, though muted somewhat by height. Rachel enjoyed being above street level in spite of the stairs, and today, with the little ones upstairs with Kirsty, she was enjoying a few blessed moments' peace before descending again to the office. She would be forty this year and, as James told her, was entitled to rest once in a while, if she felt the need.

Today she had felt it, not so much from physical fatigue but in order to assemble her thoughts and, as always, count her blessings, with gratitude. James her husband and Jamie her son were both at sea, but they would soon be home, God willing, as would dear Tom. The twins, too, would reappear, regular as clockwork with the London sailings, and Maitland was a mere stretch away at the Yard. With Kirsty upstairs and Alex back from St John's they would be a family again, complete. Almost complete. She thought with the usual sadness of Pearl, homesick and lonely, half-way across the world. But Davy, Matt and little Martha continued to thrive. A family of my own, she thought, with no cold corners. It had been her childhood ambition.

Of course there were small draughts . . . she remembered Tom's love for Amelia and that uncomfortable business with Jamie and the Abercrombie girl. Jessie Abercrombie, her old rival and one-time friend, was at the back of that particular trouble, she was sure. But Jessie's mischief-making dated from way back . . .

At that moment in her thoughts, there was the sound of a step on the stair. Rachel looked up in surprise as the door opened and Tom came in, with India beside him. For a moment she did not recognise the girl, thinking it some elegant stranger, perhaps wanting to book a passage to London. Then, as she took in the red hair and eager eyes, she scrambled to her feet and held out her hand.

'India! I'm so glad to see you. And how charming you look. I had not heard you were coming home.'

'No.' India looked to Tom for help.

'That's why we came to you, Ma,' he said, closing the door behind them and motioning India to a chair. 'India came home without telling anyone. By great good fortune, she found the *Jessica* in London and begged a passage. But her father does not know.'

'And you want me to tell him?' said Rachel, coming straight to the point.

Tom and India exchanged glances, then Tom said firmly, 'Yes.'

'Yes please, Mrs Christie,' said India, looking a little shamefaced. 'And I am sorry to cause you trouble.'

'That is quite all right, dear. It is time your father and I sorted out a few things anyway.' She sighed with a hint of private sadness, before saying, more briskly, 'But first let us have a little tea together, while you tell me everything I ought to know.'

Rachel's messenger, one of Alex's boys, found Fenton Abercrombie in the warehouse on the Quay, where he was checking a consignment of tobacco for the Union Street shop, and handed over the note in person, as he had been told to do. The handwriting meant nothing to Fenton and he was expecting it to be some new business order: but when he read the short contents his face lost all colour and his heart beat uncomfortably fast. 'Please come to see me at your earliest convenience on a matter concerning your daughter, India.' The note was signed 'Rachel Christie' and the word 'earliest' was underlined.

Whatever could it mean? India was in Bath, young Christie at sea. At least . . . All sorts of possibilities churned through his agitated mind. He had forbidden his children to go near the Christies, had himself vowed never to set foot in their house again. Yet once, many years ago, he and Rachel had been at ease together. That was before he had married Jessica, when she and Rachel were still friends and he had gone courting in North Square. So many years ago. He had not spoken to Rachel since his own son's christening, and Finlay, he recalled with shock, was eleven years old. Eleven years.

But he would have to go. Whatever Rachel knew concerning India was obviously urgent. He gave the hovering lad a penny, with a mumbled 'Thanks' and finished what he was doing with all speed. If he had to go, he had best go soon and get it over with. But he hoped to God James Christie was not there.

He found Rachel alone in the front parlour of the Christie apartment. She was dressed neatly in a soft blue dress with a lace collar and looked little older than when he had known her in Fisher Square. She held out a hand to him, saying, 'I am glad you came, Fenton. It is time you and I had a talk together.'

Reluctantly he took her hand in his, but when his eyes met her steady grey ones and he saw the understanding and compassion, his antagonism fell away, leaving only anxiety.

'India is not hurt, is she?'

Rachel shook her head. 'No. She is safe enough. But there are things we must talk of, you and I, before you see her.'

'See? Is she here?'

'Yes. She arrived this morning, with Tom. The poor girl has been so homesick and has endured so bravely for such a long time.'

'She had no business to come home before I sent for her!' Fenton was white-faced with anger. India had run away – and to *James Christie's house*. 'What was the school thinking of?'

'I don't think the school was consulted,' said Rachel solemnly, but her eyes were alight with humour. Reluctantly, Fenton managed a smile before saying, with returning anger, 'My wife always said she was a "disobedient wee tyke".'

'Perhaps, Fenton, but your daughter is a wee tyke no longer. She is a remarkably striking young woman who has been very unhappy, among strangers, and far from home. She is an affectionate and loyal girl who deserves your love and understanding.'

Abruptly, Fenton turned his back and stared, unseeing, out of the window across the sunlit harbour basin which bristled, as always, with ships' masts and derricks and all the paraphernalia of the sea. On the Quay below the window were the usual seamen, shore porters, merchants and touts, the usual trundling barrows, heaped bales, coiled ropes and ubiquitous seagulls. The usual cheerful bustle of a busy port. But Fenton saw none of it. He was remembering his wife's admission, all those years ago, about herself and Rachel's husband.

'It is James, isn't it,' said Rachel quietly. 'James and

Jessica?' He made no answer, but she knew by the stiffening of his shoulders that she was right. 'I thought so. But there is no need, Fenton. It happened years ago, before James and I were married.'

'But not before I was!' The viciousness of his voice was like a physical blow.

'Poor Fenton,' she said quietly. 'You should forgive and forget. Besides, it is not fair to punish the girl for her mother's imagined wrongdoing.'

'*Imagined?*' He whirled round to confront her. 'She confessed, woman! She told me herself!'

'What did she tell you?' Rachel was as white-faced now as he was.

'That she and he were alone together in the Christie office and . . .'

'And?' prompted Rachel, though her fingers dug so hard into the palms of her hands they should have drawn blood.

'And "no harm done",' quoted Fenton bitterly, remembering his wife's words. 'But I did not believe her.'

'No,' agreed Rachel sadly. 'There was harm enough. But it is *over*, Fenton. Remember, he is my husband.'

At the pain in her voice, Fenton was brought up short, then suddenly ashamed.

'I am sorry, Rachel. I had forgotten how painful it must be for you to talk about such things. I have been unutterably selfish. Please forgive me?'

'If you will forgive India,' she countered. 'She should not have left school as she did and she knows it. She expects to be punished – but do not send her back. There is no reason why she should not stay in Aberdeen and surely no reason why she should not see Jamie if she wants to? They are young and happy together. That is all that matters.'

He would like to have believed her, but the old worm

of jealousy would not die. Suppose James Christie had lied to his wife? Suppose the association had continued with Jessica after James's marriage? Suppose Rachel had been deceived, as he had been?

'Will you forgive her?'

'India, yes. Jessica, no.' He looked at her bleakly and she was filled with such compassion for him that she took his hand in both hers, reached up and kissed him gently on the cheek.

'I hope one day we can be friends again?'

Her affectionate kiss had brought with it the memory of that other life in Edinburgh and his secret joy. He would have liked to tell Rachel about it, to confide all his hopes and fears for his beloved little bastard son, to tell her how sweet and loving and faithful his Mary was. Instead, he pushed the memory aside and said brusquely, 'Perhaps. But I would prefer it if your son and my daughter did not meet. Please tell me where India is so that we may go home.'

The Coronation of Queen Victoria took place on Thursday, 28th June, 1838, and was celebrated in Aberdeen with proper ceremony and great jubilation. Even the heavens blessed the occasion with clear skies and a refreshing breeze to temper thc sun's heat. At dawn, bells were rung all over the city. The Union Jack was unfurled on the Town House. Multifarious banners of every hue and device festooned the city streets and every shop and business house, though naturally closed for the day, contributed to the patriotic fervour. Hadden's premises on the Green ran a Union Jack to the top of their new 200-foot chimney and every vessel in the harbour was decked with pennants, flags and bunting of every conceivable colour and design.

There were two splendid *jets d'eau* to add to the wonder

– the one in Castle Street in the shape of an Imperial Crown with the letters 'VR' underneath, the one on the Green more obscure, but undoubtedly framed on the latest principles of hydraulic science.

By 10 o'clock the city was agog, the streets packed with citizens of all ages and callings, all in their best holiday clothes – to be rivalled only by the splendid spectacle of the Trades Procession which they had gathered to see. 'Kings' in triumphal cars, 'Princes' on foot, 'warriors', 'clerks' and all kinds of fancy dress, horses, fire engines, a band of musicians sweetly playing. The Gardeners' cart was particularly fine, being fragrant with every kind of flower, and the 260 carpet weavers outshone everyone with their decorated carriage and their costumes, all the products of their own works and no doubt swelteringly hot in the benign June sunshine.

The procession set off at 10 from the Inches on a twelve-mile route which took them past the Town House, where they paused to give the Provost three cheers, then on to cover most of the town and take in Old Aberdeen as well before winding up, exhausted, some six or seven hours later at their original starting point, to disperse gratefully to the Green where Hadden's of the splendid chimney had laid on suitable refreshment.

At mid-day the Military fired a splendid *feu-de-joie*, the *Duke of Wellington* steamer answered with a royal salute and there were celebratory dinners everywhere. The Civic authorities assembled in the Town House to drink toasts to the Queen in three-times-three, the Trades similarly celebrated in the Trades Hall, and officers from the 74th Regiment graced a Grand Coronation Banquet in the Public Rooms.

Then at 7.30 the bonfire was lit in Castle Street with half the town's young folk there to see it, as well as half the town's old. Christies, Nobles, even the Abercrombies joined the crowds who streamed into the Castlegate in gathering numbers to watch the celebratory fire leap higher and wait for the evening's fireworks display to begin.

It was Tom who first spotted India. He was standing with Amelia Noble and her brother near the Athenaeum when he saw her through a gap in the shifting crowds and called to attract her attention. She saw him almost at once and came pushing through the throng to join them, her brother Finlay trailing behind.

'Hello, Tom. Isn't it exciting? Have you seen the fountain? And the crown of little gas lamps above the Adelphi? And Grandpa says there's to be a grand triumphal arch with a portrait of the Queen all done in fireworks! I can't wait to see it.'

'You are looking lovely, Indy,' said Amelia admiringly. 'You bought such elegant clothes in Bath.'

'Maybe, but it's not worth going all that way for them, 'Melia, believe me.'

But it was not just the clothes, though India's white jaconet muslin dress and double pelerine trimmed with lavender ribbons were elegant enough and certainly in the forefront of fashion. There was a freshness and eagerness about her which was strangely appealing and which gave added lustre to her creamy skin and added brightness to her eyes. Now she looked around her and said, 'Where's Jamie? I thought he was to be home in time for the Coronation?' She had not seen him since the night of the fire in the Christie yard, almost two years ago, when her father had forbidden her to see him ever again and had banished her to Bath.

Her father had been more lenient with her than she had expected in the matter of her flight from school, merely confining her to the house for a week, on meagre rations, and requiring her to write an abject letter of contrition to the school. After the first rebellion, she had enjoyed that, knowing she would not have to return, and had produced a splendidly obsequious composition which, she thought with glee, anyone with any intelligence would realise was a hoax. She had had a nervous moment when she presented it to her father for approval, but he barely read it before folding it neatly with his own and despatching the packet to the mail coach. Then he had told her she was free to go about her business as usual, 'As long as you do not associate with the Christies.'

That had been a shock. She had understood, from her father's meeting with Mrs Christie, that whatever feud there had been between them was over. Apparently not. But India had learnt circumspection if nothing else in Bath and had said meekly, 'Yes, Papa.' She had been sure she would see Jamie at the Coronation – unless, of course, his ship had been held up.

'Is he not here after all, Tom?'

'Oh, yes, Jamie's somewhere around,' said Tom, putting an arm round Amelia's shoulders to protect her from the crush. 'Probably with that crowd from North Square.' Then the first firework exploded above the Castlegate in a brief splendour of sputtering colour and India forgot even Jamie in the wonder of it.

So it was that Jamie Christie's first view of her was of a girl in a white dress, with an upturned, rapturous face, her red hair falling loose from a little straw bonnet with trailing ribbons and her mittened hands clasped tight in front of her. Behind her, in the satin evening sky, a trail of coloured stars hung briefly overhead, then disappeared. And she turned her head and looked at him.

Jamie swallowed, blinked, and with a surge of excitement and a nervousness he had never felt in her presence before, realised that the vision was India Abercrombie, his childhood friend. Then she was pushing her way towards him, laughing, and he could only stand there, open-mouthed, and stare.

'It's only me,' she said, breathless with a happiness that made her light-headed. 'Don't you recognise me after so long?' Still he looked at her with an expression that brought the colour racing to her cheeks and made her suddenly self-conscious and shy. 'Have I changed so much?' she finished in a small voice, not looking at him.

'Yes,' he said and swallowed before saying boldly, 'You've grown beautiful.'

'But I'm only *me*.' She looked up to see he was still studying her as if he had never seen her before. He too had changed. He was no longer a boy but a man, she realised, with a man's voice, a man's physique, and a man's neat beard which would be soft as breast feathers against her cheek. She looked away quickly lest he read the thought in her eyes.

'It's a "me" I like,' he said quietly and took her arm to support her as a crowd of children ran buffeting past.

'Who's a fine lady, then,' jeered a voice from behind them and Eppie of the mussel beds appeared out of nowhere and stuck out her tongue. 'Struttin' like a peahen in her fancy feathers!' She tweaked India's skirts and skipped nimbly out of reach. 'And all togged up for the mussel scarp – or is it the Town Sergeant ye're ready for this time?' and she winked and leered with unmistakable suggestion. Jamie clipped her swiftly round the ear.

'You'll not speak to Indy like that or you'll get more where that came from. Now away with you or I'll give you another, here and now.'

Eppie merely grimaced, but from a safe distance this time, and turned her attention elsewhere. 'Fatty Finlay Townie! Fatty Finlay Townie!' she jeered and Finlay, who had been trailing in India's wake, turned and fled for the safety of the crowd. With a crow of delighted laughter, Eppie followed.

'I suppose he will be all right?' said India doubtfully.

'Of course he will. He's a grown lad and it's time he learnt to look after himself. Besides, isn't your Grandda hereabouts?'

'Yes,' said India gratefully and promptly forgot Finlay for the rest of the evening as Jamie strolled with her up and down the Castlegate, through the Adelphi and out again, along Union Street and Broad Street, scarcely noticing the competing decorations above the shops, the evergreen arches and flamboyant devices, the 'V's and 'VR's' everywhere, while Jamie told her of his adventures and experiences at sea and India confessed the miseries of her time at school in Bath. After the first awkwardness it was like old times when they had been childhood friends. Yet not quite the same, for there was a new awareness between them, a new excitement, and when Jamie drew her into the shadow of a darkened doorway away from the crowds and hesitantly kissed her, India realised what it was. It was what her sisters had whispered and giggled about on those tedious afternoons so long ago, what Victoria hinted at when she came home, late, from some dance or other, a little too pink-cheeked and ruffled, her eyes a hint too bright. But with India it was more than just sexual attraction. It is love, she thought with wonder, and his beard *is* soft as breast feathers, just as I expected. She felt her arms creep up around his neck, and when her lips needed to find his, she let them. But only for a brief, sweet moment.

'We'd best go,' she said, breaking away, suddenly shy. 'We'll miss the end of the fireworks.'

'Not yet,' murmured Jamie. 'Please? I've never kissed a girl before and I think I like it.'

India did not quite believe him on the first count, but

when he added in a soft voice, close to her ear, 'And I *know* I like you. Very much,' she gave in. She had never felt so jubilantly happy in her life.

But she made him take her back to the fireworks just the same, at first with arms entwined, then hand in hand, then, more decorously as they reached the Castlegate, with her hand in the crook of his courteous arm.

They were standing together whispering and laughing when George Abercrombie came upon them unexpectedly and beamed his pleasure, though there was anxiety behind the smile. 'My, but you're a rare sight for an old man's eye, Indy love,' he said, giving her a hug. 'See you look after her, young Christie. There's thugs and cut-throats in any crowd and I'll not have my favourite grand-daughter come to harm.'

'I will, sir.' Jamie grinned cheerfully and, when he thought Abercrombie was not looking, winked at India.

'I saw that, lad,' growled the old man. 'So mind you behave yourself, you young stirk. Which reminds me, have either o' you seen young Finlay? His Ma's asking for him.'

'Is Ma here?' India's face fell. That meant her father must be here too. But tonight she did not care. Let him see her with Jamie, she thought defiantly. It is a holiday, after all. 'I thought Ma was staying at home, to "keep away from yon stinking crowds".'

'Aye well, she's changed her mind, hasn't she?' said Abercrombie tartly, 'and she's wanting Finlay, and him not to be found the length and breadth o' the Castlegate.'

'It's all right, Grandpa,' said India, taking his arm. 'He'll be with Eppie and the Footdee crowd. I expect Nana Brand'll be there, too, so you needn't worry. Stay with us and watch the grand finale.'

So it was that India, arm in arm with her grandfather Abercrombie on one side and Jamie Christie on the other, watched the sky above the Castlegate explode into colourful splendour as a thousand fireworks coruscated in the shape of a grand triumphal arch, in the centre of which dazzled a half-length portrait of Her Most Gracious Majesty, with the sparkling motto, 'God Save the Queen'.

Then the last firework fizzled into darkness and it was over, but for the lingering tang of gunpowder in the air and the floating ash of burnt paper.

'Time to go home, lass,' said Abercrombie and led India away, but not before Jamie had whispered, 'When shall I see you again?' and India, sparkling-eyed, had promised 'Soon.'

'Best not see too much of that lad,' said her grandfather gruffly as they walked back together to the Broad Street house. 'I didn't want to spoil your pleasure by speaking in front o' the lad, but your father doesn't approve and nor do I.'

India bit her lip with shock, then said, in a small voice, 'Why not?'

'Never you mind why not, lass. Just remember what I tell you. Keep away from yon Christie. There's good reason, believe me. Why else would I have let your father send you off to yon daft school? Ask yourself that. But now you're back, see you remember, lass. I'm fond o' you, Indy love. I only want what is best for you.'

And I want Jamie Christie, thought India, setting her jaw with determination, but she had sense enough not to say so. Whatever her father's and grandfather's reasons, she knew they were invalid. Some ancient family prejudice, of no concern to her or to Jamie. But daft or not, the Bath school had taught her how to conceal her thoughts. So she merely said meekly, 'Yes, Grandpa,' and turned the conversation to the evening's entertainment and the family gathering which was to follow when they had all assembled at old Abercrombie's house.

* * *

That was the beginning of an enchanted time for India, a time of clandestine meetings, of sweet, snatched moments, and a secret happiness which sustained her as nothing else could have done throughout her mother's nagging and her sister Victoria's confidences, designed, India knew, merely to elicit similar from herself

In October, Victoria was engaged to the Pirie boy – 'And had best marry quick,' rumour had it, 'afore it's too late.' Only time would prove the truth of that particular rumour, though India suspected it was not without foundation and that more young men than Gordon Pirie could have given evidence to prove it. But at least Victoria's imminent wedding took the attention, meantime, from her younger sister and though, as the autumn season swung into motion, Jessica insisted on pairing India off on all occasions with a succession of 'suitable' city youths, she no longer expected India to emerge from each encounter with an engagement ring. That could wait till Victoria was safely transmogrified into Mrs Gordon Pirie.

Then, India knew, it would be her turn. She regarded the coming conflict with apprehension, but with unwavering courage. Whatever they threatened, she would not give in. Meanwhile, Jamie was sailing the *Firebird* regularly to Canada, sometimes with his father as captain, more recently with Alfie Baxter, and was away for two months at a time. But when he was home, India managed, somehow, to meet him and the memory of those brief, snatched moments sustained her through the long weeks of his absence at sea.

Mairi, happy in the possession of Miss Indy's silver chain to which had been added a pretty horsehair bracelet and, most recently, a small cameo pin, entered as eagerly as her young mistress into the spirit of the intrigue and, untouched by love herself and at an age now where she no longer expected it, found a vicarious excitement in the smuggling of secret notes from India to young Christie and enjoyed his teasing compliments – and the odd coins she managed to extract from him – as she took his messages back.

Jamie was a practical lad, not given overmuch to penmanship, and these were usually verbal and of a strictly practical vein. 'Athenaeum, noon', or 'The Green at four', though once, when his sailing was unexpectedly brought forward, he had written her a note. Though it consisted only of two lines, 'Sorry, Indy. We must catch the tide. See you next time. Jamie,' India kept it folded small inside her bodice, next her heart, and at night took it out to read and kiss before tucking it happily under her pillow, to fill her dreams with thoughts of Jamie.

Victoria was married at Christmas and removed to the Pirie mansion in the West End, leaving India to bear the full force of her mother's matrimonial intentions.

'Now, India, it's your turn,' she said one February morning when the day was particularly dreary with a lowering sky and incessant rain, varied only by occasional sleet. The street outside was running with water and the carriage wheels sent up bow waves of spattering mud so that the skirt hems of any women unfortunate enough to be out on foot were sodden inches deep in slush. In the Abercrombie drawing room the fire still smoked in spite of all Mairi's efforts with candle ends and newspaper and there was a depressing chill in the air, due in large part to the draughts which wandered freely round the window frames and under the door.

India was reminded uncomfortably of Bath where she had been required to practise dance steps in a draughty ballroom while clad in the skimpiest of muslin gowns. Her hands and feet had been permanently blue, her nose red and her ears numb. But at least here she could wear several layers if she chose, and top it all with a good old-fashioned plaid.

'I wish you would not wrap yourself up like a fishwife!' grumbled her mother, noting India's attire. 'You looked real nice when you came back from yon school.'

'I'm cold,' retorted India, then added hastily, 'But I'll take this off when the fire burns up a bit.' It was not worth annoying her mother unnecessarily.

'If it ever does,' grumbled Jessica. 'And me with guests expected. I've asked Archie Grant's ma, wi' Mrs Mack-enzie and Mrs Hunter. They have lads about the right age. I thought we'd make up a party later, for the theatre maybe, or the Assembly rooms.'

India sighed with resignation. She'd have to agree of course; have to dance with them and smile and make silly conversation; she'd have to look as if she was enjoying herself. The trouble was, if she did all that, the boy – whichever partner her Ma had allotted her – would take it to mean she was willing. Then she would have to fight him off in some undignified scuffle in the corner of a balcony, or behind a potted palm. She was adept now at making excuses for not looking for 'a breath of fresh air', for not wanting to 'admire the stars' or 'watch the sunset', and she refused flatly to 'stroll in the moonlight', but it meant always being on guard and sooner or later she would fall into another trap and have to extricate herself as best she could without giving offence. That was the trouble, of course. If she could have said what she thought, acted as her instinct prompted, told them all outright that she found them silly, puerile and ridiculous, and, if necessary, clouted them smartly, the full weight of her Ma's anger would have thumped down on her, hard. That she could have coped with, except that her father would be brought into it and would know, without a word being spoken, why she acted as she did. No, to protect

Jamie she had to go along with her mother's plans as far as she could without betraying herself, or him.

'Well?' demanded Jessica. 'What do you say?'

'Yes,' said India hastily. 'I think the theatre is an excellent idea.'

'Good. Then the next thing to settle is which of them to set your cap at. I favour Archie Grant myself. The Grants are in granite and there's good money in that. Yon Marischal College they're rebuilding is going to be solid wi' the stuff and then all the best headstones are in granite.'

India feigned amazement. 'But Mamma, surely you do not want me to choose a husband just to get a free headstone when I'm dead? Or is it for you?'

'Course not, ye daft quine. But granite's money and there's no call to sneer till you're drowning in the stuff!'

India resisted the urge to point out that you could hardly drown in granite and instead said meekly, 'No, Mamma. But Archie Grant's small.'

'Nought wrong wi' that! Though you may be right,' she conceded, studying India with her head on one side. 'A nice-looking lass like you might be better wi' a man whose head reached higher than your shoulder, right enough. But the Grant lad's only twenty. He'll maybe grow a bittie yet.'

'Then I'll wait till he does,' retorted India, 'before I make up my mind.'

'Of course, there's Willy Mackenzie,' went on her mother. 'He's taller, and in the law, too. I've always fancied the professions. But then the Hunters' manufactory is doing real well and there's two Hunter boys to choose from . . .'

India ceased to listen, but drifted off into the familiar reverie of herself and Jamie Christie, one day, on a deck together in tropical seas, with the flying fish he talked of and the dolphins and the flap of clean sail in the wind, until she was jerked back to attention by her mother saying, 'That's settled then. Mackenzie's first on the list. You'll sit next to him at the theatre and be real charming to him – or you'll have me to answer to. Then we'll maybe have a small supper party, wi' dancing. Then an outing o' some sort, in the carriage. I reckon you could be engaged by Easter, if you play your cards right. You've grown into a nice-looking lass in spite o' your tempers and if you do as you're told, I'm prepared to wager you'll be wed by June. And Mrs William Mackenzie's a real nice name.'

India looked at her mother in gathering alarm. It was one thing to evade unwelcome attentions in a crowd, quite another to escape when her own mother was planning to hand her over to the youth in question, like a bone to a hungry dog. She would have to tell her.

'I'm sorry, Mamma. I don't mind going to theatres and suppers if I must, but I'll not marry Willy Mackenzie.'

'Nonsense. You don't know him yet.'

'It does not matter whether I do or not, Mamma. I don't wish to marry anyone.'

'Maybe not now, Indy, but when you've met the boy you'll feel different.'

'No, Mamma, and it's a waste of your time and Papa's money to try and make me.'

'Is it indeed! We'll soon see about that.' Jessica heaved her ample bulk off the sofa, with a great twanging of springs, and stood threateningly over India. 'Your father says you're to marry and so do I. *So marry you will!*'

At that moment the door opened and Fenton himself came in, having arrived on the morning boat from Leith on what had become his regular weekly trip. He looked from Jessica's irate face to India's obstinate one and said coldly, 'I could hear your voices from the hall. Kindly reserve family discussions for family ears – unless you want to advertise our domestic discord to the entire town.'

'I'm sorry, Fenton,' said Jessica, 'but she makes me so angry. Here's me bendin' over backwards to do my best for her, finding her a good husband like you said, and the young miss refuses to marry *anyone!*'

'Is this true, India?' said Fenton, shoulder to shoulder with his wife and glaring down at her where she sat, huddled in her plaid, on the window seat.

India stood up to face them, letting the plaid slip from her shoulders and as she did so revealing the sweet, innocent curves of her breasts and hips, and, thought Fenton with a twist of the heart, the lovely vulnerability of her graceful neck and clear grey eyes. He felt at the same time afraid for her and achingly protective. Then she spoke and all other feelings were drowned in the familiar anger.

'Yes, Papa. I will marry no one.' But truth required her to add, 'Except Jamie Christie.'

'Then you will remain a spinster,' said Fenton, with cold fury, 'for I swear to God you will marry no Christie.'

'But *why*, Papa?' cried India in anguish. 'I do not understand. Mrs Christie said . . .'

'Your mother knows why,' interrupted Fenton and slammed out of the room.

Jessica opened her mouth to shout after him, changed her mind, bit her lip, looked down at her hands, turned her back on India and said grimly, 'That's that then. No Christie.'

'Why, Ma?' wailed India, tears unashamedly standing in her eyes. 'Please tell me why?'

'Never you mind, lass. Some daft idea of your father's, that's all. It's wrong, it's stupid, but you'll not shift him. I *know*,' she added bitterly. 'So you'd best accept it. And you'd best accept a husband, too, if you know what's good for you. There's more fish in the sea than Christies and bigger fish too. Ye'll not need to seek a nunnery yet awhile.'

But India was as obstinate as her father. She had said Jamie Christie or nobody and she meant it.

'What call had you to tell the girl that?' demanded Jessica, finding out Fenton in his study and closing the door behind her. 'Dragging up that ancient old tale. It's nae fair. I've put up wi' your obstinate jealousies long enough. You're *obsessed*, Fenton. That's what it is. You dinna see the truth when it stares you in the face.'

Fenton did not answer, but deliberately turned the page of his book and continued, conspicuously, to read.

'I'm sick of it!' declared his wife, abandoning caution. 'Punishing me for years on end for *nothing*. And it was nothing, whatever you've blown it up in your mind to be. The way you've been on at me all these years anyone'd think I'd been in and out of every bed in Aberdeen – and I wish I had, the way you've treated me. I'd have been no worse off *and* had a bit o' fun into the bargain! You and your high and mighty ideas. But they don't apply to *you*, do they? Oh no.' She paused for breath, before finishing, 'You're nothing but a *hypocrite!*' There, she'd said it at last, and waited in trepidation and excitement to see how he would react. For a moment she thought he was going to ignore her, then he said quietly, without looking at her, 'And what do you mean by that?'

'You ken fine what I mean. All those clean shirts to go to Edinburgh. "Courting" Mairi said, and she's nay far off the mark, is she? Maybe we should look in Edinburgh for a match for Indy? It seems a right fair town for "attachments".'

'What I do in Edinburgh is my affair.'

'Oh, "affair" is it? I'll bet it is. Some scheming tart with her claws into your purse, buttering you up wi' "darling Fenton" this and "sweetest Fenton" that, till she's got you just where she wants you, all panting to get her into bed.'

'But then I am used to that, remember? I have had years of training, from you.'

'Well I wish her joy of you,' cried Jessica in fury. 'And I hope she finds more under your precious clean shirt than I ever did.'

That needled him, but to her own disadvantage as she should have known it would. 'She does,' he said. 'But then you were too busy looking elsewhere, as I recall.'

'If I was,' blustered Jessica, 'which I *wasn't*, it was because I got little enough from you!'

'Ah!' pounced Fenton. 'But who did you find, tell me that!'

'I've telt ye a thousand times, ye daft fool! *Nobody!*'

'I do not believe you. And if you raise your voice to me again, woman, I shall remove myself permanently to Edinburgh, and the Town may think what it chooses.'

Jessica subsided instantly, all bravery spent. It was what she had dreaded. Not that she would miss her husband – he was little enough company to her – but she would be the laughing stock of the town. They would whisper behind her back, 'Yon's the Abercrombie woman who couldn't keep her husband,' and worse. And without a husband she'd likely not be respected any more, not asked to serve on committees or to make up a table at cards. She'd be ostracised, ignored, or merely quietly dropped. She'd rather be widowed!

'One more thing before you go,' he continued. 'I meant what I said about India. There is to be no hint of a Christie liaison. Do you understand me?'

'Yes, dear.' Meekly, Jessica removed herself, but the look she directed at the closed study door would have curdled the milk in a whole herd of cows.

* * *

'We will have to elope,' said India on a day in early summer. 'There is no other way.'

'But that's not right,' protested Jamie Christie. 'It would upset our parents dreadfully.'

'Yes,' agreed India with relish. 'It would. But they would not be able to do one thing about it, and it would serve my father right. It's been weeks now since we've even met and when we do, we can only snatch a few minutes together in secret. I can't bear it much longer, Jamie. I want to be with you always, proudly, with all the world to see us. So I thought I could stow away on *Firebird* the very next time you sail, and your captain could marry us at sea! Oh Jamie, it would be so romantic and right. I do love you so.'

Jamie held her close and kissed her gently before saying, 'And I love you. But it is still not right. My Da would be angry, my Ma hurt. I don't want our marriage to begin like that.'

'But what else can we do? They will never let me marry you, I know they won't.' India was supposed to be at her grandfather's house where Mrs Abercrombie's dress-maker was waiting to fit her for a new ball dress for the autumn season, but she had managed to send word to Jamie to meet her on the way, under the bridge by the Green. They had found a quiet corner in a nearby wynd where, for the moment, they were safe, but India dared not stay long. She had hoped to settle their elopement, here and now. She knew *Firebird* was to sail for St John's in two days' time and had not dreamt that Jamie would refuse. She had thought he loved her, thought he would have welcomed her idea, thought he wanted her as much as she wanted him. Her joy drained away, leaving a grey and choking misery.

'It's not right,' repeated Jamie gently, seeing her face. 'Besides, I am still apprenticed. Wait until my time's up.

It's not long now and I'll have my own master's ticket before you know it. Then we'll marry.'

'But he won't let me,' cried India. 'Don't you understand? He'll *never* let me and I can't bear it.' She buried her head in his shoulder for a brief, intense moment, then drew back and looked at him from bleak eyes. 'They will marry me to someone else, Jamie, and it's you I love.'

Jamie's resolution wavered. He loved her, there was no question of that. He wanted her with a healthy lust he found difficult to control, and would not have tried to had she not been India and innocent, and now she was offering herself to him. In less than a week she could be his wife. At the mere thought, he felt desire harden. He wanted her more than anything – except, he admitted, his father's approval. And he knew he would forfeit that, if he married India in secret, without her father's consent. He would lose his father's trust and with it the chance to captain a Christie ship, perhaps even the tea-ship Maitland was building. His dream of sailing that tea-ship to China would vanish for ever.

'Wait, my darling,' he said gently, his lips close against her ear. 'Just a little longer? Just till I have my papers? Then we could sail to China together.'

India drew back and studied his face. His eyes were dark with love, his expression serious with responsibility, and she knew she would not change his mind. 'Do you promise me, Jamie?' she managed. 'Do you promise I may come with you to China, whatever my father says?'

Jamie swallowed, then made his decision. 'I promise.'

'Truly? Because otherwise I cannot bear it.'

'Truly. Or may my boat be a bonnet to me,' he added, committing himself beyond retreat. 'But do not look at me like that, Indy, or I'll not be able to bear it either, and I must, if we are to be honourably man and wife.'

Man and wife. He had actually said it aloud. India's heart suddenly sang within her, her misery forgotten.

'So promise me you will wait for me,' he was saying.

'I promise.' They looked into each other's eyes for a solemn, timeless moment, before India became aware of a movement beyond Jamie's shoulder, in the shadows where the wynd joined the Green. 'There's someone coming! I must go.' She reached up and kissed him, with brief intensity, before turning her back and walking with apparent unconcern up the cobbled stretch of Flourmill Brae towards Broad Street and the Abercrombie house. Dear Jamie. She knew he loved her, knew he wanted her, knew he was acting only for her good, and, being Jamie, could do no other. It would be another six months before the tea-ship was ready, but with Jamie's promise to sustain her, surely the time would fly by?

As she walked, light-footed, over the cobbles she hardly noticed the gradient or the freshening wind which always funnelled with mischievous force along Broad Street, teasing her skirts and plucking at her pelisse. Jamie loved her, and they were promised to each other, for ever.

'Oh Mairi,' she confided, late that night when the maid came to collect her clothes for the wash tub. 'He is so honourable and so true. I wanted to run away with him, but he wouldn't, for my sakc – so I promiscd to wait a little longer – and he promised to marry me. Mairi, we're hand-fast! Really, truly engaged!'

'Oh Miss Indy, how romantic,' sighed Mairi. 'Just like onc o' thcy fairy storics.'

'But you'll not tell, will you?' said India, suddenly anxious. 'Promise on your honour?'

'Course I promise, miss. Will you be wantin' your white muslin or your blue sprigged for tomorrow?'

'I don't care which, Mairi. It's only Willy Mackenzie and I'd happily go in sackcloth – only Ma would be "black affronted".' She gave a wicked imitation of her mother, in dudgeon, which reduced Mairi to helpless laughter. But when the maid had gone, still snorting and giggling into her pile of linen, India remembered Jamie's promise to marry her and to take her to China.

'Or may my boat be a bonnet to me,' he had said. India knew that was a fisherman's most solemn oath, and binding to the grave.

The Christie tea-ship was steadily taking shape. Once it became plain that she would not be completed in time to reach Macau for that year's tea crop, the first hectic pace had eased to a meticulous progress in which every nail, every inch of planking was scrutinised, sometimes with as few as three men at work, while on the other slipway, the commercial shipbuilding forged ahead under the combined efforts of the rest of the Yard. In spite of the advancement of steam transport, with a new steamship making the journey from Liverpool to New York in as little as thirteen days, the Yard had a full order book and continued to launch a succession of sailing ships, some as small as eighty tons, the majority around 200 for the profitable coastal trade. At the same time, the small Christie fleet traded regularly to St John's and the Baltic as well as up and down the east coast from Aberdeen to London. Business was good, the Christie enterprise flourishing.

Then in August letters came from Macau. There had been trouble at Canton. The Chinese had blockaded the Factories where the foreign trade took place and when eventually the blockade was lifted, all foreigners had been ordered back to Macau. But, Pearl said, the trouble was not over, and soon even Macau might not be safe. But they were not to worry about her. If the worst happened, she and Robin would put to sea with Duncan, and, in company with all the other wives, wait out the troubles on board ship till it was safe to return. Her only anxiety, she said, was for her poor little Chinese orphans as she doubted they would be allowed to leave. Her own daughter, she added, in one bleak sentence, had died of a fever.

'You must go to her, James,' Rachel said, 'as soon as you can.'

'Yes,' agreed James, frowning. 'But I wish I knew more about these troubles she mentions. If the Factories are closed and the tea-trading suspended, we may find ourselves with an empty hold.'

'Nonsense,' said Maitland. 'Trade never stops. The Chinese need the tea-revenue too much. The Factories may be closed, but there are other ways of doing business, through a third party. Trans-shipping, they call it, and Pearl would have told us not to come if it was to be a wasted journey.'

'Da, we *must* go,' put in Jamie. 'Pearl is waiting for us. Uncle Maitland's building the ship specially. So many things depend on it,' he finished and added, silently, and with the usual twinge of apprehension, including India's happiness.

'When will she be finished, Maitland?' asked Rachel quietly. That bleak sentence in Pearl's letter haunted her and, in private, she meant to suggest to James that he persuade Pearl to come home. At home, she was sure, Pearl's child would not have died. She deliberately put the thought of Pearl's husband out of her mind or, if she thought of him, it was to persuade herself that he would only want what was best for Pearl, as she did.

'I think we might launch her in a couple of months,' he said, with suppressed excitement. 'Three at the most. Then there will be sea trials, of course, and the final fittings to the deck and cabins – but I reckon she'll be ready to sail for the China seas in the spring.'

There was a moment's awed silence before everyone spoke at once – but the question that was not asked and which was at the forefront of everyone's mind was who would captain Maitland's ship to China, and who else would go along with him, as crew.

If Da chooses me, thought Jamie with a mixture of jubilation and awe, then whether her father consents or not, India comes with me, as my wife. I have given my word.

Mealtimes in the Fenton Abercrombie household were quiet affairs since the departure of the two eldest daughters, so when one or other of them arrived to share the family board Jessica, for one, was delighted. Today it was Victoria who had popped in to show off her new bonnet and to recount the latest exploits of little Georgie, her six-month-old son. 'Premature too, the poor wee mite,' as Jessica told anyone who would listen. 'Scarce a fingernail on him and no bigger than a kitten when he was born. It's a wonder he survived at all.'

'And a wonder anyone believes a word of it,' said Mairi, behind her mistress's back. 'It's not the child that was premature, but the begetting of him.'

'That's enough, Mairi!' said India. The thought of her sister and Gordon Pirie embracing made her somehow ashamed.

'Aye, it *was* enough,' giggled Mairi. 'But he's a grand wee fellow for all that. And 'Toria's made a better ma than I'd have thought. She seems real proud o' the laddie.'

A bit too proud, thought India sourly as Victoria launched into yet another tale of infant genius involving gurgles and clutchings and emerging teeth. Fenton had long ago retreated into his usual book and was waiting only for the meal to finish to remove himself. Even Jessica was beginning to be satiated with baby talk, especially as

Victoria insisted on referring to the child as 'your wee grandson' on all occasions. It made Jessica feel old.

'You'd best not get "narrow", 'Toria,' she interrupted sharply when her daughter said it once too often. 'You don't want to turn into one o' they *boring* women wi' nothing to talk about but teeth and wind.'

Victoria flushed, then countered with, 'Any talk's better than no talk at all, like *some* people. It's no wonder you're still not spoken for, India, in spite of your precious red hair and your boarding school manners. Men don't like a girl with nothing to say for herself and you'll be left on the shelf if you don't watch out. Believe me, I know.'

India ignored her.

'India has plenty of admirers,' said Jessica nervously, one eye on Fenton's bent head.

'Aye, she does that,' agreed Mairi, sawing away at the mutton on the sideboard, ready to refill Finlay's plate.

'Well they're not exactly falling over each other to take her to the altar,' said Victoria spitefully. 'Not that I can see.'

'That's 'cos you can't see everything,' retorted Mairi. There was a time when she'd been fond of Miss 'Toria, but she'd got awful stuck up since her marriage, whereas Miss Indy was real nice these days. 'If you could, you'd know better.'

'Know what?' prompted Victoria, scenting gossip.

'I'll have some more mutton, please, Mairi,' said India quickly, 'if there is any.'

'Let Finlay have his first,' put in Jessica. 'You know he needs his meat.'

'He does not!' snapped Fenton unexpectedly, looking up briefly from his book. 'You feed that boy far too much already.'

There was a shocked pause – the master rarely spoke at meals – before Fenton apparently resumed his reading.

Then Mairi tiptoed round the table with exaggerated caution, bearing the ashet, and lifted three generous slices on to Finlay's plate. 'And there's plenty for you too, Miss Indy,' she said, offering the girl the platter.

'Remember you *promised*,' whispered India fiercely, under cover of helping herself to meat.

'Promised what?' pounced Victoria, leaning across the table towards her sister with a conspiratorial gleam in her eyes. 'Go on, Indy. You can tell me.'

'Tell you what?' countered India innocently. 'There's nothing to tell.'

'Oh yes there is,' teased Victoria whose shrewd brain had worked out the connection. 'You've a secret lover, haven't you?'

'Don't be ridiculous,' snapped Jessica. 'Course she hasn't. I've never heard ought so daft! If that's what comes o' living in the West End, then you can keep it.'

'I reckon you're right, Mamma,' sighed Victoria, changing tactics. 'Who'd fall in love with *her* except some ancient old widower, maybe, too blind to see straight.'

India chose to ignore her sister, but not so Mairi. 'Yon Christie boy's better-looking than your husband and Miss Gussie's put together,' she declared, jumping, as she thought, to India's defence. 'And if anyone's blind it's you, Miss 'Toria – blind jealous!'

With that, Mairi swept triumphantly out of the room, bearing the empty ashet like an offering before her. There was a moment's appalled silence, then Fenton pushed back his chair and stood up.

'I will see you in my study, India. Now.'

Amelia Noble chose her moment with care. Her father was deeply involved with the plans for a new hospital at Woolmanhill, her brother 'Booky' Andrew, newly graduated from Marischal College, was studying with her father, as a medical apprentice. In theory, he should have relieved his father of some part of the work, but in practice they did everything together, the one ever eager to teach, the other as eager to learn. Since Booky's graduation, Amelia had seen less of him, but her own studies were so far advanced now that she had little need of her brother's help, except as a provider of books. She was now fifteen, and as determined as ever to achieve her goal.

'Papa,' she ventured one evening at dinner. 'The Christies' tea-ship is to be launched next week and if the sea trials are satisfactory, they plan to sail for China in the New Year.'

'Oh yes?' said her father absentmindedly and turned to Booky with some question concerning the Clinic.

'I would like to go with them, Papa.' There was something in Amelia's voice which made both father and son look at her with startled interest, while her stepmother laid aside her spoon and said quietly, 'Explain what you mean, Amelia dear.'

'I mean that I would like to sail to China, in the Christie ship, to join my sister Pearl,' said Amelia in a voice which left no doubt that she had considered the venture from every angle and made her plans accordingly. 'I wish to help her with the work of her orphanage, and I know she would welcome both my help and my company. Besides, I have skills to offer and can earn my keep.' In the pause that followed, she added, 'I have been studying the Chinese language for some years now and I believe I have a certain degree of proficiency.'

'You have *what?*' said her father in astonishment.

'It is true,' put in Booky. 'I obtained the books for her and not without difficulty, Papa. She has made good use of them.' He smiled quickly at his sister and said, 'Let her go, Papa. It is what she needs to do.'

Andrew Noble looked at his daughter with a mixture of pride and dismay. 'Is this true, Amelia? Have you really taught yourself a version of Chinese?'

'Yes, Papa. You said years ago that I could not go to China because I was too young and because I did not know the language. But I am now in my sixteenth year and I know far more Mandarin Chinese than Pearl did when she left us. Please, Papa? I know there is work for me to do there, and I am waiting to do it. I will be safe enough with the Christies. It is the perfect opportunity, Papa, almost as if it were heaven sent.'

'But a young girl, alone,' protested Andrew. 'It does not seem right. And there is talk of trouble to come, even war if the Chinese continue to block trade as they have been doing.'

'But that is at Canton, Papa. Pearl says Macau is not affected. And besides, by the time we get there, things may be entirely different.'

'Hmm,' said her father thoughtfully, then, with affection, 'But what would we do without you?'

'You have Booky to help you now,' pointed out Amelia, 'and as for being alone, as you put it, I will not be alone. The Christies will take me and as soon as I arrive, there will be Pearl.'

'I think you should let her go,' said Louise, when her husband did not speak. 'She has worked hard for years, just as her brother has. It would be unfair to deny her her goal just because she is a girl.'

Andrew was torn between justice and inclination. He loved his daughter and did not want to part with her, especially to an unknown and dangerous life half-way across the world. But Louise was right. Amelia had earned his consideration and deserved her reward. And Pearl, after all, would welcome and watch over her young sister. Pearl was homesick and, he suspected, lonely. Perhaps he owed it to Pearl, too?

'Very well, Amelia,' he said, with sadness. 'I will speak to James Christie about it. But it must be only for a year. As to supporting yourself, there is no need. I will give you money so that you can help Pearl with her orphans, with no worry of having to make ends meet. But you must understand here and now that unless Mr Christie sails the ship himself you may not go.'

'Thank you, Papa!' Amelia's face was radiant as she ran to embrace her father. 'You are a dear, sweet Papa whom I will sadly miss. But I will write often,' she hurried on, smiling away the threatening tears, 'and Pearl will be so happy to hcar I am coming. I will write to her at once.'

'Best wait till I have settled your passage,' warned Andrew, but Amelia had no such reservations. She knew James Christie planned to sail the tea-ship himself to China – and had no doubt that he would take her, if her father asked it.

Tom Christie was desolate when he heard the news. Amelia go to China? It was unthinkable.

'Could you not wait?' he begged her. 'Wait till I have worked out my indentures? It is not long now, then I will have a ship of my own.'

'I am sorry, Tom,' said Amelia, looking at him from resolute blue eyes. 'But I must go now. Pearl needs me. Perhaps you could come and visit me one day?' she added kindly, seeing his distress. 'I expect I will be there for some time and any visitors from home will be especially welcome.'

'Any visitors', thought Tom bleakly as he walked beside her through the gloomy winter streets. She thinks of me as just one of a crowd. I am nothing to her whereas she is . . . but the thoughts would not form in his mind, just as the words would not form on his tongue. What was the use of even trying to tell her? She would not listen to him. She would smile and listen to the words perhaps, but not to his thoughts, not to the consuming ardour of his heart.

'Do not look so dour, Tom,' she said, taking his arm for support as they turned a corner into an unexpected gust of winter wind. 'I expected you to be happy for me. You know I have worked and dreamt of this for years.'

He wanted to say 'I love you,' wanted to add, 'I want you for my wife,' but he dared not. It was too soon, Amelia too absorbed in her own plans. If he did speak, he would risk losing her friendship as well as her presence. Instead, he said, staring straight ahead into the grey mist of the distance, 'Happy for you perhaps, but not for myself.'

'And why not?' She skipped aside to avoid a puddle and laughed up at him. 'You said yourself you will have a ship of your own soon. Then you can fix one of those splendid engines you are always telling me about into your own ship and steam your way to China! Except that you had best put the fires out before you reach Macau or the Chinese may call you a smoke-ship and fire their guns at you, like they fired on the *Jardine*.'

'Yes,' agreed Tom, but he sounded preoccupied. Her words had reminded him of the latest news from China. There had been trouble at the Factories, then after the Factories blockade was over, the British had been expelled not only from Canton, but for a while from Macau as well. They had been obliged to take to the sea and lie low in the roads off Lintin and Hong Kong. It was no time to send a young girl. What was Dr Andrew thinking of? As if reading his thoughts, Amelia said, 'There have been troubles there, Papa says, and even talk of war. But those things are confined to the Factories and the menfolk. They will not affect Pearl or me. Besides, the troubles are probably over and done with by now and I would wait for ever if I waited for a time when there was no unrest anywhere, wouldn't I?' Again she looked at him with the expression he found irresistible. He turned away from her and lengthened his stride towards the Quay till she had to scurry to keep up with him.

'Do not be angry with me, Tom. I *have* to go, you know that. I told you years ago,' she panted, clinging to his arm. 'Do not make it harder for me, please?' Still he said nothing, but glared ahead of him with an expression she could not read. 'Please, Tom? I thought you would be happy for me,' she finished, in a small voice which pierced his heart.

He could not trust himself to speak until they were almost at his mother's door. Then he said, with quiet intensity, 'I will come one day, Amelia, *to fetch you home*.'

'Remember you will be at least four months at sea, my dear,' said Rachel, drawing Amelia nearer the fire. It was a raw day in early December, the days short, the nights long and cold. But in the Christies' rooms above the shipping office it was warm enough, with a good fire burning and the lamps already lit though it was barely afternoon. Through the unshuttered window one could see the bustle of the quayside, the lamplight from cabin or workshop piercing the general half-light of a laden sky.

'It will snow before the day's out,' said Tom absently and left them to their women's talk of clothes and medicines. Rachel was advising Amelia on the contents of her cabin trunk and there was no place for Tom, had he wished to stay. But Amelia's company was a stone on his heart since the announcement of her imminent departure, and except for the words he could not speak, he had nothing to say to her. He left without a word, closing the door behind him.

Rachel looked after him with concern, but Amelia was already talking of camomile, oil of citronella and the relative merits of cambric and lawn. Rachel pushed Tom's troubles aside and concentrated on the girl's travelling list.

'I am so lucky to have an understanding father,' said Amelia later when they paused to take tea and some of Rachel's oven scones. 'Not like poor India Abercrombie.' It was common knowledge that Fenton Abercrombie kept his daughter a prisoner 'to keep her away from the Christie boy'.

'Poor India,' said Rachel sadly. 'It seems so unfair.'

'Tom says Jamie is very angry,' ventured Amelia, not wishing to hurt Mrs Christie's feelings yet at the same time curious to hear the Christie side of things.

'Yes, poor boy. He believes Fenton considers him not good enough for India, but it is not that.'

'Then what is it, Mrs Christie? They are both young and healthy and well suited in so many ways. Besides,' she blushed prettily before adding in a soft voice, 'Tom says they love each other.'

'There is obviously some obstacle of which we are unaware,' said Rachel carefully. 'Now where had we got to on your list? Slippers, wasn't it?' But though she turned Amelia's thoughts into other channels, her own worried away at the problem of India and her son. Too many years of bitterness had separated the two families – but once, long ago, Jessica had been her friend and so had Fenton. She had thought the matter settled when she had met Fenton on India's behalf, after the girl had run away from school. She had explained to Fenton that there was no impediment and had thought that he believed her. She *knew* he did, but belief could not always conquer inclination. Fenton had been deeply hurt and the result was an antagonism so implacable that no amount of truth could shatter it. Nevertheless, she owed it to her son – and to poor India of whom she was fond – to do what she could towards their happiness.

When Amelia had gone, escorted once again by a silent Tom, Rachel took up pen and paper to write to Fenton Abercrombie. The letter took her several bleak hours and many drafts to compose, but eventually she was satisfied and sent it the following morning, by messenger, to Fenton Abercrombie's office.

She expected – and received – no answer.

'Be kind to them. Do not make them suffer because you have suffered. Forgive . . . Forget the past . . . and give them your blessing. They are young and in love. It is cruel to separate them for no reason . . .' The words of Rachel's letter sounded over and over in Fenton's mind though he tore the original to shreds and burnt it on the fire. They stayed with him all the way to Edinburgh and haunted his days there, till at last, with shame and relief, he confessed everything to Mary. And she spoke as Rachel had – in almost the same words. Forgive and forget. But Mary added another argument – 'Suppose you and I had been separated, and with greater reason? I could not have borne it.'

Nor I, thought Fenton, nor I . . . It was because of Jessica that Mary and he had met. And because of Jessica that he had forbidden young Christie and India to meet. 'For no reason,' Rachel had said. If only he could believe her. 'In your heart you do believe her,' Mary had told him. 'So for my sake, put aside your pride and forgive?'

She pleaded so prettily, his little son in her arms and both of them smiling, that in the end he had capitulated and as he did so, a great weight seemed to lift from him and he felt younger and happier than he had done for years.

'You are right, my sweet,' he said tenderly, kissing her forehead, then her little son's. 'Who am I to deny anyone such happiness as I have found with you?' Then, too soon, it was time to set out to Leith to catch the Aberdeen packet.

'Goodbye, my love, till you return.' She waved to him as she always did, from the upper window, and he saw her sweet lips frame the words, 'Take care.' Then she blew him a kiss, he smiled and made to catch it, then held his fingers to his lips in the private, loving ritual they had developed over the years.

He was singing as he turned the corner and as light-footed as a man half his age. He was going home to tell his daughter she could marry whoever she chose – even young Christie – and already he could see the joy that would illuminate her face. It would be as it had once been between them, years ago, before jealousy had eaten into his soul. She would forgive him and would be as happy with her Jamie as Fenton was with Mary. More so, for they would be legally married, whereas he and Mary . . . Fenton felt the old sadness creep over him, but this time he accepted it as part of his love. Mary was happy, he had made provision for her, and for his son. As long as Fenton lived, she would lack for nothing. It was second best perhaps, but bliss compared with the unthinkable alternative. Bliss, he reminded himself firmly and allowed the smile to return to his eyes.

The wind off the sea had a knife edge of ice, and the water's surface was rugged and grey. Fenton turned up the collar of his heavy overcoat and set his back to the wind as he waited with the rest to board the steamship *Brilliant* en route for Aberdeen. He had travelled on the

Brilliant often, preferring her to the *Jessica*, although the latter was a newer ship and, moreover, part-owned by his father. But the *Jessica* had unpleasant connotations, being named for his own wife, to commemorate the birth of his son Finlay, and though a faster, more comfortable and certainly more modern vessel, he always chose the older *Brilliant* when he could. Built in Greenock, she had been the first regular steam vessel on the Aberdeen–Leith route and after eighteen years of faithful service was still going strong.

So Fenton felt no unease when he embarked with the rest on that blustery December afternoon. It was 3 p.m. on Wednesday, December 12th, when the *Brilliant* left Leith for Aberdeen, and nightfall before the wind gathered strength enough to change from a chilling if blustery nuisance to a sea-lashing, rope-shredding, ship-plunging enemy. The passengers huddled below decks, those lucky enough to have cabins prostrate and groaning, those with none crowded into the saloon and clutching hand rail or each other for comfort and support while the ship lunged and rolled, the wind shrieked and the noise of the seas was deafening against the timbers. But throughout the buffeting storm the engines continued their steam-hissing, thudding power and in spite of all hazards the captain and crew wrestled to keep the ship on course for Aberdeen.

The heat from the engines was sickening below decks, and the violent lurching of the vessel more so, but those passengers who braved the howling winds to venture on deck in search of clean air were threatened with instant drowning as seas swept without warning across the bows or smacked down on the quarterdeck in a swirl of green and deadly waters.

Fenton, like most of them, was green-faced with fear and nausea. All his life he had been haunted by a recurrent dream in which his eyes were underwater, his mouth full of sea-bubbles, his limbs weightless. Now, he thrust the memory brutally aside and tried to think only of his daughter India and what he would say to her when he arrived home.

It would be morning when they reached the Quay. He would go straight to the Union Terrace house and, before he had even washed or attended to his toilet, he would call India and . . . No, first he would go to his dressing room as he always did, wash and shave, put on fresh linen. Then, when he was refreshed, he would order tea in his study, and send for her. She would come nervously, resentfully, hating him, but she would come. Then he would pour tea for them both and tell her. He could see her sweet face light up with happiness, hear her voice as she cried, 'Dear Papa, I do love you so.'

At the thought, Fenton almost forgot his fear – until he heard a shriek behind him in the lee of the wheel-house and saw a distraught woman with a child in her arms and two more clinging to her skirts, while a fourth slid helpless across the tipping deck towards him. Fenton snatched up the child and, clinging to the rail with one hand and the child with the other, fought his way back against the wind into the comparative shelter of the wheel-house.

'Thank you, sir,' gasped the woman, her eyes swimming tears, though whether from gratitude or the stinging wind Fenton could not tell.

'You'd best go below,' he said. 'The wind's gaining strength every minute.'

'But the heat's something terrible,' she moaned, 'and I'm that sick, wi' the stench.'

'Nevertheless, go below,' he said sternly. 'It is better to be sick than drowned – and you'll lose those children overboard if you stay up here. See, I will help you,' and he lifted two of the children down the steps to the saloon before holding out a hand to assist the woman.

'Maybe you're right, sir,' she groaned. 'But I wish to God we was in Aberdeen.'

So do I, echoed Fenton as the heat hit him, then the ship plunged and he forgot all else in the single-minded business of keeping his balance.

But as the night progressed the wind increased to gale force, to batter them relentlessly from the south-east, and furrow the sea with mast-high troughs of black water, crested with foam that was merely a sinister grey in the murk of that moonless night. The saloon was packed with helpless travellers, some too ill to do more than moan, others praying, others white-faced, wide-eyed and rigid with silent terror. Ropes were slung across the saloon and more on deck, to help the crew go about their necessary duties without fear of being swept overboard or dashed against the deck. And all the time the engineers kept the boilers fired and the engines turning. At least that gave them some control. Had they had only canvas, thought Fenton, they would have lost it hours ago, shredded to tatters in the wind. Sleep was out of the question and when the heat and the smell of terrified humanity became too strong, Fenton ventured back on deck, in spite of his fear, to brave the wind and the sea face to face.

There was something exhilarating, exciting, even beautiful about a storm at night. He found a spot near the quarterdeck, as sheltered as anywhere could be, and, twisting his arm firmly through a nearby rope for support, prepared to wait for dawn and a safe haven.

And at last, a little before five in the morning, the thin beam of the lighthouse on Girdleness became visible ahead of them. Home, at last. In another hour they would be rounding the headland and making for harbour. Another half-hour after that and they would be tying up in the calm waters of the inner basin. And a half-hour after that, he would be home, with his dear daughter whom he had wronged and who would happily forgive him.

He was still thinking of India when they rounded the headland at Girdleness, still seeing her laughing, loving face, when a huge wave struck the *Brilliant* amidships, washed over the ship in a solid wall of water and swept the captain from the quarterdeck into the sea. As the cry went up from the horrified crew, the same wave, unnoticed, snapped the deck rope and carried Fenton Abercrombie after him. Only the woman with the children, peering through a spattered porthole, saw him briefly struggle and disappear, but though she shrieked hysterically 'Man overboard' until someone slapped her, there was nothing anyone could do for Fenton or the captain, whom they thought the woman meant.

Captain Wade was drowned instantly, and, after the first terrified struggle, Fenton too gave up the fight and let the water carry him where it willed. He felt strangely calm as the green foam closed over him. It was, after all, inevitable – and only a dream.

The *Brilliant*, captainless, fought for her life as she was overtaken by a succession of heavy seas which carried her, helpless, over the harbour bar to smack into the south side of the north pier. The engineers deserted the engine, steam escaped rapidly, and what with the darkness of the morning, the roar of the waves and the general confusion, no one knew where the vessel lay.

Then she hove up on the supports of the pier and keeled towards the north, to settle finally against the pier itself in a position which enabled passengers and crew to scramble ashore from the fore quarterdeck with comparative ease. One poor fellow broke a leg, but there was no other accident. Even the mother of four, still telling anyone who would listen about the 'poor gentleman', managed to convey all her children safely ashore.

But the crew had escaped so precipitately that the fires were left still lit. The boilers, having been emptied of water by the buffeting, overheated and set the bulkhead alight until the fire spread to the whole vessel. It was 9 o'clock before the fire engine arrived, in company with a party of soldiers from the 91st Regiment, sent to keep order. But in spite of all their efforts, the *Brilliant* burnt to the waterline, and the fire was extinguished only by the flowing tide which broke up what remained and scattered the wreckage piecemeal up and down the coast.

A blackened spar was beached two days later, above Balmedie, with an assortment of other flotsam – and the body of Fenton Abercrombie.

The funeral party had dispersed, the guests gone home and the married members of the family returned to their respective houses when old George Abercrombie took Jessica aside and said, 'There's something I'd best tell you, lass. In private.'

Wearily Jessica led her father-in-law into Fenton's study and closed the door behind them. The room was still full of Fenton's presence. His book lay open on the small table beside his chair, his pipe was in its accustomed place on the mantelshelf, his pens in a neat row on his desk top. Jessica felt a huge sadness well up inside her – grief for the idealistic boy she had once known, for the worshipping bridegroom she had married, and a different grief for the long, wasted years of acrimony and resentment which lay between that bridegroom and the sea-tossed corpse which the waves had finally returned to her. Fenton had always been afraid of drowning, she remembered. Poor sod. She tried to retrieve her usual scathing indifference and failed. Instead, she wanted only to weep. For in spite of everything, she grieved for her husband with genuine sorrow and, despite all the bickering years, she missed him. There was an emptiness in the house without him, and a chill at her back.

But her anger and resentment came flooding back as she realised what her father-in-law was saying.

'Fenton made provision for them, of course. An annuity for Mary during her lifetime and a sum in trust for her son. The house is also hers so she'll not be destitute, poor lass, and Fenton has appointed a lawyer to take responsibility should Mary die before the child comes of age. He did all he could to fulfil his responsibilities and to spare us trouble, but I'd best go myself to see her just the same and tell her I'll see them right. She'll be grieving, likely, and he is my own wee grandson, after all.'

'Grandson? That whore's bastard?' cried Jessica. 'And what about Finlay? Isn't he grandson enough for you, and *legitimate?* You're no better than he was, wi' your hypocrisy and your whores. And to think Fenton had the nerve to accuse *me* of adultery! Me, who was pure as the driven snow compared to him. *I* didn't keep a mistress in Edinburgh, *I* didn't say I was on business when I was in a whore's bed, *I* didn't spawn bastards when I couldn't find time for my own legitimate children. Oh no. But I was wicked. I was beyond forgiveness. I was scorned and punished and had my nose rubbed in it over and over – and for what? To be cast aside for an Edinburgh whore and an Edinburgh whore's brat. And he had the nerve to tell Indy she couldna have the Christie boy. Well I'll put that right for a start.'

'Not so hasty, Jessica lass,' said Abercrombie, much troubled, both by the extent of his son's commitment to Mary Ballantyne and by Jessica's reaction. 'You're upset, I know, and . . .'

'*Upset?* And what wife wouldna be upset, tell me that,' she demanded. 'It's nae right. And if they lawyers knew what they were at, they'd see that whore didn't get a penny o' Fenton's money, nor his brat neither. What about our Finlay? The money should be his. I've a good mind to see a lawyer myself and dispute it.'

'I wouldn't if I were you,' said Abercrombie wearily. 'There's money enough for Finlay and all o' you. The woman has a claim, after all, and it's not the wee laddie's fault he's been orphaned. But it's a sad business . . .' He turned away and it took a moment for Jessica to realise the old man was crying. She had forgotten Fenton was his son, forgotten that he would be grieving. The anger drained away. She felt awkward and ashamed and weary with an overwhelming grief.

'I am sorry, Da,' she said, putting her arm around his shoulder. 'He didna deserve to die like that,' and suddenly, unexpectedly, Jessica found she too was crying.

'But you're right about one thing, Jessie,' said the old man later, when he had dried his eyes and hers on a large linen handkerchief. 'You'd best tell me the truth o' that old business between you and James Christie, so we can decide what is to be done about Indy. She's taken it hard.'

It was then that they heard a stirring from the window recess, the heavy curtains parted and India's ashen, tear-streaked face looked out at them through the gap.

'I heard what you said. I couldn't help it.'

There was a long moment's silence in which the ghost of Fenton seemed to fill the room and overshadow them all. Then India said, in a trembling voice, 'Is it true Papa had a mistress, and another child, in Edinburgh?'

'Aye lass, but . . .' Abercrombie spread his hands in a gesture of helpless acceptance. Then, seeing her face, he added gently, 'But it doesna mean he loved you any the less, Indy.'

'Why did Papa accuse you of adultery, Mamma?' said India quietly, looking her mother in the eye.

To her own consternation Jessica blushed, a deep

unlovely purple mottled with red. 'It was a mistake, lass. Years before you were born.'

'Best tell her,' said Abercrombie wearily. 'She's old enough and she's heard most of it anyway.'

'Your father thought,' began Jessica uncomfortably, then with defiance, 'your father found out I'd once had a bit of a fling wi' James Christie. Before he was married,' she went on hastily. 'When Augusta was a baby. Your father thought there was more to it than there was, and he mistrusted me after. In fact, he got himself into such a state o' jealous suspicion he imagined you children were not his . . .'

India gasped in horror and clasped a hand over her mouth.

'. . . That's why he went on so about you and young Christie, but there was no need. You were Fenton's right enough, and I'll swear it on any Bible – and so would James Christie if required. So you see, India, now your father's dead, you can do as you please. Marry the Christie lad if you choose. There's no impediment. None at all. And I dinna care what ye do.'

India did not speak. She stood rigid, colourless, her red-rimmed eyes staring at first her mother, then her grandfather.

'Aye, lass,' sighed old Abercrombie, seeing the question in her eyes. 'Your ma's right. That was the reason, but seemingly it was nought but blind jealousy on Fenton's part, so take her word for it – and be happy.'

With a strangled gasp, India pushed past them and ran from the room. When her mother went to India's bedroom some time later, she found the door locked and when she put her ear to the crack, she heard the muffled sound of uncontrollable weeping.

* * *

India had wept ever since the news of her father's death. She had not realised till then how much she loved him, or that her hatred had been merely a different version of that love. She had vowed never to forgive him for coming between her and Jamie and now she would never have the opportunity to do so. Poor Papa. She had been so cruel to him, so unforgiving, and he had been so lonely. She remembered him reading at mealtimes, in a solitary world of his own, remembered him in his study, spectacles on nose, looking up from a book if she entered the room, remembered him years ago taking India and her sisters to the fireworks in the Castlegate. She even thought she could remember him bouncing her, as a tiny child, on his knee . . . And now he was drowned. At home they had carried on exactly as usual, laughing, gossiping, eating and drinking, while all the time Papa was rolling and turning, alone in that icy sea, dead.

They had not known he was travelling on the *Brilliant* and it was not until late in the afternoon, after some woman had insisted that a gentleman had been washed overboard, that inquiries had been made and the name of Fenton Abercrombie put forward. 'A kind and courteous gentleman,' the woman had said and had given a description which fitted Fenton, but they had not known for certain until his body was washed up on the shore.

The funeral had been torment, the hushed voices and sympathetic murmurings of the guests an insupportable burden on her already tremulous control, and at the first opportunity India had fled to the only sanctuary she knew – her father's study.

But once there, the grief had been worse. She had wandered blindly about the room, touching his pipe, his chair, his books, until finally, weary with grief, she had curled up on the window seat behind the curtain to cool her cheeks against the cold glass and to gaze at the darkened heavens where somewhere, perhaps, her father was looking down at her, loving her.

She had been almost asleep when the voices had aroused her, then, as she listened, she had become immobilised with shock and it was too late to move. Her father's 'mistress', her mother's 'adultery' – the known world fell in splinters about her feet until the mention of her own name drew her out of darkness into the glare of cruel light.

Her mother had said there was no longer any impediment to India's marriage. *No impediment* when on her own admission Jessica had had 'a bit of a fling' with Jamie's father! And her own father had not known whether his children were his own. Jessica swore that Fenton was their father, but suppose . . . the very thought raised the hairs on the back of India's neck. Suppose it was James Christie who was? That would make India and Jamie step-brother and sister. No wonder her father had forbidden it! Oh God in heaven, no wonder! But Jessica had offered to swear on the Bible and even her grandfather had agreed that Fenton had imagined things, out of jealousy and suspicion. Nevertheless, India owed it to her father to respect his fears, however ill-placed, and to obey his wishes, even after death. Especially after death. But oh Jamie, Jamie, she mourned. I love you so terribly. The thought of him was anguish and pleasure, terror and melting delight – until the spectre of her own mother and Jamie's father loomed dark and fearful to obliterate all other thoughts in a shameful, writhing pantomime of illicit coupling. She stopped her ears, closed tight her eyes, bit hard on her lips till the blood ran, but she could not blot out the picture from her mind – and the worst of it was she felt an answering excitement deep in her loins and knew she wanted Jamie in the same way. And the temptation had been offered her by her own mother, as i were, on a funeral plate. 'Marry the Christie lad if you choose. There's no impediment.'

But there was. Her poor, drowned Papa was the greatest impediment of all. So India wept and prayed and tossed in torment while the arguments whirled in her mind like a relentless blizzard and the pictures loomed and changed and formed again till at last the torment stilled and she knew exactly what she must do. Then, drained of all emotion, she slept.

She awoke to the sound of Mairi sniffing, as she carried the heavy water jug to the wash-stand. Mairi had known Fenton Abercrombie since he was a child and had taken his death hard.

'Poor Master Fenton,' she had sobbed, over and over, and not even Jessica had had the heart to tell her to compose herself. But Fenton had mentioned her specially in his will, which had brought some comfort.

'Here you are, Miss Indy,' she said now, 'though whether you'll have the heart to get up at all with your poor father . . .' She gulped and hurried from the room before India could say 'Thank you' or even begin to comfort her.

India washed, dressed except for her gown, and, with a fine wool peignoir wrapped tight over her undergarments, sat down at her writing desk under the window. She lit her lamp the better to see, took pen and a clean sheet of paper and wrote, in careful copperplate script, *Dear Jamie, Since my father's death I find I cannot marry you. I wish you well on your voyage to China*. She signed it simply *India Abercrombie*, folded and sealed it, and despatched it by messenger to the Christie house. That done, she bathed her swollen eyes once more, brushed her hair into as severe a knot as it would succumb to, put on her black woollen mourning dress and went downstairs to face the first day of her new, bereaved life.

iii

Three months later, the *White Bird*, as Maitland had called his long-awaited tea-ship, sailed for China with Amelia Noble as passenger and young Jamie Christie as first mate. His father was to have captained the ship, but two days before *White Bird* was due to sail, James Christie slipped on a patch of oil on the Quay and broke his leg. Some said it was fate, others, more malicious, that Alex Christie's hand had spilled the oil, but whatever the reason James Christie's leg had snapped as it had snapped years ago, in that shipwreck off Riga, and Alex Christie, fulfilling his life's ambition, was allowed to take his place.

'Do not worry,' soothed Rachel as James Christie fumed and protested from the confines of his bed where Andrew Noble had ordered him to spend the next few weeks 'unless you want to be permanently crippled and never set foot on a deck again. Alex is a good and competent captain. Trust him, James, as I do. He'll manage fine. Besides, there'll be Jamie to see him right.'

Rachel's face saddened at the thought of Jamie. She did not know what had gone wrong between India and her son, but whatever it was, it had made both of them miserable. It was understandable that India should mourn her father, and Jamie was good-hearted enough to know that. But you would have thought such a loss would have made a girl turn to her lover for comfort. Instead, it seemed that India had severed all connections. Rachel did not understand it.

But perhaps when the mourning time was over, and the *White Bird* returned from China, all would be well? Meanwhile India looked increasingly dejected and only the prospect of China kept Jamie remotely cheerful. Kirsty was quiet, too, though since James's accident and his sudden promotion, Alex had been transformed. He exuded enthusiasm, confidence, energy, hope and enough plain cheerfulness for all of them. It was clear that he enjoyed the prospect of a year away from Aberdeen – and equally clear that Kirsty did not.

Rachel felt guilty on Kirsty's account, and guilty on her own for welcoming James's accident which meant she could keep him at home instead of losing him to China, with Jamie. She would miss Jamie terribly, but at least she had her husband, and Tom.

Tom, like Jamie, had completed his apprenticeship and was back in the Christie fleet. Fortunately so, for it meant he could shoulder his father's responsibilities in the Company while James's leg healed.

But Tom, too, had his sorrows. Rachel saw the pain in his face on that last day as they assembled on the Quay to speed *White Bird* on her way. She saw the way his eyes followed Amelia Noble as she went aboard with her hat box and portmanteau and her neat cabin trunk, saw his blush as Amelia kissed him goodbye, saw his expression as Jamie took Amelia's hand to steady her as she stepped aboard. And Rachel felt guilty on that account, too.

For when news of James Christie's accident spread, Andrew Noble had come to see her. It seemed he had made it a condition of Amelia's travel that she go under James's protection and was planning to prevent her now that James was confined to bed. But Rachel had reassured him, had promised Andrew that Alex Christie would be as responsible a guardian as James, and that Amelia would be in safe keeping. Alex himself had promised the same. Reluctantly, Andrew had withdrawn his opposition and given his consent.

Again Rachel looked at Amelia where she stood on deck, beside Jamie. The girl was radiant with excitement and purpose and a sort of shining hope which held no regret and which was apparently infectious, for already Jamie, beside her, looked less disconsolate . . . Remembering Tom and poor India Abercrombie, Rachel's doubts increased. Four months was a long time to be at sea together.

India Abercombie saw them too. She had not meant to come, but in the event had not been able to stay away, though she stood well back from the gangplank in a group of curious spectators and made no attempt to go close. She was close enough, however, to see Jamie's expression as he handed Amelia aboard, and to see Amelia's sweet, answering smile.

'No matter,' she told herself firmly. 'If they fall in love on the voyage, it will be only for the best. Jamie means nothing to me any more. I have renounced him, for ever.'

Then the gangplank was drawn up, the last ropes loosed from the restraining bollards, and the Quay rang with the clamour of final farewell.

'Give my love to Pearl,' called Rachel, through her tears.

'We will,' cried Amelia and Jamie together. Then *White Bird* slipped smoothly into the channel where the ebb tide carried her straight and true towards the harbour entrance and the open sea.

Part IV

Macau 1840

i

From the beginning 1839 had been a troubled year in the Canton river. The Chinese ban on the opium trade which they had till now openly condoned blocked the supply of silver with which to buy tea and left the business community frustrated and uncertain of Chinese intent. Then the hanging of a man in the Factory square, for opium dealing, added insult to frustration and the foreign flags were universally struck in protest. The tea trade was affected. The opium ships, loaded with the new crop from Bombay, hung around Lantau, well away from Canton, and were steadily joined by more and more. The Chinese authorities grew angrier. Lin, the new special High Commissioner at Canton, ordered the confiscation of all opium and forbade the foreigners to leave Canton. Elliot, the British Chief Superintendent, eventually agreed, but not before the Factories had been cut off and the foreign community imprisoned in a virtual blockade. It was April before the surrender and destruction of the 20,000 chests was under way, and May before the blockade was lifted and the foreigners could leave. This they did, with their entire belongings, including a life-size portrait of King George IV and forty dozen bottles of wine, and the Chinese began to wonder if, when the new tea season opened, any of them would return.

The confiscated opium, however, was worth an estimated £2½ million. It was a logical step to require compensation from those who had confiscated it. Britain could not foot the bill so Peking must pay – or be made to pay. Talk moved inexorably to the possibility of war.

But the opium habit was too deeply rooted to be destroyed by one act of confiscation, the profits too good for the traders to be long deterred. Surreptitiously the opium traffic picked up again, with Manila now as a clearing house, and the dealers using codes and stealth.

Then a fracas between drunken British sailors and Chinese villagers left a villager dead. Lin cut off all supplies to the British, by land or sea, and expelled them from Macau, while the war junks gathered. Two hundred and fifty British decamped into eighteen merchantmen and left for the barren little island refuge of Hong Kong, where at least there was a sheltered harbour: the typhoon season was imminent. There were skirmishes with war junks, but nothing serious – how could it be when every day reports confirmed that the Chinese soldiers were armed with bows and arrows, pikes, matchlocks and even halberds! The balance of numbers might be overwhelmingly on the Chinese side, but the balance of weaponry was ludicrously unequal, if not downright unfair. And the British gunboats were gathering.

The British traders still refused to sign Lin's new 'bond' which allowed any ship entering the river and found to contain opium to be confiscated and the smugglers executed. They did not trust the Chinese not to make mistakes, muddle names, seize the wrong ships or people. So legitimate trade remained at a standstill, except for the Americans. They accepted the 'bond' and did a steady business in trans-shipping up and down the river. Meanwhile, Elliot continued patiently to negotiate some sort of permit which would allow normal trade to resume – until a British ship signed the bond and ruined their collective bargaining power. War became inevitable – when the ships and forces arrived from Britain to fight it. But with correspondence taking four months or more each way between London and China such things could not be hurried. In London, the China lobby presented their case, the anti-opium lobby theirs, while the Treasury quietly considered theirs, with that £2½ million opium debt high on the list. By November secret instructions had gone out for war with China, but it was mid-February 1840 before Elliot in Macau heard the news, and then in secret – with orders to keep it so. No one wanted the new season's tea trading to be disrupted.

For in spite of all antagonisms, the trade of 1839–40 was much as usual, though all trans-shipped via American vessels carrying cotton, rattan and English cloth to Whampoa and returning with teas, silks and tubs of sugar candy.

While the London *Times* announced 'War declared on China', the British community in the Canton river continued to buy and sell, if not as usual, as near usual as possible in the circumstances. And as usual, when the trading was over, they removed to Macau. Then in June the Chinese, made angry no doubt by rumours of approaching enemy ships, attacked the anchored fleet with fire-boats – they did little harm, but it was declaration enough. That same night, the first of the British invasion fleet arrived. By the end of June they had blockaded the waterways to Canton.

Pearl was dismayed. The Christie ship was on her way to buy tea and now the river was blocked, Canton cut off. There would be no tea trading till the war was over – if then. Everyone knew the British Commissioner wanted more free ports than Canton – and everyone knew the Chinese would resist the foreign devils till the last. So Pearl worried, on the Christies' behalf more than her own, for by now she was used to living with the threat of war.

Duncan Greig, however, was elated. 'Captain Elliot plans to move straight on to Chusan and Peking. He has asked for skippers who know the China coast,' he told Pearl. 'Jardine's have volunteered me. It'll be a change from the "greys" and "chintzes" but I'll maybe manage to combine a bit of both.' 'Whites', 'greys' and 'chintzes' were the code names for types of opium. 'So pack your bags, lass. We leave today.'

'We?' Pearl could not keep the dismay from her voice. She had heard no more from Aberdeen since Rachel's letter, written in February, which had told her that *White Bird* was launched and undergoing the first sea trials. But Pearl believed Rachel's written word: 'She will sail by April without fail.' Rachel had added the astonishing news that Amelia would be a passenger. Amelia herself had written and confirmed it.

Ever since that letter's arrival Pearl had counted the days until she could begin to scan the eastern approaches for the azure pennant of the Christie ship. Then, as the ship drew closer, she would be able to make out the green and silver mermaid motif and the silver 'C' in the north-west corner. Closer still and she would see Amelia's dear face, with Uncle James beside her, and her cousin Jamie. He would be a man now, not the gangling boy she had said goodbye to five years ago. They would have five years' news to talk about, five years' affections to renew. Pearl could scarcely contain the excitement which filled every waking moment.

But suppose something should go wrong? Suppose there were storms? Pirates? Shipwrecks? Or simply Chinese war junks on the hunt for foreign heads? Her uncles did not know what was happening here and it was too late to warn them. In vain Duncan told her impatiently that Christie was a shrewd and competent master, that merchantmen were not warships and therefore safe. Pearl would not cease worrying till *White Bird* was anchored safe in Macau roads – and probably not even then, for what of the war? They said the Chinese could not hold out a week against the British weaponry, but China was vast, its population inexhaustible, its hatred of the *fan kuei*, or foreign devils, stronger than any weapon. So she hid her anxiety as best she could, in stories.

She told little Robin over and over about his Christie relatives and his pretty young aunt, of the Christie shipyard and the tea-ship they had built, 'especially to come and visit us in'; of the harbour, the house on Trinity Quay, the office; and the memories no longer brought the familiar ache to her heart. Instead, she felt jubilant, every sense alert, and happier than she had felt for fully five years. For was not the Christie ship at last on her way? How could Duncan expect her to leave Macau at such a time?

'But Duncan, suppose the Christie ship arrives and I am not here?'

'They'll not be here for weeks yet,' he said and added deliberately, for Pearl set too much store on this visit, 'if at all. They'll likely hear in Bombay of the Expedition and decide to trade elsewhere.'

'No! They're coming *here!* I must meet them, Duncan,' she finished, pleading.

'Aye, well,' frowned Greig. But he added, more kindly, 'We'll likely be back here afore they arrive and I want you and the boy with me. I'm not happy about these Chinese devils. They're angry because we've blocked their river and there's a rumour they've put a price on English ships – and that means Scots too. Five thousand Spanish dollars for a man-o'-war's captain, down the scale to $100 for a common soldier, sailor or merchant taken alive, and $20 for a head.'

Pearl shuddered. She had seen enough to know that the Chinese would not scruple at claiming that $20, roughly equivalent to a mere £5.

'No mention of women, of course, but you can be sure those thieving devils will try anything to injure the *fan kuei* and with the fleet and most of the soldiers on their way to Peking and out of reach, who's to say they won't come over the Barrier and plunder Macau for their blood money? So Christie ship or not, you will come with me, lass, and the boy too. I'll not risk either of your heads by leaving you here. Besides,' he added, 'if the ship does come before we get back, they'll hear where you are and they'll wait. Leastways, till the tea season's here and that's months ahead.'

'Perhaps you are right.' But she sounded so dejected that Greig added, more brutally than he intended, 'No "perhaps", woman. They've murdered one poor devil of a missionary already, and captured another. When the news gets out, Macau will empty soon enough. So you and Robin come with me – unless you want your heads sold.'

Pearl blanched. 'Do you really think . . .?'

'Aye. I do.'

'Then I will tell Ah May to pack at once.' Had it been only herself, she would have braved the danger, but not with little Robin. He must be shielded at all costs. Then she remembered. 'Will the seas be rough? I am sick enough as it is.' Pearl was pregnant again and beginning to show the strain. She looked sallow, wan, and, when caught unawares, almost haggard.

Duncan looked at her with fleeting pity. 'I'm sorry, lass. I'd forgotten. But you'll be no worse off aboard ship.'

He did not need to add, and no less likely to bear a healthy child. Pearl remembered him saying of his first wife, with a note of personal outrage in his voice, 'I thought her strong.' He had thought Pearl strong, too. And she had been, until he and the climate between them had drained her of vitality. For a while she had fought against both of them, then her little daughter had died of a virulent fever within a week of birth and she herself had taken months to recover. A miscarriage had not helped. Even so Pearl might have regained her usual equanimity in time if she could have stifled the memory of Duncan's tales, years ago in Aberdeen, of female infanticide, and the nagging doubt that, had the child been a boy, she would have lived. But when she said as much to Duncan he roared, 'Ah May? Murder my daughter? She wouldn't dare!' He had looked at Pearl strangely and for a while was particularly solicitous and kind. 'You must not get ideas into your head, lass. It's not good in this climate. Things get distorted. Out of proportion. You are weak and sad, that's all. When your strength is back, you'll see things differently. And wee Robin thrives.'

Robin was the joy of their lives, and of Ah May's. Remembering, Pearl said now, in a carefully expressionless voice, 'Will Ah May come with us?'

'No.' Ah May had disgraced herself by disappearing the previous summer, at the evacuation of Macau, and when the Europeans returned and the servants crept out of their hiding places, only her devotion to Robin had won Ah May's restitution. Now Pearl was delighted to hear the woman was to be left behind. After five years she felt no closer to her, no more at ease, had no clearer understanding of thought or language, and no less mistrust.

'Good,' said Pearl and secretly smiled. 'It will be just like old times, Duncan, to be aboard ship with you again.' And, she added silently, I will have my son to myself.

But in the weeks that followed, Robin spent more time with his father than with Pearl. At first, she was afraid the child would fall overboard or be struck by a swinging boom, but she need not have worried. Duncan took good care of him, strapping him into a little rope harness and tethering him neatly at his father's side. Robin loved it. He was learning to be a sailor, like his father, and only hunger or exhaustion could prise him from his father's side. Then he would clamber on to Pearl's knee, curl up neat and small, thumb in mouth, and close his eyes. Pearl loved those moments, with her darling son curled against her breast, his hair petal-soft under her lips, his small face angelic in sleep. But, surprisingly, she enjoyed other moments too.

After the first disappointment of leaving Macau before the Christie ship's arrival, her natural optimism asserted itself. She had spoken at length to her friend, Mrs Morton, the missionary's wife, then to Ah May, giving instructions for her family's entertainment should she not be there to greet them. She had written a welcoming letter, made Duncan do the same, and left them with Mrs Morton to deliver. There was no more she could have done. She allowed herself to relax and look about her.

The *Corbie* was larger than the *Jardine*, and had been used to carry stores from Madras to Tinghai until hired to help Elliot's fleet in surveying the area. She had been armed with six carronades and manned with a squad of marines and a navy lieutenant, but Greig remained the master and Pearl, as the captain's wife, received both courtesy and friendship. Their quarters were small and airless compared with the house in Macau, but once at sea the breezes soon freshened and made the sun's heat tolerable. One of the seamen rigged an awning aft so she could sit in the shade and watch the distant shore slip by as they made their way northwards, following the line of the China coast.

Pearl would sit, contented, under her awning, the sea a dancing mirror of turquoise and silver, the land a misted heat haze of dove-grey mountains and pearl-grey shore. They kept close to the shore, though not too close for safety, following the coastline northwards towards the island of Chusan where the British forces were already established.

It was a tranquil voyage in spite of the martial circumstances, though these were brought sharply home when some four days out of Canton, they approached the island of Amoy. The wide, shallow bay looked peaceful enough. The still, green sea was dotted with little islands and sampans and here and there a larger junk. Bright painted eyes dazzled from the prows. Sunlight flashed in tiny stars from the gently stirring water.

But when Greig was tempted to sail closer, perhaps with an eye to private trading, everything changed. The lookout called from the shrouds that the Chinese devils were dragging guns into a small fort on the promontory, that there were more guns in the harbour and people collecting, some apparently soldiers.

'Are they, by God,' growled Duncan, and Lieutenant Sharp ordered the men to the carronades, but prudence prevailed. Their supply of shot was limited, their mission explicit. They were to proceed north with all speed and avoid confrontation. Regretfully, Greig altered course and they sailed west around Amoy, then onwards towards Chusan.

But the incident was an unwelcome reminder of the so-called 'war' and revived all Pearl's anxieties. She remembered the blood money, the threats, and held her sleeping son tighter. At least here, at sea, they were out of reach of those hostile hordes she had seen gathering on Amoy's shore, and of those other crowds, beyond the Barrier in Macau. But every peak and bay they passed carried her further away from Maitland's *White Bird*.

She thought of the Christie ship with mingled joy and dread. She longed to see them with all her heart, yet at the same time she feared for them. They were innocent of the ways of China, naive as she had been and trusting. They expected the difficulties of trading in a foreign port, perhaps, but not this. They should be at Bombay by now. At least there they would be warned and put on guard. But $100 for a sea captain! And if the *fan kuei* resisted, then $20 for a head. Even £5 was a fortune to a man with nothing.

'Please God, keep them safe,' she prayed over and over. 'Please God protect us all,' she prayed more fervently as they negotiated the scattered rocks and islands that choked the approaches to Chusan. Off Buffalo's Nose they paused to take fresh soundings – there were rocks everywhere and the currents were strong – before nosing their careful way into harbour. But at Chusan she repeated the prayer with extra vehemence. For when Greig saw the state of things he instantly took the ship into deeper water and forbade the crew to go ashore.

'Dysentery,' he told her bitterly. 'Half the Cameronians down with it already. What a stinking, gut-rotting humiliation for a fine body of men.' When Pearl asked to go ashore and help, he forbade it. 'The harm's done, lass, and no amount of help can undo it. They drank foul water, in a foul and stinking land.'

But Chusan in the evening light was beautiful. A large island in an archipelago of hundreds, some no more than pinnacles of jutting rock, it lay just off the mainland opposite a long finger of high land known as Keeto Point, a hundred miles or so south of the Yangtze river. The chief town was Tinghai, in whose harbour they lay. Hills, temples, straggling villages, lush greenery and dazzling light; the bright reds, greens and golds of temple carvings, and, above the town and incongruous in the oriental setting, the fluttering colours of the British expedition.

Somewhere in the hills a temple gong sounded clear across the tranquil water, bats swooped silently in the evening shadows and there was a scent of flowers in the air. Greig, however, shattered any illusions of peace.

'It's hell in the town,' he reported. 'Stinking open sewers, swimming with ordure and that brutalising poison they call *samshu*. The officers smashed every jar, but the men got at it just the same. Poor sods. It's likely the last enjoyment many of them will have. Oh, there's mandarin houses elegant enough, with little gardens and carved doors; silks too and ornaments if the looters haven't got there first. But for the most part it's a squalid, godless place. And thanks to that fool who holed the seventy-four, the fleet's stuck there till the vessel's repaired. That'll mean careening and several weeks of work.' The *Melville* had struck bottom in the approach to harbour and narrowly escaped foundering.

It was swelteringly hot. The expedition's stores were rancid or rotten, the water foul. Mosquitoes swarmed in whining clouds over swamp land and flooded rice fields. Soldiers, digging the hillside to make a fort, unearthed scores of coffins whose rotting contents added to the foulness of the air. The natives were surly and hostile, thieving and finally violent. A Chinese *comprador* working for the *fan kuei* was kidnapped in broad daylight and could not be found. Greig kept a tight rein on his crew, but some contact with the shore was inevitable and no prohibition could keep out the flies. One by one, the crew fell ill and Pearl's anxiety for Robin grew unbearable. For herself it did not matter, or for Duncan who was strong, but for little Robin, barely four years old and vulnerable, a fever could be fatal. And, as if they knew the dwindling strength of the enemy, the Chinese grew more daring. They kidnapped a captain of the Madras artillery out walking with his Indian servant, and smuggled him in irons to the mainland, to prison. Next, who knew what they would do?

The idea of that blood money beat louder and louder in Pearl's head – one hundred Spanish dollars for a sea captain. Suppose they took Duncan next? Or, far away off Macau, Uncle James?

So it was with a sense of relief that she heard the news that the *Corbie* was to put to sea at last. Greig was to take his ship north with three other vessels, to survey the lower reaches of the Yangtze river.

Thank God, thought Pearl as they weighed anchor and pulled away from that hated shore. She knew there were hazards still to be faced at sea, submerged rocks, storms, even enemy junks, but at least at sea there was freedom and clean air. At sea there was not the sense of enemy eyes watching from paddy-fields or temple, not the ever present threat of alien Chinese. The sea was clean and free. The sea was theirs.

Yet it was the sea that betrayed them.

The channel between Chusan and the mainland was familiar now and presented no problems. Duncan took the helm, and, his breakfast over, wee Robin asked to take his place beside his father and 'steer the ship'. Smiling, Pearl slipped on his little rope harness and tied him securely to the rail. She kissed him lightly on the top of the head. 'Who's my fine wee captain?' she said and he answered proudly, 'Me.' Pearl looked up, caught Duncan's eye and saw the pride in his face before he could conceal it with his usual brusque frown. She smiled and for once he allowed himself an answering grin.

'Aye,' he conceded. 'He'll make a fine captain one day. Now away with you, woman, and leave the men to their work.'

That picture of father and son, side by side at the helm, one grizzled, scarred, middle-aged, the other small and sturdy, dressed in a diminutive copy of his father's nankeen breeks and short coat, but with the unblemished bloom of babyhood still on his skin, was to stay with her a lifetime. That and the sea's spray and the wind's song as the ship sped northwards under a blue sky, on a bluer sea.

Till she struck a submerged sand bar where no sand bar should have been, swung broadside to the tide and in the same instant keeled over with a crash that snapped the mainmast, stove the hull and flooded the decks with swirling, cloying water.

'*Robin!*' screamed Pearl before the water closed over her. Not cold, she thought with momentary wonder as she sank and rose again, but warm like milk. Then she was screaming '*Robin!*' over and over and fighting to gain a hold on the slippery, tipping surface of the deck while the water dragged her under every time she fought clear, filling her ears and eyes and mouth with bitter, relentless waves. She surfaced once to see the crippled *Corbie* twenty feet away and fought with all her strength against the dragging current, to reach the ship again and the wheelhouse and the rope where little Robin was tied. Tied! And the *Corbie* was already on her side, half under water, and sinking fast.

'*Robin!*' she screamed again in anguish and her mouth filled with choking foam as her head went under and surfaced again and her hands clawed helplessly at that treacherous water while the weight of her saturated clothing pulled her inexorably down . . . Then a hand struck her face, an arm clamped round her throat from behind, and someone was dragging her backwards into darkness . . .

She woke to find herself in a jolly boat with the Lieutenant, the chief mate and three of the crew. Someone had rigged a piece of cloth over her head, to protect her from the sun, and when she opened her eyes, the glare from the empty sea burned them. But she opened them again nevertheless and made to struggle to her feet.

'Best keep still, Mrs Greig,' said the Lieutenant wearily. 'Or you will capsize the boat. We're helpless enough as it is.'

'Robin?' she managed, her lips dry, her voice a croak, her eyes two pools of dread. The Lieutenant bit his lip and looked away.

'My husband?' He shook his head, then managed, 'I am sorry, Mrs Greig. One of the seamen saw him with wee Robin in his arms, the lad was clinging to him, the man said, then both of them disappeared, with the rest. Perhaps . . .' but seeing her face, he stopped. What was the use of empty speculation? Nothing and no one could survive in the sort of currents which were still snatching at the jolly boat and sending it racing this way and that, in spite of the oarsmen's efforts.

'They are safe,' said Pearl over and over inside her head. 'The Chinese cannot claim their $20 now. Duncan and Robin are together, safe, where the enemy can never get them. Duncan will look after my little boy. He loves him as I do, though he pretends to feel nothing. They are safe together, somewhere far away . . . Not lost, but *safe*.'

She clung to the word as a talisman in the days that followed, dry, burning days of drought and fire, of blazing sun and tossing, turbulent nights. No land was visible, no island, not even a pinnacle of rock. Only endless sea. Like a great, green cradle, rocking, thought Pearl on the morning of the third day, or was it the fourth? Only sometimes it is not green but blue. Stars danced under her eyelids, her skin burnt hot to the touch, her lips were cracked and sore, her tongue swollen. There had been water in the jolly boat and dry biscuit, but both were gone. So, she noticed, was one of the men. He must have died and gone overboard while she slept. He, too, was safe now. Safe . . . She closed her eyes and felt the sea's motion through the thin boards of the little boat, rocking, rocking, like a child's cradle.

It was then that she remembered. Her hands moved to her womb, still hard and firm, still nurturing her growing child. Duncan's child. Robin's little brother or sister. The numb inertia which had crept through her with grief and despair scattered and dispersed under the small light of hope. She had lost her husband, but she carried his seed. The child in her womb was all that bound her to those two drowned souls and she would fight to keep it and to give it birth. Let sea and sun and China try to stop her.

They must sight land or shipping soon. Then she would return to Macau, to await the Christie ship. In the turmoil of the past days she had quite forgotten *White Bird*. Now she thought of the ship as a guiding light, a lode star which she must keep in sight always, and strive to reach. There, in the Christie ship, her pain would ease, her sorrows wash away, and she would find peace. She thought of Rachel, so many thousand miles away across the world and knew, with blinding certainty, that if she escaped, if she survived, she would go home.

And if she did not survive? Then at least she would give them all at home no cause to be ashamed. Slowly, imperceptibly, the old spirit flowed back into her heat-drained body and she held her head at a different, prouder angle.

Lieutenant Sharp estimated their position as somewhere west of Chusan, not far, he said, from shore – and in the afternoon of that day they sighted it – a thin, grey shadow on the southern skyline. The crewmen took the oars and pulled with what energy they could muster towards the land which, as Pearl strained her bloodshot eyes against the glare, grew green and flat, with the glint of water, the outline of one or two low brick houses, and a little grove of trees.

'There is a village of some sort,' she said, apprehension drying her already parched lips.

'Yes,' said the Lieutenant quietly, 'and, I am afraid, a reception committee.' Figures were moving on the shore, jabbering, gesticulating, one of them at least with a sword. More appeared from among the huts, brandishing bamboo poles, staves and even a spade. The Lieutenant's hand moved to his pistol belt.

'Do not fight,' cried Pearl. 'They are too many and they will surely kill us. But we're worth more to them alive. You must tell them so.'

'Perhaps you are right,' said Lieutenant Sharp, his eyes on the shore. 'The murderous, yellow devils. Ship the oars, dammit. We'll let them come and fetch us. If they dare.'

'Forget your training,' said Pearl urgently, 'and tell them we are worth good money. Or if you do not, I will.'

The enemy were wading through the shallows now, wiry, pigtailed men in cotton loincloths and wide hats. Others, in flapping trousers, grouped at the water's edge, jabbering menaces, snarling, shaking clenched fists. They were very close. Pearl could see blank, inscrutable eyes, in blank, inscrutable faces, and suddenly she saw them all as Ah May – untrustworthy, resentful, taking what liberties she could get away with, scoring over her foreign mistress whenever the master was away and telling slanted tales behind her back. But she had beaten Ah May before and she would do so again.

When the first hand grabbed the gunwales and the first face mouthed some spitting threat into her face, she stood up in the little boat with what dignity she could muster and said clearly, 'Do not touch me. Taipan Greig very important man. Worth much money. Plenty, plenty money.' She stared unflinchingly into the blank eyes while her heart thudded high in her chest and the fear almost choked her.

Another hand grabbed the boat, then another, till they were surrounded by gibbering, snarling faces. Beside her, Lieutenant Sharp said, with aplomb, 'Good afternoon, rabble,' and added, quietly, 'Well done, Mrs Greig. I rather think it would be fatal to show fear.'

Pearl swallowed, thought hard of her unborn child, and said clearly, 'Queen Victoria sent us.'

'*Kwee Tau Ya*' or some such mangled version of the Queen's name mingled now with '*Fan kuei*' as more and more crowds gathered, streaming into the water, surrounding the little boat and finally manhandling it out of the shallows and on to the beach. Sharp took Pearl's hand and helped her out; the others followed. For a moment the crowd fell silent, all eyes staring in open curiosity at the group of long-nosed foreign devils: the small, proud woman, the soldier, and the three sailormen.

Then from somewhere at the back of the crowd a woman's voice jeered, another cackled with derisive laughter and the tension snapped. The villagers swarmed forward in a chattering mass, four or five to each foreign devil, and Pearl felt her arms seized and twisted, her legs lashed with bamboo, her head forced downwards, till she knelt, helpless in the sand. A metal collar was clamped around her neck and chains, linking her to Sharp and the others. Her hands were bound behind her back. Finally, when all five were similarly imprisoned, their captors tugged the lead chains and jerked them to their feet.

Then to the monotonous beat of a village drum, the procession set off, whipped into motion by a phalanx of bare-chested, pigtailed thugs in loose flapping trousers and splayed bare feet, each with a bamboo switch of deadly aim, and accompanied by a crowd of derisive villagers, jeering and taunting, or merely moving backwards in front of the procession, the better to stare, with unnerving intensity, at the strange white skins and ghostly hair of the foreign devils the sea had brought them.

A score of capering juveniles, more daring than their parents, skipped nearer, tweaking the foreigners' clothes and retreating again, till, emboldened by their captives' helplessness, one of them tugged Pearl's hair, another spat, while more pelted the sorry procession with rotting vegetables and stones.

"Oh dear,' said Lieutenant Sharp quietly. 'Things do not look altogether promising.'

They looked even less so as the day progressed. They were led from the shore to the village – a collection of bamboo contraptions, rattan matting and one or two low, windowless buildings of brick. There were ducks on a sluggish pond, a banana tree or two, a patch of pineapple palms, then they left the village behind and moved inland, paddy-fields on either side now, with here and there a duck farm or a fish farm, indicated by a sudden tangle of bamboo poles or a rattan platform over water. They passed a pair of water-buffalo up to their haunches in water the colour of their weathered hides, and roped by nose-rings to their wiry, straw-hatted owners who squatted, knees behind ears, on the bank, chewing grass. A low hill was dotted with half-moon graves. A pagoda on the skyline. Then a watch-tower, and another, glinting in the evening light of a vast, flat, alien land.

It was no surprise to find the next village alerted and

ready for them, but the row of cages waiting in the dirt of the village square was both unexpected and ominous.

It was evening now, the shadows long and cool, the mosquitoes lifting in whining trails of mist over the waterways, the buffaloes drooping long-lashed eyes, the singing birds still. Evening fires tinged the air with wood smoke and the tang of strange cooking, but the crowd that had gathered to welcome them was far from tranquil. After the first moment of silent wonder, the village erupted into an excited turmoil of jeers, jabs, stares, and surreptitious snatching at hair or clothing. Someone grabbed Pearl's hand and, before she knew it, had torn off her wedding ring. Lieutenant Sharp shouted angrily in protest, but a smart whack on the cheek from a bamboo cane silenced him in a spurt of blood and Pearl begged him again not to resist.

'We must remain calm,' she said, 'and dignified. A ring is nothing.' But it was. She had lost her husband, now the outward pledge of their marriage was gone. The only thing remaining was her unborn child. By morning, she knew that, too, was in jeopardy.

At first light, after a sleepless, wretched night spent chained in the open square, while dogs and pigs roamed scavenging, too close for comfort, mosquitoes preyed on bare flesh and the only privacy was the half-darkness of the night and the watchman's lantern, the villagers emerged, blinking and scratching, from their huts and gathered for the day's entertainment. Children prodded the captives with long sticks. One offered Pearl a slice of melon and when she opened her mouth to bite it, snatched it out of reach, laughing.

Then someone opened the lid of the first cage, a bamboo structure some three feet square. First, Pearl's hands were untied then, before she could move, she was seized from behind by two burly villagers, swung aloft and crammed into it. Her neck chain was locked to the lid and the lid closed, forcing her head down, her knees up and her back into an uncomfortable bow. But at least Pearl was small. The Lieutenant's six foot length was more uncomfortably 'folded' into his cage and the sailors fared little better. Then a length of bamboo was thrust through each one, a man took either end, and they were lifted aloft to the cheers of the village.

'Where are we going, Lieutenant Sharp?' called Pearl in alarm as she felt her cage lift and sway with a motion worse than any ship, while the lid pressed against her head and the bamboo slats dug into her back and arms.

'Who knows? Perhaps to Peking and the Emperor himself.'

But one of the village elders had understood the reference to the capital of the Flowery Land and shook his head.

'Ningpo,' he said.

'A town in Chianking province,' explained Sharp. 'Unfortunately at least twelve miles away.' But the elder had not finished.

'Ningpo,' he said again and grinned, showing a fine array of broken yellow teeth. Then, in slow pantomime and with great relish, he made the unmistakable motion of cutting his throat.

As if to set the seal on their fate, the heavens opened and loosed the rain.

ii

The winter monsoon was blowing in earnest when *White Bird* reached Macau in early October. They had been delayed at Bombay by adverse weather and again at Singapore where they had heard increasingly disturbing news about the progress of the China campaign and its effect on the tea trade. Canton, apparently, was blockaded, the river closed. There were prices on Englishmen's heads. Though the Army had captured Chusan, the troops were sick with fever and dysentery, and the British commander's trip to Peking had so far brought no agreement with the Emperor.

'What will we do, Uncle Alex, if we canna buy tea?' Jamie had asked, when they heard the first news in Bombay. 'Should we turn back?'

'Turn back?' Alex had sounded almost exultant. 'Never! Maitland's built this ship to take us to Canton and to Canton we will go! And if we canna buy tea, then we'll find something else to take home with us – silks, maybe, or spices, or Chinese gold.' Alex Christie had not enjoyed himself so much since the first time he sailed to Greenland, before he was married. A new ship on new seas with a new and unknown challenge was meat and drink to him. He found the tropical seas enchanting, the tropical storms spectacular and worthy adversaries, the tropical sun a blessing after the northern cold.

Jamie, too, was exhilarated. Had it not been for the

memory of India and her unaccountable rejection, he would have been completely happy. Amelia was sweetness itself and no one could dispute that she was lovely and an asset to any lad. But after the first week or so of her company he found himself longing for India's liveliness and wit, for her unruly red hair and her freckled nose, for her honest, loving eyes.

Why had she rejected him when she knew he loved her? And he knew, or had thought he knew, that she loved him? 'Since my father's death,' she had written, 'I find I cannot marry you' – when it was her father who had been against the match. Jamie would have thought his death would have cleared the way instead of blocking it. It was beyond him to unravel the mystery and when, one evening of particularly romantic moonlight, he strolled the deck with Amelia on his arm, the sea a soft midnight velvet laced with spray, and the breeze warm as breath on his cheeks, he asked her.

'Why did India refuse to marry me?'

'I do not know,' said Amelia truthfully, and added, equally truthfully, 'You are a man any girl would gladly marry.'

He almost kissed her. Almost, until he remembered Tom. Tom thought no one knew of his love for Amelia Noble. Poor, simple Tom. When the whole Quay had known it for years. Instead, he said lightly, 'And you? Would you marry me, Amelia?'

'Oh no,' she said, very serious. 'I can marry no one. I have other work to do, with Pearl.' After a moment, she went on, troubled, 'Aunt Rachel said we were to ask Pearl to come home.'

'Ma did not really mean it. She's just worried, that's all. She thinks that Pearl is not happy. But Ma doesn't see how anyone can be happy away from Trinity Quay,' he finished, grinning.

'No,' agreed Amelia. 'She has not seen the moon on a tropical sea, or the flying fish, or the curl of blue water on golden sand with palm trees instead of bent grass behind it.'

'Or the sea-snakes and mosquitoes and red ants big as cockroaches,' teased Jamie. 'Or the weevils and maggots and rats.'

'Stop it!' cried Amelia, clapping her hands to her ears, but she was laughing and, before he knew it, Jamie had forgotten Tom and kissed her, there in the moonlight, on the deck beyond the wheelhouse.

Alex saw them, but the ship's bell did his work for him and shattered the moment. Later, Alex had a private word with his young nephew.

'Remember I am *in loco parentis* for both you and Amelia,' he said with unusual sternness. 'I will have no liberties taken on my ship. Even a Christie is not above punishment and by God I'll see you get it if you so much as lay one finger on that girl again. Do you understand me?'

'Yes.'

'Yes, *sir!*' roared Alex and Jamie, chastened, repeated the words meekly – and fled. But in a way he was grateful to Alex: he had not really meant to kiss Amelia anyway, and for the rest of the voyage they remained, by order, purely friends.

The wind was blowing strong when they neared Macau roads, but there was little shipping in the harbour. Those British ships that were not at Chusan were in the typhoon shelter off Hong Kong, or with the merchantmen upriver, at Capsingmun. Macau had a closed and wary feel to it as of a city under threat. Alex dropped anchor in deep water and prepared to send a boat ashore.

'Where is everybody?' asked Amelia. 'Surely Pearl had

heard we are coming? I had expected her to meet us. We must have been sighted hours ago.'

But there were no welcoming crowds – merely a handful of spectators on the Praia Grande, most of them Portuguese by their colouring and dress, the only British woman a middle-aged figure in dull alpaca grey. There were sampans in the harbour, one or two larger fishing boats, and a couple of brigs.

Jamie Christie was hurt. 'What's the good of our very own agent on the spot if she had not even the time to meet us,' he grumbled. 'It is not as if we drop by every day.'

'No,' said Alex thoughtfully. He studied the shore briefly through his eye-glass, then said, 'But Pearl's cer tainly not there. Nor Greig neither. He'll likely be at sea of course, with the expedition, but I had expected Pear to meet us. We're relying on her for letters o introduction.'

'At least we know her house,' said Amelia, tying he bonnet strings more firmly. In spite of the sun there was a brisk wind blowing and she was having difficulty keeping her skirts in order. 'I for one intend to go ashore and seek her out.'

'Not alone.' Swiftly Alex gave the necessary orders fo the ship's safety as well as that of his men – so far the had escaped the attentions of both pirates and fevers an he hoped to keep it so – and helped Amelia down int the jolly boat. Jamie followed. Then the oarsman pulle briskly for the shore.

It was not the arrival any of them had planned. Amelia had imagined Pearl running towards her with outspread arms, Jamie much the same, and even Alex had expected his niece's beaming welcome as of right. Instead, the stepped ashore ungreeted, on to the esplanade of the Praia Grande. A pair of Chinese coolies trotted by with swaying sedan chair. A boy, naked to the waist and barefooted, staggered under two great pails of water suspended from a carrying pole. Two women wearing mantillas turned their regal Portuguese backs as Jamie stared and their accompanying menfolk glared above threatening black moustaches.

'No trouble, remember,' warned Alex. 'So keep your eyes off the ladies.'

'You too,' retorted Jamie, with a wink at Amelia. But they were all uneasy. Alex raised a hand to summon a passing rickshaw. 'Captain Greig,' he said with deliberate emphasis. The man's expression remained blank and Amelia was summoning up the courage to try a word of spoken Chinese for the very first time, when a voice behind them said, 'Are you the Christies, by any chance? Pearl's Christies?'

They turned to see a middle-aged woman in grey, with kind but troubled eyes. She was gaunt and dry-skinned, her hair colourless where it was not actually grey, but her voice was warm and, when she saw their recognition, welcoming. 'I am Elizabeth Morton, her friend.'

'You poor dear,' she said, taking both Amelia's hands n hers. 'Travelling all this way in such heat and yet ooking so fresh and lovely and no one here to meet you. You must have been so disappointed. You are Pearl's sister Amelia, aren't you? I thought so. And even prettier han she said you were. And you must be her cousin ames? And her uncle . . .?' She faltered, studying Alex who was not at all as she imagined. 'Pearl said I would know you instantly by the mis-matched eyes and the limp, but . . .'

'My brother,' said Alex and briefly explained. 'But where is Pearl?'

'All in good time,' repeated Mrs Morton firmly. 'Save our breath for the climb.'

But when they had reached the Mortons' apartments, on an eminence at the south end of the Praia Grande, high above the water, even the magnificent view over what looked like half the south China seas could not content Amelia.

'Please, Mrs Morton, tell me where Pearl is.'

Mrs Morton took a deep breath, looked steadily at Amelia and said quietly, 'You must be strong, my dear, and brave, as Pearl has been required to be.'

Amelia blanched. 'But what has happened? Is she ill? Or injured? And where are Duncan and little Robin?'

'You had best tell us,' said Alex, his face grave.

'Then . . . Captain Greig is dead and little Robin with him.'

'No!' Amelia clapped a hand to her mouth in horror Jamie put an arm round her for support, his face as white as hers, and this time Alex did not intervene.

'I am afraid so,' went on Mrs Morton. 'I am sorry to have to be the bringer of bad news, but there is more to come. There was a shipwreck, you see, off Chusan Captain Greig and his son were drowned.'

'And Pearl?' It was Alex who spoke.

'In prison, in Ningpo.'

'Good God! Wait till I get the bastards who . . .'

'No. You must be calm,' soothed Mrs Morton. 'Viol ence is useless. And she is not alone. There were othe survivors. They managed to get ashore, but were capture and taken in chains to . . .'

'In *chains?*' cried Amelia, her eyes dark with horro 'Oh poor, poor Pearl.'

'First in chains,' said Mrs Morton deliberately. It wa best that they knew everything from the start. 'Then i cages, for the entertainment of the populace along th journey. Now she is in prison with the others.'

'Is nothing being done to rescue them? How long ha

she been imprisoned? Is she well? How is she treated?' The questions tumbled out in a stream of outrage and anger and Mrs Morton stood quietly waiting until they slowed and finally ceased before saying, 'There are several dozen prisoners, I believe, here and there. My own husband is imprisoned in Canton.'

'I am so sorry.' Amelia's eyes brimmed with tears and she put her arm around the woman in spontaneous comfort. 'You have troubles enough of your own, Mrs Morton, without shouldering ours.'

'Oh no.' Mrs Morton smiled with sad resignation. 'I am used to it and it was no more than Robert expected. If you defy a country's laws, even in the name of God, you must accept the punishment if you are caught. My husband is a missionary and handed out his tracts although they were forbidden. It is different for Pearl, a woman, newly bereaved and in so dreadful a way, so far from home. And I believe she is pregnant.'

There was a silence as the full horror of Pearl's predicament sank in, then Alex slammed a hand down hard on he table. 'Then we'd best rescue her, by God, before hose devils kill her and her child. Where is this Ningpo? 'amie, back to the ship with you at the run and fetch the charts!'

'Fetch your charts by all means,' sighed Mrs Morton, eaning back in her seat and closing her eyes, 'but it will do no good. What can you do against so many? You had ar better leave such things to those with power and nfluence. The British Commissioner has been to Peking nd there is talk of a settlement in the air. Such things equire delicacy and tact. Months of careful egotiation . . .'

'*Months?* When Pearl is pregnant?'

'We have Chusan and the Canton river,' continued Mrs

Morton, ignoring the interruption. 'They have our pris- oners. By next month the first of the season's tea will arrive in Canton, but until the blockade is lifted there will be no foreigners to buy it. The Chinese need trade. The merchants need trade. It is a question of who will concede what. You must remember that "face" is of the utmost importance to the Oriental. He must never be put in a position where he might be seen to lose it.'

'And what about Pearl's position?' demanded Jamie 'I'm damned if I see why she should suffer so that a pig- tailed, yellow devil can strut about with his hands in his sleeves and . . .'

'I understand your feelings,' interrupted Mrs Morton 'but you must allow the Commissioners to know thei job.'

'Aye. It's not their cousin who is rotting in jail!'

'Who said she was rotting?' She waited till she had thei attention, then went on, 'Rumour has it that your cousi Pearl has persuaded her captors she is related to Quee Victoria. That she is, in fact, her sister.'

There was a moment's astonished silence, then Ale gave a great shout of laughter. 'Our Pearl the Queen' sister? What does that make you then, Amelia? Or you Jamie? Or me, come to that. I reckon I'm a Knight of th Garter at least. Probably a Duke or an Earl. Earl Christie at your service, ma'am,' and he made an elaborat pantomime bow. They were all laughing now, for the firs time since they sighted Macau. But when the laughte subsided, there was much of urgency to be discussed. was agreed that *White Bird* need not linger in Macau With tea-trading two months away at least, maybe mo if the blockade continued, she must look for other trad and why not in Chusan? There they would be on the sp when Pearl was eventually released. And, was the unsp ken thought, closer to the scene of retribution if she we not . . . There was a constant need of stores for the garrison, said Mrs Morton, and once *White Bird* had disposed of the goods she had brought from home, there was no reason why she should not load again with rice or flour if she could find it, and with beef, chickens, pigs, anything that would bring useful profit which could, when the time came, purchase tea. Based at Chusan, *White Bird* could sail the islands, trading as the opportunity arose. Stores for the garrison, Mrs Morton had said, but Alex had heard privately of a more lucrative market in 'chintzes' and 'greys'. He kept the idea, however, to himself. Stores it should, officially, be.

Jamie had a brief twinge of conscience. What would Maitland say if he knew his precious tea-ship was shipping *hens*? But Maitland did not know, and anything that took them closer to Pearl was welcome.

'Amelia must stay here,' said Alex. 'Perhaps Mrs Morton . . .?'

'Of course,' said that lady. 'She will be safe with me till you return and . . .'

'No,' said Amelia firmly, in the voice Jamie was beginning to recognise as her particular brand of immovable obstinacy. 'I shall go to Chusan. Pearl will need me.'

'Then, if you will allow me, I will come too,' announced Mrs Morton. 'For company. I can be of help to you, I am sure, and my dear Robert will be released no sooner than Pearl. And if I am not here to greet him, he will understand. He at least is not pregnant!'

'But you have not opened your letters,' she reminded them later, when they had drunk her tea, eaten her cakes, and thrashed out over and over the preparations they must make before putting to sea again on the 800-mile journey north.

One letter was from Pearl. 'My dear Amelia,' it began, 'If I am not here in person to greet you it does not mean you are any less welcome. I have longed for your coming for months – no, years – and you are to live in my house, as my dear sister, until I return, which, please God, will be very soon. Mrs Morton, my dear friend, will look after you till then and though our poor orphans have all dispersed as the result of the troubles, I am sure you will give help wherever it is needed. As for the tea-trading, Duncan has made what provision he can for Uncle James and has explained everything most fully in his letter. My darling Robin would have written too, but he is only four and can write no more than his name, but he is already quite the little sailor . . .' There was more in the same vein and Amelia was moist-eyed when she finished. Quietly she folded the letter, saying only, 'I wish I could have seen her little boy.'

Duncan Greig's letter was purely practical. Short and to the point, it enclosed a bundle of letters of introduction to be presented at various shipping offices and warehouses, including that of Jardine Matheson and Co. Alex could not have asked for better and, leaving Amelia in Mrs Morton's care, he and Jamie left as soon as propriety allowed to present the first of the letters and arrange as swiftly as possible the disposal of one cargo and the taking on of another. Five impatient days later, *White Bird* left Macau roads, in defiance of the winter monsoon which was set to blow in earnest for the next two months, and prepared to battle northwards, to Chusan.

iii

Pearl arranged the garish Chinese gown over her swollen figure and settled as comfortably as she could manage on the silken cushions. Opposite her across the low table, the high mandarin's wife did the same while pigtailed servants hovered in the background. The elegantly carved window looked out on a little courtyard and a miniature garden where caged canaries sang. The mandarin's wife wore a splendidly embroidered gown with a writhing dragon in gold thread, the sleeves of which were lined with peacock silk. Her face was porcelain pale, her eyes narrow almonds which gave nothing away. It was difficult to judge her age – her feet were no bigger than a four-year-old's. Robin could have worn her little embroidered slippers with ease, except that Robin was a sailor like his father and would have scorned such femininity.

Pearl was glad Robin was not here, glad he was with his father, safe. For Duncan would not have liked it here either. He would have scorned the food – rice, vegetables and weak tea served without ceremony, twice a day. Scorned the accommodation which was, for the first cramped week, in prison cages and after that, an unused joss-house. He would have fretted at the constriction, been irritated by the company: captured soldiers, Lascars, a sailor or two, and a trio of officers, many of them sick, and all of them uncomfortable. No, Pearl told herself over and over, it was best that *she* was the one to be in prison, best that Robin and Duncan were together, somewhere safely out of reach. She closed her mind firmly against the idea of death, knowing that if she once let the smallest drop seep through the dam gates, the torrent of grief would overwhelm her. She had not wept. And, she thought with satisfaction, Ah May had not beaten her.

Duncan had been right. 'Show her from the start who is mistress,' he had told her when she arrived in that dreadful, alien house in Macau, and she had remembered his advice. From the start she had spoken with authority to her captors and it was not her fault if they chose to misunderstand. 'Queen Victoria will be angry,' she had told them. 'We are her people.' When their faces remained blank, her cage locked, she had insisted, 'My Queen will punish you if you do not treat me with respect.'

At the end of a week, in a small and dirty cell with grating on two sides and no privacy, she had simplified her message further.

'Queen Victoria,' she said with dignity, 'loves me like a sister. If you insult me, you insult my Queen.' Whether it was the words, for the name of the foreign devil's Queen was familiar to them, or the unbending spirit of their captive that impressed them, was never known. But Pearl had been taken out of her cell and moved, with the officers, to an unused joss-house where they had greater space and privacy. The mandarin's wife had sent her clothes, for her own were dirty and splitting at the seams as her pregnancy advanced, and later, a female attendant.

Later still, as negotiations between the Commissioners of the British and the Celestial Empires manoeuvred delicately towards a truce, the mandarin's wife had invited the foreign Queen's 'sister' to dinner.

The female attendant had made Pearl ready, binding her hair, powdering her face with rice flour, decking her in a long, loose gown of peacock silk, with lotus flowers and garlands in gold and black. Pearl's feet had displeased the attendant, whose own were half the size, and she had muttered something no doubt disparaging about *fan kuei* as Pearl pulled on the white cotton stockings, but she nodded with satisfaction as she finally handed Pearl a delicately carved ivory fan. Pearl was glad there were no mirrors. She was sure she looked like one of the waterfront whores at home in Aberdeen and was glad none of her family could see her.

The *White Bird* would be in Macau by now.

But the mandarin's wife was speaking. A respectful Chinese with drooping moustaches and a pigtail interpreted, 'Honourable Lady welcome. Honourable Lady please to eat.' Then he stepped back into the shadows again and Pearl inclined her head in acknowledgement, and waited. She knew protocol was important, knew, as representative 'sister' of a queen, she was under scrutiny. Dignity, she hoped, would serve. Apparently it did. The mandarin's wife inclined her head in turn, smiled a delicate, painted smile, and motioned to Pearl to begin.

Between them on the low table servants had set out an array of porcelain dishes and, studying them from under carefully lowered lashes, Pearl recognised with a surge of relief the savoury dumplings and other delicacies of the *dim sum* which Mrs Morton had introduced her to all those years ago when she was newly arrived in Macau and had been invited to lunch at the missionary's house. When the mandarin's wife selected a morsel from the best plate, lifted it between ivory chopsticks and laid it courteously on Pearl's plate, Pearl knew exactly what to do. Carefully, and with great dignity, as befitted the sister of a Queen, she took up the chopsticks from her own place and, blessing Mrs Morton's instruction and foresight, began to eat.

Afterwards, there were questions. Through the interpreter the mandarin's wife asked why the Queen allowed the Queen's sister's husband to carry opium on his ship. Pearl replied that the Queen approved of opium no more than the Emperor did and that there was no opium on the *Corbie*. Both statements, she hoped, were true. It was certainly the correct answer to make. Next, the mandarin's wife asked why the Queen's ships were blocking the Canton river so no tea could be sold. Did not the Queen like tea?

Yes, replied Pearl. Her Queen liked tea. The tea of China, such as the mandarin's wife had served her today, was a drink fit for the highest Queen. That, thought Pearl, was fine. But what on earth could she say about the other part of the question? She had not known there was a blockade. That meant no tea could be sold. That meant no tea-ships. That meant that *White Bird* had sailed halfway across the world for nothing and would lose every shilling invested in her. But the mandarin's wife was waiting for an answer.

'My Queen wishes to buy tea,' she began carefully, then remembered Duncan swearing and shouting when the first blockade was broken and the British bargaining position spoiled. 'My Queen wishes to buy more tea. She wishes to send her ships to many Chinese ports, as friends. But it is not dignified to be asked to sign a "bond".' She knew that dignity, or 'face', was of paramount importance. With relief she saw her answer was the right one. A matter of 'face' explained everything.

It was a matter of 'face' which had kept Pearl from screaming aloud her fear and anxiety and terrible, haunting grief. And a matter of 'face' that sustained her, though she was seven months pregnant now. How much longer would they keep her? She could not face the humiliation of giving birth here, in a Ningpo joss-house prison, amid a crowd of staring Ah Mays. And if, by some miracle, she survived that ordeal, what would they do to her child? 'Please God,' she prayed over and over, 'let me go free before my child is born. Please God, let them arrange a peace.'

But the saving of face was a delicate matter and vital to any peace settlement. Negotiations could not be hurried, even in that winter of frustration and simmering hostility. In Canton, the British merchant community was dissatisfied and angry. What was the use of dragging regiments and ships and ammunition all the way to China if they did nothing when they got there except sit about and wait for the Chinese to make up their minds? The men-o'-war, including three seventy-fours, were assembled off Boat Island, below the Bogue in the Canton river, in a pointed demonstration of strength. Troop transports joined them. And still the leaders negotiated, as offer and counter-offer were exchanged in the state-room of the *Wellesley*, the Commissioner's floating headquarters. $5 million offered, $7 million asked, $6 million eventually agreed. Then came the question of the trading ports.

Christmas passed and still there was no settlement while by the back door as it were the Americans quietly trans-shipped a steady flow of tea through the blockade – at a price. It was insufferable. When were things going to get back to normal? It was all very well to say the Chinese must be handled carefully and not antagonised by excessive force, but something should be done, and soon.

It was an iron-built, 660-ton paddle-steamer, with a flat bottom and a respectable array of weaponry, that finally tipped the balance. With a draught of less than six feet, a couple of 32-pounders, several six-pounders and a rocket launcher, she was a formidable adversary and achieved more in a week than the rest of the Navy together could have hoped to do. She was called, appropriately, *Nemesis*.

This smoke-ship was far more lethal than the little *Jardine* the Chinese had banned from their waters five years ago. This smoke-ship would not 'spread her sails and return to her own country' at the wave of an edict from the Emperor. Instead, she would range the innermost waters of the Canton river, where no *fan kuei* boat had penetrated before, spreading fire and destruction until the foreign devils had achieved their aim. It was time to come to an agreement.

iv

Chusan, by November, was a healthier place. The troops were quartered more sensibly, many in houses in the town. Supplies were more plentiful and of better quality. Ships, including *White Bird*, went northwards to Korean waters and returned with beef and flour, while in Chusan harbour the ships of the line were careened and repaired. Captain Christie took *White Bird* wherever he scented profit and by the end of the year both Alex and young James had developed all the daring, agility and plain nautical skill of any China captain. *White Bird* was a joy to handle, the enemy coast an exhilarating challenge, and the trade among the offshore islands lucrative, if dangerous. Once they narrowly escaped capture by a pirate junk, once they ran aground, but always *White Bird* answered sweetly to the helm and led them out of danger. In the captain's cabin, the strong box grew heavier and went some way to ease the ever-present anxiety about Pearl – and the tea they had come so far to buy and which continued to be officially withheld.

For negotiations with China remained inconclusive, particularly where the prisoners were concerned, though a truce of sorts was arranged on the Chekiang coast and more lenient treatment promised. In Chusan itself, the British position was consolidated, unruly Chinese flogged or shorn of their precious 'queues', and a semblance of normality imposed. The town filled not only with a variety of fresh produce, but with British missionaries, merchants, the families of seamen and officers. When the weather broke and the first frosts came, there was even duck-shooting. But there was still dysentery among the soldiers, particularly the Cameronians, and by the end of the year only 1,900 men remained on the island out of the 3,300 who had landed.

'If peace is not settled soon, my dear,' Mrs Morton told Amelia, 'I fear there will be few men left to fight our battles for us. And Pearl's time is running out.' Neither of them spoke their doubts as to her chances of surviving childbirth in a Chinese prison.

'At least *White Bird* is here and can whisk her away to Macau the moment she is freed,' said Amelia. 'We must have faith.' But even her faith waned as the grey days passed and still they heard no news of peace.

It was mid-February before the message came, and another week before Pearl and the other surviving prisoners were released into a waiting frigate of the British Navy and whisked across that treacherous, island-ridden channel to Chusan.

It was almost the meeting they had dreamed of – Pearl and Amelia embracing on the quay – only this time Pearl was the long-awaited traveller and Amelia the anxious waiting one. But in spite of the years and the tribulations they recognised each other instantly, though Amelia was no longer a gawky, nervous child, but a self-confident young woman, and Pearl was no longer a lively-faced older sister, but a small, drawn matron whom heat and hardship had prematurely aged. But something of the old spirit remained, for Pearl defiantly stepped ashore in a long-flowing Chinese gown of brilliant blue silk with dragons of gold thread and flowers, and deep scooped sleeves lined with imperial purple. 'A present from th mandarin's wife,' she explained, when they had laughed and cried and embraced and Mrs Morton had done the same. 'I know I look like some quayside whore, but it would have been impolite to refuse, and I will change it as soon as I can find something more appropriate. But as you see I . . .' She spread her hands and began a smile which was suddenly halted. Quickly she wrapped her arms across her swollen womb as if to keep the child in place and asked, in a small voice, 'Where is *White Bird*?'

'Coming,' soothed Mrs Morton, taking her arm.

'As soon as they can get here,' added Amelia on Pearl's other side. Over Pearl's head the two exchanged glances of mingled alarm and relief. At least Pearl was home now and free. 'They went north on Company business, but are due back any moment. All the ships are summoned to Chusan for the evacuation.'

'Evacuation?' faltered Pearl. 'But I thought . . .' Oh God! Not more travelling, not more flight from the inevitable Chinese. But if they did not go . . . she could not face captivity again. Mrs Morton was kindness itself, but suddenly, with overwhelming longing, Pearl wanted only Rachel and James and the sure comfort of the house on Trinity Quay.

'It is all right, dear,' explained Mrs Morton kindly. 'It is not an attack, but merely part of the Treaty. We are to leave Chusan to the Chinese and return to Macau. Most of the colony has gone already. We waited only for you, but now that you are here, we can leave as soon as you feel able. Our luggage, such as it is, is already packed.'

Oh God, thought Pearl again, with momentary desperation, as she remembered the 800-mile sea journey to Macau. I shall be ill and how can I hold on to my child when I am ill? She knew she was past her time. Her body knew it too, and only single-minded concentration had kept the child in place. But it was only a matter of time now before nature won.

'I want *White Bird*,' she said with a note of desperation to her voice. 'I want my uncle and my cousin.'

'What you want is peace and comfort and, I very much suspect, a bed,' said Mrs Morton, eyeing her shrewdly. 'Amelia and I expected as much and you need have no fear on that score. We have everything arranged for you and the house is not far away. A mere matter of yards. I am sure you can manage it.'

Disconcertingly, Pearl sat down suddenly, on a nearby chest, part of the little colony's luggage awaiting shipment to Macau. Tinghai harbour was small and at the moment in turmoil as troops of soldiers and civilians milled about, shifting baggage, loading it into sampans to be ferried to the larger ships, at anchor in deep water. Chinese coolies scurried here and there, officers shouted, somewhere across the water a bosun's whistle sounded, and there was the distant chanting of a sea shanty as men hauled on the capstan to raise anchor. The evacuation was well unde way. Pearl felt a moment of panic. Suppose she gave birth here, on the quay? And Chusan, Mrs Morton said, wa Chinese land again. Pearl had sustained herself through-out her captivity by the determination to give birth o British territory, among her own people. She would no be beaten now.

'I prefer to stay here, Mrs Morton,' she said, 'and wai for *White Bird*. I am sorry, but I dare not leave the quay If *White Bird* does not come soon, then I will go aboar the nearest British frigate and . . .' but at that momen she saw what she had seen so many times in her dreams the graceful, swooping outline of Maitland's tea-ship, wit the azure pennant of the Christies at its mast-head. Sh was coming into harbour, at last.

The next hours passed in frantic activity as the Christie

took over. The joy of reunion turned to instant anxiety as it became plain even to young Jamie that Pearl was in an advanced state of childbirth. But no one had the heart to refuse her when she begged to be allowed to give birth on the Christie ship. Jamie was white-faced as he helped her into the jolly boat, with Amelia at her side. Alex ran with Mrs Morton to collect what was necessary from her lodgings, then they followed the others in a second boat and the oarsmen of both were ordered to row as never before. They skimmed the water with commendable speed to reach the smooth, varnished hull of *White Bird* where she lay at anchor under the eastern arm of the harbour, within minutes of each other. Then Pearl was lifted carefully aboard and half-carried to the captain's cabin. While Amelia held her sister's hand, sponged her brow, soothed her with what words she could, Mrs Morton took charge of practical arrangements and Alex relayed her orders with a sharp authority which grew fiercer as anxiety increased. Messengers were sent ashore to collect what luggage remained and any lingering 'refugees', for the last of the evacuation fleet was preparing to put to sea.

'We'll need to sail with the others,' reported Jamie in an anxious whisper, when his knock on the cabin door had made it open six inches and Amelia's face appeared in the gap. 'Alex says he's sorry, but we canna risk staying on alone when . . .'

'No, of course not,' interrupted Amelia, glancing swiftly over her shoulder into the tiny cabin. 'Pearl will understand.'

James glimpsed Pearl's sweat-drenched, contorted face above a mound of heaving white linen and swallowed. 'Will she be . . .? Is she . . .?' He faltered to a stop. Amelia took pity on him.

'Mrs Morton says everything is normal,' she said gently.

'There is no more to be done but wait, and pray, and above all, have faith.'

When at last, some five hours later, Pearl's daughter was born, that was the name she chose for her fatherless infant – Faith Duthie Noble Greig.

'I can tell you now that it is over,' said Pearl, exhausted, but triumphant and looking ten years younger in spite of her shadowed eyes and sweat-drenched hair. She looked first at the tiny, blessed infant who lay sleeping in the crook of her arm, then at Amelia who sat on the edge of the narrow bunk, her young face glistening with sweat, her fair hair limp and straggling free from its ribbon, her clothes dishevelled, but an air of quiet satisfaction emanating from every pore of her weary body.

'What can you tell me?' she prompted, smiling.

'That . . . that my greatest fear was that I should bear a daughter, in Ningpo, and that . . . You remember that dreadful tale of Duncan's all those years ago, at home? When you ran crying from the room?'

'I remember.' How could Amelia forget when that had been the beginning of what had become her overriding ambition?

'It was illogical, I know. Perhaps even hysterical,' admitted Pearl. 'But I could not help it. I imagined over and over what might happen to my little daughter and I knew I could not bear it if . . .'

Then at last, after months of valiant suppression, the grief burst through the dam and overwhelmed her. Gently, Mrs Morton removed the baby, lest she be crushed, and left Amelia to comfort her sister as best she could, while Pearl wept herself to sleep and woke and wept again, for Robin and Duncan, over and over, until exhaustion drained her even of tears. For the first time in their lives together it was Amelia who took charge and urged her sister back to responsibility and strength. 'What good is it to little Faith if her mother has carried her safely out of harm's way, only to starve her!' she said, teasing. 'So drink this – there's good brandy in it – and eat up your chicken broth like a nursing mother should. Your poor wee daughter's wailing for her breakfast and there's none of us can provide it. Or shall I ask Alex to put in to the nearest fishing village and look around for a wet nurse?'

'Don't you dare!' But Amelia's threat, though barely serious, gave Pearl the jolt she needed to shake her out of despair and back on to the long path of recovery.

'Duncan was not always an easy man,' she told Amelia later, as she lay, propped on her pillow, wee Faith suckling contentedly at her breast. 'But he couldn't help it. He had had a hard life, and it was difficult for him. Poor Duncan. I am glad he and Robin are together, at least they will have each other.'

'And you,' said Amelia gently. 'You have Faith to remind you of them both.'

'Yes.' There was a pause while the baby suckled, Amelia stitched quietly at the tiny garment she was sewing for her niece, and from overhead came the gentle sound of wind in spread canvas and the ripple of parting seas. Through the porthole they could see a stretch of turquoise ocean, the comforting shapes of a British frigate and an armed brig, with, in the distance, the misted outline of the shore. They were somewhere off Amoy, more than half-way to Macau.

'It's strange, isn't it, Amelia, that Faith's father should die before she was born, just like mine did? I know now what our mother must have felt.' After a while, she said, 'I shall have their names added to the stone in the Protestant cemetery. It is only right. But the sea is their real grave, and the sea stretches far.'

'She was thinking of Aberdeen,' Amelia told Jamie that

evening, when she had left Pearl sleeping. She had joined Jamie on deck, for a welcome breath of air after the heat of the cabin, and together they leant on the rail of the foredeck, looking out across the dark sea to the lights of the convoy and, overhead, the smaller, brighter lights of the stars. The bow wave curled in silken folds under the prow leaving a trail of misted lace.

'At least you will have no trouble persuading her to go home,' said Jamie, staring ahead into the darkness. 'The wonder is that she ever came here in the first place. It's strange, isn't it,' he went on after a moment. 'You know someone all your life and then suddenly they act quite out of character, for no reason.'

Amelia knew he was thinking not of Pearl, but of India Abercrombie.

'Not entirely for no reason, Jamie. Circumstances change.'

'And people with them. Aye, that'll be it. But you wouldn't think that just because someone dies . . .' He stopped, then went on in a different voice, 'But what are we thinking of, brooding like this, when we've a new wee Christie among us? At home the whole Quay would be celebrating till the small hours. So, how is my wee niece? And Pearl?'

'Sleeping, both of them.'

'And you look as if you should be doing the same, Amelia. You have shadows big as saucers under your eyes.'

'I'm tired,' she admitted, looking up at him, 'and I've been so worried.'

'As we all have.' He put his arm around her and drew her close. 'But it's over now, lass, so put your head on my shoulder and rest.' After a moment he added softly 'Thank you for looking after her. Pearl has been like a sister to me, for as long as I can remember.'

'And to me!' teased Amelia. 'Does that make us brother and sister?'

'Hardly!' Lightly he kissed the top of her head and drew her closer. With a sigh of pure exhaustion, she relaxed gratefully against his comforting strength. They stayed a long time together, leaning on the rail in the moonlight, with the wind singing in the shrouds and the soft spray flying, murmuring together of past times shared, of future hopes, of family and friends at home.

Alex saw them from the wheelhouse and Mrs Morton too, when she came on deck to say goodnight.

'They make a lovely couple, don't they?' she said sentimentally, beaming her approval. Alex Christie merely grunted. He had enough on his mind already without Jamie complicating things.

When they reached Macau there would be the question of the tea he had sailed *White Bird* from Aberdeen to buy. He had commissions to fulfil and obligations. But there was also that other trade in 'chintzes' and 'greys' which had proved so lucrative and which, rumour had it, was brisker than ever among the offshore islands and promised rich rewards. Any man with a growing family would welcome such an opportunity. But the tea-trading season was already late, because of the war, and once it was opened to them they would need to load up, turn, and speed for home as fast as the wind would take them if they were to make any reasonable profit. Then Pearl would need passage home, with her baby, and would have to be provided for on board, though with Amelia to help that should be little problem. He narrowed his eyes towards the couple on the foredeck and amended, 'unless . . .' But Pearl would be there as chaperon and before they set sail for home he, Alex, would take Jamie aside and play the heavy uncle. Remembering, Alex grinned. He had never thought that when he took the place of his brother James, he would also assume his brother's moral rectitude. But circumstances changed a man.

'I reckon it's time you sent Amelia to bed, Mrs Morton,' he said now. 'Because if you don't, I will!'

They found Macau buzzing with activity. There had been further skirmishes with the enemy, but another visit by the devil-ship *Nemesis* almost to the doors of Canton had prefaced a general assault on the city's river front. Forts were overwhelmed, guns silenced, river-craft sunk or scattered piecemeal and the factory square captured. The flag was raised over the New English factory once more.

Trade had resumed at last.

Raw cotton and piece goods were shipped in chop boats one way, silks and teas the other as merchant ships were unloaded and loaded again at Whampoa. Trade had never been so brisk, nor teas moved so fast, till they were shifting at the rate of half a million pounds a day.

Already in the background the Chinese were gathering for another attack and the British making preparations to meet it, but in the Canton river the merchantmen concentrated solely on the business of trade.

In Macau, the British community settled in again after the months of disruption. Pearl found her house intact, but Ah May gone and, with her, the little pouch of gold sovereigns Mr Abercrombie had given her years ago and which she had hidden away 'for emergencies'. After the first moment's anger, Pearl accepted the loss as a small price to pay for her freedom. Mrs Morton lent Pearl her own maid till she found a reliable replacement, and, in the intervals of caring for her baby daughter, Pearl set about putting Duncan's affairs in order. Robert Morton was back in Macau, a free man again, thinner perhaps for his ordeal, but otherwise unchanged. When he learned that Amelia had studied Chinese, he was delighted and the pair of them had long discussions about the exact translation of various of Mr Morton's tracts, while Mrs Morton and Pearl made arrangements for Duncan's headstone, and disposed of such of his effects as were not to be shipped home to Scotland.

By the end of April *White Bird* was loaded and ready to leave. Alex Christie brought her down from Whampoa to Macau to collect Pearl and the others. It was only then that Amelia made her announcement.

'I am sorry, Uncle Alex, but I am not coming home.'

'Not coming?' Alex was taken aback, then angry. 'Of course you are, girl. Pack your bag and do as you're told. I promised your father, remember?'

'Papa told me I might stay for a year,' pointed out Amelia, with sweet reasonableness. 'And Mrs Morton says I may stay with her. Mr Morton has translation work for me to do and when things are back to normal again, I intend to revive the orphanage for little blind girls.'

'Oh you do, do you? Well *I intend* to take you home, if I have to carry you on board myself!' He glared at her with the fury that cowed grown men on shipboard, but Amelia remained unmoved.

'I am sorry, Captain Christie,' she said, politely. 'But I must refuse. Perhaps next year, when you return?'

'It is no good,' said Jamie, laying a hand on Alex's arm to restrain him. 'When Amelia decides something, a herd of elephants could not shift her. Believe me, I know.' He caught Amelia's eye and winked in private understanding.

'Jamie is right,' said Pearl quietly. 'And if it is what Amelia wants to do, who are we to stop her? She came here with a purpose, and must carry it through. But I will miss you, dear,' she said, turning to her sister. 'Promise me it will not be long before we meet again?'

'I promise.' Amelia hugged her in quick affection.

'Damn women!' cried Alex with heartfelt exasperation. 'What's to be done with them?'

'I suggest, Captain Christie,' said Mrs Morton, 'that you leave Amelia in our care. We will guard her and love her like a daughter, I promise you. And isn't it time you were sailing your precious tea-ship home?'

'Aye . . .' But Amelia's decision had created problems. 'You see, Mrs Morton,' he explained after a frowning moment, 'I am responsible for her. Her father expected her to stay a year, right enough, but with her sister. It is not right to leave her here with strangers. I know you will forgive the word, Mrs Morton, but it's the truth.'

'You are right,' said Jamie Christie slowly. 'We'd best think what Da would have done if he'd been here.'

'If you'll excuse us for a moment?' said Alex, with a jerk of the head, and he and Jamie stepped outside and closed the door. It opened after a few moments, but only to summon Pearl. All three were back within five minutes.

'Pearl says there's a half-share of Duncan Greig's ship to be claimed and his job, likely, with the Jardine fleet,' said Jamie, his eyes bright.

'This war business is not over yet,' added Alex, 'and there'll be more trouble before it's finally settled.'

'So, if Amelia stays, then a Christie had best stay too to see her right.'

There was a startled silence as Amelia looked from Jamie's radiant face to Alex Christie's frowning one.

'Not Pearl?' she faltered. Pearl, she knew, longed to g home, but Pearl had always been unselfish and brave.

'No, not Pearl.'

'Then . . .?'

'Yes, Amelia,' he said. 'I will stay here, in Macau, wit you.'

V

The progress of the 'Opium' War had been followed with close attention on Trinity Quay, albeit their news was inevitably several months out of date. *White Bird* had already set sail for home when they heard about the blockade of the Canton river and the exploits of *Nemesis* and, fortunately for their peace of mind, no reports of Pearl's capture reached them through public channels. The Christie letters home, by common consent, had contained no mention, though Amelia wrote to her father, telling him Pearl's story and explaining why she was staying on. But she sent her letter via *White Bird*. So their worries, apart from the natural ones of any sea journey, related principally to trade.

For many local businessmen as well as the Christies themselves had invested in *White Bird* and the responsibility lay heavily on James Christie's shoulders. It made him short-tempered at times, and, as Tom put it, crotchety. But then James still fretted that it was Alex who had ailed to China and not himself and no amount of reassurance could persuade him that Alex would handle things s well as anyone. Though his leg had taken months to heal and still pained him on occasions James would thump the floor with the stick he often used now and growl, 'I should have gone myself.'

'Next time,' Rachel would soothe and Tom would add, 'Come with me, Da, on my steamship,' and they would launch into the usual discussion. Though since the news of the *Nemesis*'s triumph both James's and Maitland's hostility to steam had mellowed. They were prepared to concede that, in certain circumstances, steam might have its uses, though for the China run, sail was still best.

Maitland's next ship, with a new bow and even more graceful lines than *White Bird*'s, was already on the stocks, but while Maitland could lose himself entirely in the creation of the second tea-ship, James still worried about the progress and business success of the first.

Rachel, however, had a different and private anxiety on her son James's behalf. She knew he had taken India's rejection hard, suspected he was hoping that a year's absence – and a year's mourning for her father – would change it, and feared further hurt in store for him on his return. For India Abercrombie was engaged to be married and the wedding set for September.

'I don't understand it,' Rachel told Kirsty sadly as they worked together in the Christies' office one summe afternoon. Since Alex's departure for China Kirsty had been a great help to Rachel, one way and another, and if ever Rachel protested, said only, 'Don't be daft. I enjo helping, and it passes the time.'

It was fifteen months since *White Bird*'s departure, and though they knew the tea season in Canton had bee delayed and the sailings with it, surely it could not b much longer before Alex and Jamie came home?

'I am sure India Abercrombie feels nothing for th Mackenzie boy.'

'No,' agreed Kirsty. 'And I would never have though that girl would marry for money. She always seemed s honest. But then, with a mother like that, I suppose it only to be expected.' Kirsty had disliked India's moth since they were children together in Footdee. Jessie Brar had given herself airs even then, when she was only fisherman's daughter and no better than the rest of them. 'Silly cow,' she added now, with feeling.

Rachel did not need to ask whether Kirsty referred to mother or daughter: the description could apply equally to either. But she had done her best, she reflected, remembering her attempts to persuade Fenton to abandon his prejudices. With the lingering coolness between the two families, there was little more she could do.

For Jessica Abercrombie had used her widowhood to consolidate her position in Aberdeen society. She knew the whole town had heard of Fenton's mistress in Edinburgh and his little 'by-blow', knew the tea-tables had buzzed delightedly with the scandal for weeks after Fenton's death, and had decided to adopt a dignified course of uncomplaining nobility and sorrowing forgiveness. She grieved for her dear, wayward husband, she implied, and grieved the more that he had been so sadly led astray. Above all, she *understood* . . . and if anyone dared even to hint at the subject in her presence, she froze the unfortunate by a look of such noble reproach that the victim invariably retreated into blushing silence, leaving Jessica more firmly entrenched than before in what she called 'best society'.

It was into this society that she had led India, when the year's mourning for her father was over, and from this same society that India, to her mother's private astonishment, had accepted the Mackenzie boy, as suitor.

Remembering past declarations of devotion to young Christie and refusal to marry elsewhere, Jessica had been both gratified and suspicious. It was not like India. But then India had changed since her father's death and that embarrassing scene in Fenton's study when the girl had overheard Jessica's admission. Jessica had told her it meant nothing, of course, had even given her consent for India to marry the Christie boy, but India had merely buried her head in her grandfather's chest for a brief, sobbing moment, then fled to bed. The subject had not been mentioned again, nor the name of Jamie Christie.

Jess, for her part, intended to forget the whole incident. Nevertheless, when, twelve months after Fenton's death, she had said, 'It's time we were looking for a husband for you, India,' she had expected the girl to mention the Christies' tea-ship. Young Christie wouldn't stay in China for ever and folk said *White Bird* was due home, any time. But all the girl had said was, 'Very well, Mamma.' Just like that. No argument, no contradiction, nothing . . . It made Jessica uneasy, but in spite of her suspicions, she could find nothing amiss.

India went to the parties her mother arranged for her and if not actually vivacious, was invariably smiling an polite. She danced when required to do so, attende theatres and dinners, and, when Willy Mackenzie dul approached Jessica for permission to ask India to marr him, India agreed. The only hint of opposition had com over the date of the wedding. Jessica had wanted June - 'The flowers are real pretty in June and we'd maybe ge early strawberries for the reception' – but India ha preferred September, for no reason that Jessica could se except awkwardness. But the girl had been so docile ove everything else that Jessica thought it best not to pres her on the matter. Besides, as she told anyone who woul listen, it was more seemly, 'with the family bereavement India, of course, was no longer required to wear mour ing, but Jessica herself knew better than to discard blac till she'd been widowed at least two years. But she coul dispense with the crêpe at eighteen months, so a Septen ber wedding would be an advantage there. Happil Jessica set about planning her own and India's wardrot in the intervals of deciding whether to dress young Finl in a pale blue velvet suit or in traditional highland dres

Finlay himself, fourteen now and beginning to shed the fat his mother had delighted in heaping on him, had privately decided that not for all the tea in China would he be seen dead in either, but that particular battle was yet to come.

Old Mrs Abercrombie was as pleased as her daughter-in-law about India's approaching wedding. George Abercrombie, however, was not.

'Think carefully, lass,' he told India one afternoon in July when, had Jessica had her way, India would have been already married. 'It's the rest of your life at stake, remember. And the rest of his.'

India was silent, staring down at her hands. They were in what had once been Fenton's study and was now known as the library. It was little changed since Fenton's occupancy, except that his papers had gone from the desk top, his pipe from the mantelpiece, and the room no longer smelt of tobacco except when, as now, Grandpa Abercrombie came visiting. The old man sat in what had been Fenton's chair beside the fireplace, filled, in recognition of summer, with a fan of pleated paper. Jessica ordered a fire whenever the fancy took her for the drawing room, but as she never used the library herself, she saw no point in wasting good coal. Of course, when Finlay went to the College and needed to study, then he could have a fire whenever he wanted, the poor pet. Meanwhile, if India chose to bury herself in all those dreary books, that was her own lookout. She could take an extra plaid with her and like it.

India did. She spent long hours in her father's study, reading and thinking. And if ever her resolution slipped and she found herself thinking too little of Willy Mackenzie and too much of Jamie Christie, she would shut herself away in the library and deliberately recreate, word for word, that dreadful scene after her father's funeral. Then, her resolution strengthened, she would take up a book at random and read, as her father used to do, till summoned by the dinner gong, or her mother's voice.

'*And the rest of his*,' repeated George Abercrombie with emphasis. 'Remember that. It's all very well for you to sacrifice yourself, lass – and don't protest. You know as well as I do that that's exactly what you are doing. You think by renouncing young Christie you will make it all right wi' Fenton, in heaven. But what about young Mackenzie, on earth? How's he going to feel when he wakes up in the morning and finds he's married a stranger? And that's what you'll be, lass, make no mistake. That's what you'll always be.'

India bit her lip and looked away. She fixed her eyes on the bookcase on the far wall and remembered Fenton saying, 'I swear you will never marry a Christie.'

'You'd far better stay a spinster,' Abercrombie was saying, 'than ruin some poor fellow's life.'

'I will not ruin his life!' she said, with dignity. 'He loves me and in return I intend to be his loving, loyal wife.'

'Rubbish! All you intend to do is martyr yourself ever after at that poor lad's expense. I'm ashamed of you, Indy. Black ashamed!'

'Then I am sorry.'

'Aye, and so am I,' said Abercrombie bitterly. 'I'd thought you the best of the bunch, wi' more straighforward good sense than the rest o' them put together. Now I see you're worse than all of them. They may be empty-headed, but at least they're honest.'

'But Grandpa, I . . .' How could she explain that only by marrying someone else could she keep her resolution? That only by marrying Mackenzie could she be true to her father's wishes? She said, with a hint of desperation, 'I am only trying to do what my father wanted. At least *he* would approve.'

'I doubt it,' growled Abercrombie, heaving himself painfully to his feet. He was almost seventy and this business with India made him feel his age. 'He knew what it felt like, remember, to be unhappily married. Oh, give me my overcoat and have done. I've no patience with you, India. I'm away to Edinburgh. At least Mary Ballantyne's not a fool!'

Since Fenton's death George Abercrombie had taken over supervision of the Edinburgh branch and while there had fallen into the habit of visiting the flat in the New Town, at first on business matters relating to Fenton's will, then for his own pleasure. He liked Mary, liked the neat way she kept the flat, liked the intelligent, loving care she gave her son. He was a fine wee lad, a credit to her, and to his old grandpa. Abercrombie loved the lad as much as any of his legitimate grandchildren and when the boy was grown, intended to take him into the business. If Jessica objected, she'd have to lump it, and as for Finlay, it would do him good to have a bit of healthy competition. He'd had life far too easy . . . but it wasn't too late to save him. Not like Indy who seemed dead set on hurtling along the road to self-destruction.

'Damn the girl,' he grumbled as he stamped off home, to collect his bags and prepare to take the ferry. 'Damn her for an obstinate young besom! But I'll not trouble wi' her again. I've better things to do wi' my time.'

But in spite of the old man's irritation, he could not get India out of his head, however hard he tried. The poor, misguided lass was set on ruining her life and no one else was going to stop her if he didn't. He brooded throughout his inspection of the Canongate shop, and was still brooding when he called at the New Town flat. When Mary Ballantyne asked him, gently, what was troubling him, he told her.

* * *

India Abercrombie sat listlessly in her bedroom, an open book in her lap, while Mairi folded linen and layered it neatly in the open chest which contained India's wedding trousseau. There was a scent of lavender in the air, from the ribbon-tied sachets which interleaved the clothes, and a bee droned lazily at the window pane. Dust motes danced in the afternoon sunlight. It was four weeks and two days to India's wedding.

'They say yon Christie ship's due any time now,' Mairi said, breaking the silence. 'Sixteen months they've been gone, and no saying what's happened to them meantime. Mind yon *City of Aberdeen?* When *she* came back from China half her crew were dead and the rest so weak they could scarce lift a glass o' whisky! In China there's diseases folks here have never heard of – and nae wonder. They say yon Chinese eat anything that moves, even dogs! Fried, with fancy bits o' this and that. And birds' nests! So what can a body expect? No, I reckon half yon Christie crew'll be dead and gone and that's why they've been so long coming back. Couldn't get more crew, likely. I wouldna be surprised if Christie himself was . . .'

But India could take no more. 'Be quiet, Mairi! Can't you see I'm trying to read?'

'Hoity toity,' bridled Mairi, hurt. 'It's books now, is it? People aren't good enough, I suppose? Or is it only *county* folk you're interested in now, wi' you marrying a step up the ladder? I remember a time, Miss High-and-Mighty, when you'd have paid me good money for news of a certain Christie.'

India slammed shut her book and stalked out of the room. It was hard enough for her to keep her resolution without Mairi tormenting her day in, day out, with things she preferred to forget. And her mother had another of her dreadful tea-parties this afternoon. It was a clear case for her father's study.

She was at the top of the stairs when she heard the front door open and a great roar of 'Indy! Come here this instant!' Then her grandfather was mounting the stairs towards her. 'Get your bonnet, lass, and whatever fal-de-rals your Ma makes you wear in the carriage. You're coming with me.'

'Where to, Grandpa?' India's heart beat suddenly faster. Her grandfather looked angry and determined, and joyful at the same time. She had never seen him like that before.

'Never mind where to. *Do as you're told!*'

Obediently, and with a strange excitement mounting inside her, India obeyed.

Five minutes later she was in the carriage at her grandfather's side.

'Trinity Quay!' he snapped, and the coach rumbled into motion. 'And before you ask,' he said, turning to India, 'we are going to the Christie office. *White Bird*'s been sighted off Greyhope Bay and you, lass, are going to join the welcome committee.'

'No!' protested India, suddenly shaking. 'I can't, Grandpa. You know I can't! You've no right to try and make me.' She reached for the door of the carriage with some wild idea of jumping out.

'And you've no right to behave like a blind fool!' He pulled her roughly back and held her firmly, both hands in his. 'Listen to me, lass,' he said, forcing her to meet his eyes. 'I said *listen*, woman! Because this is the solemn, gospel truth. I've been talking to Fenton's Mary. Do you know what she told me? That Fenton was coming home to tell you he'd been wrong and foolish, to say he'd let jealousy blind his judgement. He was going to tell you, India, that you could marry Jamie, with his blessing.'

India stared at him with huge, disbelieving eyes, not

daring to hope – while hope gathered and grew stronger in spite of her fear as her grandfather continued.

'Mary says he went away so happy on that last day, thinking of how happy you would be when you heard. She was horrified when she heard what you'd done. If I hadn't thought it might upset her to hear about Fenton's other family, I'd have mentioned it sooner, but I'm that glad I told her, Indy. Your Da *wanted* you to marry Jamie Christie, do you hear me? And if you don't believe me, I'll take you on the next packet boat to Leith and she can tell you so herself.'

But India was scarcely listening. Misery peeled away and the joy welled up inside her till her whole body came alive again, after its long, dreary sleep.

'Oh Grandpa, do you think Jamie will still have me?'

Then she remembered her last sight of Jamie, with Amelia on his arm, smiling . . . and Mairi's tales of illness and danger. Her joy left her as suddenly as it had come.

'Nay, lass,' said Abercrombie with new concern. 'Dinna look so fearful. It'll all sort out for the best, you'll see.' But something of her anxiety had spilled over on to him. *White Bird* had been gone a long time. Anything could have happened.

The entire Christie clan was assembled on the Quay to meet the returning tea-ship. James and Rachel, with Tom and the three youngest children; Alex's wife, Kirsty, with her six, though Kirsty's Annie was a strapping nineteen year-old and walking out with a sailor, and the rest scarcely 'children' any more; Maitland, tense with expectation as he waited to have his life's work confirmed – or to return to the drawing board to start all over again. William and George, the unmarried Christie twins, had managed to be ashore together and were as excited as any of their nephews and nieces. 'Like a pair of overgrown children,' grumbled James Christie, watching them capering about in a group of small fry. Dr Andrew was there, with his wife and son, expecting news of Amelia, if not Amelia herself, and the entire work force of the Christie yard had been given an instant holiday, so they too could join in the welcome. Even Alfie Baxter was hovering on the edge of the throng which swelled by the minute till it looked as if the whole of Footdee had turned out as well as most of Shiprow and the Quay. After all, it was not every day that a ship sailed home from China, and a Christie ship at that.

She was very close now. They could see her figurehead, her pennant, the coiled ropes on her deck. Sailors swarmed the shrouds, as sails tumbled in rippling folds and over the water came the sharp bark of command. There were figures on the deck, waving. A woman? A small woman, with a bundle of some kind. Could it be . . .

Rachel felt excitement beat through her breast with unbearable intensity, and behind the excitement, dread. Any moment now they would know the worst . . . who had died, who survived . . . She could not bear to look at that group of figures amidships, could not bear the suspense. Biting her lip, she turned her eyes away – and saw, close by in the crowd, old George Abercrombie with his grand-daughter India on his arm. The girl was ashen, with a look of such harrowing anxiety on her face that Rachel felt first compassion, then a surge of joyous relief. The girl had seen sense at last! There could be no other explanation. Then a great cheer rose from the crowds as the first rope snaked across the gap between ship and shore, then another, and *White Bird* slipped smoothly and with quiet grace to rest against the Quay. The gangplank was lowered and to a great welcoming roar the first of the sailors stepped ashore.

James Christie pushed his way through the crowd,

Rachel beside him – and stopped short with a gasp of astonishment. Before he could recover, Rachel had pushed past him and was running, arms outstretched, towards a small, smiling woman with a child in her arms. 'Pearl!'

The next moments passed in a whirl of tears and joy as the Nobles joined them, and a crowd of clamouring children, for Pearl had always been popular. Then Rachel brushed her eyes with the back of her hand, laughing, and looked around her. 'Where is Amelia? Jamie? And Alex?'

But a bronzed and bearded man with sea-blue eyes and an air of command was shouldering his way towards them.

'Captain Christie reporting, sir,' he said, coming smartly to attention in front of James. '*White Bird* delivered safely, all present and correct. Sir!' His voice was formal, curt, but trembling with pride – and something else. 'Oh Da! It's good to see you!' he cried, embracing his father with spontaneous affection. 'And Alex's nae dead so ye needn't look like that. And I didn't organise a mutiny, neither. I'll tell you all about it later,' then he swung his brother Matt high into the air, tried the same with nine-year-old Davy, but settled for a playful jab in the chest instead, clipped Tom lightly round the ear and received a similar greeting in return, kissed little Marth and tickled her with his beard till she squealed wit delight, and finally hugged Rachel in a great, bear-hu while she wept, openly, for joy, and his own eyes gre suspiciously moist. But after a few happy moments Rache felt him stiffen and looked up to follow the line of h gaze. He was staring solemnly at India Abercrombie wh was staring as solemnly back. Anyone would think the were at a wake, thought Rachel with momentary anxiet Then George Abercrombie pushed forward, draggir India with him.

'Well go on, ye great gowk!' he said to Jamie. 'Give the lass a kiss. Or have ye forgotten how after so long away?'

They were no longer looking at each other with blank faces: the joy and love and plain, naked longing which transformed them both was evident to all. Then Jamie stepped forward and, in full view of half the town, took India Abercrombie in his arms and kissed her, at first tentatively, then with jubilation as she clung to him and kissed him and would not let him go.

'Thank goodness for that,' said old Abercrombie, taking Rachel's arm. 'I thought that daft lass would never see sense.'

But Rachel had forgotten, in the joy of her son's triumph and his reunion with India, that there were those among them with little to celebrate. 'I must find Kirsty,' she said, 'and comfort her.' Tom, too, would need compassion if Amelia, as Pearl told them, was determined to work in Macau.

'Aye, right enough,' said Abercrombie. 'But there's nae comfort like a good family gathering, with food and whisky and wine. And if I know the Christies, that's exactly what's arranged.'

They celebrated *White Bird*'s return with a party that spilled from attic to basement of the house on Trinity Quay and lasted till the small hours of the following day. India and Jamie were inseparable as they moved from one group to another, Jamie recounting tales of the China seas, and Alex's trading in the offshore islands. 'He made s a fortune,' he told them proudly, over and over, and if nyone asked what Alex sold, he answered solemnly, Chintzes.'

'Fancy yon flowered material being so valuable,' said irsty's Annie, and Jamie snorted. Kirsty's Annie didn't otice. In company with her mother and her brothers and sters, she was still lost in wonder at the presents Alex had sent home to them – silks, little ivory boxes, jade statues and jewellery, an ornamental Chinese dagger, even a huge straw hat. 'And he'll be home himself in a year or so,' Jamie had reassured them, 'when Amelia's settled.'

Amelia, Pearl told everyone, was working in the Prot- estant Mission. Her family were sad not to see her home, but proud of her. Booky talked of joining her one day, as a medical missionary perhaps. Tom said nothing. He hac decided long ago that if Amelia did not come back witl *White Bird* then he would fetch her himself. Preferably ir the next Christie ship. If not, then in the steamshij Abercrombie talked of ordering. But by steam or sail, h would seek her out one day and fetch her home.

'Alex did the right thing,' said James Christie, when h and Rachel found a quiet moment together. 'I'm proud o him. It cannot have been easy to send Jamie home wit all the triumph of success and stay on in that place, jus to do his duty by Amelia Noble.'

'No,' agreed Rachel, but she added, eyes sparklin 'Though by Jamie's accounts Alex doesn't waste time ou there. That strong box couldn't have held a single extı gold piece.'

'Aye, they did well.' The tea profits had not bee spectacular – the late trading and Pearl's baby had mea they missed the early market at home – but more tha adequate. And with the extra profits Alex had made t his own private trading the Christies had netted a sm fortune.

'I am not entirely happy about that coastal tradin said Rachel. 'Jamie is very evasive about it and I am n even quite sure what they sold. Are you?'

'I have a good idea,' said James, who meant to find o later from Jamie exactly what they had been up to. 'Bu think it's best not to inquire too closely. Best just to thank God for *White Bird*'s safe return.'

'And for the first of the next generation.' Rachel looked across the room to where Pearl, her baby asleep in her arms, sat with Dr Andrew and Louise and a group of Footdee folk, including, Rachel noted thoughtfully, Alfie Baxter. 'The first survivor,' she amended, remembering Duncan Greig and his little drowned son. 'Poor Pearl. She has suffered terribly.'

'And come through, indomitable as ever. And if that daughter of hers has half her mother's spirit, she'll be a credit to us.'

'It will be Jamie's turn next,' said Rachel. Jamie and ndia, arms entwined and emanating happiness, were at he centre of an animated group of young ones, all tale-elling and laughter.

'And I am prepared to bet the contents of that strong ox that a mere seven thousand miles will not long deter ur Tom!'

At that moment there was a disturbance at the door nd the crowd parted to reveal Jessica Abercrombie, in a rilliant blue flowered gown ('One o' they chintzes, kely,' said Kirsty's Annie, with awe, 'and her supposed be in mourning!'). There was a moment's astonished lence as all eyes turned to the intruder.

'I heard as how you was celebrating,' she said, with hat Kirsty later described as 'brazen cheek', 'and being Footdee lass mysel', I thought I'd drop by.'

ssica Abercrombie had been entertaining ladies, includ g Mrs Mackenzie, at tea when Mairi had burst into the om without ceremony and announced, 'Yon Christie's a-ship's home! She took so long, folks say, along of ving her hold so full o' gold bars she almost sank! And ung Christie's back a captain and Mr Alex still in China

'cos that 'Melia Noble's set on being a missionary . . .
She had paused to draw breath, but only momentarily before rushing on, 'And Miss Indy was that delighted t see young Christie she ran and kissed him, in front c everybody. Jamie Christie always was real handsome, lik his Da, and now he's rich, too. Oh ma'am, it's th romantic!'

There was silence. An awful stillness had settled ov the room so that even Mairi felt the chill of it, for she ha said, blustering and belligerent, 'Well, it *is* romantic whe two young people love each other and Miss Indy's bee that miserable, the poor quine, since her father died, reckon she deserves a bit o' happiness at last.'

Still no one spoke, though Jessica's mind was racing the double to find a way out of the awful situation. would be an uphill struggle even to begin to extrica herself from this one. As for keeping a toe-hold in Go Society . . . But hadn't Mairi mentioned something abo gold?

'Well, she does deserve it! Poor Miss Indy.' Mairi w apparently hell bent on ruining every chance Jessica ha 'And I reckon if a girl can choose between a lad she lov who's handsome and rich into the bargain, and a lad s doesna love who's no great shakes that I can see, she'd daft not to take the first, just because her ma wants her take the second. Indy's the one who's got to bed him, n you!'

With that parting shot she had slammed out of room, only to reappear, two seconds later, as Jessica h known she would, with the inevitable postscript.

'And ye'll nae even need to change the wedding – j the bridegroom!'

Goodbye to Good Society, Jessica had thought grin The Mackenzies, for one, would never speak to her ag Probably not the Hendersons either. Or the Piries. Bu least, if even half what Mairi said were true, the Christies were not poor. With a long sigh, Jessica Abercrombie had accepted the inevitable.

'I am so sorry, ladies,' she had said, with what graciousness she could muster, though even Jessica's courage had not been enough to meet Mrs Mackenzie's eye. 'I must ask you to excuse me. I have urgent family matters to attend to.'

'Well?' she said now, surveying the crowd in the Christie home with an unexpected quickening of the pulse. She hadn't been at a gathering like this since she didn't know when. 'Is naebody going to give me a drink?'

'I reckoned,' she announced some time later, mellowed by several tots of whisky and a slab of mutton pie, 'that if my Indy and your Jamie are going to be wed, our families might as well be on speaking terms, at least. What do you say, Rachy?'

Rachel and James Christie exchanged glances over Jessica's head. James winked.

'Why not?' said Rachel carefully and added, with only a hint of irony, 'We are, after all, old friends.'

It was not quite the wedding Jessie Abercrombie had planned. The wedding itself was elegant enough, even without the carriages of county folk, though Augusta and Victoria had deigned to come, with their families, and actually seemed to be enjoying themselves, and she had to admit that Jamie Christie made a real handsome bridegroom. The reception was real nice, too, in the new Assembly rooms, but when it came to the dancing afterwards, if it hadn't been for the marble pillars and the chandeliers, you'd have thought it was one o' they weddings in Footdee, years back. The Christies were all there, of course, and the Baxters, and Jess had bowed to India's request – after all, what had she to lose? – and invited Nana Brand who had brought, by the look of it, the whole of North Square with her. With the Nobles and the Abercrombies it made a right cheerful crowd.

'I reckon folks are enjoying themselves,' she said smugly to Rachel, at the table set aside for parents of the bride and bridegroom. 'It reminds me of when you and James were married, years back.'

'Yes,' said Rachel, smiling at her husband. 'But that was more than twenty years ago.'

'And you don't look a day older,' he said gallantly. He slipped an arm around Rachel's shoulders and drew her close. 'I don't see why young Jamie should have all the fun, do you?' Deliberately, he kissed her.

'And what about me?' said Jessica archly. 'Do I get a kiss too?'

Solemnly, his arm still round Rachel's waist, James leant forward and kissed her on the cheek.

'I suppose that'll have to do, but you're not the man you were, James Christie. You'll be telling me next your dancing days are over, too, or I'd remind you that you ought to ask me, as mother of the bride.'

James looked at Rachel. The unspoken question hung between them as she remembered past conflicts, past pain. Then after a long moment, Rachel nodded. James stood up and bowed with mock solemnity.

'Mrs Abercrombie, may I have the pleasure of this dance? That is, if you will make allowances for an old man's gammy leg.'

'Old? You're nae older than I am, ye daft loon!' Gleefully, Jessica seized his hand to take their places for the eightsome reel.

Rachel watched them merge into the swirling, joyful pattern of the dance and waited for the old jealousy to bite. Instead, she felt her troubles and anxieties melt away, like summer snow.

'No cold corners?' said a quiet voice at her shoulder and she looked up to see Dr Andrew Noble, friend of her childhood, standing beside her.

Slowly, Rachel surveyed the bright elegance of the ballroom and the throng of friends, all enjoying themselves, all sharing the happiness of the young bride and groom. Alex was not there of course, but she had no worries for him, and Kirsty seemed content to wait. She was dancing with Maitland, Pearl with Alfie Baxter. Even Tom was joining in, with one of the Brand girls on his arm, and young Finlay Abercrombie, to Rachel's amusement, was surrounded by a gaggle of teasing lassies from Footdee, led by Eppie Brand. Her dear friend Louise was not dancing, but talking happily with her stepson Booky, no doubt about medical matters – and the younger children, down to Martha Christie and Pearl's baby, Faith, were in good hands. As for Jamie and India – they were radiant with a love that brought a lump to Rachel's throat.

'No cold corners?' repeated Andrew quietly in the private language of their shared childhood, when it had been orphan Rachel's ambition to own a house and family of her own, and Andrew's to be a distinguished doctor. He had known sorrows as well as joys, as she had, but her adoptive brother had more than achieved his ambition, as she had hers.

'No cold corners,' said Rachel, and knew that it was true.

'Then I intend to break the habit of a lifetime,' he said, smiling, 'though I fear we may both regret it. Mrs Christie, would you care to dance?'

More Compulsive Fiction from Headline:

Agnes Short

THE FIRST FAIR WIND

A delightful family saga of Scottish fisherfolk

The warm-hearted Christie family take in orphan Rachel and raise her as one of their own. Like other fisherwomen, Rachel gathers bait, coils the lines, wades into the icy sea at dawn to launch the boat, carries full creels to the market – and dreams that one day she might have a house and family of her own.

James, the handsome eldest Christie son, longs for a different way of life, more prosperous and more secure than fishing – he dreams of building a fine stout ship that will carry him to the trading ports around the world. But his ambitions bring him into a near disastrous conflict with a local merchant.

Set in the bustling fishing community of Footdee, *The First Fair Wind* is the first in a trilogy of novels that follows the fortunes of the Christie family.

"Agnes Short has created a memorable picture of daily life in a Scottish fishing community nearly two hundred years ago . . . She has a feeling for the period, and a nice sense of humour." *Irish Times*

FICTION/SAGA 0 7472 3179 6 £2.99